BREAD
OF
LIFE

DIARIES AND MEMORIES OF
A DAKOTA FAMILY
1936-1945

by
MARIAN KLEINSASSER TOWNE

289.7092
Tow
C 1
Bangor Women's Corner

Copyright © 1994 by
Marian Kleinsasser Towne

Library of Congress Cataloging-in-Publication Data

Towne, Marian Kleinsasser

    Bread of life : diaries and memories of a Dakota Family / by
Marian Kleinsasser Towne. Indianapolis, Ind. : the author, 1994.
    p. cm.
Semi-fictional account based on the diaries (1936-1945) of John
P. Kleinsasser.
ISBN 0-9642666-0-1
1. Hutterian Brethren – South Dakota – Fiction. 2. Hutterian
Brethren – South Dakota – Diaries. 3. Kleinsasser, John P.,
1896-1984 – Diaries. 4. South Dakota – Hutchinson County –
Fiction. 5. Mennonites – South Dakota – Fiction. I. Title.
BX8129.B68 K5 1994
289.7092

                              94-90344
                               CIP

      ISBN 0-942666-0-1

Printed in United States of America

PINE HILL PRESS, INC.
Freeman, S. Dak. 57029

Preface

I wrote BREAD OF LIFE; DIARIES AND MEMORIES OF A DAKOTA FAMILY as a grateful response to my family and to the community of relatives and friends which nourished and sustained us following the death of our mother, Katherine Tieszen Kleinsasser, in 1937. It is a memorial to the strength and perseverance of South Dakota pioneers and their descendants. But the book should be of interest to all who are concerned about the future of middle America—its agriculture, human ecology, and structures—social, economic, and political.

BREAD OF LIFE may be read as a story of one family's struggle to survive set in the context of major historical events such as the Great Depression and World War II. But it may be read also as a daily record of social and economic life between the years 1936 and 1945.

BREAD OF LIFE gives a semi-fictional response to factual occurrences, kneading story, vignette, biography, history, correspondence, and speeches into the loaf of diary entries to rise with the yeast of the reader's imagination. It is both fact and fiction, transforming facts into truth.

The story takes place in a tightly-knit Hutterite Mennonite community north of Freeman, South Dakota. Its main character is Morgan (John Pierpont Kleinsasser, 1896-1984). He was a husband, father, farmer, rural school teacher, state legislator, ecologist, religious and civic leader, and perpetual student. As his youngest daughter, I wish to share his vision with a larger world.

I am indebted to the members of my family, especially my sisters, Pearl (Mrs. Peter A. Hofer) and Ruth (Mrs. Edwin E. Pollman), and my brother, Cal Kleinsasser, who live in the Freeman community and have shared in shaping this record.

Marian Kleinsasser Towne
5129 N. Illinois Street
Indianapolis, IN 46208-2613
(317) 253-7973

Diarist

John P. Kleinsasser
(Morgan)
Freeman, South Dakota
1896-1984

Foreword

Families and communities are the building blocks of human societies. They nurture in each generation the skills and disciplines essential to human intercourse in the larger society. Marian Kleinsasser Towne's and her father's participant-observer accounts here offer a remarkable demonstration of the function of family and community in South Dakota in the 1930s and 1940s.

Here individuals learn to accept responsibilities within the family enabling them to cope with the chores of everyday and the crises of illness and death. Personal and community life come together in experiences of work, education, worship, politics and mutual aid. They take responsibility for one another in a burial association, the Mennonite Aid Plan and are called on to help some neighbor almost daily with chores, with transportation, with equipment.

This Mennonite community participates in the larger world. It enters into federal programs of drought relief, economic planning in the Agricultural Adjustment Administration, and the Soil Conservation Service. It responds in its own unique way to World War II. Children go away to colleges and return either to work or on frequent visits. Mr. Kleinsasser ventures into state politics, holds office in the Crop Improvement Association, and the County Education Association. Family and community relate to the world "outside" and remain the source for the strength and renewal of society.

But this is not written nor should it be read as a case study in social organization. This is the story of two persons in a particular time and place. Their memories and records are the sources for BREAD OF LIFE. Reading it is to enter into the life of this family and this community.

Edwin L. Becker
Professor Emeritus, Sociology of Religion
Christian Theological Seminary
Indianapolis, Indiana

v

Table of Contents

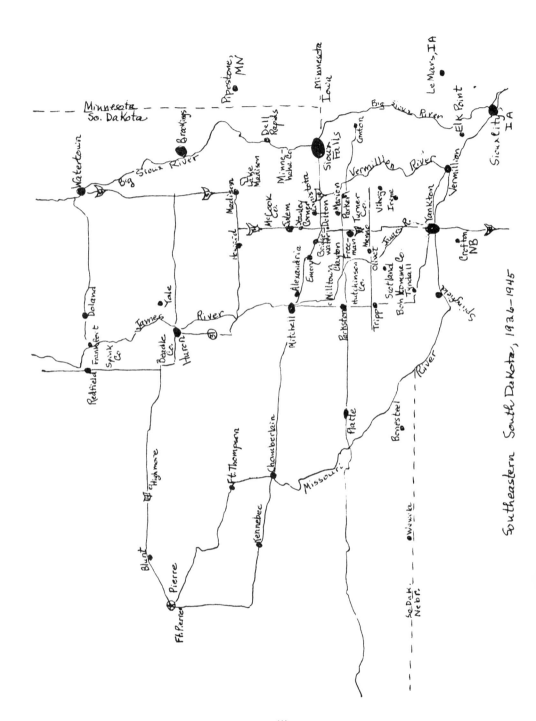

Southeastern South Dakota, 1936–1945

Part I

1936
The Big Snow

Wednesday, January 1, 1936

All in church this morning. After dinner we went to Grandpa Tieszen's place. Abe Tieszens and Henry Tiahrts were there too. The children said their Christmas poems for which Pearl got a half dollar, Cal a quarter, Ruth a dime and Marian a nickel.

Max Walter brought the ice cream freezer back while we were gone.

Thursday, January 2, 1936

Wheat meeting was postponed 'til Saturday. Had exams in District #98 today. Ma and I went to church in the evening and got a flat tire. Pearl and Cal fixed it after we got home.

Friday, January 3, 1936

Ma washed clothes after supper. Pearl and Cal worked in the barn all afternoon.

Saturday, January 4, 1936

Had all-day wheat meeting at Merchants State Bank. Committee members are nephew John L. Hofer, Emanuel Auch and I.

Sunday, January 5, 1936

Whole family in church. Got there on time twice in a row. The New Year's resolution is holding so far.

Monday, January 6, 1936

My pupils this year at #98 are Paul, Elizabeth, Sarah and Esther Hofer; Bertha, Max and Marie Walter; and Melvin Ratzlaff.

The AAA was declared unconstitutional today by the U. S. Supreme Court. Six judges in favor and three dissented. Very bad feeling among farmers.

Tuesday, January 7, 1936

Could not get Oldsmobile started, so I walked to school. It was 18 below zero.

3

Wednesday, January 8, 1936

Had Silver Lake Co-op Telephone meeting at nephew, Joe L's place. Heard Roosevelt talk over Joe's radio. I was elected secretary.

Thursday, January 9, 1936

Drove to town after school to have oil changed at Phillip's 66 station. Paid $1.15 for 6 quarts.

The windmill does not pump. I accidentally dropped a piece of an iron file down the pipe that had broken.

Friday, January 10, 1936

Ruth lost her first tooth and put it in a cup of water on the window sill so it would grow.

It thawed today. I drove to town after school to get Pearl and Cal, who stayed in town to practice basketball. Cal is attending Freeman Independent grade school and Pearl is attending Freeman Academy. Our home school, Sunshine #26, is closed this year for lack of pupils.

Saturday, January 11, 1936

Bought 1650 pounds of coal at Freeman Lumber Yard @ $12.50 per ton.

Sunday, January 12, 1936

I stayed home from church to thaw out the well pipes. Pearl and Cal drove the car to church.

Max and Marie Walter came over with their Shetland pony. They take turns leading and riding. The children played dominoes.

Nephew Jake L. Hofer, Jr., and his Mrs. visited us in the evening.

Monday, January 13, 1936

This is Ruth's sixth birthday. She was born at 5 a.m.

Tuesday, January 14, 1936

Gave quite a few tests in school today. The 8th graders got 100% in Language, so Max and Marie were peeved. Paul still has his sore ears.

Wednesday, January 15, 1936

Went to town for Pearl and stayed for a basketball game at the College.

4

Katherine Tieszen Kleinsasser

Friday, January 17, 1936

This is Mrs. John P. Kleinsasser's birthday. She was born in 1899. Could not have a birthday party. Money very scarce. In fact, I have none at all today.

Went to Olivet to the Hutchinson Co. Federal Land Loan Association meeting. I got stuck with my car in John L.'s driveway and then we got stuck with his car driving out. Shoveled out both cars and took mine to brother P.P.'s to put in his barn. Went to Olivet with John L.

The meeting was postponed because only 35 were present. Whiskey and wine were passed around. I drank my first glass of whiskey since the repeal of Prohibition. It burned my throat and affected my head but not seriously. Gottlieb Haar treated those there. Haar is secretary-treasurer of the Association.

Saturday, January 18, 1936

Butchered a sheep in the morning. Cal is getting the "hang" of butchering, but he says he does not want to be a butcher. Had liver for dinner at 1:30.

Went to town in the afternoon and bought apples from the truck.

Sunday, January 19, 1936
All home today. Roads are blocked.

Monday, January 20, 1936
Pearl, Cal and I went to see a basketball game. Ma, Ruth and Marian stayed home. Springfield Normal played Freeman College. The College led all the way until the last few seconds of play. They played overtime and Freeman won 35 to 31. Simon Unruh's brother is the coach. Two Springfield boys fouled out but they were permitted to play because Springfield had brought only five men along.

Tuesday, January 21, 1936
The well is still not fixed. Heckenlaible says the weather is too disagreeable to fix it.

Wednesday, January 22, 1936
27-30 below. I am keeping the fire going in school, burning briquets.

Thursday, January 23, 1936
We emptied the supply tank of water. There is no water for livestock.

Ran out of gas driving to school in 20 below weather. Pete Ratzlaff and Jake M. Hofer helped me get started. Both are on the school board with Fred Thomas. Pete and Jake tried to go to Olivet for the School Officers' meeting, but they got stalled two miles south of Freeman.

Friday, January 24, 1936
Jake M. Walter took me to school this morning. I walked home in the evening. The snow is 12-14 inches deep in the stubble field.

Max visited Cal. The radio battery is getting weak. We are using Abe Wiens' old battery radio.

Saturday, January 25, 1936
Had a meeting with J. C. Graber concerning politics.

Manured out the barn. Elmer Glanzer bought Abe Wiens' radio we had been using.

I sent $65. interest to Olivet on the land loan. Got stuck in a snow drift coming home from town.

Sunday, January 26, 1936

Roads blocked. Did not go to church.

I am reading THE SOUND WAGON by T. S. Stribling. It is about rotten politics.

Cal is thawing out some fish. We still have a good supply of frozen fish which we bought from Joe L. for $8.

Monday, January 27, 1936

Walked to school. The children got there before I did.

Max got notice that he won a radio at the Webb filling station in Sioux Falls.

Tuesday, January 28, 1936

Walked to Jake Walter's and drove to school with him. Jake M. Hofer visited school and took us home with his sled.

Horse & sled.

Wednesday, January 29, 1936

Drove to school with the car. Could not get it started after school, so Ratzlaffs pulled it. Went to town after taking the children home. Got some coal and my warrant for teaching.

Marian said the "Bo Peep" poem when I got home. She is 2 1/2 years old.

Cal had no school today because of a declam contest. He is working sixty day 6% problems in the 7th grade in town. Old time stuff!

Thursday, January 30, 1936

Jake M. Walter took me to town after school. The doctor told him he probably has stomach ulcers.

Friday, January 31, 1936

Walked to school. Stove smoked, so I cleaned out the stove pipes after school. Rode home with Hofer's sled. Had to have Daisy pull the Olds to get it started. Oil would not circulate. Put fire under the car to warm up the oil. Took radio battery back to Julius Albrecht.

Saturday, February 1, 1936
Went to Olivet for the County Farm Loan Association meeting. John L., John J. Gross, brother P. P. went along with me. It had been postponed from January 17. The officers elected were the same as last year with the exception of Henry Goehring.

The oil did not circulate in the Olds on the trip to Olivet, so it burned out the connecting rod. But we drove home with it anyway, going 20-25 miles an hour.

Sunday, February 2, 1936
No car, so did not go to church. Heard that Jacob P. Maendl's chicken barn burned down.

Monday, February 3, 1936
Weather cold. Art Becker did not drive on our place to get Pearl and Cal. There was too much snow just east of our driveway. It turned into a blizzard. Pearl and Cal stayed in town at Mrs. Ike Kleinsasser's. I walked to school in the morning and came home with the sled.

Ruth asked Jesus to forgive her sins and take her heart. She wants to be a child of God.

I got another book from the Literary Guild of New York. It is LAFAYETTE by Latzko. Very interesting.

It is 11:50. I must shave and hurry to bed. Ma and the little girls are sleeping.

Thursday, February 6, 1936
Plenty of snow. Pearl stayed in town and Cal walked home from the gravel.

The mail carrier came north out of town today. He walked to our mailbox to deliver our mail.

Friday, February 7, 1936
Very cold this morning. Pearl stayed in town last night at Aunt Emma's. Cal started out walking to the gravel because Becker cannot come west on our south road. But I told Cal to stay home.

I walked to Jake Walter's and then the Walter children and I walked to Jake M. Hofer. Hofer took us to school in the sled.

It was blowing and snowing all day. All the east-west roads are blocked. North-south roads have quite a bit of snow on. Cannot get through with cars. The mail carrier did not go today. Becker

*took Pearl and the Walter girls, Clara and Elizabeth, home from
town with his sled.*

*Politics are getting hotter. There has been no farm bill passed
yet to follow the AAA.*

Saturday, February 8, 1936

*It blizzarded all day. The wind from the northwest is very cold.
Some reports say 35 below zero.*

Heard that Joe L's have a baby boy named Delmar.

*Just did the chores and went back to the house. The wind is
so strong that one can hardly get his breath. We cannot even see
the windmill from the house.*

"Hurry up, Daddy, come in and close the door! You're letting
the cold in," cried Ruth as she greeted him at the door. He was
dressed in a big brown sheepskin coat. Icicles formed around his cap.

"What are you doing out here on the porch? Get in where it's
warm!"

"Marian and I were watching at the parlor window for you. We
scratched away some of the frost and saw you coming." Then,
laughing, she said, "You look funny. You look like Santa Claus."

"Tell Ma I gathered the eggs. I gotta go check on the hogs
now," Morgan said, brushing the frost from the flannel scarf tied
around his neck.

"Okay! Mama, the eggs are here," called Ruth, slamming the
door to the porch and rushing into the warmth of the dining room.

Katherine, their mother, stepped out on the porch. "Be careful,
John," she said, and took the tin pail of eggs packed in straw.
"Chickens can't even lay in this weather. Barely enough eggs for
our own needs."

Sunday, February 9, 1936

*Blizzard still raging, but not as cold as yesterday. Roads are
all blocked. Jake M. Walter and Max rode over on horseback to
see whether we'd have school tomorrow.*

"You don't want to have school, do you, Max?

"Not patically."

"Sure, we'll have school. If we don't have school, we'll have to
make it up on Saturdays or after spring planting starts," said his
teacher.

"Can Cal come to our school tomorrow, then? I heard over the
phone that town school's not gonna have school."

"Really? Hey, that would be fun!" exclaimed the young blond Cal.

9

"No, if town school is closed, Cal's gotta stay home and do the chores so his Ma doesn't have to tramp through the snow."

"Aw, shucks!" moaned the boys in unison.

Monday, February 10, 1936

The day is calm. No wind to drive the windmill but our windmill hasn't been fixed yet anyway. Livestock are eating snow.

I walked to the mailbox, where Jake M. Walter picked me up with his sled. Pearl and Cal stayed home. College and High School both closed.

The road north of our place past John P. Gross farm is in bad shape. People can hardly get to town for coal. Nearly everybody is out of coal. I heard Freeman sold more coal so far this winter than it has sold for many years.

Tuesday, February 11, 1936

I walked to school today. The drifts are deep but do not hold my weight, so I break through most of the time. I was sweating when I got there.

Pearl and Cal are still at home. Public School is open but College is not because they are out of coal. No coal has come to town for quite some time. Dealers are rationing the coal 500 pounds to a customer.

Clara Walter came over this afternoon to visit Pearl with her Shetland pony. Going home she sure made headway!

The children were sledding on the big drift in front of our house.

"Let me take your picture standing on top of the snow bank," called Morgan to Cal, who was pulling Ruth and Marian to the top of the bank in a large grain shovel.

"I gotta rig up a harness so Beauty can pull you guys up," said Cal, panting.

"Can I get in the picture too?" asked Ruth.

"Sure! Everybody, get in the picture. You too, Clara. Cal, take off your leather cap for a few minutes so I can get a better picture of your face and hair."

"Naw, I wanna have my Lindbergh cap on," he protested.

"Okay, then, keep your cap on. But whatever you do, be sure to obey me!" Morgan laughed.

"Want me to take my cap off?" offered Marian.

"No, keep your cap on. That was a bad idea. Okay, everybody smile!" Click went the shutter on the black box Kodak. "People won't believe, in years to come, how much snow we had this year."

10

"I believe it, and it's not artificial, either!" shouted Pearl as she and Clara sailed down the embankment on the Red Flyer sled.

Wednesday, February 12, 1936

Lincoln's birthday. I read a number of stories about Lincoln to the school children. Jake M. Walter took us to school. I had walked nearly to his place. My time was about 15 minutes fast. We passed Jake M. Hofer's place at 8 a.m. He said it was too early and if we did not come later, he would take his children to school himself. Usually the patrons want the teacher there too early.

Katherine said Jake M. Walter was here at noon waiting for Pete Pankratz, who was supposed to fix the well.

I received another book from the Literary Guild. It is O'Henry's COMPLETE WORKS, priced at $1. The print is a little too small for me. My glasses should be changed.

Republicans were to meet in Tripp. I am not there.

Thursday, February 13, 1936

Jake M. Hofer took us to school by sled again. A terrible blizzard blew up by going home. All the roads are blocked again to auto travel. It is colder this year than it has been for the last fifty years, they say. The College has no school because they have no coal.

We have moved into the parlor for most activities to conserve fuel. The hard coal burner keeps us warm.

"This is fun, eating breakfast around the library table!" exclaimed Ruth.

"Be careful so you don't spill your milk on Daddy's papers," cautioned her mother. "He'll be angry if his school papers get all messed up."

"Like he got mad when Marian cut up his red dictionary?"

"Yes, something like that."

"Daddy *laughed* when I cut up his book," protested Marian.

"Only later was he able to laugh about those missing pages in the Thorndike-Barnhart, when he showed the dictionary to his friends," said Mother, who was arranging their clothes on chairs near the hard coal burner. "When you've finished your breakfast, you may get dressed in front of the stove. I've warmed your clothes on the stove fenders."

"I'll get my toes warm first," said Ruth, sitting in a wooden chair before the stove and propping her feet on the chrome fenders.

"Me too," said Marian, following suit.

"And then you may help me knead the bread dough," said Mother, preparing a work place near the stove.

Friday, February 14, 1936

Jake M. Walter took us to school this morning. The official temperature was 36 below. Jake was so cold going to school that he ran beside his sled to keep warm.

We finished the fourth period six weeks tests. Afterwards the children made Valentines.

Heard that State College at Brookings has no school because of no fuel.

Cal drove the cows and horses over to Walter's place to water them because our windmill is still broken.

Saturday, February 15, 1936

No teachers' meeting because the roads are blocked, including 81. I wanted to go to Sioux Falls to have my glasses changed but could not because of the roads.

Went to town in the forenoon with Walter's sled to get Pete Schmidt to fix the well. Three of the pump rods are bad. He could not complete the work today. He pulled the independent pump out.

Sunday, February 16, 1936

No church today. Pete Schmidt came out and we finished fixing the well. The last two pump rods are new, also the second one from the top. But there was no wind to start the windmill.

I took Schmidt to the gravel road and nephew Ted Kleinsasser came up and took him back to town.

We had fish for dinner from our supply of frozen fish.

Beauty had pups. Nice little rat terriers.

Monday, February 17, 1936

It was very windy. I walked and had a hard time getting to school. It took me an hour to walk a mile and a quarter.

It got more windy all day long. By 4 p.m. we had a regular old-time blizzard. Jake M. Hofer took all the children home. He took me to my road on the section line.

Cal stayed in town. He had gone to Public School with Becker's sled. Pearl is still not in school. She had the windmill going for about an hour.

Snowbanks are getting higher right along. We can hardly see the horse barn from the parlor windows.

Many schools are closed on account of no coal. We have very little coal left at #98.

Tuesday, February 18, 1936

Weather very bad this morning so I phoned Jake M. Hofer whether he wanted school. I walked to Jake M. Walter's place and then Walter took us to school.

The weather was not so bad in the evening. The windmill was pumping until 10:30 p.m. The supply tank contains much ice.

Jake Walter brought the mail out from town because the mail carrier has not been able to get through.

Wednesday, February 19, 1936

Very beautiful today. However, the windmill will not run because there is practically no wind.

The children played outside at recess and noon hour.

We have no mail. Cal is still in town, staying with Aunt Emma. He phoned home about 4 p.m.

Towards evening it started snowing and the wind came up. We started the windmill and let it pump water into the small tank. I tried to thaw out the pipes leading from the big supply tank, but it seems it cannot be done.

Ruth has been sleeping with me upstairs for two nights. She likes it. Enough warm air rises through the ceiling register to keep the room warm.

Pearl did all the chores today. She is a good worker.

Thursday, February 20, 1936

Max came for me in the sled this morning. Cal came home from town with John P. Gross. Public School has had no school on account of no coal this week except for Monday. Gross wanted to get some coal but no coal has come to Freeman for quite some time on account of the train not being able to get through. We still have a little coal. Some people are getting coal in Bridgewater.

Friday, February 21, 1936

Jake M. Hofer took us to school this morning and then went to town to get some coal with his sled. He could not get any because the train has not come in yet. Our coal in school is just about all gone.

Paul took me home after school. The relief workers are shoveling snow off the county road running past my place on the south. They got as far east as Jake Walter's corner today.

Jake Walter went to Sioux Falls to exchange the radio Max won at Webb's. Highway 81 is still blocked.

Chickens are finally laying. Got 27 eggs today.

Saturday, February 22, 1936

Most roads that had been opened were drifted shut again when the wind came up this morning.

Walters and we went to town using our team and their sled. I got 690 pounds of coal, my ration. Freeman got in seven railcar loads.

Today is my birthday. I am 40 years old. The children made ice cream. Ruth gave me a kiss for a birthday present. Max and Clara were here to help us celebrate.

Sunday, February 23, 1936

No church today although the weather is very good. The wind was from the southeast and it was thawing nearly all day. There was enough wind to pump water.

Marian sings "Rock-a-bye, Baby." She carries the tune beautifully.

Pearl and Clara walked to the Peter M. S. Waldner place on Highway 81 for a visit.

I am reading O'Henry's short stories.

Monday, February 24, 1936

It thawed all day. Jake Walter took us to school with his sled. He wanted to go fishing in the James River. People have been spearing a lot of fish there.

Becker drove his car to town and took Cal along. The Public School opened today after four days' vacation on account of no coal.

We still have plenty of feed for the livestock and the chickens are beginning to lay fairly well, considering the weather. We have no lambs yet. We are milking two cows.

Marian ran with a fork, fell, and rammed it into her chin, the same place she cut open when she jumped in bed and fell against the bedspring.

Tuesday, February 25, 1936

The College and Academy opened today after two weeks of vacation. Pearl and Cal went to town with Becker's car. Highway 81 is just passable. Cars can hardly meet and pass each other. The road needs to be widened.

Wednesday, February 26, 1936

Worst blizzard we've had this year. Drifted all the snow into the opened roads.

Jake Walter took me home after school with his sled. I hitched up the wagon to go for Pearl and Cal, who had walked out to the highway this morning, but Becker did not go, so they walked to Waldner's place. The drifts were so high on the road that I could not go through with the team and wagon, so I went through Thomas's land inside the highway fence. I drove 'til Waldner's place and walked across for the children.

It was some drive home! Pearl claims she froze her legs. At least she had Ma grease them with goose fat. Maybe she will put on enough clothes from now on.

"Why didn't you walk home when Becker did not come?" asked Ruth of her big sister.

"We were already frozen by then and it was shorter to go to Waldner's place than to walk back home," answered Pearl, trying to hold back tears.

"She kept wanting to stop and rest. I had a hard time keepin' 'er goin'," put in Cal to all assembled around the pot bellied stove.

"Well, I was all played out, sinking into the drifts. You had pants on but I didn't," said Pearl, defiantly. "When we got to Waldner's, they had to rub my legs with snow."

"Didn't that make 'em colder?" asked Ruth.

"You gotta raise the temperature gradually," explained Cal.

"Didn't they give you anything to warm you up inside?" asked Ruth.

"Sure, we had hot cocoa and dipped stale bread into it."

"Oh, that's my favorite!" cried Ruth. "Don't we have some hard bread we can dip in cocoa, Mama?"

"Sure, right there in the bread box," said Mother. "I'll stir up some cocoa and it'll be warm in a jiffy."

"Yippee!" shouted the little ones, chasing each other around the stove.

Thursday, February 27, 1936

Nice day. Cold but not stormy. Turned out the livestock early in the morning.

Pearl and Cal rode to school with Becker's sled. The gravel 81 is blocked entirely now since the wind was from the southeast. Around 9 p.m. the road crew was opening 81 with a rotary snow plow.

Friday, February 28, 1936

Cal drove to Freeman with Becker in the sled in the morning and came home by car. Pearl stayed in town. The Academy and College will have school on Saturdays to make up for the time lost.

Saturday, February 29, 1936

The Mrs., Ruth and I went to town using Walter's sled. Ruth had two baby teeth pulled, one upper and one lower. Dr. Wollman checked my teeth and charged 25¢ total.

Sunday, March 1, 1936

There was church today but we did not go. Hofers reported only 27 people present.

Monday, March 2, 1936

Snow is melting fast. Hofer took us to and from school with the sled and part of the time we were on mud. The mail carrier went with his team today.

Tuesday, March 3, 1936

Today was the township election. Mrs. Walter, Katherine and I tried to get to Freeman to vote. P. P. was supposed to come north to the Marion gravel, but nobody came. Our phone does not work, so he could not call us or we call him. We drove south with the team past Charley Schrag's place. It got too late to vote so we turned back toward home.

Got our first pair of lambs today, a ewe and a buck.

Wednesday, March 4, 1936

Got the report of the Grandview Township election: Elias Pollman, supervisor; John L. Hofer, clerk; Edwin Mendel, treasurer; Albert Koerner, assessor. An upset!

Thursday, March 5, 1936

Walked around on the road to and from school. I was afraid of getting wet by cutting through the fields.

Saturday, March 7, 1936

My Mrs., Jake L. and his Mrs., Evelyn and Melvin and I went to Sioux Falls to see Dr. Basset. He said I did not need to change my glasses and should use Murine. Jake's children did not need a change of glasses either. He claims their trouble is with the eye muscle. He suggested using a stereoscope with picture to remedy the problem.

There was so much snow on 81 and 16 that some banks are still higher than the car.

Sunday, March 8, 1936

Did not go to church. Went to Marion with the Olds to visit Grandpa and Grandma Tieszen. They were not at home so we went to Mrs. Marie Tiahrt's place. She said that Katherine's brother Jake was in Mt. Pleasant, Texas. Saw two flocks of wild ducks.

Monday, March 9, 1936

It was our turn to take the children to school in town. The following go with our car: Pearl and Cal, Clara and Elizabeth Walter; Luella, Linda and Elmer Ratzlaff; and Gordon Schmidt. District #26 pays for transportation for Cal, Elmer and Gordon because they are still going to grade school. I rode with them 'til #98.

Saw a meadowlark.

Started delivering eggs to Fensel's Hatchery.

Tuesday, March 10, 1936

Cal got stuck in our driveway because he did not stay in the middle of the road.

Christ Schmeichel and nephew Ed Kleinsasser butchered a steer for us in about two hours. We cut up most of the meat in the evening. Ma wants to can most of it. We gave a little to Aunt Emma, P. P. Tschetter, and brother P. P.

I bought a paper, HOUSEHOLD JOURNAL, that Melvin Ratzlaff was selling in school.

Katherine's brother George had supper with us.

Wednesday, March 11, 1936

I walked to the gravel after school and caught a ride to town with a trucker. Told the printer to print 250 letterheads and envelopes for me. Had my petition made out for State Representative. Clarence Gering typed up the necessary information. John L. will circulate it for me.

John L. and I went to a basketball game between Nettleton College and FJC. Nettleton won 44 to 37.

Rode home from Freeman with the Becker boys. They had a blowout so I walked home to get my car, drove back to take them home, but they had already fixed their tire and gone home.

Aunt Emma and children Jerome and Virginia were here for a visit. Ma served beef steak and ice cream.

Thursday, March 12, 1936

County Agent Harold Roth, Davies and brother P. P. came to my school in regard to starting a 4-H sow litter club. Pearl and Cal might join.

Sold some Durham wheat to Sam Ratzlaff @ 85¢. He got stuck on the yard and I had to pull him out with the team.

Saturday, March 14, 1936

Had teachers' meeting at #21 this afternoon. There were 22 present. I was supposed to be on the program, but four meetings were held in one so lots were drawn. It fell to Anna Gross to discuss our subject—recreational reading in 4th-6th grades. Rosamond Schamber discussed spelling very interestingly. Co. Sup. Rose Perman was present.

John L. is circulating my petition.

Sunday, March 15, 1936

In church for the first Sunday since January 5. Some record! Went home at noon to gather eggs, then to John J. B.'s for dinner. Came home at 8 p.m. Pearl did not milk tonight. She claims she is too busy studying "Lady of the Lake." Miss Pankratz makes them work.

Monday, March 16, 1936

Got 6 lambs today. One ewe has a bad teat, so we have to bottle feed both of her lambs.

Tuesday, March 17, 1936

Got warrant for teaching and for attending Teachers' Institute.

I drove to town to get Pearl, who had stayed in to practice for Glee Club. She ranked first in English class.

We all went to Grandpa Tieszen's tonight. He had no objection to my coming out for State Representative. Got home at 11:30, and took care of the lambs. It is now 12:30 a.m. I still have some announcements of my candidacy to send to Tripp, Parkston and Menno papers.

Sold 15 doz. eggs to Fensel Hatchery.

"How's come you asked Grandpa if you could run for the legislature?" asked Cal on the drive home from Marion.

"More of a courtesy than anything else," replied Morgan.

"What would you have done if he'd said NO?" Cal persisted.

"Prob'ly run anyhow."

"Why should he care if you run?"

"Well, if I win, Ma will be home alone a lot with you guys. Grandpa would care about that. Then, too, Mennonites don't go in much for politics, especially the Low Germans."

"Haven't there been any Low Germans that ran for public office in South Dakota?" asked Pearl.

"None that I know of. There've been Schweitzers like Gering and Hutters like Wipf and Uncle P. P."

"Uncle P. P. ran for office?"

"Sure, ran and won. Served in both the House and Senate. Served first when South Dakota was still a part of the Dakota Territory."

18

"That must've been a first for a Hutter."

"No, actually not. A Wipf, David D., served as Secretary of State in the early part of the century."

"I thought only women ran for Secretary of State," said Pearl.

"That's a more recent phenomenon," said Pa. "Why, would you like to run some day?"

"No, I don't like politics."

Wednesday, March 18, 1936

Two more lambs today. One came dead. Ferd Thomas came to my school to see if he could borrow a barrel to treat seed grain. Some people are already sowing.

Thursday, March 19, 1936

Went to town for harness repair and stayed for a basketball game between Flandreau Eagles and Freeman College. Flandreau won 34 to 27. Our College team consists of John Neufeld, Kurt Wipf, Archie Ellwein, Elgin Wollman, Oswald Schrag, Amos and Paul Kleinsasser, and "Bulger" Kaufman. The boys played good ball but were tired out in the last quarter. Some of the boys smoke. "Bosco" Unruh is their coach.

Friday, March 20, 1936

Got two more lambs. We now have 15 from 9 sheep. Oiled harness in the evening.

Marian is starting to stutter. She must have gotten hurt.

Our snowpile is still 2 feet high. It was not artificial.

Ma fixed up the davenport. She is real artistic.

"It looks beautiful, Katherine!" said Morgan. "I almost didn't recognize Father's *Schlaf Bank*."

"That's the idea, John."

"What's a *Saf Bak*?" lisped Marian.

"It's a sleeping bench, like a day bed. Your Grandpa Kleinsasser always rested on it during the day. That way he didn't have to get the bedding dirty," explained Morgan. Then, turning back to his wife, he asked, "How'd you pad it?"

"Well, the corn husks were all gone, so I used straw for the mattress part and padded the edges with an old feather tick."

"Well, well, well. Too bad we didn't get it fixed up while Father was still alive. Many's the time I had to lift him off his *Schlaf Bank* and transfer him to the bed."

"That's why I didn't get it padded. He was always on it, watching every move I made."

19

"Oh, now, he was just following the movements of a beautiful redhead."

Saturday, March 21, 1936

Last night one ewe wanted another ewe's lambs, and this morning she had a pair of dandy twins.

I am getting the drill ready. Dragged one field of plowed ground.

I tried to have my wheat fanned at Park Lane Feeds but all Kaufman's bins are full.

Put a new Lee tire and tube on the Olds. I had bought it last year.

Sunday, March 22, 1936

Pearl, Cal and I went to church. I taught a Sunday School class.

Rev. P. P. Tschetter visited us today, and we visited at John L.'s He has 58 signatures on my petition.

Gave a donation of $5. to Jac. Mendel for the new church piano.

"Well, Katherine, I paid our pledge for the new piano in church."

"Good! That should improve the singing considerably. We should have had one long ago."

"Well, you know the older people wouldn't have allowed it too long ago."

"I know. Like they objected to my wearing a hat to church instead of a *Tichele*. All those old ladies looking like they just got off the boat from Russia."

"Well, you won, didn't you?"

"Sure, but not without a lot of stares!"

"They were just jealous that they didn't have such nice naturally curly hair under that flowered hat," teased Morgan.

"The piano will help us learn our parts and keep us in tune when the choir practices too."

"In tune with the piano, maybe. Now we'll have to pay for a piano tuner too. The fancier you get, the more expensive the upkeep. The old timers knew why they kept things simple."

Monday, March 23, 1936

Pearl's and Cal's Poland China sows came from a breeder near Inwood, Iowa. They look pretty good.

I got Bill Gross to sow for me at $1.25 a day.

Wednesday, March 25, 1936

I took my pupils on a field trip to the College for an art exhibit and then to the Co-op Creamery. Walt Bruun, the manager, showed us around. He is from Denmark and really knows the creamery business.

Bill Gross seeded 12 acres of barley this afternoon. We are sowing it 2 bushels to the acre.

There is a new farm program out – the Soil Conservation Program – to take the place of the AAA.

Thursday, March 26, 1936

Blizzard today, so Bill Gross went home. There will be no seeding for a while.

The Hofer children were absent for the first time this winter. Up to this point we had had perfect attendance.

Pearl and Cal and others started for home and got stalled a mile north of town. They went back and stayed at Emma's.

One of the Poland China sows had 11 pigs. A wonderful mother, very tame and gentle.

Friday, March 27, 1936

Nice but a lot of snow on the ground. I had to arrange transportation for Gordon Schmidt today since he was not along yesterday when the children stayed overnight in town. Julius Albrecht of Square Deal Garage came out to get Gordon. The children tried to drive home tonight but the Olds stalled at Floyd Graber's place. Graber pulled the car to Albrecht's garage but they could not fix it. So one of Albrecht's boys took the children home.

Saturday, March 28, 1936

Had Jake Walter drive me and Leon Weier to the Fraternal Burial Association board meeting in Viborg. My car was in the shop. Got home at 12:30 a.m. Albrecht had brought the Olds out by the time we got home.

The second Poland China club sow had 9 pigs. She is not as gentle as the other one.

Before I left for Viborg I prepared the garden for Mrs. She and the girls planted quite a field while I was away.

"Why do we have to plant such a big garden?" asked Pearl. "We'll never be able to hoe all of this."

"We need the garden stuff to feed the family. You all are eating more every year. Besides, this year we're going to make the rows far enough apart so we can cultivate between the rows with the corn cultivator. And now everyone can help with the garden."

"Ruth and Marian are going to have to help more this year. I've got all the milking to do, and Cal and I both have to take care of our 4-H club pigs."

21

"We like to help," piped up Ruth.

"You like the idea of helping. When it comes to sticking with a job, that's another story," asserted Pearl.

"Tie on your bonnets. It's easy to get a sun burn on spring days like this. And cover your arms with jackets," directed their mother.

"I hate to wear a bonnet. Makes me feel all cooped up. I like to feel the breeze," complained Pearl.

"I like the spring air too, but you don't want to get brown. Looks un-ladylike. Light complected people like us have to be careful of too much sun. Makes the freckles come out too," said their mother, pointing to a permanent feature on her face.

Sunday, March 29, 1936

Took Marian to Chiropractor Emil Tiesen for a treatment for stuttering. It snowed 6 inches.

Monday, March 30, 1936

One of the club sows killed one of her pigs, so she has only 8 left.

Pearl could not get the Olds started at the College, so Albrecht poured some gas into the vacuum tank to start it.

I went to town later for coal and to deliver the hatching eggs. Got 840 pounds of Montana coal @ $12.25 per ton from Thompson Yards.

I began my last six weeks period of school today.

Tuesday, March 31, 1936

Snowed. Had to pull the Olds with Daisy to start it. Jake M. Hofer told me to put in my application for teaching again next year.

Wednesday, April 1, 1936

April Fool's Day. The tire on the front wheel came off and tore a new valve stem on the inner tube. The nuts of the tire lug had come off.

Snowing today. We drilled on spelling for the elimination meet on Friday.

Had Soil Conservation meeting in Freeman tonight. John L. was elected chairman. I could not get on the committee because I am a candidate for state office.

Thursday, April 2, 1936

Drove to Olivet with Jake Walter to file my nominating petition. Many cars were stalled along the road in the snow. They had tried to pass each other where there was only one track to follow. At two places near Menno between 15 and 20 trucks and cars were stalled.

Got to Olivet after the court house had closed, so I gave my petition to Attorney William Metzger, who also notarized it. Saturday, April 4, is the last date to file.

The unruly sow killed another one of her pigs, so she has only 7 left.

Friday, April 3, 1936

Our school was host for the spelling and declamation contests. Districts #98, 54, 56, and 49 participated with teachers Jacob B. Hofer, Anna Tschetter, Elizabeth Hofer and me. First places in their grade went to Esther Hofer, Esther Graber, Melvin Ratzlaff, Eugene Graber, Jeanette Merk, Florine Waltner, Lorene Merk, and Elizabeth Hofer. In declam Lois Graber, Marie Walter and Fae Graber got firsts.

I drove to Sam Schmidt to get a warrant for transporting three children from #26 for $6 each per month. Had to go to John P. Gross to get it signed and then to John M. S. Hofer to get a check. Went to town to cash the check after that.

Saturday, April 4, 1936

Had 1,000 campaign cards printed and started electioneering. Atty. J. C. Graber told me to introduce a bill for more exemptions from farm foreclosure.

Sunday, April 5, 1936

Went to church and taught a class. Paid Jake L. for twine and Joe L. for fish.

Monday, April 6, 1936

Congratulated winners in spelling and declamation.

Went to Marion to try to get new fenders for the Olds. Bill Rapp said he could fix both old ones for $4.

Tuesday, April 7, 1936

Jake M. Kleinsasser started working for me @ $25 per month. Sold some barley @42¢ to the elevator. Ordered 400 Leghorns from Fensel to be delivered April 23 in exchange for eggs.

School children collected and sent $1 for YOUNG AMERICA.

Wednesday, April 8, 1936

Took Marie Walter to Miss Pankratz at the College to drill her piece, "Edith Helps Things Along," and commended Miss Pankratz on her teaching. Marie has a few words that seem to trouble her.

Jake is sowing barley 2 bushels to the acre.
Did a little campaigning in town.

Thursday, April 9, 1936
Cleaver put fenders on my Olds for $1. Pete Ratzlaff had bought them in Sioux Falls at $2 a piece.

Took Marie to Miss Pankratz again for more help on her declam piece.

Friday, April 10, 1936
Good Friday. No school. Went to church and to Marion after dinner. Dave J. R. and Susie were visiting with the folks also.

Saturday, April 11, 1936
Took Elizabeth and Esther Hofer, Melvin Ratzlaff and Marie Walter to Olivet for the county spelling and declam contest. Nobody placed but it was good experience.

Campaigned in Olivet. Prospects look very good.

Cal and Pearl signed their notes for the 4-H club sows $47.70 @ 8% interest for 7 months.

I paid my personal taxes in full—$7.50.

Sunday, April 12, 1936
Easter Sunday. Pearl, Cal and I went to church. Katherine stayed home to prepare dinner for the Joe J. Hofer family, Paul E. Hofer family, Sam J. and Sarah B. Hofer, and Orphan Gladys and Sammy. We made out the program for the youth meeting on June 21st.

Monday, April 13, 1936
Easter Monday. I rode to school with Cal. Pearl stayed home. College was closed in observance of Easter Monday.

Our church observed the Lord's Supper but I had school.

Jake Walter got Durham wheat from me and is sowing it. I did not have my man working in the field today.

Cal took Butcher Tschetter's trailer back and lost it on the road. He did not have the cotter key in the pin.

Ted Mettler wants some Durham wheat to make puffed wheat. A man on Minnesota Avenue in Sioux Falls manufactures it, he said.

Jake Gross wants $1.10 per acre for plowing.

Tuesday, April 14, 1936
Got $40.50 salary from #98 and $5. from Mrs. Abe Ratzlaff for transportation. Jake finished seeding wheat. Had pigs out sunning. Ma planted more garden stuff.

"When are we going to plant the tomato plants that are growing on the window sill, Mama?" Ruth asked.

"When all danger of frost is past."

"When's that?"

"Around the first of June. We've had snow in June. But we can plant the cabbage plants. They're more hardy."

"When are we gonna plant these?" asked Marian, pointing to the seed packages on the ground.

"What are they?"

"I don't know. They look like beans, but they're black, not white."

"Those are string beans. We'll plant them later too, in May."

"*String* beans?"

"Sure, they're green beans but they have strings that we have to pull off. You remember, we make *Strankel Zup* with potatoes and onions out of these beans."

"But I don't like the strings, do I?" asked Marian for confirmation.

"Me neither," piped up Ruth. "They get stuck in my teeth."

"Where'd we get all these seeds?" asked Marian.

"Daddy bought most of them from Preheim's Feed and Seed store because we can buy in bulk. It's cheaper that way. Some seeds we got from my sisters and Daddy's sisters. Some we saved from last year's garden, like the Little Russian cucumber seeds. We saved flower seeds too."

"That's what I like best—the flowers!" exclaimed Ruth.

"We'll plant the flowers up by the house so you can see them more easily."

"By the holly hocks?"

"Yes, we'll have moss roses and four o'clocks between the house and the garage."

"Oh, goodie! Then we can tell what time it is, when the four o'clocks open and close."

"That's right. When you see the flowers close, you'll know it's time to help Pearl bring the milk cows home from the pasture."

Wednesday, April 15, 1936

Regular dust storm. Jake finished sowing barley in cornstalk land and in south lake. Sowed 21 acres.

Went to town after school and changed a few more Democrats to Republicans.

Cal has a bad ear ache. He wanted me to take him to a doctor during the night. I blew cigar smoke into his ear instead.

John J. Gross, Henry's father, predicted that I would win as State Representative. Henry Goehring bought me a beer. I got home quite late, around 11:30.

"Well, it's about time," said his wife. "We waited for you quite a while before we ate supper. But I couldn't keep the children waiting any longer."

"I was politicking downtown."

"I know. I can smell it."

"You can? That's funny. I had only one beer."

"That's all it takes. I guess you think you have to join the crowd to get elected."

"You can't give the impression you think you are better than everyone else if you want them to like you."

"Maybe you shouldn't worry about their liking you. Maybe they'd respect you if you didn't take their beer."

"You're making a big fuss about one beer."

"I just don't approve."

"There's a lot you don't approve of. I'm going to bed."

Thursday, April 16, 1936

Had our athletic contests in school. Winners were:
Elizabeth Hofer, 1st High Jump, 1st Ball Throw, Class B
Bertha Walter, 2nd High Jump, 2nd Dash, Class B
Marie Walter, 1st High Jump, 2nd Dash, Class C
Sarah Hofer, 2nd High Jump, 1st Ball Throw, Class C
Esther Hofer, 1st High Jump, 2nd Ball Throw, Class D
Max Walter, 2nd High Jump, Class B
Melvin Ratzlaff, 1st High Jump, 1st Dash, Class C

Saturday, April 18, 1936

Got a lot of encouragement while campaigning in Parkston. Made a bet with Doering. He bet me a dollar I would win, so I called him on it. He is the stake holder. He has the money in an envelop in his desk.

Wm. Friedrich promised to support me. Got support of Solomon Tiede and Wm. Isaak too. Henry Rempfer wants to play neutral. Got home at 12:30 a.m.

Sunday, April 19, 1936

Whole family in church. Taught a class of 13 young ladies, including Pearl, Evelyn and Marjorie Hofer, Grace and Gladys Hofer, two Elizabeth Hofers, Caroline Tschetter, Mary Glanzer, Annie Gross, Marjorie Pollman, a Gross girl, and someone I do not know.

Had Christian Endeavor program in the evening. Collection was $4.76.

Tuesday, April 21, 1936

John R. Hofer was here to have me sign a Soil Conservation agreement. There are 186 crops considered to be soil depleting.

Josephine Zehnpfennig was here campaigning for Co. Sup. of Schools. Her father, who was with her, said I would be elected.

Went to town after school and got dried beef from Butcher Miller.

Wednesday, April 22, 1936

Took the car to school and went home for dinner.

Jake, the hired man, had a runaway with Bullet and Daisy. He finally got them stopped on Joe L. Wipf's land south of the church.

After school Jake, Clara and Pearl fanned about 70 bushels of oats. Cal dragged land after school.

I went to Menno campaigning. Ted Mehlhaf said if I don't carry Menno, it won't be his fault.

Thursday, April 23, 1936

Planted 5 bushels of potatoes after school. Should have done it on Good Friday.

Ray Hirsch was here about my Federal Land Loan interest, which was due April 1. I will have to make some arrangement for money or get an extension on the loan. Interest on the loan is 3 1/2% until June 1, 1936, and 4% from then 'til June 1, 1938. The Commissioner loan is 5%. I have a $7,000 Land Bank loan and a $4,000 Commissioner loan.

Friday, April 24, 1936

Pearl is home sick. She caught a cold celebrating Clean Up Day at the Academy.

My eighth graders do not have their book reports in. Bertha has drawings and essay ready, but Paul and Elizabeth do not.

Frank Wilde bought 39 bushels of barley @ 50¢.

Saturday, April 25, 1936

Went to Olivet to hand in required drawings and bought some new books for the 2nd and 4th graders. Miss Perman did not permit me to count as books read the WEEKLY READER or YOUNG AMERICA.

Got only a fair reception while campaigning in Kaylor. Possibly made a mistake by asking the banker to take a personal interest and hand out cards for me.

Had some nice contacts in Tripp. Tiede will probably run strong there. Lichter thinks Tiede will lose west of Tripp.

Met Johnson in Menno. He says the fight is between him and me. Got home at 12:30 a.m.

Sunday, April 26, 1936
Got to church late. The church clock was fast. Went to Emma's in the evening but she was not home so we visited at Jake W. Gross's for the evening.

Monday, April 27, 1936
Did not have school today. Campaigned in Parkston, Dimock, Starr and Cross Plains Townships. Theo Zehnpfennig went with me. I expect a lot of votes out of Cross Plains.

Came back by way of Lindeman at Old Elm Spring Colony. Car stalled four miles west of Clayton. A Johnson pushed me to Clayton where I roused up Boehmer. He poured gas into the vacuum tank. Car ran 'til Joe J. Walter's place by pouring gas into tank. Stopped across from Nachtigal's and then walked home. Got home at 3 a.m. That's politics.

Tuesday, April 28, 1936
Took car to town to have it timed and to have a fuel pump put on.

Wanted to go to Sioux Falls after school to hear Theodore Roosevelt, but Dr. M. M. Hofer backed out. Instead I heard him speak over Jake Walter's radio. He addressed the Young Republicans. Leslie Jensen, candidate for Governor, introduced Roosevelt.

Wednesday, April 29, 1936
I hit Max in school with a stick. I had wanted him to count the counties in South Dakota but he claimed he didn't know how after I had just told him.

Haar took me to Olivet to make out an extension on my Land Bank loan. The extension is for June 1.
$100-September 1, $69.27 + $100 Commissioner loan interest.

I mortgaged 500 bushels barley, 100 bushels wheat and entire this year's crop.

Thursday, April 30, 1936
Went to town for more sweet clover. Jake had opened the seeder too much and for a while was seeding 37 pounds per acre. We are sowing sweet clover with the oats as a nurse crop. The oats was sown quite a while ago.

Had about an inch of rain last night, so conditions are just right for sweet clover and alfalfa. We are sowing 15 pounds to the acre now.

Max helped Cal clean out our cistern.

Friday, May 1, 1936

Hired man sowed 11 acres alfalfa after coming home at 4 a.m. He was in Milltown for a dance. Got a warrant for $18 for transporting pupils from #26. Had to visit three Board members again to complete the transaction.

Saturday, May 2, 1936

Campaigned in Molan Township and Tripp. Craig had a news item in his paper about me.

Handed in the school children's book reports, essays and drawings and paid the Young Citizen League dues at Olivet.

Sunday, May 3, 1936

All went to church. I taught a class. The hired man stayed home.

We visited Rev. D. S. Wipf in the afternoon and went to the Salem K. M. B. Church in the evening, where the College faculty gave a program.

Monday, May 4, 1936

Campaigned in Pleasant Township, Parkston, Foster and Milltown. Had lunch with Elmer Haar at Milltown. August Kayser of German Township said he had campaigned for me. It looks as if Tiede will be first and I second.

Tuesday, May 5, 1936

Election Day. Hauled some votes in Grand View Township. Zach Wipf campaigned hard against me for the precinct committee man job. He won 46 to 44. He promised the ballot box to some people.

I went to Silver Lake to haul in some votes. It takes the women too long to get dressed. One spends too much time waiting.

Wednesday, May 6, 1936

Over the tension. Can relax a little. The big campaign is ahead.

The kids are taking Test F in school. It seems as though they have a chance to pass.

Chas. Preheim is testing our seed corn by germinating it. There seems to be a scarcity of seed corn. Every other year it seems to be scarce. I don't know whether I have enough.

Friday, May 8, 1936

School picnic today. Had sandwiches, ice cream bars, fudgsicles, cookies, bananas and oranges.

Last day of school for lower grades. Upper grades will have a 3-day review and then final exams on May 28 and 29.

College gave an operetta, SYLVIA, to a packed house. Pearl played a minor part, a hay maker. Ma did not use her ticket because she was sick, so we took P. P. along.

98% of the seed corn that we had stored upstairs in the house germinated, according to Preheim.

Saturday, May 9, 1936
The boys shelled and graded seed corn. I worked on school reports – quite a tiresome job.

Got 500 Leghorn chicks from Fensel @ $6.50 per hundred.

Sunday, May 10, 1936
All in church but Pearl and Marian. Got there too late to teach my class.

Ma took a treatment from Emil Tiesen and then we went to Marion to visit the folks. Abe Wienses and Henry Tiahrts were there.

Tuesday, May 12, 1936
Sold some barley @ 33c per bu. to pay the hired man. Chicks are coming fairly well. We have lost a few.

Wednesday, May 13, 1936
Bought some mercury solution to treat the seed corn. Ma planted beans.

I tried to shear sheep but could not find where I had stored the knives. By the time I found them, I could get only two sheep shorn.

Got high school graduation announcements from John J. Kleinsasser from Doland High School, Jerome Kleinsasser from Freeman High School, and Ed. S. Tieszen and Helen Tiahrt from Marion High School.

I had Chas. Gering re-sole my shoes for $1.

Thursday, May 14, 1936
I finished spring plowing using Jake M. Hofer's gang plow. I fell from the plow and hurt my back badly.

Friday, May 15, 1936
Started planting corn. Treated seed with "Merko." We are using the small plates that throw 3 kernels to the hill. We plan to plant 40 acres in the northwest field.

Saturday, May 16, 1936
Alfred Hofer is planting corn for me @ $1.50 a day.

30

Took 7 pupils to Rally Day in Tripp. Melvin Ratzlaff placed 1st in Class C High Jump (4 ft., 2 in.) and Elizabeth Hofer placed 1st in Class B Ball Throw.

Sheared two sheep after I got home at 6 p.m. Went to town later. Pearl was a waitress at the Academy Junior-Senior Banquet.

Sunday, May 17, 1936

Ma, Cal and I were in church. Alfred Hofer called me from Emery to get him and Bingo. They were in a bad car accident with a Juhnke on Highway 35. Both cars were badly damaged.

Tuesday, May 19, 1936

Senator Dickinson said, "In 1932 we had FDR, in 1933 NRA, in 1934 IOU, in 1935 SOS, and in 1936 it will be GOP."

Finished planting corn this forenoon before it rained. Planted sunflower seeds too.

Wednesday, May 20, 1936

Sold wool to Elias Wipf @ 25¢ a lb. We had 15 sheep.

County Agent Roth was here to weigh Cal's lambs. The boys organized a 4-H lamb club.

My eighth graders all passed their daily work.

Thursday, May 21, 1936

Went to the Freeman High School Commencement because Jerome graduated. Atty. A. C. Miller from Kennebec spoke. He said, "The two sins of education are indifference and ignorance. Think or perish. Think right and do right."

Saturday, May 23, 1936

Pearl and Cal went to Menno to practice livestock judging for 4-H. I worked on my school reports and ditched water out of our many lakes standing in the fields.

Sunday, May 24, 1936

After church Cal and I went to Lake Charles. The spillway had torn away. Quite a few fish had swum out of the lake. We then went to Wolf Creek Dam, which also had broken through.

Monday, May 25, 1936

Started 8th grade review. Cal plowed with the sulky. He passed the 7th grade.

Pearl is learning to drive the car.

31

Ma and I planted sweet corn in the garden. We had fresh onions and lettuce. Ruth and Marian ate quite a few onions. I hope they do not pay for it later.

"You dig the holes and I'll drop in the seeds," said Katherine.

"Tryin' to take the easy path again, I see!" Morgan teased. "Don't you remember I hurt my back?"

"Don't you remember I just got a treatment myself from Emil?"

"Tieszens aren't supposed to get sore backs. They're supposed to cure sore backs."

"This sweet corn ought to be good, at least better than eating field corn," said Katherine, changing the subject.

"Yeah, I wonder why the other corn we planted didn't come up. Prob'ly too cold or maybe the cut worms got it."

Seeing her youngest daughters approach the garden, Katherine said, "Come here, girls, you can help me plant the corn."

"Boy, I'm gonna have trouble keepin' up with three women!"

"Ruth, you help Marian count out three kernels. One, two, three. No more than that in each hill," said their mother.

"Okay, Mommy," she said, taking charge. "One, two, three. Count them, Honey."

"One, two, tree."

"One, two, *three,* Honey," said Morgan. "One, two, three. Say it after me."

"One, two free."

"Don't rush her, John; she'll get it," cautioned the mother.

Tuesday, May 26, 1936

Reviewed with my 8th graders again. They have forgotten plenty.

The WPA toilet crew of four men was here and put in a sanitary, fly-proof toilet over a concrete floor. We used our old building. Most of the construction had been done in Parkston.

Paid my Mennonite Aid Plan insurance. A. R. M. Hofer charged 1% again for district expenses. The levy was 10c per $100 valuation. My insurance was $8.72.

Wednesday, May 27, 1936

Took Pearl, Clara and Elizabeth to town to catch a ride in Kaufman's truck to their Academy picnic at Milltown. He charged the 63 students a dime a piece. They rollerskated most of the time and kicked about the lunch when they got home.

Cal covered a leafy spurge patch with straw that was packed around the windmill during the winter. The weed seeds came across to our land from Deckert's land.

32

Friday, May 29, 1936

I graded the exams for my 8th graders. Unofficially, Paul averaged 81.5, Elizabeth 82.1, and Bertha 81.7.

Saturday, May 30, 1936

Started cultivating corn. Corn a good stand. Creepers are coming fast, especially on early plowing. Corn in low places is fair where seed was treated with Merko.

Got John J. K. Stahl's Poland China boar. Pearl and Cal want to raise some fall pigs.

Sunday, May 31, 1936

All went to church. The floor had been varnished Friday and was not dry so we had church outside. Sunday School was not held.

Tuesday, June 2, 1936

Reuben Glanzer was here trying to sell Banker's Union life insurance out of Denver. I told him I had enough.

Wednesday, June 3, 1936

After I finished cultivating, Katherine, Pearl and I went to church to practice singing for Jacob B. Hofer's ordination. There were 15 or 16 of us. It is easy practicing since we have the piano.

Ruth went along with Rev. P. P. Tschetter for German school at District #51. She said she made A + today. She got quite a thrill out of going to school.

Thursday, June 4, 1936

I was called to Freeman on account of the seed and feed loan. I have to pay $110 with this year's grain and have the rest extended until next year. Gave 1936 crop mortgage for $100.

Cal is cultivating corn with the double row cultivator.

Friday, June 5, 1936

Ruth wanted to go to German school. Cal took her out to the section line with the car so Rev. Tschetter could pick her up. Soon after he got back, Ruth was home too. She could not wait for Tschetter.

Cal and I went crabbing with Math Kleinsasser north east of Stanley Corner. We caught 4 gunny sacks full. The whole family ate crabs for supper, but I ate too many.

"Here, I'll help you, Honey," said Cal to Marian. "What you need to do is pull the tail out first. Then take this little band off the

33

tail at the top where it was attached to the body. Then just pull the soft, cooked flesh out of the shell."

"You do it. I can't."

"Yes, you can. Try it!"

"I did try it. I can't do it!" she insisted.

"*Ormst Ding!* Here, I'll clean some for you," said Morgan, who already had a huge mound of red shells in front of his place at the oilcloth-covered dining table.

"I can't believe I'm eating all these crabs," said Katherine. "I never used to be able to stomach them."

"You Low Germans have missed out on a lot of delicacies," said Morgan.

"Some I'd just as soon never heard of."

"Like what?" asked Pearl.

"Oh, *Nukele Zup, Gashtel Zup,* all those fattening foods. Why do you think Hutters are fat while Low Germans are thin?"

"Not all Hutters are fat and not all Low Germans are thin," countered Pearl.

"You're right, but as a general rule, you'll find more overweight people in the *Hutterische* community than you'll find in the *Platt-deutsch* community," pronounced their Low German mother.

"I thought heredity had something to do with it too," said Cal.

"I'm sure it does. But you watch these *Hutterische* grandmothers feeding the little ones. They think every baby has to be fat or it's unhealthy – won't make it through the winter. Watch 'em pour cream over soda crackers and sprinkle sugar over that and feed it to the babies!"

"Is that what Grandma Kleinsasser did when she was still living?" asked Pearl.

"Yes, she did, until I stopped it!"

"My mother raised nine children to adulthood, so she knew something about it!" Morgan objected.

"Well, she didn't know much about germs and hygiene!"

"Are you going to start that again?"

"Well, I think the children are old enough to learn what I had to put up with when your mother was living with us!"

"What did she do?" asked Pearl.

"When you were a little baby, she would masticate your food and then feed it to you."

"Masticate?"

"She would chew it up first, then spit it into a spoon and give it to you."

"No!"

"Yes, she'd also cool your food like that sometimes."

34

"What did you do?"

"Well, one time I got so disgusted, I just started walking home!"

"You're kidding!"

"I did! I just left!"

"Then what happened?" asked Cal.

"I went and brought her back," Morgan laughed, "where she belonged."

"Did Grandma stop then?" asked Pearl.

"Not really. You can't change those old people's ways," said Katherine.

"She thought she was doing the right thing. And look how strong Pearl is today – doing the milking, raising a litter of pigs, being first in her Academy class!" said Morgan, proudly. "There was a lot of wisdom in those old people."

"Grandma almost scared me to death. I remember that," Pearl added.

"She did? How?" asked her mother.

"With her ghost stories. She told me that if I didn't behave, the wolves would come and get me!"

"From Wolf Creek?" asked Cal.

"Yep! Did she tell you the same thing?"

"Sure, but she never fazed me a bit."

"I'll bet she scared you when she told you how the Russians used to steal Grandpa's horses, lifting them right out the door!" said Pearl to Cal.

"That's impossible!" protested Cal. "How could they lift a horse out the door?"

"I'll bet you have an image of those Dutch half doors from the old fashioned houses, where the top half is open and the bottom half locked so children can't wander out," surmised their mother.

"Maybe so. But I remember she definitely said children who didn't behave would be carried off by wolves," insisted Pearl.

"Doesn't seem to have worked," smiled Morgan, cracking a crawfish claw and sucking out the tasty morsel. "They did have a lot of wolves in Russia to contend with. You're lucky she didn't tell you about throwing children out of the sleigh to distract the wolves."

"Now, John, that's enough!" said Katherine with finality.

Saturday, June 6, 1936

Gave a pail each of crabs to Jake Walter, P. P. and Mrs. Ike.

Pearl and Cal had their sow litter club meeting at P.P.'s. Cal furnished the ice cream bars.

Some teachers are helping to grade 7th and 8th grade tests in Olivet. I got the grades for my 8th graders. Their final grades averaged 5 to 6 points higher than I had given them.

Sunday, June 7, 1936
We were the first ones in church for a change.
Pearl and Cal went to a shower for Sam J. Hofer and Sarah Gross at Joe A. Hofer's place.

Monday, June 8, 1936
Roland Haar's truck is still stuck in our driveway at 9 p.m. Four horses couldn't pull it out. He came for a load of barley.

Tuesday, June 9, 1936
Cal replanted some corn that had drowned out and I cultivated for the second time.
Had County Republican organization election. Wm. Metzger was elected chairman and Ted Mehlhaf secretary by the precinct committeemen. A. J. Waltner was elected to the patronage committee.
I sent $100 to the Federal Land Bank as payment on interest due and $74.50 on my seed loan.

Thursday, June 11, 1936
Metzger is in Cleveland to nominate presidential and vice presidential candidates for the Republican Party. Landon, Knox, Borah, Vandenburg and Hoover are spoken of as Presidential timber.

Friday, June 12, 1936
Landon and Knox were nominated. The GOP endorsed a Soil Conservation program.

Saturday, June 13, 1936
Extremely hot. Grain suffers for lack of rain.
Went to town in evening. Sold eggs to Fensel Hatchery for last time this season. I was well satisfied with the treatment we got from Fensel.

Sunday, June 14, 1936
Went to Olivet for 8th grade graduation. Jake M. Hofer went with us. Two of the three graduates from #98 were his children.

Tuesday, June 16, 1936
School election today. #98 will have a fight on. Ben Ratzlaff and Zach Wipf were the candidates for treasurer. Ben won 13 to

11. *Zach is supposed to have gotten mad as a bull. He wanted to hit Fred L. Thomas. Jake M. Hofer was chairman. He had to quiet Zach down a number of times. It is reported that Zach swore in the schoolhouse.*

Our election in #26 was a tame affair. The Thomases stayed at home. John P. Gross is chairman, John M. S. Hofer treasurer, and Sam J. Schmidt clerk. The officers and Katherine and I were the only ones present.

We might not have school again in #26. The only pupils would be: Ruth and Cal, Gordon Schmidt, and Janice Ratzlaff.

Friday, June 19, 1936

Got two sacks of crabs. Ma got tired of cooking them. Took some to John L.'s and Ted Haar.

"Pearl, you're going to have to learn how to cook crabs sooner or later anyhow; it might as well be now," Katherine instructed her eldest daughter.

"Oh, Ma, do I have to?"

"Well, if your father keeps bringing all these crabs home, somebody is going to have to clean and cook them."

"These are so muddy and tangled up in weeds."

"That's because of where they come from—out of the mud. Here, I'll help you carry them down to the windmill. We'll hose them off down there."

Katherine and Pearl loaded the burlap sacks of squirming, clawing crawfish into the faded red coaster wagon and pulled them to the windmill, where a leaking galvanized round bath tub (a "Number Three") awaited them on the wooden platform under the windmill.

"Let's hose them off in the sacks first before dumping them into the tub," said Pearl.

"Fine!"

Pearl took the hose fastened to the water hydrant on the wooden supply tank and turned the water on full force.

"Be careful! You'll drown us both!" cautioned her mother.

"Just wanted to get as much mud off as possible." That completed, Pearl loosened the binder twine holding one sack closed and the two women dumped the sack full into the water-filled tub, causing the crabs and water to overflow.

When the little girls heard the squeals at the windmill, they left their play in the dirt under the elm tree and ran to see the excitement. "Can we help?" asked Ruth.

"You'd better just watch or you might get pinched by some of these Granddaddy crabs," said their mother. Gingerly Pearl and

37

Katherine picked up the escaping crayfish by their hard-shelled torsos and threw them into the milk pails which had been sun-bleaching upside down on wooden fence posts near the windmill.

"There's one getting away," cried Marian, pointing.

"Look at their eyes sticking out of their heads," said Ruth, wrapping her hands in her skirt.

"See their feelers? That's how they know where they are and how to stay out of danger," instructed their mother.

"Well, they're in danger now," said Pearl, exultingly, "and there's not much they can do about it!"

When a milk pail full of crayfish had been cleaned, the women carried it back to the house where a copper boiler of water was simmering on the three-burner kerosene stove in the kitchen. They turned up the burners and dumped in the crawling, struggling crayfish.

"We'll have to watch these burners so they don't flare up. Now, we'll put in a hand full of coarse pickling salt and add a few red peppers," said Katherine, demonstrating.

"Is that what makes the crabs red—the red peppers?" asked Marian.

"No, they turn red from the hot water," answered Pearl. "The red pepper flavors them."

"You mean they turn red when they're dead," observed Ruth.

"You might put it that way."

"Don't they hurt when you throw them in the hot water?" asked Ruth.

"We prefer not to think about that," said Katherine. "You girls go back to the windmill and repeat the process. I'll watch the boiler."

"I want to stay here with you, Mama," said Marian.

Saturday, June 20, 1936

The Burial Association Board decided we'd let our loudspeaker be used free of charge for any church doings.

Sunday, June 21, 1936

Jacob B. Hofer was ordained to the ministry in our church. Brother J. W. and Rev. P. P. Tschetter spoke in the morning, and Pete Stahl and Alfred Waltner in the afternoon. We had a Christian Endeavor program in the evening. Evelyn Hofer gave a good pianologue. The collection was $4.83.

Monday, June 22, 1936

Ruth is memorizing a verse of the Bible. She is such a puzzle to her teacher in German school that Rev. Tschetter had her memorize the following: "Wass meint ihr wird aus diesen Kindlein werden?"

Pearl is 16 years old today. No rain. The crops look worse every day.

Went to Henry Tiahrt's to celebrate Pearl's birthday.

Tuesday, June 23, 1936

Pearl's 4-H pigs have "necro." One died. Cal plowed for the Soil Conservation program.

Wednesday, June 24, 1936

Pearl went to 4-H camp at Mitchell. Cal did not go.

J. W.'s Johnny hitchhiked down from Spink County. Spink is burned out again. He will work for us.

Sprayed the potato bugs with Abe Wiens' spray pump. It is slow but does good work.

Friday, June 26, 1936

Cal cultivated with the double row cultivator. Very hot and sultry – 100 degrees.

Tschetter's German scholars gave a program tonight in our church.

Saturday, June 27, 1936

Johnny and I are fencing up a piece of sweet clover and oats for pasture. The oats was seeded too late. Ground is so hard that we have to soak it before we can dig the post holes.

Had new potatoes for the first time – as big as chicken eggs.

Sunday, June 28, 1936

Sam J. Hofer and Sarah Gross were married in church this morning.

Johnny will work for Joe L. and Abe Wiens this week.

Adjusting loss at John J. B.'s for the Mennonite Aid Plan. His barn burned.

Thursday, July 2, 1936

Started cutting grain. Cal and Pearl are shocking. Barley is very poor in high places. Green as grass in lakes but good. Had half inch of rain in the evening.

Saturday, July 4, 1936

In the evening we went to Marion with a freezer full of sherbert [sic] for Grandma's 79th birthday. Rev. & Mrs. Derk Tieszen were there too. It was 111 degrees today.

"Okay, you may walk to the business district," said Morgan, after the children had finished their sherbet. "Just don't stay too long. We got to get up for church tomorrow morning."

Pearl, Cal and the two little girls walked the two blocks west to Marion's Main Street, which was lit up for Saturday night shoppers. They walked past Hieb's store, the Tieszen Clinic and the Tieszen Hotel. "That's where the bonesetters work," said Ruth, knowingly.

"I know. I've been there plenty of times," said Pearl, impatiently.

"Where can I buy some firecrackers?" Cal wondered aloud.

"Firecrackers? You're not going to buy firecrackers, are you? You can get your fingers blown off that way," said Ruth.

"Naw, that's sissy talk. I know how to handle firecrackers. Done it lots of times."

"If you buy firecrackers, I'm gonna tell Pa," Ruth announced.

"Go ahead, be a tattletale! That's all you're good for!"

"She's right. They're very dangerous," confirmed Pearl. "I heard of a boy who lost his eyesight."

"Oh, you're all a bunch of spoilsports."

"You can go ahead and get firecrackers if you want to kill yourself," said Pearl. "But I am not going to be a party to it. Come, girls, let's go back to Grandma's house," said Pearl and took the two young ones in hand.

"Will Cal get a spanking?" lisped Marian as Pearl hurried the girls back east on Grandma's street.

"I don't know. What's worse, he might get hurt – seriously hurt!"

"Aw, gee, I thought we could see what Marion looks like on July Fourth, and now we gotta go back already," pouted Ruth, as she dragged her feet on the sidewalk.

"It looks just like Freeman on a Saturday night – just lights and lots of people crowding the streets, gossipping," said Pearl.

"I bet they have a band playing. I think I hear music," said Ruth.

When the girls got back to their grandparents' cottage, the adults were all sitting on the screened porch, fanning themselves. Bugs buzzed around the street lamps and flew against the screens. "Let's just sit here on the steps for a while," said Pearl, not wanting her parents to know that Cal was not with them.

"I can hear kids playing on the Maypole across the street in the school yard," said Ruth.

"Me too. Can we go over there?" asked Marian.

"No, it's too dangerous to play in the dark. You might get hit in the head by the chains when they swing out and back."

On the screened porch the grownups were talking about crops, the heat, their church activities, relatives. The conversation, mostly in *Plattdeutsch* for Grandmother's benefit, was hard for Marian and Ruth to understand. However, when Marian heard the words, "*Schlopa gona*," she agreed. It was time to go home and go to bed. Soon her parents and Rev. and Mrs. Tieszen appeared at the door and said farewell to their elderly hosts. The girls called out their good-byes to their grandparents as the family walked to their 1928 Oldsmobile.

"Where's Calvin?" asked Mother, surprised that he was not in the car.

"He's still downtown; he wanted to buy something," answered Pearl.

Just then the figure of a young man appeared in the lamplight. It was Cal! "Boy, you're lucky you didn't miss your ride home!" admonished Morgan from behind the steering wheel as Cal slipped into the back seat.

"He has such a smirk on his face, he must have gotten his firecrackers," surmised Pearl.

Sunday, July 5, 1936

Not in church. Very hot—110 degrees. Went to Henry Tiahrt's in the afternoon. When we got home, the cows were out. Got to bed after midnight.

Monday, July 6, 1936

Finished cutting rye. Ma, Pearl and Cal shocked.
Took cream to town. Sells @ 31c lb. butterfat.

Tuesday, July 7, 1936

Started cutting at 5 a.m. and cut 'til 6:30, when the binder broke.

Wednesday, July 8, 1936

Started cutting at 7 a.m. Broke a pinion and took 'til 5 p.m. to get started again. Grasshoppers cut off half of the barley heads in the field I cut today. Very hot and windy all day. Went to town in the evening. Stores are open on Wednesday nights as well as Saturday nights now.

Thursday, July 9, 1936

Ma was shocking for a while. She is having a wonderful appetite. We will have to let her shock all year.

41

Friday, July 10, 1936

Paul Decker asked me to go in threshing with him and John R. Hofer. I consented gladly.

Saturday, July 11, 1936

Finished cutting grain. Family went to town in the evening. I hauled a load of hay after it got cooler.

Sunday, July 12, 1936

4-H club picnic at Riverside Park on the James River in Olivet. The whole family was there.

Monday, July 13, 1936

Johnny and I pitched "bouquets" at Paul Decker's. Pearl and Cal hauled two loads of barley bundles into the hay mow.

Cal got sick in the afternoon. His legs got stiff.

Republicans had a meeting in Olivet, but I did not care to run my own car. Atty. John C. Graber did not go and Atty. Henry L. Gross had already left by the time I came home from threshing and phoned him.

Threshed 10 1/2 hrs. at Decker's.

Thursday, July 14, 1936

Pitched 11 3/4 hrs. wheat and rye bundles at Decker's. Rye bundles very heavy but yield poor, about 8 bu. to acre.

Wednesday, July 15, 1936

Pitched bundles 5 1/2 hrs. at Decker's, then moved to John R.'s and pitched 4 1/2 hrs. Terrific heat—over 102 degrees. Had a little stubble fire at Hofer's. Must have started from the John Deere tractor. Johnny pitched too.

All in town in evening. Sold $4.39 worth of cream from four days' milking of five cows.

Thursday, July 16, 1936

I got overheated yesterday and felt bad this forenoon. Butch Hofer came out looking for a job, so I gave him mine.

Got a ram from Abe Tieszen, who wants $5 if I keep it.

Got oil from Joe L. Changed oil at 5,625 miles.

Friday, July 17, 1936

I was home getting ready for threshing. Very hot. Butch and Johnny pitched for me. I am taking salt tablets to avoid heat stroke.

Saturday, July 18, 1936

I set up the elevator in the morning. The machine moved to our place and we started threshing here about 3 p.m. Threshed 98 bu. rye and a little barley.

Sunday, July 19, 1936

All in church. Very hot. P. P. Tschetter preached. Rained about 4 p.m. Very much wind and dust.

Monday, July 20, 1936

Finished threshing today. Had a good run all the way through. Threshed 348 bu. barley and 68 bu. wheat. Josh Tschetter was here to help elevate grain and set the straw stack. I paid him $2.

Tuesday, July 21, 1936

Cal took a load of barley to Park Lane Feeds to be ground for his pigs. I fixed fence so the pigs don't get out on the yard. Ma does not like it when the pigs get into the garden.

Wednesday, July 22, 1936

Very hot. Cal and I got up at 4:30 a.m. and drove to Alexandria to exchange a ram with Saunders. Got back at 8 a.m. Terrific wind.

Thursday, July 23, 1936

Pearl is helping at Henry Tiahrt's while they are threshing. Ruth got her arm caught in the Maytag wringer while helping Ma. She has quite a bit of pain.

Saturday, July 25, 1936

Went to town in the evening and had Ruth's arm looked after at Emil Tiesen's clinic. It is not out of joint.

Sunday, July 26, 1936

Home in the forenoon. Tiahrts brought Pearl back. Had half inch of rain.

Monday, July 27, 1936

Started fall plowing. Moved 207 pullets on new range and sprayed chicken barn for lice and mites.

Thursday, July 30, 1936

Johnny was pitching at Jake M. Hofer's. The horse (Lena) got her tail in the belt and tore off most of the hair and a piece of the tail. We culled out 26 old hens. Ma canned 17 today.

"How can you tell if they're not layers, Daddy?" asked Ruth as she watched him stuff the chicken crate with the rejects.

"If I can't get three fingers between their back bones where the eggs come out, then I know they're not laying. And we can't afford to keep feeding hens that aren't producing."

"What if you make a mistake?"

"Well, we do make mistakes some times. Then you and Marian get to eat the little yolks in the soup."

"So, whenever there's an egg in the soup, that's a sign you made a mistake?"

"That's right!"

Friday, July 31, 1936

Cal and I went crabbing and fishing with Melvin and Kenneth Hofer. Got 4 gal. crabs and 139 fish. We gave 20 to Elmer Tiahrt and 25 to Rev. Jacob A. Tieszen. Most of the crabs have gone into their holes. Only one was big, the others small.

Saturday, August 1, 1936

Plowed in the morning with the sulky and all afternoon with the old gang plow. The gang was quite rusty, but it worked all right. Ground is very dry for plowing.

Sunday, August 2, 1936

Not in church. I am reading FOLDED HILLS by Stewart White.

Monday, August 3, 1936

Plowed up some sod with the gang. Johnny relined the brakes on the Olds.

Tuesday, August 4, 1936

Dr. Pullman vaccinated the pigs for erysipelas.

Wednesday, August 5, 1936

Dug 25 bu. potatoes with Grandpa Tieszen's potato plow. Sold 108 lbs. to Butcher Miller @ $3.50 per cwt. A real price for potatoes.

Thursday, August 6, 1936

Cal was chosen to represent the 4-H lamb club in Brookings on the livestock judging team.

Tuesday, August 11, 1936

Sold 270 lbs. potatoes to Schamber's store for 3 1/2¢ per lb.

Made out the Christian Endeavor program at Joe J. Hofer's. We intend to get Rev. P. R. Schroeder to speak on the Mennonite World Conference in Holland.

Thursday, August 13, 1936
Grandpa and Grandma Tieszen brought some apples from Mrs. Regehr's tree. Katherine's sister Susie was along. Dave J. R. does not having a teaching job yet.

"Who is Mrs. Geer?" asked Marian as she bit into her apple.

"Mrs. Regehr is Grandpa's sister. She lives in the little house next to Grandpa and Grandma. You know, the one with the apple tree we climb in," answered Ruth.

"She's the one who wears the fancy black satin cap with the ruffle on it," said Pearl.

"*Tante* Regehr is your great aunt," Katherine instructed the little ones.

"She likes children, doesn't she?" asked Ruth.

"Oh, yes! She was never able to have any children of her own, so she takes a special interest in other people's children."

"Is it true that she wears a cap because her shawl caught fire when she was lighting a fire with cobs and kerosene?" asked Pearl.

"That's right. You have to be very careful around fire."

Saturday, August 15, 1936
Cal dragged the potato patch and found about 3 pails more. Sold 96 lbs. Bought a bushel of tomatoes @ $1.50 and windfall apples. We plowed the potato patch leaving dead furrows to hold water, if it comes.

Friday, August 21, 1936
Went to the Co-op Creamery picnic at the College Gym. They served ice cream in Dixie cups. Mr. Brandt of Minneapolis spoke on cooperatives. He cracked a few hot jokes. Cream brings 37¢, eggs 16¢.

Saturday, August 22, 1936
Cleaned hog barn and washed the floor. The pigs will have to wipe their feet before going into the barn now.

Sunday, August 23, 1936
Miss Helen Nickel, missionary to India, spoke in our church this morning. She had an interesting talk and a pleasing voice.

Tuesday, August 25, 1936

Traded peddler Dan Graber 100 lbs. potatoes for medicine and supplies.

Our bull was quite irritated. He wanted to go visiting.

Saturday, August 29, 1936

Went to College with brother J. W. to see about a job for Johnny. President Unruh promised him a job to work off 2 quarters' tuition.

Monday, August 31, 1936

Started teaching #98 with 6 pupils: Max and Marie Walter; Sarah, Esther and Sam Hofer; and Melvin Ratzlaff.

Pearl and Johnny started at the Academy and College, respectively. The Walter girls ride with us. Freeman Public School is not in session yet, so Cal and Ruth are home. Cal is plowing.

Tuesday, September 8, 1936

Dismissed school for the Hutchinson County Fair. Melvin Ratzlaff placed 3rd in Chester White boar, Pearl 1st & 2nd in Poland China litter, and Cal 1st and 2nd in Shropshire rams and ewes.

Wednesday, September 9, 1936

Cal stayed in Tripp with the livestock while Pearl and I were in school. Pearl won grand champion boar and sow in open class.

Our cows were on Joe L. Wipf's land south of the church when I got home from school.

Johnny sowed rye after school. Very hot. Flies bother the horses.

Monday, September 14, 1936

Cal is 13 years old today. I gave him 13¢. Walters were here in the evening. Ike Tschetter brought ice and we made 2 gal. ice cream but it did not reach out.

P. P.'s Alice and Pearl went to the State Fair in Huron to show their pigs.

Wednesday, September 16, 1936

Was at Teachers' Institute in Olivet. Could not stay for the picnic because I had to take the College students home.

The Mitchell DAILY REPUBLIC printed pictures of nearly all the candidates. Mine looks pretty good but is too dark.

Thursday, September 17, 1936

I was elected vice president of the Hutchinson County Teachers' Association and alternate delegate to the South Dakota Education Association meeting at Rapid City.

John P. Kleinsasser's campaign photo. Candidate for South Dakota House of Representatives from Hutchinson County.

Cal borrowed John J. K. Stahl's corn binder and started cutting sugar cane after school.

Friday, September 23, 1936
Cal cut corn and John shocked sugar cane after school. Cannot get much work done at this rate.

I went to the Fraternal Burial Assoc. meeting at Viborg. We decided to go to Omaha to look at a hearse.

Thursday, September 24, 1936
John picked nearly a lower wagon box full of citron melons. Ma will make some jam.

Friday, September 25, 1936
We had our first county Republican rally for the season, held at #67 on Highway 81 near the Yankton County line. All the Republican candidates spoke in their own behalf. Metzger gave the main talk.

Saturday, September 26, 1936
Charles Schrag, Cal's teacher, collided with a car while driving a truck. He died this morning.

Monday, September 28, 1936
Four different teachers taught Cal's 8th grade classes at the Public School since his teacher died.

47

J. W.'s Adeline is staying at our place.

Got my first school check – $40.50. Paid K & K on account $10. and Preheim $10.

Tuesday, September 29, 1936

Richard Waltner was here to get my old carbureator. I gave him 15 citrons.

I kept Marie Walter in all day because she yelled like a heathen going home from school yesterday. She wanted me to dismiss school for Charles Schrag's funeral at the South Church. When we didn't close school, she got "bucky."

Ma, Adeline, Cal, Pearl, and Esther went to the funeral. There was an immense crowd. His picture was in the Mitchell REPUBLIC.

Pigs have a touch of flu. Gave them Epsom salts.

Thursday, October 1, 1936

I took Ma to Henry Tiahrt's after school. She has a piano deal on. They went to Canistota to see a Mr. Eucker, a piano tuner. He is to look the piano over in Mitchell and report to Ma concerning it.

Friday, October 2, 1936

John J. Gross and I went to Kaylor in my car for a Republican rally. We got there after the first two speakers had been introduced. I was then presented. Main speaker, Weller from Mitchell, criticized the WPA. He gave an example of 8 men unloading a 28-ton railcar of coal. The last man just says, "Load 'er up, boys." It was quite tiresome.

Saturday, October 3, 1936

John and Cal hauled corn fodder. I cut and raked spring-sown alfalfa in low places.

Brother J. W. came down from Doland for the Sunday School Convention and stayed with us overnight.

Ma got her piano for $40. Paid $10 down and $3 for transportation.

Sunday, October 4, 1936

Went to church three times today for the Sunday School Convention in Freeman. Mr. & Mrs. Iky Tschetter stayed overnight.

Found first pullet eggs.

Monday, October 5, 1936

Relief workers made a sanitary toilet for us at #98.

Cal and John hauled a sling of corn fodder into the hay mow.

Tuesday, October 6, 1936

John J. Gross and I drove to Olivet with my car for a Republican rally. Atty. Lammers of Madison was the main speaker.

Wednesday, October 7, 1936

Took John to Sioux Falls after school to be fitted for glasses by Dr. Bassett. After that we heard Repr. Lemke of North Dakota, candidate for President on the Union Party ticket. He is a forceful but sarcastic speaker.

Thursday, October 8, 1936

Eucker tuned and cleaned our new piano. He charged $4. for work from 9 a.m. to 2 p.m.

Hauled a load of alfalfa and Russian thistles mixed. Cal got pretty scratched up.

Friday, October 9, 1936

Hauled squash home from the field. The vines are killed off but the squash are not frozen.

Went with J. C. Graber, A. J. Waltner, and Chas. Kaufman to a Republican rally at Milltown. Attys. Graber and Metzger spoke.

Saturday, October 10, 1936

Pheasant season opened. I shot 4 roosters in 15 minutes.

"Boy, did I have fun today!" Cal told Max when the boys met in town that night. "I was ridin' with my Pa when we saw a pheasant in the ditch. Pa cocked his old 20-gauge shotgun and shot out of the window on the driver's side. Then he said to me, 'Go get 'im.' Well, I thought I was jus' gonna pick up one pheasant. But when I got there, I saw four roosters lyin' there dead."

"Four?"

"Yeah, Pa says they line up like that sometimes. Most he ever killed with one shot was six."

Sunday, October 11, 1936

Had church three times today. Rev. P. P. Tschetter baptized 11 in the morning. Rev. Mike Hofer and Rev. Albert Claasen spoke in the afternoon, and Rev. Jacob A. Tieszen spoke in the evening.

Monday, October 12, 1936

Heard Alf Landon, candidate for President, speak over the radio from Cleveland. He spoke against relief.

There have been strange cattle here for several days — a Guernsey, a Holstein and a Hereford.

Tuesday, October 13, 1936

J. C. Graber amd I went to German Township for a rally. All the candidates were there but Dave Tiede, candidate for State Senate. They gave me a good send off. I expect a good vote out of that community.

Metzger was not there, so Graber gave a fairly good talk and introduced the candidates.

Wednesday, October 14, 1936

Went to John J. B.'s for supper. Sister Katherine put on a big feed. Got home early for night hawks.

Friday, October 16, 1936

Got late to a Republican rally at Summit, #51, on account of measuring pasture land for Mrs. Marie Tiahrt. That was not much of a good impression, but I still expect a big vote out of Silver Lake Township.

Max was not in school today. He was looking for their white cow, which has been missing for several days.

Saturday, October 17, 1936

Finished measuring Marie Tiahrt's pasture with John L.'s wheel at 3 p.m. Ordered a pair of high-top kangaroo shoes, size 585 (8 1/2 E width) from Wollman's store.

In the evening P. P.'s Walter took me and Rocky Borman to Dimock for a Republican rally. Got a good send off.

John J. B. and
Katherine Kleinsasser Hofer

Sunday, October 18, 1936

J. W.'s Anna (Mrs. Joshua B. Stahl) and Adeline were here over-night. Emma (Mrs. Ike) and her children were here for dinner and supper. Stahl of Aberdeen predicts a complete Democratic victory.

Monday, October 19, 1936

A man from Ford Motors in Sioux Falls was here trying to sell me a 1932 Pontiac. He wanted $225 out on mine.

Rev. P. P. Tschetter and family were here for supper. He is supposed to leave for Canada to teach in a Bible school this winter.

Tuesday, October 20, 1936

Republican rally at Freeman. Gurney and Bushfield spoke. Other candidates were introduced and asked to bow, except for me. Metzger asked me to give my alphabetical arrangement spiel.

Wednesday, October 21, 1936

Two men were here from Sioux Falls with a Ford V-8 and a Plymouth. I took a ride in the Ford and had Julius Albrecht try it out. He told me to leave my hands off the Ford.

Thursday, October 22, 1936

My high-top kangaroo shoes came in at Wollman's. I took them to Chas. Gering to have heels put on.

Friday, October 23, 1936

Good crowd at Republican rally at Clayton. Metzger spoke. Democrats had rallies in Parkston and Freeman.

Saturday, October 24, 1936

Ma and I tried out a Chevrolet that Andrew Schaefer has at Freedom Garage.

Campaigned in Parkston. Prospects look pretty good there. Put an ad in the Parkston paper. Cost $1.

Had J. J. Mendel print 1,000 campaign cards for me for $3.25 and put an ad in the FREEMAN COURIER. Cost 75¢.

Sunday, October 25, 1936

John and I went to Sioux Falls with Schaefer to get a Chevy. Made the deal. Figured their car $450, my Olds $100. Finance and insurance, $83.

Rev. P. R. Schroeder reported at our church tonight on the Mennonite World Conference in Holland. He is concerned about the modernists.

Monday, October 26, 1936

Had a good crowd at the rally in Menno. I told the story about Rex Tugwell, BS, Ph.D, and the 4-H club boys. It sounded pretty raw to some, especially after Ackerman told his story about Jacob and the Christmas stockings.

Karl Mundt and Chan Gurney spoke too. Mundt had a very bad cold and could barely speak. He tried to urge his voice along with lemon and water.

Tuesday, October 27, 1936

Had a fair crowd at Parkston rally. Handed out quite a few cards. Clark thought Gross was out campaigning with Tiede, but he was not. It was his brother, who is running for the Senate. Republicans do not get such a good reception in Parkston, a Catholic area.

Wednesday, October 28, 1936

Campaigned in Tripp after school. Got a very good reception. Many said they would vote a straight Republican ticket. Even the relief workers are not afraid to vote the Republican ticket there. Our Hutterische people are afraid to vote Republican or say they would.

Thursday, October 29, 1936

Campaigned in town after school. Saw all the people on the east side of Main Street. Intend to see all those on the west side. Expect a good vote out of Freeman unless the Democrats desert me.

Friday, October 30, 1936

Taught 'til noon, when John brought Louise Schroeder to school to substitute for me. Campaigned in Menno and Olivet, then to Tripp for rally. Had 350 people there. The College girls' trio sang.

Saturday, October 31, 1936

Stayed overnight with Pete Hofer in Tripp and had breakfast with them. Campaigned in Kaylor. Prospects fair. D. J. Tiede came to Kaylor also, and we went together to a road crew in Kulm Township. Then we drove to Olivet and later to Paul Stahl's sale.

Campaigned in Freeman in the evening, where the Democrats had a rally in the College Gym. A Dr. Clark from Sioux Falls spoke. Lots of bunk!

Sunday, November 1, 1936

John and Cal went to College to sweep the Gym. I suppose sweep up the cigarette stubs.

Went to Marion to visit grandfolks. Got home after sundown and found Johnny had done all the chores.

Monday, November 2, 1936

Had school. Had planned to go campaigning but changed my mind. Glad I did because the snow turned into a bad blizzard. Had the car at school and couldn't start it. Mrs. Pete Ratzlaff helped me pull it with one horse and finally it started.

Went to town and had Schaefer put in the battery that had been in the Olds and changed the oil.

Heard that a number of Freeman Democrats would vote against me because I called Clark's speech a lot of bunk. I suppose I said too much. Better to think a lot and say nothing.

Tuesday, November 3, 1936

No school. Election Day. I got most votes in Sweet, Grand View, Silver Lake, Pleasant, Freeman and Olivet. Came in second to Tiede but we'll both serve from our district.

Wednesday, November 4, 1936

Had quite a time staying awake in school. Pupils seem glad I won. Maybe they are glad to get a different teacher.

There was a terrible skunk stink in the school house.

My total vote in the county was 2,918. Tiede got 3,165. Democrats Boehmer and Dannenbring got 2,160 and 2,532, respectively.

Every Republican, except Paul B. Hofer, won. Ed Weidenbach beat him for Auditor.

Thursday, November 5, 1936

Children came home early from school so we could butcher a 250-pound hog. We could not get the water hot enough, so after fooling around with the scalding for an hour we skinned it. It went better after that. The hog is quite fat. We did not clean the head and feet. Ma will have to do that tomorrow.

Friday, November 6, 1936

John stayed in town after school to practice basketball. He is on the College team. I went to town after school for supplies and got many congratulations.

Saturday, November 7, 1936

Snowing and cold. Manured barns and hauled in straw.

Dug open the well pipes. Part of the hold had caved in. We do not have the well or supply tank packed with straw yet.

Sunday, November 8, 1936

Did not go to church. Boys were thawing out water all forenoon.

Monday, November 9, 1936

Children got home late because John played basketball. Water was frozen up this morning but all right in the evening. Cows froze their teats. Red cow's teats are badly swollen.

Tuesday, November 10, 1936

Rev. Walter Gering brought Rev. J. M. Regier out to speak at our church but the meeting was called off. Regier stayed at our place all evening. We made ice cream and served it after Gering came back to get him.

Wednesday, November 11, 1936

Johnny's glasses cost $4.16 to fix. He had broken a lens playing basketball.

Friday, November 13, 1936

Marian said I should write her and "Uffie's" names in my diary.

I shot a skunk under the school house after 4 p.m. Melvin Ratzlaff came over with a long stick to get it out. I offered it to him and he took it.

Saturday, November 14, 1936

Leon Weier and I went to the Burial Association Board meeting in Viborg. We bought a 15-year-old house and lot from Chris Jensen for $2500 to use as a funeral home. Some alterations must be made.

Cal made a door by the storage tank. He acts like a carpenter.

Sunday, November 15, 1936

Cal took Nelly (horse) to Pete Ratzlaff's to be bred.

John J. Gering of Marion got a room in Pierre for the session at $5 a week. He is the Turner Co. Rep.

Monday, November 16, 1936

Schaeffer took our Chevy to Wold Auto Co. in Sioux Falls to be checked over. We had so many complaints that they said it might take them 2-3 days.

Am getting letters from people wanting jobs during the legislative session.

I did all the chores but milk, which is Pearl's responsibility. Cal and I sawed wood with the two-handled saw. John went to bed after supper.

Tuesday, November 17, 1936

Schaeffer came out to take the children to school with a '28 Chevy because our car is still in Sioux Falls. The children did not enjoy the ride.

Otto Wildermuth was here about a job in the tax division. He took up so much of my time that I couldn't do the chores.

Ma is still sick. She has stomach trouble.

Wednesday, November 18, 1936

Went to Sioux Falls with Schaeffer to get our '34 Chevy. Wold Auto Co. put it in good shape free of charge.

Thursday, November 19, 1936

I filed my campaign expense report. It was $28.16 for the November election.

Johnny went home to Spink Co. The College has a 10-day vacation between quarters.

Sunday, November 22, 1936

Visited Henry Tiahrts. Urged Arnold to attend FJC.

Tuesday, November 24, 1936

Paul Tieszen brought 2 tons of ash and hackberry firewood from Nebraska for $7 a ton. Bought a little coal. Can't get much in the trunk.

Regular old-time dust storm today.

Thursday, November 26, 1936

It is Thanksgiving but I had school because I will miss a lot of days during the session. The Hofer children did not attend.

Dorothy and Rebecca Tschetter are staying here during their school vacation. They attend Engbrecht's Sunnyside Bible Academy in town.

We had roast duck, broasted potatoes and rice dressing with giblets and raisins for supper. Ma butchered six ducks this week.

Saturday, November 28, 1936

Hank Borman wants the game warden appointment.

Sunday, November 29, 1936

Ten girls were baptized at Pete Stahl's church this morning. A teacher in Engbrecht's school, Rev. Jacob B. and Pete Stahl preached. Big crowd in that little church. Stopped at P. P.'s a little while to hear the College singers over radio WNAX.

Johnny came back from Spink Co. with Prof. D. S. Wipf.

Monday, November 30, 1936

Got transportation warrant for $11.40 from #26 for driving this month. Sam Schmidt deducted 60¢ because we did not drive on the Friday after Thanksgiving, when there was no school.

Pearl and Cal paid off their sow litter notes at the First National Bank.

Katherine's brother George brought back the ram. He did not like it. I sold him my old ram for $12. I am not sure that all of my ewes are bred.

Tuesday, December 1, 1936

Johnny traveled to Yankton College with the FJC basketball team. He will stay there overnight.

We visited John J. K. Stahl tonight. A horse kicked him on Nov. 17 and broke his leg. He is still in bed. He paid me $30 for the boar. I paid him $5 for using his corn binder.

Wednesday, December 3, 1936

Pearl is working on her SILAS MARNER booklet for English.

Sam Mendel wants to insure the house he moved up from Menno for $1600 in the Aid Plan although he bought it for only $600 and paid $150 to move it.

Saturday, December 5, 1936

Took Susie Stahl along to Olivet for Teachers' Institute. Bought Ruth a PETER AND PEGGY workbook and crayons.

Sunday, December 6, 1936

The Harlem Globe Trotters played the FJC team. Had a regular circus. The Negroes won.

Could not get our Chevy started this morning after pulling it around with the horses. Phoned up three garages (Schaeffer, Albrecht, Waltner). Herb Koster finally came out to transport the children. He charged 50¢ each way. After school I got the car started and drove to town. Had Waltner clean out the carburetor and change the oil.

Tuesday, December 8, 1936

Had to pull the car with horses to start it. Our battery is being charged by Albrecht.

Had Burial Assoc. Board meeting in Viborg. Got $50.80 from Assoc. this year ($25.80 per diem and mileage and $25 salary as secretary). I was re-elected secretary. Got home before midnight.

Wednesday, December 9, 1936

Bertha Walter did not go to Freeman with the children this morning. She wants to quit school. Her brother Max has quit building the fire for me in the mornings at #98.

Johnny stayed in town for basketball practice. His ankle must be better.

Ma and I went to town after school. We spent a lot of money for just a few things.

I collected and sent $6. to YOUNG AMERICA and $2.70 to WEEKLY READER.

Thursday, December 10, 1936

Max had built the fire when I got to school this a.m.

I am still getting many letters from job seekers.

Got a letter from Tiede about a room in Pierre for the session. They have a big room with one double and one single bed for $150 for the 3 of us.

Friday, December 11, 1936

Marian told me to write her name in my book.

Jake M. Hofer, A. R. M. Hofer and I had a meeting about Sam Mendel's insurance on his new house. We decided to insure it for $1200 instead of $1600.

In the evening Johnny, Cal and I went to a basketball game between Freeman High School and Olivet. Freeman won 27 to 18. Johnny thought he would take Elizabeth Kautz to the game, but she was not at home.

Saturday, December 12, 1936

All home today. John and Cal built a straw loft in the west chicken barn.

Gottlieb Schmeichel oiled and greased the windmill.

We carried the hard coal base burner into the parlor.

Sunday, December 13, 1936

All in church this morning. The children practiced for their church Christmas program this afternoon.

We audited the telephone company books. The bookkeeper claims we owe him $62.05.

John J. B.'s were here for dinner and stayed while the children practiced.

Monday, December 14, 1936

College Founders' Day. Yankton College and FJC played basketball in the evening. Yankton won, 37 to 20.

Ma went to the musical program during the day. Mrs. Herman-son, the new music teacher, did some outstanding work, Ma said.

Heard the prize fight over the radio. Joe Louis, a Negro, knocked out Sims in 18 seconds. 12,000 people were in the arena.

Wednesday, December 16, 1936

FJC basketball squad went to Springfield to play the Normal school. They got beat 48 to 8. They hit a horse going over and ran into the ditch. They did not kill the horse.

Thursday, December 17, 1936

South Dakota University graduates had a banquet in the Congregational church in Olivet for the senator and representatives from this county. Nathaniel S. Tiede and I were there. The University big shots were all there giving talks. They are looking for some big appropriations out of the legislature.

Tom Berry, outgoing Governor, called a special session to convene December 21, 1936. Tiede is going up. Glad I don't have to.

I signed my Soil Conservation contract.

Friday, December 18 , 1936

Co. Sup. Rose Perman visited school.

John is not going home to Spink Co. He will work off his tuition at the College during Christmas vacation.

Saturday, December 19, 1936

Bought hard (Montana) coal for the base burner. It will keep the house warm during the night.

Sunday, December 20, 1936

All in church this morning. Rev. P. P. Tschetter is back from Canada where he was teaching in a Bible school. The children practiced for their church Christmas program in the afternoon. Had Christian Endeavor in the evening. Paul L. was elected chairman and Mrs. Paul E. secretary. Program committee: Paul Decker, D. D. Glanzer. Joe J., song leader, and Mrs. Ed A., pianist.

Heard that ex-Gov. Norbeck died.

Monday, December 21, 1936

Special session convenes at Pierre today. It concerns the arrest of Lt. Gov. Peterson for embezzlement. His bank at Centerville is short $170,000.

I am having school.

Tuesday, December 22, 1936

Very nice weather.

Marian memorized a German piece and Ruth memorized "Away in a Manger." She cannot get the German.

Wednesday, December 23, 1936

The boys found the horses after school close to the church.

Went to Parkston to be measured for a suit by Mr. Schlimgen. It will cost $35 for two pairs of trousers.

Dentist Hofer approached me with a bill that is to come up this session. It is designed to weed out charlatans and quacks from the dental profession.

Thursday, December 24, 1936

Had school today. College and Freeman Public School were out. I bought 50¢ gifts for each of my pupils. I got a box of candy from the Walters, a milk pail from the Hofers and a five-year diary from Melvin Ratzlaff.

Ruth and Marian said pieces at the children's program at church tonight. Ruth's was "Little Lord Jesus" and Marian said a German piece. It was her first time and she did fine for a three-year-old. The program lasted 1 1/2 hours. We passed out sacks of nuts and candy afterwards.

"I was proud of you girls tonight," Mrs. Kleinsasser said to her two youngest daughters as she sat between them in the back seat of the '34 Chevy which Cal was driving home.

"Stop pulling the horse hide blanket off me," demanded Pearl, sitting next to Ruth. "I'm cold."

"The blanket is big enough for all of us. It won't be long before we're home. Then you can warm up in front of the base burner," said their mother. "I thought Marian did very well, considering it was her first piece, and German to boot!"

Cal put in his two cents' worth: "Better than Pearl did at that age, that's for sure!"

"How would you remember? You were only three months old!" Pearl retorted.

"I heard about it. Somebody in church told me. You burst out crying and Ma had to walk up and get you!"

"Now, who would have remembered a thing like that for so long?"

"One of my friends."

"It was all those pairs of eyes staring at me. Any sensitive child would be frightened."

"I remember that too," said Morgan. "You had pig tails then. Ma had sewed you a pretty blue dress with a big white collar. And the program was entirely in German – one German poem after the other. Now at least we have a few verses in English."

"I remember when Cal got a bawling out at church in front of all the kids," said Pearl.

"From whom?" asked Katherine.

"From Pa."

"Now, that's awful hard for me to believe, John," said his wife.

"Sure. Cal refused to learn his German piece at home and didn't want to stay after church to practice for the program because he knew he didn't know it. So Pa said, 'You're gonna learn it one place or the other. If you can't learn it at home, you can learn it at church'."

Friday, December 25, 1936

All in church. Had beef steak for dinner.

In the afternoon we visited Grandpa and Grandma Tieszen where the girls said their pieces. The Henry Tiahrt, John Tieszen and Abe Tieszen families were there also. Ma got a dollar from her mother. The children all got some money.

Johnny Klein had his foot set by Dr. Derk Tieszen. He has a lot of pain. Dr. Tieszen talked to me about the "Basic Science" bill and said we should pay him another visit.

"The so-called 'Basic Science' bill will probably come up in the legislature again, Morgan," Dr. Tieszen said as he manipulated Johnny's ankle. "It's a very dangerous bill. We managed to defeat it the last few years, but the medical society and the medical college keep bringing it up."

"What would it do?"

"Well, in effect, it would compel the public to take their treatment from medical doctors. It would eliminate chiropractors and osteopaths and all those practicing drugless healing."

"I don't think you have to worry about that passing. Our South Dakota people are not a herd of sheep."

"Well, combined with the Social Security Act, it could be really dangerous. The state medical board could control all federal allotments to the state for maternal and child health services, for example, and force people to get their treatment from drug pushers."

"I'll certainly vote against that."

Saturday, December 26, 1936

Did not go to church this morning. It rained a quarter inch during the night.

Had township meeting concerning the 30% car tax that the townships are getting now. A bill is supposed to come up in the legislature concerning this tax. The boys are afraid that the townships will lose this revenue.

P. P.'s Anne is home from Platte, where she is teaching.

Sunday, December 27, 1936

Ma did not go to church this morning. She was sick.

Caroline Tschetter would not sign a Sunday School class list because we sometimes read the Scripture in German in that class. There is a lot of anti-German feeling arising.

Monday, December 28, 1936

We sent two hogs to Sioux Falls with Roland Haar's truck. Top hogs are now bringing about $10 per cwt.

We were supposed to have a Republican meeting in Olivet tonight about appointive jobs. It sleeted most of the day and roads were very icy, so we gave up the idea.

Tuesday, December 29, 1936

Children are taking tests in #98. I paid up my bill with the peddler, Dan Graber. He told me about a bill that is coming up in the legislature to increase the tax on peddlers.

January, 1937-July 8, 1937
The Family Intact

Friday, January 1, 1937

Had school for the last day before the legislature meets. It was Melvin Ratzlaff's birthday. He gave me a five-year diary for Christmas, but I bought this one because I need more room to write.

Cal and P. P.'s Edward took Johnny Klein to Parkston this morning to catch a ride to Huron with the Tiedes, who were planning to leave for Pierre. But they changed their minds and went by train, so John came back. They ran off the icy road at Milltown and had to get pulled out by a truck.

It was snowing and drifting most of the day. It is still doing so at 11 p.m.

Saturday, January 2, 1937

Terrible blizzard. Phone does not work. Cannot understand a word. I am wondering how to get to Pierre.

Pearl has a toothache but is reading HUCKLEBERRY FINN. We cut up the pork and put the hams in brine.

Made out secretary's report for the Silver Lake Telephone Co. and a grade report for the Co. Sup. of Schools.

Sunday, January 3, 1937

Did not go to church. Most roads are blocked.

Johnny and Cal took me to John Weier's place. From there we went to Praven Christensen's. His boy took us to Hurley, where Weier's brother-in-law took us to Parker.

We are staying in separate rooms at the hotel which charges $1 for a single room. Had soup for 15¢.

Leon Weier is quite sick with a cold. I gave him some antiseptic solution.

It is almost 9 p.m. Am going to bed. We leave for Pierre by train in the morning.

Monday, January 4, 1937

Left Parker at 5:20 a.m. The train was due at 4:07. Got to Huron at 9 and left at 10:09. The ticket from Parker to Huron was $1.90 *and from Huron to Pierre $2.39. Leon Weier stayed in Parker because he was sick.*

Got to Pierre about 1:30. Had Republican caucus at 3 and elected all our officers. A. C. Miller is slated for Speaker. So far I have not missed anything. Pierre is alive with politicians.

Bought a meal ticket for $5.50 at the State House Cafe. Rep. Nathaniel Tiede, Sen. David Tiede and I from Hutchinson Co. have a room together. Each of us pays $45 for the session.

Tuesday, January 5, 1937

Had session at noon. Members all took oath of office. I affirmed.

We had a joint session of the House and Senate after that. The old and new officers appeared. Ex-Gov. Berry gave a very short talk, but Gov. Leslie Jensen gave a wonderful address. I hope we can follow his suggestions.

The Inaugural Reception was held at the State House. The hand shaking lasted until 10 p.m. After that we went to the Inaugural Ball. They had a beautiful grand march. The Hot Springs High School Band played.

Wednesday, January 6, 1937

Had short session. It stormed all day. Had breakfast at 10 a.m., no dinner, and supper at 6 p.m. Very cold. I am wearing Ma's fur cap when it gets too cold.

Our landlady's place is one block north of the St. Charles Hotel. Her name is Georgia Sommerside and her mother, who is 88 and the oldest woman in Pierre, stays with her.

Thursday, January 7, 1937

15 below this morning. I was appointed to the Apportionment Committee.

The Soil Conservation group met in Pierre. Joe Hill and Eberle were here.

Saw a movie, "Bengal Tiger," for 40¢. Not much to it.

Tiede got on the Appropriations Committee.

Friday, January 8, 1937

Got up at 10 a.m. because we had waited at the train depot last night 'til 1:10 a.m. for a Mogck girl to come from Parkston to be a page in the Senate, but she came this morning instead. There are two girl pages in the Senate.

House met at 2 p.m. Bishop, Speaker pro tem, had the chair. Alt introduced a resolution concerning the federal Child Labor Amendment.

Saturday, January 9, 1937

Met at 10 a.m. for about 20 minutes and then adjourned 'til Monday at 8 p.m. so some of the fellows could go home over the weekend. I wanted to go to Doland to see brother J. W., but changed my mind.

I worked on the reapportionment all day. I do not know what would be the best way to connect up Hutchinson Co.

Went to a basketball game in the evening. Pierre beat Ipswich 29 to 17, and Blunt beat Fort Pierre 16 to 13.

Sunday, January 10, 1937

Went to the Congregational Church for Sunday School and church. Doane Robinson, the historian, was in our class. Rev. Bessel preached.

Had dinner at 1 p.m. and no breakfast. Saw "Come and Get It" in the afternoon. The picture is not complete. The book was better.

Talked to Ben Strool, Commissioner of School and Public Lands. He is a very interesting man. His mother was a German Jew.

Monday, January 11, 1937

Wrote quite a few letters concerning apportionment of representatives and senators, including one to Karl Mundt. I have not gotten a letter from home yet.

Session convened at 8 p.m. Voted for a resolution to Congress regarding the Child Labor Amendment. We are opposing it. Looks like a way for the labor unions to get control of Congress. It might be all right in an industrial state, but it would hurt us as an agricultural state. Got letters from both Joe A. Wollman, a Democrat, and Rev. John Dewald, a Republican of Tripp, against it.

I was appointed to the Auditing and Charitable Institutions committees.

Had a nice talk with Henry Gierau, the blind representative from Wewela. He is a Democrat.

Tuesday, January 12, 1937

Got my first letter from home. Cal, Pearl, and Mrs. all wrote. I was glad to hear from them.

Met Oscar Fosheim from Miner Co. He is quite an orator.

Wednesday, January 13, 1937

Ruth is 7 years old today.

Was appointed to the Education Committee. Bettelheim of Spearfish is chairman.

I introduced my first bill concerning redistricting the state Congressionally (two districts north and south instead of east and west to even up the population). Spoke with "Speed" Travis of the Rapid City JOURNAL. Earl Hammerquist likes my bill but says he might have to vote against it. He is from the West River district and they like having a representative for a small population.

Got a letter from fisherman Math Kleinsasser about the net bill.

Thursday, January 14, 1937

Got our first pay today, $24.90 for mileage and $55. per diem.

I sent $55 for auto payment and $10 home. Paid $5.10 for meal ticket and $1 for new shirt.

We passed just one bill today, on floating bonds in a county. Quite a number of bills are being introduced.

Had Republican caucus in St. Charles Hotel basement at night. Gov. Jensen and Speaker Miller spoke. Kundert bought me a beer.

Saturday, January 16, 1937

Passed no bills today. I worked on the rural credits map. The state owns quite a bit of land. The new fieldmen are not yet appointed. Banker A. J. Waltner of Freeman wants to be appointed in our district.

We were in the Secretary of State's office for signing of the resolution to Congress on the Child Labor Amendment. Secretary of State Goldie Wells was not there. Her assistant, Iweena Stewart, was.

Miss Johnson of the Senate staff, Marian Lewis of the House staff, Sen. Wilson and I, of the Engrossing and Enrolling Committee, take the bills from our respective chambers to the Governor to be signed.

Sunday, January 17, 1937

This is Ma's birthday, but I am not home. Got a letter from home this morning.

Went to the Methodist Church this morning. Rev. Bullock is the pastor.

Had no breakfast, but did eat lunch and dinner. Met Gov. Jensen in a restaurant and also at the hotel. His wife, two children, and male secretary, Jamison, were there for dinner.

Saw the show, "Ramona," at the Bijou for 25¢.

Monday, January 18, 1937

Got a number of letters from constituents, including one from Pres. Unruh of Freeman Junior College.

Session convened after 8 p.m. Some of the Reps. could not get back from home in time.

Took bills to the Governor to be signed, but his secretary did it. He can write Jensen's name almost identically.

Only one bill was up for passage, but the sponsor thought it would lose so he referred it back to committee.

Saw "Charge of the Light Brigade" at the Grand for 40¢. Quite a show. Went after 9 p.m. and got home at midnight. Gierau, the blind representative, was there.

Tuesday, January 19, 1937

Snowed all day. Roads are badly drifted.

Had a joint Game and Fish Committee meeting and also the House Education Committee meeting. The Spearfish Normal bill was up for discussion and also a bill to permit the teaching of religion for a certain number of hours.

Wednesday, January 20, 1937

Had quite a talk with Mr. George of Spearfish and Rep. Haynes of Lawrence. Might have a bill introduced to abolish Springfield and Madison Normals. We are having a tough time supporting all these Normal schools set up under Territorial government. They were first intended for two-year teachers' training and now they all want to go to four-year colleges with full courses of study.

Passed two bills. One was to pay coroners' jurors and the other to legalize payment to a Beadle Co. man by the County Commission.

Met Jamison, the Governor's secretary, in a restaurant and had a long talk with him.

Had a big snow storm today, so we postponed our recess.

Thursday, January 21, 1937

We voted down the bill to abolish the sales tax. The Senate passed the death sentence for murder. Two ministers, Rev. Sen. Johnson of DeSmet and Rev. Sen. Hove of Colman, spoke in favor of the bill and voted for it. One senator changed his vote so the question can be taken up again.

Friday, January 22, 1937

Session convened at 12:01 a.m. and lasted 'til 1:30. At 4 a.m. we left Pierre by train for Wolsey. Ticket was $2.13. From Wolsey to Mitchell to Dolton, the ticket was $1.88.

Got to Dolton at 3 p.m. Walked to John J. B.'s for supper. John J.B.'s Johnny took me to Jake L.'s, from where George M. Hofer tried to take me home, but we couldn't get through. I walked to Adrian's filling station to warm up. Johnny Klein and Cal came to get me from there. We got home at 10 p.m.

Saturday, January 23, 1937

Home for legislative recess. Took a good rest in the morning and went to town for hard coal in the afternoon, using Bill Isaak's trailer. Got stuck with the trailer on the north road out of town. Andy Schrag helped me out but tore off the rear bumper.

Johnny and Cal came to Highway 81 to pull the trailer home with horses. I got stuck several times.

Was told to look after several things in Pierre—the road past my place, auto licenses, Game and Fish Commission.

Sunday, January 24, 1937

Home today. Well is frozen up. I trimmed wool from a few sheeps' eyes. Had windmill going in the p.m. At 4 p.m. it started to blizzard. Cannot see a thing.

George M. Hofer and Jake L.'s Maggie were to be married today but I think it was called off due to the blizzard.

Monday, January 25, 1937

Drove to town with horses and wagon to take the children to school. Gave a talk at College Chapel.

"Good morning, Students, Teachers.

"When I asked Pres. Unruh if he would let me speak to you when I was home on recess, he said, 'Yes, if you have something to say.'

"Reminds me of a story I heard about two politicians who died and went to heaven. When they got there, they found no cheering, no flag waving. They were really disappointed. Things went on like that for a while. But one morning there was a big commotion—the angels were singing and soaring around. Everyone seemed especially pleased. Finally the politicians said to St. Peter, 'Just what does this mean? When we came here, there was no such uproar.'

"Well,' said St. Peter, 'the man that came here this morning was a college president, the first one we've had in a century.'

"I thought you might be interested in the composition of the legislature. In the House we have 38 farmers, 5 lawyers, 11 merchants, 1 railroad engineer, 1 civil engineer, 4 newspapermen, 1 contractor, 1 doctor, 1 minister, 2 hotel keepers, 6 insurance men, 1 city fireman, and 2 oil jobbers. As you can see, the farmers are in the majority, but we seldom vote in a bloc.

"The President of the Senate is the Lieutenant Governor, but the Speaker of the House is elected by its members. This time it is A. C. Miller of Kennebec. It takes about a week to get all the committees appointed. I'm on the Apportionment Committee, the Education Committee, the Game and Fish Committee, to name a few.

"Members of the legislature may write their own bills, which are proposed laws. The lawyers usually write their own bills. But most bills are drawn up by the Attorney General's office.

"Many people wonder about lobbyists and whether the citizen has any real input into the legislative process. There are lobbyists of all kinds. One I think of is a member of the Federated Women's Clubs. She is primarily interested in the welfare of our young people. Another is Mr. Steele, the lobbyist for SDEA, which is trying to improve the quality of public education in South Dakota. Another form of lobbying is what goes on in Room 120 of the St. Charles Hotel. I went to a big party there the other day put on by the oil dealers. We had everything from tomato juice to something stronger and bologna to shrimp rolled up in meat. Then there are the lobbyists in the lobby, outside the House and Senate Chambers. They literally buttonhole legislators about a specific bill up for consideration. We had to make a rule to keep them out of the House Chamber after noon.

"People wonder if legislators actually read constituent mail. The answer is YES. Even penny postal cards make a difference. But I have gotten very little mail so far this session. I have had to write letters to the editors of our county's newspapers, like the COURIER and the Parkston ADVANCE, requesting that the editor sample opinion about which form of taxation (and there will be a tax increase) would be least onerous. We have to raise some money to match the federal Old Age Pension mandated by Congress. Should we do it through a gasoline tax, an increased sales tax, an increased ore tax, a net income tax, or what?

"I just got a note from Pres. Unruh. It says, 'You may speak as long as you wish, but Chapel is only 20 minutes long.'

"So, thank you for your attention. If there's anything I can help you with, such as a copy of a bill or a report, please write me. Just address it to Repr. John P. Kleinsasser, State House, Pierre, South Dakota, and I'll get it."

Took home 2,440 pounds of briquets ($15.75). Nearly got stuck several times. There are some pretty high banks.

Tuesday, January 26, 1937
Worked at home. Pearl, Cal and Johnny had stayed in town overnight but Gordon Schmidt was still at home, so I walked over to Schmidts and then Gordon and I caught a ride to Freeman.

The snow plow went through this morning and again this after-noon. The snow banks are higher than the cars.

Got a number of letters concerning legislation.

Gordon Schmidt and Pearl stayed at Aunt Emma's. Cal and Johnny and I came home with Zach Wipf.

Wednesday, January 27, 1937

Cal and Johnny went to school and back with Andy Wipf. Pearl stayed in town. Gordon came home with the boys.

Unloaded the briquets. Jake M. Hofer castrated a boar for me and Jake Walter helped us.

Storming this afternoon. Wind came from the southeast in the morning and the northwest in the afternoon. The tank is full of water.

Our county telephone tax is $3.74.

Chickens do not lay at all.

Thursday, January 28, 1937

Worked all forenoon thawing pipes of the tank and then learned that the tank had run dry. A hydrant was open in the hog barn. The water all soaked away.

I caught two cottontails. Ma made stew.

Highway 81 was blocked again. Cars are beginning to go after dinner. Johnny and Cal rode with Andy Wipf but Gordon stayed home. We had figured on going back to Pierre today.

Friday, January 29, 1937

Went to Freeman with the children in the morning. Got stuck going out to 81. Saw Sam Schmidt in town. He said he would make out the transportation warrant in full.

Got $10 cash from Merchants State Bank.

Went to Stanley Corner with an agent. The Stanley guys wanted $1.50 to take me to Salem. I gave Henry Engbrecht $1 to take me. Left Salem at 7 p.m. by train.

Saturday, January 30, 1937

Got to Pierre at 1:10 a.m. and went to bed at 3 a.m. Brother J. W. was in my bed when I got there.

Had session today. Adopted the minority report on SB 29 (death penalty for murder). John J. Gering and Oscar Fosheim brought in a DO NOT PASS report. The lawyers got their ears knocked down on that bill as they expected to pass it without much trouble. The vote for the minority report was 51 to 45. It will come up again, I suppose.

I made a speech against the death sentence. Got a very good letter on it from Rev. Walter Gering of the Bethany Church. He said the Mennonite Church had taken a stand against willful, deliberate taking of human life for over 400 years and that we cannot conscientiously interpret God's Word in any other manner than to uphold the sacredness of human life whether it's the life of a criminal or not.

Sunday, January 31, 1937
J. W. and I went to the Congregational Church in the morning and were home all afternoon. DeBoer came over and read a sermon by Spurgeon. We listened to the Freeman College quartet over WNAX.

Talked with Attorney Wm. Metzger, Klatt and Clark from Hutchinson Co. Metzger came up to get some jobs for Hutchinson Co. people.

Monday, February 1, 1937
Session convened at 2 p.m. Death penalty bill came up again, but there were 55 votes against having it reconsidered. The "cinch" motion was put on so it cannot come up again. There will be no death penalty!

J. W. was still here today. He is looking for a job as Gas and Scale inspector as soon as the division is transferred back to the Agriculture Department.

Tuesday, February 2, 1937
Passed the T. B. test for cattle bill. I voted NO on that bill. It will be a hardship on us farmers.

Metzger is still here. He called me and Rep. Tiede off the floor concerning the abolition of a judgeship.

Got a letter from County Agent Roth.

Wednesday, February 3, 1937
Had a joint Education Committee meeting. Education will ask for 50% of the sales tax money. A T.B. test for teachers was introduced.

Had a House Education Committee meeting at 8 p.m. We passed out of committee the Spearfish Normal four-year course bill and the joint resolution concerning a statue to Gen. Beadle, who was Territorial Superintendent of Education, responsible for preserving school lands. He was brother P. P.'s teacher.

Monday, February 8, 1937
Convened today at 2 p.m. and again at 7:30 p.m. It was the last day (35th day of session) to introduce bills personally.

The boys had a Dutch lunch stag party last night but I did not go. I was afraid it might develop into a booze party. I was told they had plenty to eat and plenty of beer but that no one was drunk.

Tuesday, February 9, 1937
Had a routine session.

Went to the Methodist Church for a church supper for 35¢. Did not get much to eat.

Steele of the SDEA gave a good speech on education.

Wednesday, February 10, 1937
Met at 2 and worked 'til 5:30. Passed a 6% gross tax on ore mined. The original bill called for 10%. The vote was 68 aye, 33 nay, and 2 excused.

Got a letter from home, the first since returning from recess. Weather seems to be better here than at home.

Thursday, February 11, 1937
Had session at 2 p.m. Drove home with Wesley Neufeld, who was up to take a civil engineering exam. Left Pierre at 5:45 and got to my corner on 81 at 12:30 a.m. Friday. I was disoriented in directions but got my bearings after I got to my mailbox.

Friday, February 12, 1937
The children drove to school with the car. I thawed out pipes. The windmill pumping pipe burst.

Saturday, February 13, 1937
Everybody home. Terrible storm. Got stuck early in the morning. Roads were already badly drifted at 9 a.m. It started thawing at 11 a.m. and then quit drifting.

Pete Schmidt helped me fix pipes on the windmill. He charged $2 for labor and $1 for parts. The upper pipe is now 7 1/2 ft. long.

Sunday, February 14, 1937
Went back to Pierre with Atty. Henry L. Gross and Banker A. J. Waltner. Stopped at Mitchell where we met Ray Hirsch, who drove with his car to Pierre. The road was very bumpy. It started to drift west of Miller.

I am at the State House now at 7 p.m. Talked with quite a few Reps. I was glad to see them.

Tuesday, February 16, 1937

Session at 2 p.m. Passed a few bills but did not hear the committee report of those that had gone to Washington, D. C. about the Child Labor resolution. It had been set for a special order of business at 2:15, but we did not hear it because the Speaker forgot about it.

Heard a man from Yankton discuss the bridge situation over the Missouri River.

I was invited to the Waverly Hotel for a Farmers Union meeting and a good feed on a man from Sioux Falls. Met ex-Gov. Schober.

Wednesday, February 17, 1937

House passed the Sims money or "Baby Bond" bill by vote of 61-38. The bankers were fighting the bill.

Had a talk with a member of the Certification Board in the office of the Sup. of Public Instruction.

Got a letter from Ludeman, Dean of Springfield Normal.

Thursday, February 18, 1937

HB 158, the Education bill, passed by a big vote. Pension for teachers was discussed by Bell of Huron. HB 19, Spearfish Normal bill, was reported out of committee without recommendation.

Session tonight at 7:30 will be last opportunity to introduce committee bills.

Friday, February 19, 1937

Passed two banking bills apparently necessary to conform to federal law.

Oscar Fosheim claims that a substitute Speaker cannot take a motion to adjourn.

Many members are absent. It is 5:50 p.m. and everybody is ready to quit.

Saturday, February 20, 1937

Session at 9:30. Quit at noon sharp.

Had Third District Farmers Union meeting in the afternoon. Most of the Farmers Union members in the legislature were called on to speak. I spoke also. Democrat Emil Loriks gave me a good send off. He said, "Kleinsasser always votes right." I am not so sure about that. And I'm not sure that will stand me in good stead if some Republicans get hold of it.

The ore tax passed in the Senate. I wanted to go home but gave it up.

Sunday, February 21, 1937

Got a beautiful birthday card from home. Was at the Methodist Church this morning. Capalli, an Italian soloist and preacher, was there. He'll hold meetings all week.

Having beautiful weather. I am working in the State House this afternoon. Tollefson of Lincoln Co. is getting quite some publicity on account of his speech against the Democrats.

Monday, February 22, 1937

Today is my 41st birthday. Had no session because of Sen. Feeney's funeral in Fort Pierre. The funeral was held in the Catholic Church. The priest certainly went through a lot of formality. He gave a 15 min. eulogy, which was good.

Tuesday, February 23, 1937

Session at 2 p.m. John Gering got back from Marion before the session started.

Spearfish Normal is still fighting for its four-year program. Madison and Springfield Normals want to hook on.

Wednesday, February 24, 1937

Very busy day. Some 25 bills up. There was much argument about the reapportionment bill. It passed with the Senate apportionment set up and the House set up. It will likely go to Conference committee. Hutchinson Co. loses one Representative.

Thursday, February 25, 1937

Brother-in-law Joe M. Hofer of Huron is here staying with Judge Polley. 30 bills on the calendar today. Brother-in-law Peter G. Hofer came up from Sully Co., where he had business.

I worked quite late last night and then went along with Weier because I let Peter G. have my bed.

John Gering's family came up from Marion for a visit.

Friday, February 26, 1937

Acted on 38 bills. Passed many appropriation bills.

Spoke before and after noon. I have to be careful not to talk too much. The ARGUS LEADER man wrote: "Rep. John P. Kleinsasser, Freeman rural teacher, says he 'hates firecrackers.' However, he declared he could not vote for a measure intended to abolish the use of fireworks except on July 3 and 4 unless the exceptions include the State Fair. Kleinsasser is one of the most 'heard' members of the House and opines on nearly every question from Good Friday to firecrackers."

The press are to put on the Third House tonight.

Saturday, February 27, 1937
Had sessions at 11 and 2. Acted on many bills. I came in for a lot of ribbing last night at the Third House. The ARGUS man impersonated me speaking on every issue.

Sunday, February 28, 1937
Went to Baptist Church this morning.
I wrote home again but have not heard from the children about coming up. Worked on bills late into the night.

Monday, March 1, 1937
Gov. Jensen addressed joint session at 2:45 about HB 13, the ore tax bill, and HB 133, the 100,000 ton exemption bill. He spoke in favor of the net income tax.

Tuesday, March 2, 1937
Republicans caucused in the Governor's office concerning tax measures. We decided to have a 3¢ sales tax and a 2 mill property tax with a Homestead exemption of $5,000.
Gov. Jensen is very tired and so are the legislators. Gov. visited the House for about 1/2 hour.

Wednesday, March 3, 1937
Members put on a freak uproar in the House. The sergeant-at-arms was asked to take one of the members out. Amsden made a speech and then presented Speaker Miller with a beautiful engraved watch. Miller was greatly moved.
Did not get a letter from home about whether Pearl and Cal are coming up, so I phoned at 2:20 a.m. It cost $1.40.

Thursday, March 4, 1937
Pearl and Cal arrived at noon by train and are in the gallery now at 5:30 p.m. We are still in session.

"C'mon, kids, let's go get some supper before the session takes up again in the evening," Morgan said to his eldest two as he met them in the lobby outside the House Chamber.

"Okay!" they exclaimed in unison and followed their Pa to the ground floor where the State House restaurant was located.

Along the corridors and stairs Morgan proudly introduced his children to legislators and staff members. "These are my two bosses at home. They're taking care of the place while I'm up here."

Finding a booth unoccupied in the restaurant and handing menus to his children, Morgan announced grandly, "Get whatever you want."

"Really?"

"Sure, you're not getting any younger."

"Well, I think I'd like this chicken fried steak with mashed potatoes and gravy," said Cal, cautiously.

"That's a good choice. I'll have that too. It's very good here," said Morgan.

"Okay, make it three," Pearl informed the waitress, whom Morgan called Betty.

"Three chicken fried steaks comin' right up!" she said and hurried to the kitchen.

"Well, what did you learn today?" Morgan asked the two.

Each looked blankly at the other. "Well, one thing is that they have a pretty good time," said Cal.

"I can't understand why they put everything off to the last minute. It seems to me they could budget their time better and not let the calendar get so full at the end of the session," commented Pearl.

"It's a perennial problem," said Morgan. "But there are so many things that have to happen – drawing up the bills, committee hearings, caucus meetings, amendments, conference committees, and so forth that many bills just can't make it up any faster."

"I guess it's a good thing they have a definite cut off time, or they'd dribble on and on and never get their work done," observed Cal.

"You're right about that."

When their steaks came, they ate with relish almost in silence, commenting only on how good it was to sit down to a meal without having to do the farm chores first.

"It hasn't been too hard at home without me, has it?" Morgan asked cautiously.

"Yes, it has, Pa. Ma has to cry sometimes, especially when the well freezes up," said Pearl, candidly.

"Well, it's getting warmer and the session is almost over," sighed Morgan. "Would you like any dessert?"

"I'll have a dish o' ice cream," Cal announced quickly.

"What about you, Pearl?"

"Well, I saw bananas and cream on the menu, but that's an awful price to pay for bananas and cream."

"What was it?"

"Twenty-five cents."

"Well, if you want it, you may order it," said Morgan.

"What about you, Representative Kleinsasser? Aren't you having any dessert?" asked the waitress.

"No, I have to watch my girlish figure," he said to gales of laughter.

It is 10:35 p.m. The children are in the gallery. We acted on 23 bills so far. Cannot clear the calendar any more. Just voted on a 3.2 beer bill. The Senate killed the net income tax.

Friday, March 5, 1937

Sessions at 11 and 2:30. Pearl and Cal are enjoying it here. It is 8:23 p.m. and we have not concurred with the Senate yet on the appropriations bill.

We sang for a long time and had an enjoyable time. Most of the talkative guys had something to say. Some of the boys were pretty well "soaked" up.

Saturday, March 6, 1937

Had session 'til 2:30 a.m. Stopped the clock so as not to adjourn after midnight. Some Representatives and Senators left last night but most stayed 'til this morning.

Cal, Pearl and I rode to Stanley Corner with Norsted, secretary of the State Highway Commission. I bought him 10 gal. of gas and paid for his meal in Chamberlain for a total of $2.41. We made it in five hours.

Johnny came to Stanley Corner to get us. Highway 81 is very wet and muddy.

Went to town in the evening and talked to many of the town fellows.

Tuesday, March 9, 1937

Went to Sioux Falls with Jake T. Gross and ordered the ARGUS LEADER for six months with the Sunday edition. The children like the funnies, especially "Little Orphan Annie."

In the evening Cal and I went to P. P.'s to hear F. D. Roosevelt discuss the U. S. Supreme Court over the radio.

Wednesday, March 10, 1937

Went to see George Tieszen and Henry Tiahrt concerning seed oats and to Paul Decker concerning seed wheat. Paul phoned later to say I could have some at market price.

Thursday, March 11, 1937

Got our first two lambs this morning and two more in the evening.

Started teaching again following my Pierre vacation.

Weather is fair. Snowpile in the middle of the yard is decreasing, but it is still several feet high.

Cal and I went to John L.'s to get his trailer. We burned out a fuse twice before we got home.

Saturday, March 13, 1937

Went to Olivet with Ed Weidenbach for a teachers' meeting. Miss Manning of the U. of S. D. spoke on Art and Mrs. Truax of Sioux Falls spoke on the NEA meeting in New Orleans.

There was an auction of state lands in Hutchinson Co. We have about 1300 acres of state land in this county. It rents for 40¢ to $1 an acre.

Sunday, March 14, 1937

Johnny, Cal, Pearl, Ruth and I were in our church today for the first time since January 1. Paul E. Hofer family was here for dinner.

Katherine's brother John was here too. He says his wife left him, taking all the household goods. Just left him two cats, he said. He wants a job here after a week.

Monday, March 15, 1937

One ewe had twin lambs. She does not like one of them. We have that same trouble with her every year.

Took four hams to Jake Huber to smoke.

Wednesday, March 17, 1937

Made out my Soil Conservation sheet at John L.'s. I have to sow 28 acres of sweet clover or alfalfa or eradicate 28 acres of creeping jinnies.

Jake M. Hofer visited school.

It is midnight now. Long past bed time.

Thursday, March 18, 1937

Sent $13.57 to Sioux Falls for car payment due February 26. Next one is due March 26. P. P. bought an Allis Chalmers tractor.

Friday, March 19, 1937

Drilled spelling for the district elimination meet and gave exams in spelling.

Johnny dragged after school. Low places are still frozen. It was frozen nearly all day but still people were seeding. Some just have to be the first ones out.

Saturday, March 20, 1937

Got 30 bu. Burbank wheat from Paul Decker @ $1.30, fanned. Johnny sowed 8 acres. Ground frozen 'til noon.

Elmer Tiahrt brought 75 bu. oats @ 52¢, fanned.

Sunday, March 21, 1937

John Tieszen was here. He says he cannot come to sow for us. He wants to go to Minnesota to work.

Monday, March 22, 1937

I tried to get to town for my 1935 wheat check. I had overseeded but the government decided to pay us part of the second 1935 wheat allotment.

Wednesday, March 24, 1937

Regular old time blizzard this morning. A yearling ewe had twins. She seems to have enough milk. Got the lambs started sucking before breakfast. They seem to be coming just fine.

The children did not go to school. I walked to school. Only Melvin came. We practiced spelling nearly all day.

It was hard going to school but harder coming home. Wind has abated somewhat this evening (northeast wind).

Max came for yeast.

Good Friday, March 26, 1937

No school. Jacob B. and P. P. Tschetter both preached this morning. Tschetter had just come back from Canada.

Johnny went home to Spink for Easter. He hadn't been home since Thanksgiving because of his work at the College.

Abe Wiens family were here for a visit in the afternoon. They said Mrs. Regehr died this morning.

There is quite a bit of snow. Most of the telephone lines are down.

Saturday, March 27, 1937

Tried to manure the barn but the spreader was broken. Made fence around the strawpile so the cattle can't tramp the straw down. We had made a fence earlier but the cattle trampled it badly.

Got my second payment for 1935 wheat contract for $26.26. I had overseeded but finally got it straightened out with the government.

Sunday, March 28, 1937

Did not go to church this morning because we all went to Mrs. Regehr's funeral in the afternoon. She lacked just a few months of reaching her 80th birthday on July 4. She was born in Russia and lived most of her life on a farm neighboring Katherine's folks. Her husband died in 1918, before Katherine and I were married.

On the way to the Bethesda Mennonite Church for the funeral, Pearl asked, "What was her first name? We just called her 'Mrs.' or *Tante* Regehr."

"Her name was Helena. She was my father's sister, so we called her *Tante*."

"She never had any children, did she?"

"That's right. She and Uncle John were married for forty years and never had any children. But she loved children. That's why she was always so kind to you kids."

"Yeah, she always gave us candy," said Ruth.

"And she never got mad when we climbed into her apple trees," added Cal.

"She must have been one of Grandpa Tieszen's oldest sisters. How many were there in the family, anyhow?" asked Pearl.

Taking a deep breath, Katherine said, "My grandfather, Peter Tieszen, and my grandmother, Maria Duerksen, had 13 children, all born in South Russia. But seven of them died before the family left Russia. The oldest one was Anna, who died in Mountain Lake, Minnesota. Then there was Uncle Peter. He was married twice. He died here near Marion about ten years ago. He was the father of Rev. Jacob A. Tieszen, pastor of the Bethel Mennonite Church, near where the Tiahrts live. Then came Mrs. Regehr. Then Rev. Derk Tieszen, who will preach the funeral today."

"Is he the one that married you and Pa?"

"Yes. Then came Aunt Maria. She married John Engbrecht and their first child is Rev. Engbrecht, who has the Sunnyside Bible Academy."

"So Engbrecht is your cousin, then? That's why we go to services there sometimes?"

"That's right. Then the next child was Grandpa, my father."

"Then he was the youngest child in the family?"

"He was the youngest to survive. There was another girl born after him, but she died in Russia."

"I'm the youngest one in MY family," said Marian.

"Yes, but not for long," said her mother, winking at Pearl.

"Wow! That's quite a family history. I never knew all that before," said Pearl. "Where does President Unruh's wife, Amalia, fit in?"

"She is Rev. Derk Tieszen's daughter, just as Mrs. Linscheid is."

"Who's Mrs. Linscheid?"

"Oh, I guess you haven't met her. She's married to a minister, Louis Linscheid. Ben V. and Abe V. Tieszen are brothers to her and Mrs. Unruh. So they are my first cousins."

"That's quite a family!" said Pearl, sighing.

Monday, March 29, 1937

Lost a lamb today. An old ewe, #92, had twins and fell on one of her lambs. She tried to get up but couldn't, fell back and killed the lamb.

Tuesday, March 30, 1937

Rye looks good. Fixed on telephone line, so it works now south of our place.

Wednesday, March 31, 1937

The SDEA JOURNAL carried my picture and a little write-up about my efforts on school legislation.

Had our district declamatory and spelling contests in #98. The only winner I had was Esther Hofer in 3rd and 4th grade spelling. Diamond Valley #56 had the most winners. Rev. Jacob B.'s school was not entered.

Thursday, April 1, 1937

Got fooled by the kids in school.

The old red cow had a nice bull calf. It is mostly red with a few white spots.

The yard is very muddy.

Farmstead of John P. Kleinsasser, 3 miles north of Freeman, SD.

Friday, April 2, 1937
College students are in Vermillion at the university for a music contest.
Julius Albrecht at Square Deal Garage fixed our phone for 20¢.

Saturday, April 3, 1937
County spelling and declam contests in Olivet were called off because of snow.
De-tailed 12 lambs.

Sunday, April 4, 1937
Got up too late to go to church. Got a new roan bull calf from the red heifer. Plenty of snow on the ground. There has been no seeding since March 20.

"Read us the funnies, Daddy," cried Ruth and Marian as they jumped up and down on him in bed, waving the Sunday edition of the ARGUS LEADER.

Tuesday, April 6, 1937
Pearl is having quite a time milking the young heifer.

"They kick! That's why I hate to milk fresh heifers. This one stepped on my toe, put her foot in the milk pail, and spilled everything I'd gotten out of her so far," complained Pearl through her tears.

"We have hobblers, you know. Why not try to hobble her with the chain?" asked her mother.

"She doesn't want to be hobbled either. I tried that. She just kicks the chain off."

"I don't know what to suggest, Pearl. You know my condition. I can't do it.

"You just tell me why milking is considered women's work around here! Tell me that!"

"It's not just around here, Pearl. The menfolks have their hands full with the field work. They can't leave the field work and come home to do the milking."

"They at least could help break in the heifers!" exclaimed Pearl, picking up her pail from the kitchen floor and heading back to the barn.

Once back in the dreaded milking area, Pearl scolded, "This time I'm gonna stick my head into your flank so hard that you're not gonna be able to move your leg!" With her head wrapped in a white flour sack square, Pearl pressed her head into the heifer's side. "Squirt, squirt, squirt" came the sound of success.

Thursday, April 8, 1937

Johnny came home from College with the car at noon to sow wheat. He sowed 10 acres Burbank. I took the car back after my school for the other students and bought 750 lbs. of briquets for $5.75.

Friday, April 9, 1937

Took the Freeman students in and then came back to take my #98 pupils to Olivet for the Young Citizens League Convention and spelling and declam contests. Only Esther was entered. She did not place. Ruth went along to Olivet. She enjoyed the YCL Chorus, especially "Froggie Went a-Courting."

This year Grades 5-8 sang "The Cuckoo Clock," "Swing Low, Sweet Chariot," "The Quilting Party" and "Froggie."

Grades 1-4 sang "Rickety Jig," "Lightly Row," and "Sleepy Fishes."

All the grades sang the YCL song, "Lead, Kindly Light," "The Linden Tree," and "Oh, Susanna."

Saturday, April 10, 1937

Both Jacob B. and P. P. Tschetter preached this morning. Visited folks in Marion in the afternoon. In the evening Pearl, Johnny and Cal went with me to Freeman to hear Rev. Gordon, a converted Jew, preach in the Pullman Hall. He goes through a lot of commotion but has pretty good ideas.

Monday, April 12, 1937

Cal stayed home from school to sow but it was too wet. Johnny went out after school and it worked fairly well.

Tuesday, April 13, 1937

Pearl stayed home from school this forenoon to drag. Johnny came home from College and finished sowing Durham. When Cal came home from school, Johnny went in to study and Cal sowed oats.

Ma and I wanted to go to town but the car was out of gas. I walked to Walters and bought a gallon.

Traded eggs at Fensel for three sacks of egg mash.

Heard the Jew, Gordon, speak on politics. He says Roosevelt was elected through the relief set up and booze.

Wednesday, April 14, 1937

Cal stayed home to sow oats and drag. He sowed 11 acres oats in south field. Johnny started sowing barley after school.

Thursday, April 15, 1937

Johnny came home from College to sow barley and plow a garden patch.

I went to town in the evening to hear Mr. Gordon preach. I did not enjoy it. He had quite an audience.

Friday, April 16, 1937

Arbor Day, but we did not plant any trees. Cal stayed home to disc the corn stalks. There is still a little water in the northwest lake. The wheat is coming. One can see the rows in the field sown March 20. Could use more rain.

Saturday, April 17, 1937

Sowed barley in the northwest cornstalk field and hauled 2 loads of manure.

Fixed phone line north to my land boundary. Phone works now. I called Weier and he called me back.

Went to Viborg for Burial Assoc. board. The funeral home is fixed up very nicely, almost too elaborately. It cost us over $2,000.

Sunday, April 18, 1937

Johnny took our car to take College singers to Avon and Springfield. They gave three programs. He got back after midnight.

Monday, April 19, 1937

Cal stayed home to drag. Johnny dragged Russian thistles in north field where we had sweet clover. The clover is good only in low spots. Alfalfa looks better every day. Might make a crop yet.

Had a telephone co-op meeting at A. R. M. Hofer's place. It was decided each member should fix line along his land.

Wednesday, April 21, 1937

College Clean Up Day, but Johnny drilled oats in the north sweet clover field. Some College kids came out to see him in the afternoon.

Plowed some more for potatoes. The plow scours well.

Thursday, April 22, 1937

Planted 3 bu. potatoes west of machine shed, a new place. We made rows with the corn planter.

Mr. Gordon gave his demonstration of the Jewish Passover. It was interesting but he certainly took his time. The Gym was packed. I had to stand in balcony.

Friday, April 23, 1937

Drizzling all day turned to snow in the evening.

We fed the last hay today. Not much oats left either. Horses are in poor shape, but they have been able to pull the machinery.

Ma is sick with a bad cold. It always seems to develop into something worse.

Had two flat tires and ran out of gas going to school.

Saturday, April 24, 1937
Regular blizzard. Ma is very sick. If roads had been open, we would have gone to the doctor.

Sunday, April 25, 1937
Snow banks 5 feet high and phone wires down. Saw no cars travel. Ma is a little better. She slept a little in the afternoon.

There is no feed in the barn for livestock. We still have straw in piles outside but could not get to it on account of the blizzard. Trees are breaking down.

The children made ice cream.

I am reading Wells' KAPOOT about Russia.

Monday, April 26, 1937
I walked and the children drove with the car. They had to shovel at Jonath Graber's place and got to school at 10:30.

Jake Gross (Juppa) left his tractor at Philip Mensch's place without draining the water. His radiator and head cracked. (That is, the tractor's.)

Took two cases of eggs to town. Eggs are 17¢ per doz. Bought necessary groceries and a few extras.

Tuesday, April 27, 1937
No field work. Hauled a load of rye straw to hay mow. Not very good, but that's all we have.

Hundreds of telephone posts are down. East-west lines went down this time.

Wednesday, April 28, 1937
Out of hay. Wind tore down the alfalfa fence. Cattle are eating rye straw in the barn. Sheep get enough rye pasture. Early sown rye is not good. It must have dried out last fall. Later sown rye is better but not thick enough. We should've sown it 2 bu. to the acre, not 1 1/2.

Thursday, April 29, 1937
Reviewing for Test F in school.

Reports are that many people lost cattle and sheep in the last snow storm.

Got a letter from Bushfield, state Republican chr.

Friday, April 30, 1937

Pearl and Johnny tore the wallpaper off the ceiling in our bedroom. Ma wants to calcimine it green and buff.

"What are you doing, tearing up the house again?" Morgan asked his wife as he entered the house to find bits of wallpaper littering the floor.

"We're just taking the paper off the ceiling. I want to get the room fixed up nice for the baby."

"I can't figure you women out. You're never satisfied. Always have to change things around."

"John, this paper has been on the ceiling since your mother slept in this room."

"Doesn't look bad to me."

"Well, I'm tired of it."

"What are you going to put in its place?"

"We're going to re-do it, with a new product, Calcimine."

"Calcimine!? Waddaya want with that? That's nothing but whitewash!"

"It comes in different colors."

"It's still not paint!"

"Well, I wish we could afford paint, but we can't. Finer said Calcimine would serve until we could paint it."

"You women! You can take more money out the back door than a man can bring in the front door!"

Johnny took the car without permission and went to a wedding party. He got home at midnight.

I tightened the telephone wire after school.

Got a letter from Nissen of the SDEA JOURNAL.

Saturday, May 1, 1937

Rained last night. The soil just soaks those little rains up. Some lakes have quite a bit of water. Wild ducks are still around. I hope they nest here.

Johnny calcimined our bedroom. Cal plowed and I fenced, burned Russian thistles and did general repair work.

Sunday, May 2, 1937

Not in church. It rained.

Boys played football on the old alfalfa patch.

I went to College for a Round Table discussion program, but it was called off.

Cattle graze on the field east of the hog house.

Monday, May 3, 1937

The car got hung up on ruts on the section line when children were coming home from school.

Jake M. Hofer picked me up at the school house to go adjusting storm losses for Aid Plan. George M.'s windmill is down and his steer choked at Jake Aman's place.

Wednesday, May 5, 1937

Picnic for #98 at the Jim River. Pete Ratzlaff drove his car and I took my car. Caught quite a few crappies, bullheads and sheepheads. Got a good sun burn. Had a blow out. Had to buy Lee tube and tire at Philipps 66 for $10.

Thursday, May 6, 1937

Ascension Day. Johnny used our car to take the College singers on deputation work at surrounding high schools.

I turned the horses on the rye field.

Johnny blew out another tire. They had three flats on their singing tour. We bought a tire from Rudolph Gering for $10.25.

Saturday, May 8, 1937

Rally Day in Tripp. Melvin Ratzlaff won 1st in Class C High Jump and Dash, Max won 2nd in High Jump, and Marie won 3rd in both. The MITCHELL DAILY REPUBLIC took pictures of the winners and judges.

Sunday, May 9, 1937

Visited Henry Tiahrts. Henry broke his ankle two weeks ago when a horse fell on him. They have a new radio for which he paid $99.95. They also have 1100 chicks.

Tuesday, May 11, 1937

Cleaned water tank and took out the bullheads. We ate 8 and put 27 in the lake west of the barn. I hope they grow big.

The boys picked stones off the east field.

Thursday, May 13, 1937

Finished plowing little east field. Johnny and I took down fences.

Land is to be measured by air for compliance this year. Another brainstorm of a brain truster.

Saturday, May 15, 1937

College had a track meet for 7th and 8th graders from rural schools. Cal had a hard time getting in because he attends town school. He placed 2nd in broad jump (14 1/2 feet) and 2nd in a judging contest.

Took the cattle off the rye field. We'll let them eat creepers for a while.

Sunday, May 16, 1937

Pentecost. All in church. P. P. Tschetter preached. He has accepted a call to preach for a Kingman, Kansas, congregation.

Potatoes are coming up.

I was on the Christian Endeavor program tonight. The theme was "Das Gewissen als eine Gottliche Stimme." I discussed it in English. Paul E. and Peter J. S. discussed it in German.

Monday, May 17, 1937

Started 7th and 8th grade review in arithmetic with Max, the only one this year. After school I plowed up the lake bed in the pasture.

Tuesday, May 18, 1937

Started planting corn. Bought 2 1/2 bu. Murdock seed from Preheim for $3.50 per bu.

Wednesday, May 19, 1937

Children are starting a fat lamb 4-H club. Got 180 chicks and chick mash from Fensel's. They are started chicks but don't look very good.

Thursday, May 20, 1937

7th and 8th grade exams were held at my school today. Max Walter is writing the 7th grade exam.

Cal has his school picnic today.

Friday, May 21, 1937

I sent exams to Olivet with County Auditor Ed Weidenbach. It would have cost me 39¢ to mail them.

Saturday, May 22, 1937

We planted 1 bu. "Hybred" seed corn. If it does not yield more than my other, it will cost me nothing. It it yields more, it will cost me $10 per bu.

The town fellows are still cussing about the net bill. Mr. Voss, the game warden, does a lot of arresting for use of nets at the Jim.

Sunday, May 23, 1937

Children went to church but Ma and I stayed home.

Corn might not even come up if it does not rain. Windy and hot today.

Rev. Walter Gering gave the baccalaureate sermon at the Gym tonight. He is a fine speaker and a fine man.

Tuesday, May 25, 1937

College people are taking final exams. Pearl plowed after school while we went to Tiahrts crabbing. Got 2 sacks full and a few bullheads. Cloudy all day but not too cold for crabbing.

Wednesday, May 26, 1937

Rained all day. The College kids had their picnic at Wall Lake. They went in two stock trucks.

Put the sheep in the barn for shearing tomorrow.

Thursday, May 27, 1937

Sheared 14 sheep between 10 a.m. and 6 p.m. They have good fleeces.

College had graduation exercises tonight. Johnny finished the one-year Normal course. Jake, Adeline, Mary and the Josh Stahl family came down from Spink and Beadle for the graduation.

Friday, May 28, 1937

College Field Day and Alumni Program. J. R. Thierstein, who started the Alumni Association in 1907, spoke. Alumni decided to buy 24 arm desks for FJC.

Josh Stahl family and Mary K. stayed here overnight. Johnny went back home with them.

Saturday, May 29, 1937

Planted seed corn, beans, popcorn and muskmelon in the field by the stone pile.

Started plowing for Soil Conservation program.

Cal and I and Jake L. and his boys went fishing. We caught 65 bullheads and a 3 lb. catfish.

Got my shearing knives from Juhnke and stored them in oil in the southeast corner of the garage.

Sunday, May 30, 1937

Had congregational meeting in the afternoon regarding future conduct and regulation of the church. Jacob B is to be preacher now that P. P. Tschetter is leaving for Kansas. We discussed buying

Tschetter's house in Freeman as a home for the minister. He wants $2300 for it.

Monday, May 31, 1937

All at work. Cal is plowing, I am fencing, and Ma and Pearl are weeding the garden.

"Can we help too?" asked Ruth as she and Marian approached their mother and older sister in the garden.

"Yes, you may," answered Katherine. "You may work here in the carrots. But be careful not to pull out the carrots. See what carrots look like? They're very easy to tell from the weeds. They have these fine, feathery leaves."

"I wanna work by you," said Marian.

"You may, right next to me in your carrot row."

"I'll start down at the end and meet you in the middle," said Ruth, running to the end of the carrot row.

"Isn't that risky?" Pearl asked her mother, quietly.

"What?"

"Letting Ruth in the carrots unsupervised."

"Carrots need some thinning anyway," laughed her mother.

"I hope we can get some help when the baby comes," said Pearl. "I don't think I can handle all the work, especially during harvest."

"Adeline will help, I think," said Katherine, rising from her knees with great difficulty and holding her aching back.

"Is Addy coming?" asked Marian.

"Not now. A little later."

"Little pitchers have big ears!" said Pearl, quietly.

"Pretty soon she won't be the baby any more," observed her mother.

"I'm no baby!" insisted Marian.

Wednesday, June 2, 1937

Pearl plowed and dragged corn. Cal and I and Jake L. took our wool to Mitchell. I had 320 lbs. @ 30c ($96. from 23 sheep). Three had died during the winter, so they did not have much wool. Jake pooled his wool. He got 20¢ per lb. now.

Thursday, June 3, 1937

Ervin Aman was here checking on the soil diversion acres. I have most of the weed control acres plowed.

The Hutchinson Co. Teachers' Assoc. wants to give Miss Perman a gift and I am to present it to her at the graduating exercises Sunday.

Max passed 7th grade exams. His lowest grade was in arithmetic.

Friday, June 4, 1937

Got check from government for Soil Conservation in 1936. ($36.14) Sent $27.14 to Edwards Finance Co. for car payments due May 26 and June 26.

Saturday, June 5, 1937

Mrs. Regehr's sale. All household goods sold well. The house brought $1625 with lots. Father-in-law bought quite a few articles of his sister's.

We came home at 10 p.m. A big wind blew the barn door down and our new hay rack over. It was a very heavy rack, but we had it positioned wrong.

Sunday, June 6, 1937

Went to Olivet today for 8th grade graduation exercises. I presented Rose Perman an electric clock from the HCTA. About 200 graduates heard Prof. Ludeman from Springfield Normal speak. It was very cold and windy. I wore my winter overcoat while driving.

We saw part of a ball game on the way home between Meridian and Mayhen at Meridian. At the end of 8 innings, the score was 8 to 1 in favor of Meridian.

Monday, June 7, 1937

Girls and I went to town in the evening. Marian got a pair of white shoes.

Pearl, Cal and I went to Rev. Wipf's house for visitation later. A lot of people are down from Beadle and Spink for the funeral.

Tuesday, June 8, 1937

Uncle David J. Wipf was buried today from the Neu Hutterthal Church. Young Hofer from Beadle, Mike Hofer from Bridgewater and Schartner preached. Albert Hofer was the undertaker.

"I still don't understand how we are related to the Wipfs," said Pearl on the drive home from the funeral.

"Okay, listen carefully! My father, your grandfather (Paul Kleinsasser) had six sisters, all born in South Russia. Their father was also named Paul Kleinsasser, but he died in 1877, when Father was just a young man, only eighteen, in fact. One of Father's sisters was Katharina, and she's the one that was married to Rev. David J. Wipf. So Rev. Wipf was my uncle by marriage."

"Then he was Paul K. Wipf's and Becky Wipf's father?"

"Yes! He's their father."

"What did the other sisters do?"

"Well, they married. The two older ones married men in the Colony, a Gross and a Walter. And the two younger ones married ministers named Wipf – Rev. David Wipf, who was buried today, and Rev. Elias Wipf."

"We sure have a lot of ministers in our family!"

"It's an honorable profession. But they were farmers too. Most of our ministers were not remunerated. I think Rev. P. P. Tschetter was the first one in our church who got a salary. Mostly they were farmers, and prosperous ones at that. You had to be prosperous in order to attain the respect of our people. Success was measured by the amount of land you had."

Rev. P. P. Tschetter, his Mrs., and Caroline were here for a visit this evening.

"I hate to see you go," said Katherine to Rev. Tschetter. "We'll miss your thought-provoking sermons."

"Well, Mrs. Tschetter and I will miss you folks too. But we have to go where the Lord leads."

"Yes," said Katherine.

"I hear they raise some pretty good wheat down in Kansas," observed Morgan.

"Turkey Red wheat it is, what our people brought over from the Old Country. Hard winter wheat."

"No wonder they can support a four-year college there," said Morgan.

"More than one. There's Tabor College in Hillsboro in addition to Bethel. But they're having trouble down there too. They're just coming out of the Dirty Thirties too. When the wind blows in Kansas, it blows just like here. They've planted Osage Orange along the fence rows to stop the erosion some, but the dirt still blows."

"Well, we want you to come see us when you get back up this way," said Katherine.

"I 'spect I'll be back for special meetings. But Jacob B. will need your support now."

Wednesday, June 9, 1937

Bought 4 pail-fed bull calves @ $4.50 each at Leonard Wudel's sale near Parkston.

Thursday, June 10, 1937

Cal cultivated corn after I started the field for him. Max came and fenced near the barn with me so cattle cannot get off the yard to the south. Cal took Paul L.'s trailer back. He wants 1¢ per mile for its use.

Friday, June 11, 1937

Pearl and I cocked some alfalfa that had been cut Mon. It does not dry very fast.

Cal & I cultivated the garden with a one-horse cultivator. Some of the garden stuff looks very promising, especially the potatoes.

Saturday, June 12, 1937

Smaller corn field is very poor due to cut worms and gophers.

"Let's see if we can drown out some gophers," Morgan said to his son.

"How we gonna do that?"

"We're gonna hitch up a horse to the stone boat and haul a barrel of water to the field. I'll pour a can of water down the hole and force 'em out. You'll watch for the gopher to come out the hole and clobber him with a rock!"

"Okay!"

On the way to the field, both stood on the stone boat, Morgan directing the horse and Cal balancing the barrel of water. "We used to do this all the time when I was a boy," said Morgan. "It was a great diversion."

"What else did you do?"

"Oh, we played ball, fished, told stories — whatever didn't cost any money. One time we went to a fair and Father gave me a dime. When it was time to go home, he asked what I did with the dime."

"Not too different from today," Cal chuckled.

"Maybe you can make some bounty money by selling gopher tails."

"Really?"

"Sure. Finer used to pay a penny a tail. I wouldn't be surprised if he still did that."

By the time the water barrel was empty, Cal had a dozen ring-tailed gophers to his credit and Morgan had the assurance that there would be a dozen fewer gophers eating up his "hybred" corn.

Sunday, June 13, 1937

All in church but Ma. P. P. Tschetter gave his farewell sermon in the evening. The church was filled to overflowing. Many stood outside who couldn't get in. Rev. Jacob B. spoke first. He asked *for remarks from the audience. Mrs. Tschetter also spoke. We took up a love offering of $29. for the Tschetters.*

Monday, June 14, 1937
Alfalfa is still wet. It got rained on twice.
Ma did the washing.

"I need some help carrying these baskets out to the line, Cal," called his mother to Cal, who was getting a drink at the pump.

"Yeah, be right there."

"Honestly, I don't know how I'll get all these clothes up," said Katherine, under her breath.

"We can help pick out the handkerchiefs and hand them to you," offered Ruth.

"That would be a big help if you and Marian would do that," their mother replied.

"Where's Pearl, anyway? Why isn't she helping you?" asked Cal.

"Pearl is helping Pa with the hay."

"I'll go out and take her place," said the young man.

"No, you go help your Pa too. It's more important to get the hay in before it gets rained on again."

"What's the matter with your legs?" asked Cal, alarmed. "They're all swollen!"

"They're retaining water. I really should be keeping them up."

"Well, you go lie down for a while, and the kids and I will hang up these clothes," he offered.

"Have you ever hung up clothes before?" she asked, smiling.

"No, but there can't be much to it. Just get 'em up."

"There's a proper way to do it. I don't want shirts hunt up by their collars! You go to the hay field and we'll take care of the clothes."

"Okay, Ma, whatever you say," said the puzzled young man.

Tuesday, June 15, 1937
Had school election. John P. Gross was elected chairman again. He was the only one nominated. We decided to have no school in #26 and to send the children to the Academy or High School, whichever they prefer. The grade school children will go to Freeman Independent School.

Wednesday, June 16, 1937
Jake P. Waldner borrowed our Nelly because his mare had a colt.
I took Cal, Pearl and Melvin Ratzlaff to Swan Lake 4-H camp and stayed for supper.

Thursday, June 17, 1937

Planted old cane on Soil Conservation land. It is 2 years old and very dry. I doubt it will come up if we don't have rain.

Friday, June 18, 1937

Lizzie Walter is helping Ma while children are at Swan Lake camp, but Lizzie is sick today.

Hauled alfalfa to hay mow. It is not very dry. Hope it keeps.

Saturday, June 19, 1937

Helmuth Schnaidt and I went to Mitchell for a meeting of purebred sheep breeders. I was appointed to a committee to arrange for a sale in Mitchell some time after the State Fair.

Sunday, June 20, 1937

Jacob B. preached this morning. Joe P. Glanzer asked me about teaching their school (Summit, #51). I have not decided whether I will teach again or not.

Monday, June 21, 1937

Cal finished cultivating the first time and started the second time. We had Bullet hitched up, but she is afraid to go crossways because the cultivator makes a noise.

Tuesday, June 22, 1937

Measured the soil diversion and base acres. (13 1/2 acres long field and 6 1/2 acres small cane field).

It was Pearl's birthday, so she, Clara Walter and I went to Tiahrts crabbing. Caught one sack full. Our net is too small. I bought it for 85¢ in Mitchell. It is really a minnow net.

Wednesday, June 23, 1937

Cal is cultivating. Nose flies are very bad. Got over 104 degrees.

Jake L., John L., and I went to Hurley for the Turner Co. Farmers Union picnic. Gordon Stout, Secretary of Agriculture, and Emil Loriks, President of the SD Farmers Union, spoke. Bought a screen door for $3.57.

Thursday, June 24, 1937

Cal planted cane and I cut oats, wheat and barley along the fences for hay. Put the fly nets on horses.

I got Adeline from Peter G.'s to help us.

Friday, June 25, 1937

Co-op Creamery picnic was postponed due to rain. Had a real soaker (2-4 inches), the first one this season. Many lakes have water as much as 6 inches deep.

Saturday, June 26, 1937

Rained this morning but the Co-op had its picnic in the afternoon. Metzger spoke on cooperation. An East Freeman quartet sang 3 numbers and David Melvin Wollman played guitar. They served 1500 Dixie cups and lemonade. Menno ball team beat Freeman 3 to 1 and won $25.

Sunday, June 27, 1937

Children and Adeline went to church. Mrs. P. P. and four of her children visited us in the evening. P. P. had gone to Menno to hear Gordon, the Jew.

Monday, June 28, 1937

Merchants State Bank refused to lend me money to buy alfalfa. Old Jacob Wollman said they could not take my note any more.

Tuesday, June 29, 1937

Some corn is knee high. Cal cultivated, Pearl raked hay with Lena and Bullet, and I got the binder ready to cut rye.

Wednesday, June 30, 1937

Cal and I were out in the field by 6 a.m. to haul oat, barley and wheat hay (4 1/2 loads).

Rolled up the corn planting wire. Bought 100 lbs. binder twine. John J. B. family visited here in the evening.

Joe P. Glanzer offered me $55 per mo. to teach #51. I have not decided to take it.

Thursday, July 1, 1937

Girls are shaking mulberries at Wienses.

Wheat is rusty.

Adeline went to a shower for Clifford Hofer and Anna Gross.

Saturday, July 3, 1937

Bought Cal a pair of high-top work shoes for $3 from John Wollman's store.

Sunday, July 4, 1937

Daisy had a colt. Everybody rejoicing. Adeline saw it first. Children went to church.

95

Adeline went to the Salem K. M. B. Church with Raymond Hofer, and Jake Schoenwald came for her in the evening.

Tiahrt and Wiens families visited in the evening. Henry helped me fix the binder roller.

Monday, July 5, 1937

I hitched Bullet in the binder. The line tore, which nearly resulted in a runaway. After she got used to the noise, she was the best puller in the team.

Cal, Pearl and Adeline shocked.

Tuesday, July 6, 1937

Grasshoppers are damaging the wheat. They bite the whole head off.

Wednesday, July 7, 1937

Started cutting wheat. Much smut and grasshoppers. 10% of the heads are on the ground.

Thursday, July 8, 1937

Cut the wheat field west of the tree and then started on the southwest rye field.

Adeline went to Canistota for Sports Days with Jake Schoenwald. Cal went with them. Pearl went away with Art Becker and someone else.

I cut rye 'til 9 p.m. It is now 10 and I am going to bed.

Part II

Death Visits Family

Marian

"Your mother is bread," she understood the doctor to say as he loomed above her.

"Bread?" asked Marian. What did the doctor mean? A loaf? A slice? "Where is Daddy? Where is Pearl? I wanna see Mommy."

"You can't see her now. You'll see her tomorrow. Your Daddy and Pearl are with her now," said the doctor in his white coat.

"Where's Cal? Where's my brother?"

"Did he come too? He must be parking your car."

"When is Daddy coming out?" asked the little girl.

"He'll be here shortly. Why don't you come over here and sit with me on this nice settee? Oh, dear, you got your pretty dress dirty by playing with those cigarette butts in the ash can."

Ruth

When Doc Ernest came down the corridor of the hospital wearing his white coat, Ruth recognized him. She had been to his office in Freeman several times with a sore throat or an ear ache. But what was he doing here in Sioux Falls? Had he brought Mother up here to have her baby? She thought Mother was going to have her baby in Freeman at Mrs. Schmidt's Maternity Home.

"Do I have a baby brother?" she asked Doc Ernest.

"No, you have a baby sister."

"Oh, goodie! Can I see her now?"

"No, you can't go in there now. Your mother is dead."

"Dead?"

"Yes, she died in child birth."

"My mother died?"

"Yes."

"Like my kitty?"

"If your kitty died, yes."

Ruth began to cry.

Cal

Cal impatiently swung the front doors of McKennan Hospital open and walked into the waiting room. There were Ruth and Marian with Doc Ernest sitting between them on the wicker sofa. The doctor, tall and dark, rose to meet Cal with his right hand extended.

"What's wrong? What happened? Why is Ruth bawling?" demanded Cal.

"It's your mother. She died just a few minutes ago."

"Why didn't you do something?"

"I did all I could, but she just lost too much blood."

"A few minutes ago? While I was parking the car?"

"Yes."

"Did she know we were here?"

"Yes, she saw your father and sister, gave one more gasp, moved her lips, and was gone."

"My God!"

Pearl

"You'd better go in the hospital room. Pa just fainted over Ma in bed," said Pearl to Dr. Ernest Hofer.

"Aren't there any nurses in there?" asked the doctor.

"Yes, but they said you should come in. They want some help." Then, watching Hofer rush down the corridor, she said, "I can't believe it. She was all right yesterday when she went to the doctor. Kissed us all good-bye. Now she's gone and left a baby. What are we going to do? I'm only seventeen years old. I can't be a mother to all of us," she cried, burying her face in the sofa cushion between her little sisters, who sat in shock.

Morgan

"I wish I'd left the rye field and driven with you and Katherine to the hospital yesterday. I had no idea she would have any problems delivering," Morgan said to the young doctor as they walked slowly from the hospital room. "Why didn't you insist that I go along?"

"I didn't know it would be this bad either, Morgan. I thought any complication that would arise could be taken care of here in the hospital."

"Well, it's a sad day for me and my children," he said weakly as they all gathered around him in the waiting room. "But we have a new baby sister. Her name will be Katherine."

"Would you like to use our telephone, Mr. Kleinsasser?" the desk attendant said after an interval.

"Yes, thank you. I have to call Mr. Raynie, our undertaker in Viborg."

Part III

Extended Family Rallies

As Morgan drove west through the clear night air on US Highway 16, he wished his mother were still living. If she could have lived only six more years, she would know what to do now. She had reared nine children herself, first in South Russia, then on board the immigrant ship, the *Mosel,* in 1879, and then on the Dakota plain. She had allowed him to suck from her breasts when he got thirsty in the fields until his older brothers shamed him by calling him "Baby." He must have been Marian's age then. Maybe a little younger.

Paul Kleinsasser, Sr., and John P. Kleinssaser as child.

She was a good woman, *Mutter.* Never let anyone go away from the farm hungry. Cooked whatever there was—potatoes, salt pork, eggs.

Katherine and Mutter hadn't always gotten along well. It had been hard for Katherine as a bride to move in with in-laws and, as a Low German, to move into the *Hutterische* community.

And *Vater's* long illness at home. That had been hard on everyone. Turning him in bed. Carrying him piggy-back. Morgan's back still ached from carrying his father from room to room or outside to sit under a shade tree.

What would *Vater* say now if he were alive? "Take a woman to the hospital to have a baby and she comes home dead!" All Father's children had been born at home. Mother herself had been present at the birth of many a child in the *Hutterische* community north west of Freeman. One of the best midwives around, they said.

"We'd better stop at Uncle George's and tell them about Ma," said Morgan as he passed the CANISTOTA sign on the highway.

"But they'll be asleep," Pearl protested from the back seat where she was sitting between Marian and Ruth, now asleep on her shoulders.

"They won't mind. They'll want to know. They knew Ma was due," he said as he turned into the farm of his wife's eldest brother.

The sun was just showing pink through the windows of their '34 Chevy as they drove the long driveway to Uncle George's and Aunt Bena's house. Roosters were crowing but no people were stirring. "We'll just sit here a few minutes and see if the dog's barking wakes them up."

"Where are we?" whined Ruth as she awoke and peered through the windows.

"We're at Uncle George's," answered Pearl.

"Why?"

"We want to tell them about Mother." And Ruth began to cry.

"Do you want me to knock on the door?" asked Cal.

"No, I'd better do it," sighed Morgan and lifted his large frame out of the car door. He walked to the front porch saying, "That's okay, Shep; it's only Morgan. We're not here to make trouble. Just want to talk to George and Bena."

At that, the screen door opened and George, holding a kerosene lamp before him, emerged with a "Who's there?"

"It's Morgan."

"What are you doing here at this hour? Anything wrong?"

"It's Katherine. She died."

"No! When?"

"One thirty this morning."

"Where?"

"McKennan Hospital, Sioux Falls."

"What about the baby?"

"The baby's alive."

"Come and sit on the swing. I'll call Bena."

"Come sit here on the porch swing with me, Cal," called Morgan to his son as the boy approached the house.

"Should I get Pearl?"

"No, the girls need her now."

"Morgan!" cried Bena as she moved gently through the screen door in her cotton night gown and took his hand, "I'm so sorry. What about the baby?"

"Baby's still at the hospital. They think she'll make it."

"Praise the Lord!"

"We'll call her Katherine."

"Oh, Morgan, that's as it should be. Can I make you some coffee?"

"No, thank you, we want to go to my sister Katherine's place near Dolton. We stopped there on our way to Sioux Falls last night to ask for directions to the hospital. She and Johnny J. B. will be wondering what happened. Then we'll go to Henry Tiahrts and Abe Wienses."

"Is that Pearl in the back seat?" Bena asked.

"Yes, she's with the little girls."

"Cal, I'm awful sorry," Aunt Bena said, putting her arm around the fourteen-year-old as they walked toward the car.

"Yeah," he sniffled.

"You're not alone. We'll all help. You know that."

"Yeah."

As George and Bena looked through the open windows of the Chevy, they saw Pearl and Ruth crying and Marian just waking up. When Marian saw everyone else cry, she began to cry too. "The doctor said Mommy turned into a loaf of bread," she said.

"Dead. The doctor said she was dead," clarified Pearl and Ruth through their tears.

"We'd better go," said Morgan. "It's getting light. George, would you call Grandpa and Grandma Tieszen and ask them to call the others except for Anna and Eva? We'll stop to see them."

"Do you know yet when the funeral will be?"

"Probably Monday. We'll contact you about arrangements."

"Drive careful," George cautioned them.

"God be with you," added Bena.

"You'd better drive, Cal. I'm so tired, I'm afraid I might go off the road," said Morgan.

Cal got behind the steering wheel and waved to cousins LeRoy and Ruth, who were just stumbling out of the house to investigate the commotion in the yard.

There was very little traffic on Highway 16 as the car drove west, the rising sun behind them. Morgan could see that people weren't done cutting grain east of Stanley Corner either. He was glad he was not the only one late. He had had trouble with his binder. Tore a strap on the binder platform canvas. Then the flies were so bad that he almost had a runaway with the horses. Bullet, especially, was jumpy. The binder noise seemed to scare her.

At Stanley Corner Cal turned south to Dolton. "Uncle Johnny will be up, I'll bet. He always gets up at 4 or 4:30 during the harvest."

"Best time of the day, he claims. Your uncle works from 'can't see' to 'can't see'."

When they drove onto the Hofers' yard, they saw Uncle Johnny carrying a five-gallon pail across the yard to the chicken house. "You startled me. I'm still half asleep," he explained as he walked up to Cal's window. "What are you all doing here at this hour? Anything happen?"

Morgan got out of the passenger's side of the car and walked around the front to where his brother-in-law was standing with the pail of chicken mash still in his hand. "Johnny, my Katherine died early this morning. Had a hemorrhage."

"*Gott in Himmel!*" he said, dropping the pail. "Come up to the house. I'll wake Katie. Have you had breakfast?"

"No, we just came from George Tieszen's place. We've got to go to Tiahrts and Wienses yet. Adeline's at home too. She doesn't know yet what happened."

"Well, come in and have some breakfast," he said, motioning for all in the car to come.

As Morgan approached his sister Katie, his arms opened wide and his face convulsed in agony. "Katherine is dead," he sobbed.

"*Ach du Lieber!*" sighed his dearest sister, next to him in age.

"Oh, Aunt Katherine, what am I going to do?" asked Pearl. "How am I going to take care of the baby?"

"I'll take the baby!" offered Katherine. "I can raise her."

"Oh, I just don't know."

"Is she okay? That's the most important thing! We'll all take turns raising that baby. Don't you worry about that. God will find a way." And with that final benediction, she was pumping water for coffee. "Cal, you go upstairs and wake my boys. I need their help. Don't sit in that corner over the cellar door, Ruthie. We gotta open the door to bring up the bacon and eggs to fry for breakfast. *Du ormes Ding, du,*" she clucked to Marian and drew her toward her ample breasts. "Pearl, you slice the bread. There's the board hanging on the wall." Aunt Katherine handed Pearl a large long loaf of white bread.

"The doctor said Mommy turned into a loaf of bread," Marian told her aunt.

"What?" exclaimed Katherine, dumbfounded.

Pearl explained, "Honey, Mommy is in heaven. She's with Jesus. She is happy. She is looking down from heaven now. She sees us making breakfast."

"Why didn't she stay with us and help us?"

"Oh, my God, help me with this child!"

"Let's pray," said Uncle Johnny, once all had been seated around the large oval table. "*Komm, Herr Jesu, sei unsere Gast und segnet vass du uns besheret hasst. Amen.*"

When the bacon and eggs had been passed around the table, Uncle Johnny asked, "Will she be buried in the Bethesda Church cemetery or in ours?"

"In ours, of course, where she was a member, *recht zum Vater und Mutter.*"

"Well, I'll organize the group to dig the grave today, then. Can't do it on Sunday."

"Aren't you cutting grain today?"

"John and Ted can handle the cutting. Sam and Little Katherine can do the shocking. We'll manage. Don't worry."

"Thanks, John. Try to get some help from the Tieszen side of the family too, and from the neighbors."

"I will. We'll all pitch in."

Tiahrts and Wienses had already heard the news of the death by the time Morgan and his family arrived to tell them. Anna Tiahrt, an older sister, said, "Katherine had a premonition of her death. She told me about it."

"Really?" cried Pearl, her face convulsed in grief.

"When was that?" asked Morgan.

"A few months ago, when she was so sick. She dreamed she was floating on the clouds, playing the piano in a long white gown."

"After she bought the piano," Morgan surmised.

Eva Wiens, a younger sister, said Katherine had a foreboding about the pregnancy. "At 38, you know, it was dangerous, she thought. Because little Agnes was stillborn and then she was so sick last November around election time."

"Yes, I remember that. We thought it was stomach trouble — upset over my being gone so much campaigning, we thought. If only I'd known, I would've stayed home more."

"Can't be helped now. Remember you have another beautiful little daughter to remember her by."

"Yes, I'll remember her."

When the Kleinsasser family got back to their farm, Adeline had also heard the news and was busy cleaning the house. "There's gonna be an awful lot of people here tomorrow. Have to get this place cleaned up. Besides, keeping busy will make the grieving easier."

While cousin Edward was cutting grain with the binder, neighbor Jake Walter came to drive Morgan to Viborg to pick out the casket. "How'd you get involved with this Burial Association, anyway? You could have Mike do the funeral. It would be more convenient than driving all the way down to Viborg."

"Jake, I had to bury both my father and my mother. Almost went broke. I made up my mind I wasn't gonna pay through the nose any more. We organized a fraternal association and I'm a member of the board. We pay our undertaker a reasonable salary and get a nice, dignified funeral without breaking the bank."

At the funeral home, Mr. Raynie met them at the door. "Morgan, I'm sorry. I never dreamed. . . ."

"Neither did I. You just never know. I had no idea Katherine was having troubles. But apparently she was. She told her sisters. I guess we shouldn't have had any more children. Tried not to, but you know how that goes. Couldn't really afford any more."

"Morgan, if we waited until we could afford our children, we'd be old men or the race would die out, one or the other."

"Did you see the baby when you were in Sioux Falls?"

"Yes, she seemed to be doing all right. Did they tell you how long they'd keep her?"

"Long enough to give her a good start, I expect. She seemed strong and healthy to me. Well, I guess I'd better do what I came down here for."

"You know where the caskets are, Morgan. You and Jake just go in there and take your time. The prices are all listed. No surprises. You know how we operate."

"Oh, I brought this blue dress along. Always thought she looked good in blue."

"She was a beautiful woman, Morgan, in more ways than one. We all loved her. You know that."

Morgan sobbed. "You come with me, Jake, and help me pick out something she'll look good in."

"Morgan, you were always good at picking out what your girls would look good in."

Driving back to Freeman, Jake said, "I knew you'd pick the maroon casket. With her graying hair and blue dress with the white collar, she'll look mighty pretty."

108

"Tell me, Jake, have you ever been able to figure it all out? Why do some people have all the troubles and others just sail through?"

"I dunno. Don't live right, I guess. But if anybody lived right, it was Katherine. I dunno. I got my problems too. The bank is about to foreclose on my farm."

"The bastards!"

"After all I put into that land!"

"I had some 'good news' myself the other day. Went into Merchants Bank for a loan to buy some alfalfa hay to feed my cattle until this year's crop came in. Old Man Wollman said they couldn't loan me any more."

"It figures. I hope you'll be teaching our school again this fall. Max never did so good for any other teacher. I know he's stubborn, needs a lot of coaxing. Wants to play ball all the time."

"Joe P. offered me $55 a month to teach their school, #51, on an eight month contract. I haven't decided yet what I'm going to do. That's ten dollars more per month than I made at #98. I'd be able to use that money, you know. A difference of $80 a year!"

"Can't blame you, Morgan, but that's a lot bigger school, isn't it?"

"Yes, they have 20 pupils, 10 boys and 10 girls, in 7 grades."

"Well, you'll do what you have to do. But remember the kids respect you at #98, even if they don't always act like it."

"Look at that field of wheat over there. All smut and 'hoppers, it looks like."

"*Ja.* They got grasshoppers here too."

"About 10% of my heads are on the ground. Hoppers just bite the whole head off."

"Corn looks good, though. That field sure was knee high by the Fourth!"

"*Ja,* it'll make a crop if it doesn't hail."

"Or burn up," Morgan added.

When Morgan got home, the Tieszen grandparents were in the parlor, counseling with the children. Pearl and the little girls sat with tear-streaked, swollen faces. Cal was attempting to be stoical. Rev. Jacob B. and his wife rose to give Morgan the news. "John, the hospital just called to say that the baby died too," said the pastor.

"When it rains, it pours," said Morgan.

"It's for the best, Morgan; it's God's will," said Rev. Hofer.

"How do we know what God's will is?" Morgan asked abruptly. "I better call Raynie. There's another body for him to pick up," he said, wearily dragging his body to the wall phone. "Hello, Central?

. . . . Yes, it's true. Yes, the baby died too. If anyone asks, you can tell them that the funeral for both will be on Monday at 2 o'clock at the Hutterthal Mennonite Church, one mile west and three miles north of Freeman. Visitors may call at the farm after church on Sunday. Now, get me Mr. Raynie again at the Fraternal Burial Association in Viborg."

All day Sunday the visitors poured in and out of the parlor of the homestead farmhouse located three miles north of Freeman on Highway 81 and a half mile west on the Marion road. Only Katherine lay in the casket. Baby Katherine would be brought the next day for the funeral. Women and children stood around the casket, conversing. "She looks so pretty, so natural, with her wavy graying hair and her freckles."

"You'd never know she had any pain, to look at her."

"Her earthly trials are over now. May she rest in peace."

"She's better off now. No more troubles."

"I told Joe, I said, I wished many a time I'd never been born. Nothing but pain and heart ache."

"Too bad about Morgan and the children."

"Yes, it will be hard for them now."

"It's a blessing the baby died too."

"The Lord giveth and the Lord taketh away."

Two hundred forty eight families came and went, stopping to pay their respects, drink a cup of coffee, eat a piece of cake. They chatted about the harvest, the weather, the grasshoppers, the homestead where Paul and Anna, Morgan's parents, had staked their claim in 1879.

They had come from South Russia in the last group of migrants from the village of Hutterthal, a migration that began in 1874 to seek out a new land where they would be free to practice their religious beliefs, exempt from military service.

In the farmyard men stood around in clumps, their coats off and their white shirts unbuttoned at the collar. They picked their teeth with sharpened match sticks and shooed chickens away from the few shaded spots available. "Last time I was here was when *Paulus Vetter* died. Morgan has made a lot of improvements on the place since then. Take that hog barn over there."

"Being the youngest one in the family, he was expected to stay on the farm. Old Man Paul wanted his quarter section of homestead land to stay in the family."

"I believe Paul mortgaged the land to buy cheaper land in Beadle and Spink Counties for his other children."

"You could get six times the land up there for the same amount of money."

"Well, I don't envy Morgan now."

"Teaching, into politics, and no wife. I don't know how he's gonna make it."

"Those kids will grow up fast – Pearl and Cal especially. Pearl is almost out of Academy, isn't she? She's big enough to take over."

In the evening, after the cows had been milked, the hogs fed, and the eggs gathered, relatives and friends lingered around the farmstead and around the casket. An Aladdin kerosene lamp was lit and placed on a fern stand near Katherine's head. Jacob B., himself a product of the community, himself a teacher and newly ordained and installed minister of Hutterthal Church, stood to the right of the lamp and said, "Somebody go out and tell the menfolks that we're going to have a little service. If they can get in the house, fine. If not, ask them to be quiet while we pray."

Slowly the men came closer to the house, sat down on the front steps or leaned against the porch to listen through the open windows and the screen door. It would be nothing new, just the familiar comforting words of The Lord's Prayer, a reading from the Psalms, and an extempore prayer for strength and guidance for the bereaved.

Slowly the gathering dispersed with promises of more food to be brought on the morrow. Marian and Ruth, who had been playing with other children on the swings under the elm tree, came in for a scolding from Pearl. "You've gotten your dresses all dusty. We'll have to wash them out and iron them so you can wear them tomorrow."

"And look at your new white shoes, Marian!" exclaimed Adeline. "Your Mommy bought those just a month ago, and they're all scuffed up already. They'll have to be polished in the morning."

On the day of the funeral, July 12, 1937, the winds blew hot across the plains. Mr. Raynie arrived with little Katherine, the infant, dressed in a white gown, and laid her in her mother's arms. The immediate family gathered around the casket, linked arms and wept while relatives offered words of comfort. "They look so beautiful together."

"It's a blessing that she died too."

"Their spirits are in heaven now."

"They'll be together forever."

All morning relatives from Beadle, Spink, Sully, McCook and Turner Counties had arrived to pay their respects. Pearl and Adeline were joined in the kitchen and dining room by more aunts and cousins, who brought sliced baked ham, cheese, and potato salad with boiled dressing.

Cal and his cousins Harvey Wiens and Elmer Tiahrt were busy directing traffic and parking cars of callers. At 1 p.m. it was time for another service, at which a friend and pastor of a neighboring church, Rev. Peter J. Stahl of the Hutterdorf Mennonite Church, spoke. "We never know when the Lord will take us. We must be prepared. Every death is an opportunity for us to examine our lives to see if we are ready to meet the Lord. Katherine was ready. She loved the Lord. Are you ready?"

As the family followed the hearse to the church just a mile and a half from the farmstead, they passed the cemetery where a fresh grave had been dug by nine relatives and neighbors, mostly cousins and brothers-in-law, from both *Hutterische* and *Plattdeutsch* sides of the family. Even Grandpa Tieszen had helped.

As Morgan entered the small white frame church, he recognized Gov. Leslie Jensen standing on the concrete slab porch. "Appreciate your coming, Governor," Morgan said softly, nodding. Other men, their flat-topped dress straw hats removed, nodded as the family passed by them to enter the church.

The immediate family was ushered to the front pew. Marian was dressed in her freshly laundered honeysuckle print cotton dress with smocking on the front. With her white shoes newly polished, she sat next to Ruth, who wore a blue dress handed down to her by a generous cousin, Jean. Ruth was proud that her dress matched her mother's. Pearl and Adeline wore the darkest dresses they could find in their closets while remaining reasonably comfortable. Cal and Morgan sat sweating in hot dark wool suits with white shirts and dark ties.

The windows were open to the hot winds blowing. People who could not squeeze into the church listened through the windows. Three ministers spoke, two in English and one in German. Rev. Derk P. Tieszen, Katherine's uncle and former pastor, spoke in German. Now almost blind, he had married Morgan and Katherine eighteen years before. Three groups brought special music. "I'm glad we got the piano before Katherine died," Morgan thought. "It adds so much and she had wanted it so badly for the church."

As the congregation sang "*Ich weisz einem Strom*," Morgan thought, "I wish Rev. P. P. Tschetter were here today. He always knew just what to say."

When Marian fell asleep in the pew, Morgan lifted her into his lap. Sweat formed on his face and she awoke hot and sticky. "I want my Mommy," she cried, waking to the sight of her mother and baby sister lying in the casket before her.

"It's okay, Honey. It's okay," said her father, patting her back and wiping away his own tears.

They walked across the road to the cemetery, following the hearse. Before the casket was lowered into the grave, yet another service of commital was held. "Dust to dust, ashes to ashes. . . .But I will come again to receive you, that where I am, there you may be also."

Pearl plucked blossoms off the floral spray for each of the girls to press in their Bibles later, and each child sprinkled a hand full of dry soil into the grave.

Cal drove them back to the farm where a few relatives had gathered again. "I'd be glad to take Marian and Ruth for a few days," offered Aunt Anna. "I know you're harvesting."

"No, thank you. I think it's better if they stay with us on the farm. Maybe later, when they get used to the idea of Ma not being here, they can visit you," answered Morgan. "My oldest sister, Elizabeth, is going to stay and help with the cooking while Pearl and Adeline shock. We've gotten awful far behind in the harvest. The barley and oats are leaning over already."

"Okay, Morgan, but you know I want to help. Katherine and I promised each other that we'd help the other's family if anything happened," said Anna Tiahrt.

113

Part IV

July 13, 1937-December 31, 1937
Shifting Priorities

Tuesday, July 13, 1937

Cut barley in the morning and then cut oats 'til noon. It started raining in the afternoon. Rained from 2:30 'til almost evening. Miss Katherine more when I am not busy.

"Quick, come in out of the rain. And bring your shoes. If you're gonna take off your shoes anyway when you play in the dirt under the lilac bush, you might as well take them off in the house in the first place. We can't afford to have you ruin another pair of shoes by leaving them out in the rain," scolded Pearl as she held the screen door open for Marian to enter. "Where's Ruth?"

"I told her to chase the ducklings into the brooder house," answered Mrs. Jacob L. Hofer, Sr., wiping her hands in the apron covering her cotton wash dress. "*Gott in Himmel, es ist heisz!*" She eased her plump figure into the large wooden rocker that sat before the south window of the parlor. "Looks like we're going to have a nice, slow rain. That's nice! A nice, slow rain to fall on Katherine's grave – like a blessing from above. Come here, Marian; come sit on my lap."

Marian crawled into her aunt's lap. She didn't know this aunt – her Daddy's eldest sister Elizabeth – as an aunt. She was more like a grandmother to her.

"Let me tell you how it was when we came over from the Old Country. It rained on the ocean almost every day. We had to stay down in steerage to keep dry. It was awful crowded there. And there wasn't much to eat, either. We used to hoard a biscuit or a cracker in our pocket. Do you have a pocket?"

"Here's my pocket."

"I'm going to put something in your pocket. But don't look what it is 'til you get to your bedroom and lie on your bed." She slipped a peppermint drop into Marian's pocket and heaved a sigh of relief as the little girl ran off to her bedroom for a nap.

"You're so good with children," said Pearl as she sat down at the dining room table with a pan of green string beans.

117

Harvest Picnic, 1910, at Paul Kleinsasser Farm
Morgan, age 14, stands in front, leaning on car's headlight.
The Jackson car was the only one in the community at that time.

118

"Well, I oughta be. Raised eight of my own and helped my mother, your Grandma Kleinsasser, raise many of hers because I was the oldest."

"Right here on the homestead, wasn't it? Daddy told us about how he and Aunt Katherine used to herd sheep on the section line and how they got into trouble with Grandma one day when they exchanged clothes. Grandma looked out the window and wondered why Katherine was doing all the chasing of sheep while Daddy was just sitting around."

"Well, that was after I married and left home. I was raising my own children by then. Katherine and John were the youngest ones in the family."

"Did you ever live in his house?"

"A little while. I remember the first house we had, south of this location, closer to the section line. Made it out of sod. The first winter it was so cold that Mother took us to stay with Grandpa and Grandma Tschetter."

"I thought sod houses were supposed to be warm."

"They're warm if they're built into a hill. But we had no hills on this farm, only flat prairie."

"You had school in your house too, didn't you?"

"Yes, first German school – reading the Bible, ciphering. Then we got an English teacher – *eine Fremde*."

Ruth came in, allowing the screen door to slam behind her.

"Be quiet. Marian's sleeping," cautioned Pearl. "And wipe your feet on the rug. We don't want any mud tracked in. Did you round up all the ducklings?"

"I only counted twelve. I couldn't find the rest."

"The others must have taken shelter in the tall weeds by the pond," surmised Pearl.

"Wash your hands and I'll give you a peppermint," said Aunt Elizabeth.

Ruth pumped some water into the enameled basin, dipped her fingers in it, and blotted them on the gray linen roller towel. She ran into Aunt Elizabeth's arms.

"That's a good girl. Want to sit on my lap for a while?"

"Yeah. Can you tell me a story?"

"What kind of story?"

"About the olden days."

"Oh, yes. I'll tell you a story about when I was a little girl here on the farm. We had ducks then, too, on the pond south of here. You can see it through the window. We must have had fifty or more ducks then. Hatched 'em with settin' hens. It was my job to feed and water the hens every day. I didn't like to do that because

119

I had to go through the gate into the farm yard with a pail of shelled corn in one hand and a pail of water in the other. We had ganders too and roosters and a big sheep buck in that yard. So every day I was scared that something would get me, either a gander or a rooster or that buck."

"Did they get you?"

"Usually I could run faster than the gander or the rooster. Sometimes the gander would nip at my heels and the rooster would fly and jump at me and peck me. Once the buck ran for me and actually butted me with his horns."

"Did you get hurt?"

"He knocked me down but I got up and ran away — with the corn and water spilled on the ground.

"We have a bull in our pasture. A big red one. When I get the cows, I try to stay away from him. Ma says never to wear red. . . ." Ruth stopped and began to cry.

"*Du ormes Ding, du,*" the elderly aunt said and comforted her by patting her shoulders and stroking her hair.

"Are you gonna stay here with us since Ma died?"

"I'll stay this week. I can't take it any longer than that. I'm an old lady, you know. And Uncle Jake needs me. But I'll be back, and there'll be others who'll come."

"I wish Baby Katherine was still living. I always wanted to have a baby sister."

"You have Marian."

"I mean a little baby, one I could play with, dress her up, and push her in the buggy."

"Well, maybe one day you will have another baby sister. Why don't you help Pearl trim the string beans now?"

That evening, after the chores were finished, the family sat around the oilcloth-covered dining room table to eat their supper. The Aladdin kerosene lamp blazed in the middle of the table as Morgan directed, "Uffie, you pray."

"Thank you for the food we eat, thank you for the friends we meet; thank you for the birds that sing; thank you, God, for everything. Amen."

As Aunt Elizabeth was slicing a large loaf of bread against her breast, Marian announced, "Pass the soup. I'm hungry!"

"*Strankel Zup!* One of my favorites!" said Morgan, as he passed the steaming bowls of pieces of chicken, new potatoes in their skins, onions, and string beans.

"We forgot the sour cream!" exclaimed Pearl as she jumped up from the table and rushed toward the basement door, took a match from the wall holder and struck it on the basement wall. The acrid smell of the sulphur tip permeated the air.

"*Pasz auf!*" called Morgan. "We don't need anyone else falling down the basement!"

"Who fell down the basement?" asked Aunt Elizabeth.

"I did," piped up Marian. "I fell down and hurt my arm. Cal picked me up and carried me upstairs."

"When was that?"

"Friday night, the night Doc Ernest took Katherine to the hospital. We should have known something worse was going to happen that night. You know the saying: 'When troubles come, they come in threes.'"

"Or bushels," said Elizabeth.

"First the kerosene lamp flared up, got the whole kitchen sooty. Then Marian fell down the basement. Then came the call in the night," said Pearl, soberly.

"Do you have a little bay leaf to flavor the soup with?" asked Elizabeth.

"No, but Mother sometimes put a little Summer Savory into the soup. Want me to get some?"

"You mean *Pepar Krut*? No, not now. Those herbs need to be cooked with the soup. Remind me to bring you some bay leaf. Gives it a real nice flavor. Picks it up a little. Anybody want some more bread?"

"How can you slice bread like that, without a board?" asked Ruth.

"Easy. Been doing it all my life. Have you ever seen the old men at the colonies, the *Brotschneider*? That's how they slice bread."

"Look! Somebody just turned into the driveway," cried Ruth, pushing her chair back from the table with a screech.

"Uffie, you sit there 'til you've finished your supper," commanded Morgan.

"And don't go peeking through the curtains out the window," added Pearl.

"Which way was the car coming from?" asked Cal.

"From the church."

"From the west? That's probably a date for Pearl or Adeline," teased Cal.

"I'm not expecting anyone tonight," said Pearl.

"Me neither," said Adeline.

"I think it's the neighbors. *Deutscher Jek.* Yep, it's Jake and Marie and Max!" exclaimed Cal, standing at the screen door.

Soon Marie and Max had sprung from their car and were racing down the sidewalk to the house. Marie had a cake in her hands. "Here, Ma baked this cake for you," said Marie, handing the layer cake to Pearl.

121

"Thanks! We still have quite a bit of cake left from the funeral, but this is nice and fresh."

"Why don't you all sit down and have some cake and coffee with us?" asked Morgan as he moved his chair from the head of the table to make room for three more.

"No, thanks, we just got up from the table," explained Jake. "We came to see if you need any help with shocking tomorrow."

"Sure do!" exclaimed Adeline.

"All three of us could help. We finished ours before it rained."

"Sure could use some help, Jake. I have to cut some more rye yet and a little oats. The Durham wheat will be next."

"We'll be over in the morning, after choring," said Jake, as the trio left.

"Now, that's a neighbor for you!" Morgan said as he stood inside the screen door watching them leave.

Saturday, July 17, 1937
Cal is helping Tiahrts. Mrs. Jacob L. Hofer, Sr., went home today. She had been here since the funeral—a great help.
Just a week ago that Katherine died.

"It's a good thing there's plenty to do," Morgan thought. "Bad to brood over Katherine's death too much. Both Eva and Anna said she had a premonition. She never said anything to me. Should have known, though, that something was wrong. She was reading the Bible more, singing and playing hymns on the piano. I thought it was because of swollen legs.

"I was really surprised when she told me she was in the family way. Guess I should have stayed away from her more. Knew we couldn't afford any more children – not during the Depression.

"I remember back in November, right after the election, she got so sick. Thought it was the flu. Couldn't keep anything down. Then, too, I knew she was worried about my being gone for two months in Pierre in the dead of winter with all the work to do on the farm. And all the expenses, and not much money comin' in.

"Never was sure she wanted me to run for the legislature. I even asked her father.

"Being gone so much during the campaign. I know that was hard on her. Never being able to get a steady hired man. And the windmill breaking down during the coldest snap we had.

"And the campaign expenses – how that irritated her. Having to pay almost thirty dollars just for the November campaign. Of course, that didn't cover the gas I used up traveling over half the county. And the sales I lost at home when somebody came looking for a ram.

122

"It was nice Gov. Jensen came for the funeral, though. And all the consolation cards, almost fifty of 'em. Some really thoughtful expressions of sympathy, too. People surprise you. You think you know people, but you never really do."

Sunday, July 18, 1937
In church this morning. Clifford Hofer and Anna Gross were married.

Graduating Class
Katherine Tieszen Kleinsasser is in back row, third from left.

"When we got married, it was the summer after Katherine got her Normal degree from the College," Morgan remembered. "She wanted to be a teacher, but I talked her into getting married. She would've made a good teacher, too, especially with the younger children, teaching them art and music and expression. She was a very artistic person. She could make something beautiful out of almost anything.

"Glad she got Johnny Klein to help her take the paper down in our bedroom before she died. Wish we could have afforded paint instead of calcimine. Guess she wanted it pretty for the new baby.

"We knew there could be trouble – a Low German and a Hutter getting married. 'Stay with your own kind,' Father said. 'You just shouldn't marry outside your own people.'

'But they're Mennonites, Father, just like we are.'

'But they come from a different part of the Old Country – from Holland. They didn't really suffer like we did.'

'They were in Russia for a hundred years, just like we were.'

'But they came from a different part and had some very big farms. They were never in colonies, only in villages. They always looked down on *Unser Volk*.'

'Well, you know, I never thought they were superior to us in school,' said Morgan.

'The Bonesetter, Derk Tieszen, he was always looked up to.'

'That's good, Vater! That's an advantage! Maybe we can get our backs fixed free!'

'Oh, you! I never could win an argument with you! Go ahead, but don't think it will be easy.' "

"The girl getting married is so pretty," thought Marian. "Flowers and white dress. My dress is pretty too. Cal said so. Mommy got it for me. White shoes too.

"Where's Mommy? The girl getting married looks like Mommy."

"Mommy's in heaven," Pearl said.

"Where's heaven? Is that heaven in the picture behind the preacher? I see a lady with a white dress on. She's walking over a bridge. Where is she going? Maybe she's going to heaven.

"Uffie, is that Mommy in the picture up there, behind the preacher?" Marian whispered to her sister sitting next to her in the front row.

"Sure, that's Mommy. I know it is. Looks just like her. I had a dream about her last night. She said she'd come back and get us," whispered Ruth.

"Shhhh!" came a stern voice and a finger poke from Mrs. Paul E. sitting with her daughter, Angie, in the pew behind them.

Tuesday, July 20, 1937

I plowed soil conservation land. The creepers are very bad. Pearl and Calvin were picking cockleburrs. Clifford Hofer and Raymond were here concerning threshing. They have rented a machine and tractor and want to charge 2¢ per bu. for wheat and rye, 1¢ per bu. for oats & barley for use of the machine and 35¢ per hr. for use of the tractor. We are to furnish the gas and oil.

"Well, Clifford didn't take off much time for a honeymoon either," Morgan mused. "Wonder how Anna feels about that. At least we waited until after the harvest to get married. Father-in-law thought we were in a big enough hurry as it was.

"A man's gotta make a living somehow. Prob'ly doesn't help that Doc Ernest is his brother."

"Hate to think what that doctor's bill is gonna be, let alone the hospital bill. All that expense and nothing to show for it! No wife, no baby."

Wednesday, July 21, 1937

Pearl and I were picking cockleburrs in the forenoon. We finished the long field. There were very many in the lake but practically none in the rest of the field. Calvin is plowing. He plowed 'til about 11 o'clock and then came home. The horses were played out. We set up the elevator in the afternoon getting ready for threshing.

"Glad Adeline is here to take care of the girls," Pearl thought as she walked the rows of corn. "It's good to get away from the house once in a while. Good to get out in the field even if it is hot. Forgot to wear my hairnet, though. My finger wave will be ruined.

"We're making pretty good time walking the rows, even two at a time. I thought there'd be more cockleburrs than this, didn't you, Pa?"

"One good thing about the drought is that even the weeds don't grow. The lake bed, that's a different story."

"Pa, have you thought about what we're gonna do when school starts?"

"Waddaya mean?"

"With Marian and the housework. Ruth will be in school, but who's gonna take care of Marian?"

"I can't. I'm gonna be teaching District #51, Joe P.'s school. They offered me $55 a month."

"That's better than you got at #98."

"But not much. It's also farther away, so I'll use more gas getting there."

"Well, since I'm going into my senior year at the Academy, I don't want to have to stay home."

"I don't want you to, either. Don't want you to miss any of your senior activities, either. We'll work something out. What about Adeline? Do you think she'd stay?"

"I think Adeline wants more money. She can't just work for room and board any more. She told me that when we were hoeing."

"I've been paying her a little."

"I know, but she needs more. She's having trouble with her teeth too. She'll have dentist bills."

Sunday, July 25, 1937
We were in church this morning. At Jacob L. Hofer, Jr., for dinner and supper.

After arriving at the Jacob L. Hofer estate Morgan and his two youngest children went first to the apartment of Jacob L. Hofer, Sr., and his wife, Elizabeth. *"Kommen sie hier, meine Kinder!"* said Aunt Elizabeth, drawing the two to her breasts.

"Do you have any candy?" asked Ruth.

"Ja, ich hob Kendy, ober nit jetzt. You can have candy after dinner. Run and play now. Merlin and Vernon should be outside."

Marian and Ruth ran into the large garden south of the house. "Uncle Jake always has something good to eat in his garden," said Ruth. "He grafts fruit trees and raises all kinds of berries. I bet he's got some berries."

Walking down the rows of neatly trimmed trees and bushes, they soon discovered the raspberries. "Oh, look. He's got red ones and black ones. All kinds of berries," shouted Marian.

"Let's take just a few and then go back to the house," said Ruth. "But be careful so you don't get any on your dress or Pearl will get mad."

They ate a few of the warm, juicy globes and then a few more. Soon they were stuffing hands-full into their mouths.

"Aha! Here you are!" shouted Pearl. "I thought I'd find you here! Look at your hands and faces! And your dresses! You got berry stains all over your dresses! How am I going to get that out? And your new white shoes, Marian. You've ruined your new white shoes! What would Mother say?"

Suddenly the two little girls burst into tears.

"Come up to the house, now. The menfolks and Uncle Jake and Aunt Elizabeth have sat down to the table already. You'll have to eat in the kitchen. But first I'll have to clean you up so you don't get berry juice over everything you touch."

Pearl ushered them into the Hofers' bathroom. "Don't touch anything!"

It was a treat, anyway, to get your hands washed in a bathroom. Not many people had bathrooms. "I like the pretty white knobs," Marian thought.

Soon the girls were sitting in the kitchen with the other children at a table laden with steaming bowls of homemade chicken noodle soup. "I got an egg yolk!" squealed Marian.

"Pass the jam!" said Merlin.

"You're supposed to say 'Please'," instructed Marian.

"Okay, then, PLEASE pass the jam."

"How's come you eat jam with noodle soup?" asked Ruth.

"Because I like it!" responded Merlin.

"Merlin eats jam with everything," explained his mother. "Don't you like jam?"

"Yeah, all kinds. We made a lot of jam this summer. That was before Momma died."

"Yes."

"And Grandma Tieszen has groundcherry jam," piped up Marian.

"Oh, that's good too. How about if I send some red raspberry jam home with you?"

"They've had enough raspberries already today," called Pearl from an adjoining table, where she was eating with Evelyn and Marjorie.

"Oh, can't we?" whined Ruth.

"Okay, we'll take it home, but we'll save it for a special occasion, when we want a change from mulberry and rhubarb jam."

"What's a special 'casion?" asked Marian.

"You'll see – a party or a celebration."

"Like my birthday?"

"Maybe."

"Then we should have had it yesterday already! Her birthday was yesterday!" announced Ruth.

"It was? Then we'll have to sing 'Happy Birthday'," said Annie, and led the group in singing. "How old are you?"

"Four. One, two, free, four," Marian counted on her fingers.

"*Du liebst Ding, du*," said Annie, hugging her from behind.

The last two persons at the main dining table were Morgan and Uncle Jake, who sat sucking on chicken bones. "*Nun, vie geht's?*" Jake asked.

"*Es geht, aber es geht sehr schlecht,*" replied Morgan.

"*Varum?*"

"I miss Katherine, and I don't know how we're going to get along once school starts. Pearl doesn't want to drop out of school and I don't know who will take care of Marian."

"How about J. W.'s Adeline?"

"She wants to earn more money. Wants to go to Chicago, I think, to stay with her Walter cousins and get a good job there."

"That's a big city – Chicago! She could get lost there."

"I told her there's no guarantee she's going to find a job, let alone a good job, in Chicago. There's more people in Chicago looking for work than there are in South Dakota."

"*Ja.*"

"Elizabeth did such a good job with cooking and taking care of the children the week after Katherine died. I wondered if she could help us out some during the year."

"Well, I tell you, Morgan. Elizabeth is no spring chicken! She's 62 years old. She was awful tired when she came back from your place. I just don't think she can take it anymore. She's lying down right now, I bet."

"Yeah, I know. We're none of us gettin' any younger."

Tuesday, July 27, 1937

Threshing today—Durham wheat, barley and started on Burbank wheat. Mrs. P. P. is here to help Pearl and Adeline cook for threshers. We pay our machine man 30¢ per hr. and the pitchers 25¢ per hr. belt time. Total threshing time, 4 hr., 15 min. Got 281 bu. barley.

Wednesday, July 28, 1937

Still threshing. Had a lot of trouble. If the engine does not trouble, the machine does. Threshed wheat today and also the 10 acre field of rye. Burbank wheat made 8 1/3 bu. per acre. Durham made 12 bu. per acre. Machine sieve broke. Threshing time, 7 hr., 20 min.

Thursday, July 29, 1937

Threshed rye in forenoon. Nice rain in afternoon. Cal and I repaired fence after rain. Turned horses, sheep and cattle on stubble field. They will have plenty to eat for a while. Time, 4 hr. Burbank wheat, 298 bu. Oats, 30 bu.

Friday, July 30, 1937

Threshed rye with four racks in afternoon. Got two loads of grain, 470 bu. It was rather damp. Threshing time, 2 hr.

John J. B. family visited here in the evening.

"Brought you some *Kratsivitz,* Brother John. Know how you like *Kratsivitz mit Raum!*" said his sister, known lovingly to Morgan as Sister Katherine, but less kindly to some as *Dicke Katrin.* She eased her heavy frame over the threshold and into the kitchen.

"Oh, *danke schön!*" said Morgan.

"How did you know our cucumber vines weren't bearing yet?" asked Pearl.

"I could see when your mother died that your garden was not as far along as ours was. I brought some early tomatoes too."

"They'll taste good with sutah," said Ruth.

"Sugar, sugar. Not sutah!" corrected Morgan, as they all laughed.

"We wanted to see how you were all getting along," said Katherine as they all finally settled into chairs around the dining room table.

"Well, we're making it, one way or the other. Mrs. P. P. was here cooking for threshers this week."

"We have so much work now, but later on we'll be able to help," assured his sister. "I wondered, Morgan, if we could get some well water from you."

"Sure, the windmill just keeps pumping it, now that we got it fixed. How much do you want, a tank full?"

"No, just a couple cream cans full. I want to use it for making dill pickles. Your well water is much harder than ours. Makes better pickles, I think."

"Sure, help yourself!"

"Boys," she said to Ted and Sam, "go fill up the cans!"

"Just turn on the faucet at the supply tank if the windmill's not pumping. That's the easiest way," instructed Morgan.

Saturday, July 31, 1937

Moved the wagons to Clifford's this morning. Threshed one load in the morning but it was so wet that they quit 'til noon. Rained a little at noon so I went home and they threshed alone.

Cut weeds on the section line. Cal and Max manured the barn. Sold a red cow and white faced heifer for slaughter—$85.

Sunday, August 1, 1937

In church this morning. Rev. Jacob B. invited us for dinner. Didn't stay for supper. Sold another cow and heifer.

Adeline and Pearl went to the Silver Lake M. B. Church in the evening with some Stahl boys.

"Where are you going?" asked Marian as she watched Pearl heat the curling iron over the kerosene lamp chimney and apply it to her hair.

"To church."

"Do we have church tonight?"

"No, Addy and I are going to the Silver Lake Church."

"Why?"

"They have a special musical program. A group from Kansas is singing."

"Can I go too?"

"MAY, MAY I go too?"

"May I go too?"

"No, we're going on a date. No kids allowed."

"Why not?" Marian asked, climbing on a stool to observe her big sister in the mirror.

"Because kids don't go on dates," Pearl said, pinning her glass violet corsage to her dress.

"What's a date?"

"When a boy and girl grow up and like each other, they sometimes go places together."

"Do you like a boy?"

"Uhmm, yes."

"What's his name?"

"Mikey."

"Mikey what?"

"Mikey Stahl. You know him. He gave you a nickel in town once to buy some pop corn."

"Oh, yeah, I like him too. Can I go with him too?"

"No, I told you, little kids don't go on dates," she said, turning her head and raising her leg to straighten the seams of her silk stockings. "Here, I'll give you a spit curl." Wetting her finger and twirling Marian's hair around her finger, she said, "There! I gotta go! I think they're here already."

As Pearl and Marian approached the screen door, Adeline was giving Ruth a good-bye hug. Pearl spoke through the screen door to her date, "Be ready in a minute." Then, turning to Marian she said, "Look, Honey, you can't go tonight. But I promise some time I'll take you along with me."

As Adeline and Pearl walked with their dates to the waiting car, Ruth and Marian stood at the screen door and began to cry. Then, flinging open the screen door and running down the sidewalk to the Stahl boys' car, Marian cried, "Take me with you!"

Morgan, rising dejectedly from the dining room table where he had been reading the newspaper, called to her. "Now you get back here in the house this minute!"

Then, lifting both girls to his lap, he said, "Listen, both of you. Adeline and Pearl are big girls. They can do things little girls can't. They will be going a lot of places without us and we'll just have to get used to it. I wish it weren't so, but I can't tie them up. Maybe there are some things that little girls can do that big girls can't. Can you think of any?"

"Sit on your lap?" asked Ruth.

"That's right. I can't hold Adeline and Pearl on my lap anymore, but I can hold you."

"Hugs and kisses?" asked Marian.

"Lots of hugs and kisses for you," he said. "How about eating ice cream? Would you like to go to town for a dish of ice cream?"

"Yeah!" they cried in unison.

"Cal," Morgan called upstairs to his son's bedroom, "you wanna drive us all to town for some ice cream?"

"Sure!!" And Cal descended the steps three at a time.

Wednesday, August 4, 1937

Still threshing by Clifford's. Had to stop occasionally on account of rain. There are thousands of grasshoppers in the cornfields. In the afternoon we could not get the bundle loads to the machine fast enough, so they had to wait for us. We have only four bundle racks and six men. Cal was along with me.

Thursday, August 5, 1937

Cal and I came late to threshing this morning. The alarm clock was not heard. Lost 25 min. Horse time, 10 hr., 15 min. Our time, 9 hr., 50 min.

Friday, August 6, 1937

Cal went to Brookings with the county agent. I miss him. He is a good helper. Started at 11 o'clock and threshed 'til 8:55 p.m.

Saturday, August 7, 1937

Four men quit pitching by the machine. Cliff got into an argument with them regarding the pay. He wants to deduct them pay for quitting and also charge board.

Sunday, August 8, 1937

All in church this morning. I taught the boys' Sunday School class. David Melvin Wollman came along with Cal for dinner. The boys played ball. Melvin sure can run fast.

Visited P. P.'s in the afternoon. Peter G.'s were here in the evening.

Tuesday, August 10, 1937

Katherine died a month ago today.

Finished threshing at Joe D.'s A horse got its tail torn out in the belt at P. P.'s. They had to shoot the horse. It belonged to P. P.

Wednesday, August 11, 1937

Threshed for Jake M.'s Put in 11 hrs. today. Cal & Max were field pitchers. Cal is not yet 14 and Max is younger. Good workers!

Thursday, August 12, 1937

Katherine was buried a month ago today.

Friday, August 13, 1937

Took Nelly to Andrew Hofer's place to breed her. From there to Art Ortman, the Allis Chalmers dealer. Cal & Art brought down an AC tractor with a plow. Everything rubber tired. Cal started plowing the rye field west of the house while I took Ortman home.

Saturday, August 14, 1937

Cal plowing with Allis Chalmers. Likes it.

Clifford here to settle up for threshing. I still had to pay out $16.60. My threshing cost me $49.

Tiahrts brought Adeline back. She'd been working there.

Sunday, August 15, 1937

Whole family in church. Adeline stayed home 'cause she was sick.

Hot and windy. Just scorched the corn. Muskmelons and tomatoes in the open were burned.

Had Christian Endeavor in the evening. Paul Decker's class gave Bible verses and sang songs. Pearl was in the group.

"A"

"All things work together for them that love the Lord."

"B"

"Be kind in the Lord."

"C"

"Count your blessings."

As Paul Decker called out the letters, his class responded with an appropriate Bible verse or proverb. Pearl was embarrassed. "This is so babyish! I'll bet the Schweitzers don't do anything so childish at their C. E. meetings," she thought. Later, in the car, driving home from church she repeated her views to her brother.

"They may not even have C. E.," said Cal.

"Yes, they have C. E., but it's run more like a literary society. People give speeches or themes, develop topics."

"If you have some better ideas, tell the Program Committee," suggested her father.

"I'm sick and tired of Bible verses, object lessons, and recitations," Pearl harped on.

"They have some of those things for the children," moderated Morgan.

"We should have a separate program for the children, one they can participate in, not just sit and listen to."

"Good idea, but where would you have it? We don't have a basement. We just have one room, an entry, a baby room, and the balcony. Where would you put the children, in the balcony? There'd be so much noise, we wouldn't be able to hear ourselves think on the main floor if the children moved around with their chairs in the balcony."

"We could draw the Sunday School curtains and have the children in their classes, just like we do on Sunday morning."

"Give your ideas to Paul E. or Sarah B. See what they think."

Monday, August 16, 1937

Carburetor clogged up, so had late start. Ortman was here to fix the tractor.

Tuesday, August 17, 1937

Cal plowed 14 hrs. Max is here to fool around with the tractor. He likes it.

Wednesday, August 18, 1937

Rained last night. Ground almost soaked through by plowing. Beckers got the tractor we had been using.

Sister Katherine is putting up pickles for us.

Thursday, August 19, 1937

Cal was cutting lake grass in the southwest corner and enjoyed it so much he did not come home for dinner 'til 2 p.m. Went to Fred Huber's place for weed control demonstration. They showed a duck foot cultivator.

Friday, August 20, 1937

I got the old gang plow out this morning and am putting it and an old John Deere plow I bought together to make one good plow out of them. Plowed both a.m. and p.m.

Cal is tearing down the old wash house. We want to make a tank house out of it.

Saturday, August 21, 1937

Finished plowing the west rye field with the gang plow. Put up hay in afternoon. Got three loads from the two lakes. Poor quality hay; plenty of pepper grass in it. Cal raked and Pearl leveled the loads for me. She can do a good job. Practically no hay stayed on the rack.

I picked 3 gal. pail of canteloupes in the field. Adeline canned tomatoes and then went home to Spink Co.

Sunday, August 22, 1937

Rev. D. S. Wipf from the College preached at our church. Good sermon. Also discussed refinancing the College debt.

Sunday School teachers met concerning the program for the Convention at Doland in September. Jacob B. is to bring a theme and Paul E. a biography of D. L. Moody.

Monday, August 23, 1937

Dipped sheep with Cooper's dip using Jac. Mendel's tank. Used 100 gal. water but could have used more. We first dipped the lambs *so had to dip the old sheep lying on their backs. Big job! Harvey Wiens helped. He came with his mother, who was here to help Pearl.*

"So glad you came to help with the wash today, Aunt Eva. It's awful hard to do it alone since Adeline left," said Pearl, as she took the two apple pies Eva had brought.

"Where'd she go?"

"Back home to Spink County. Got homesick, she said. I think she really wants to go to Chicago where she can make more money."

"Uh oh!"

Reminded of danger, Pearl said, "I'd better check on the girls."

"Better check on Arvel too. I'll fill the copper boiler with water while you're gone."

"If I'm not back when you're finished, you can start cutting up the soap. Here's the butcher knife and cutting board."

Pearl found the girls and Arvel at the big barn, sitting on the wooden fence and watching the sheep dipping operation. Harvey was helping to chase lambs out of the east door and into a chute which led them to the green sulphur solution. As the lambs emerged from the tank, they scrambled down the steps and shook the foreign substance from their wool. Squeals went up from the kibitzers on the fence.

"Be careful not to get too close to the tank," cautioned Pearl. "That's poison in there, you know. Kills ticks. Also stains clothes. So watch out!"

When Pearl got back to the house, she discovered that Eva had finished filling the copper boiler with water from the kitchen pump and had cut the soap into tiny shavings. "This is nice soap. Did you make it yourself?"

"No, it was left over from a batch that Aunt Katherine made for us last winter. She has a big black cauldron that she fires up outside. We saved up our old lard, took it up there, and she made the soap with Lewis lye."

"It's so nice and white."

"She strained the drippings out of the lard first. I think that's the reason it's light. But she also puts Borax in it, I think."

As they sorted the dirty clothes into piles—white shirts here, towels there, colors in between—Pearl went for the bib overalls. "These overalls are always last because they're the muddiest. But there's a reward. Daddy says whoever cleans out the pockets can keep the change." She pulled the pockets inside out and soon nails, screws, washers, nuts, bolts, wood staples, straw, dirt, paper scraps and coins piled up on the linoleum floor of the kitchen. As she picked through the pile she put the sundry hardware items into a tin can and counted the coins. "Only 28 cents today. Fair. It's been better," she said, pocketing the change and sweeping up the dirt.

"Will Cal and you both be going to the Academy this year?"

"Yes, Cal will enroll as a freshman and I'll be a senior."

"My, that must be expensive. My Harvey will go to Marion High School. We can't afford to send him to the Academy."

"Our school district pays tuition to both places, whichever the students choose. So we can go either to Freeman High School or Freeman Academy. But if we go to the Academy, we have to buy our own books. Usually we can buy them used from someone ahead of us through the Bookshop. But that's not what I'm worrying about."

"What are you worried about?"

"What to do with Marian when I'm in school and how I'm going to get all the work done, that's what."

"You expect Adeline to be gone?"

"Yes."

"And your Dad will be teaching?"

"Yes, he'll be teaching the Summit School, in the opposite direction from town."

Just then the girls and Arvel appeared at the back door where the Maytag's exhaust pipe was extended. "We wanna clean out the overhall pockets," announced Ruth.

"The overall pockets have been cleaned out already. I did it."

"Oh, shucks! How much did you make?"

"Only 28 cents."

"That's a lot!" hollered Ruth.

"How many ice cream cones would that buy?" asked Marian.

"Five," answered Pearl, "with three cents left over. Listen, we have to start thinking about dinner. I want you kids to go out to the garden and fill this pan with string beans. Pick all the dead ripe tomatoes you can find and look for about four big slicers. Hurry, now. We don't have time to play around," she said, handing them two wooden peck baskets.

"The girls are big helpers already," observed Eva.

"When they want to be. They make themselves scarce after dinner when it's time to dry dishes. They can usually be found in the toilet or playing with the kittens."

"I wish I had a girl. Just boys I got. But they help some. And Abe, he helps too."

"I never realized how much work there was to do 'til Mother died."

"You're the mother now, aren't you?"

"Yes, and it's scarey!"

"Well, I know you'll do all right. And we'll all help. When we can. You know that, Pearl."

Friday, August 27, 1937

Went to Olivet for the pre-school teachers' meeting. Miss Zehnpfennig, the new Co. Sup., spoke. She has a big job. Agents of various book publishers spoke also.

We had a special treat. Gov. Jensen spoke for a few minutes. He recognized me in the audience. I thanked him for coming to Katherine's funeral. In the evening I went to hear him again at the Bang Lutheran Church picnic 4 miles east, 3 south, and 1 east of Meridian store. He makes an interesting talk.

Saturday, August 28, 1937

Cal is plowing again with Ortman's AC tractor and plow. This morning the gas pipes and screen were clogged up. A man 3 miles northeast of Ortman had been using it. We had to clean it out in order to plow.

Cal and I went to town in the evening. Sold 21 hens we had culled from the flock for $8.28. Bought a barrel of gas for $8.10. This would have been our 18th wedding anniversary.

Sunday, August 29, 1937

Rained nearly all forenoon. Did not go to church. Pearl and Cal went to the neighbors in the afternoon. I was home with Ruth and Marian. A lonesome afternoon for me.

Max came in the evening with two big watermelons.

"Give me the heart! I want the heart!" cried Marian.

"Why do you always want the heart?" asked Pearl as she sliced the watermelon.

" 'Cause there's no seeds in it. Then I don't have to pick the seeds out."

"You can pick them out with your fingers, like I do," suggested Ruth.

"Better to do it with a fork," said Pearl. "Okay, who wants the end? Nobody? Well, then, I'll take it."

"Here, give me the bowl," said Morgan, resigned.

"Why don't you hand us our pieces so we can eat 'em outside?" asked Cal. "Want to, Max?"

"Sure!"

"Okay, you guys, here's your pieces, but the rest of us are going to eat with forks at the table," she announced as the girls were about to follow the boys outside.

Cal and Max went out the north door of the dining room and walked to the fence separating the yard from the chicken pen. "Look," said Max, "you can see the lights of Bridgewater and Canistota."

"Yeah."

"Did you go to Sports Days this year?"

"Yeah, I went with Adeline and Jake Schoenwald. That was right before Ma died. Have you ever gone?"

"Naw, the Old Man says it costs too much money."

"It does! Boy, this watermelon is good. Got a big crop this year?" asked Cal.

"Finally. They started growin' when the rains came."

"You must have 'em in a sandy patch. We have cantaloupes this year but no watermelons. Wanna take some cantaloupes home?"

"Sure."

"How far can you spit?"

"Huh?"

"The seeds. How far can you spit a watermelon seed?"

"I dunno. That's like askin' me how far I can pee. Three feet, maybe."

"Bet I can spit farther."

"Okay, try it."

Cal spat and laughed. "Where is it? I can't see it. We'll have to try that in daylight some time."

"You guys want another slice?" called Pearl through the screen door.

"Sure!" they replied in unison and threw over the fence the rinds which had already been chewed down to the green.

Leaning over the fence, Max asked, "You gonna go to the Academy this year?"

"Yeah. It starts Thursday. Who's gonna be your teacher, at your school?"

"I dunno her name. It's a woman."

"Should be duck soup."

"Easier than your Dad, that's for sure. But I still wish he was our teacher. He was tough, but he played ball with us at recess and took us to all the track meets and stuff."

"He's tough, all right. He's tough at home too. Did he ever give you a licking in school?"

"He hit me last year with a stick!"

"No! What for?"

"He wanted me to count the counties in South Dakota on the map, but I told him I didn't understand why he wanted me to do that. He said he had just told me, and that I was just being stubborn. And then he picked up the stick and hit me."

"When was that?"

"In spring, close to the end of school."

"Before the primary election, I bet. He was going pretty strong then, day and night."

"I think he was sorry for it after he did it, but he never said so. The next day he asked me to help you clean out the cistern."

"Oh, yeah, I remember that. Yeah, he has a pretty short fuse sometimes."

Wednesday, September 1, 1937

Pearl and Cal enrolled at the Academy in the p.m. I got Mrs. Jacob L. Hofer, Sr., to stay with the children.

Thursday, September 2, 1937

Pearl and Cal at the Academy. I sowed rye. One of the horses, Lena, was dead this morning. I guess we worked her too hard yesterday while dragging. She seemed all right when we quit at 7:30 last night, but she was dead this morning. The Menno rendering works came to get her because I didn't have time to skin her.

Sister Elizabeth is here. Marian has chicken pox.

Friday, September 3, 1937

I sowed in the big rye field (26 acres) west of the barn, 2 bu. to the acre. My school starts next week. Mrs. Jake L. went home.

Sunday, September 5, 1937

Marian still sick with chicken pox. Pearl and I went to Marion to try to get Grandma Tieszen to come over for a while.

Anna Kliewer Tieszen met Pearl and Morgan at the front door of her bungalow. Her diminutive figure clad in a flowery print house dress covered with an apron bowed to them. Her yellowing white hair was covered with a cotton print dust cap.

"*Kommen sie herein,*" she said and led them into the dining room where Jacob P. Tieszen was dozing in a rocker. Waking, he rose to greet the visitors.

"*Setzen sie,*" said Grandpa.

"*Ich will Vaspa machen,*" said Grandmother and hurried to the kitchen. Pearl followed and soon the two had laid *Zwieback,* cheese, butter, groundcherry preserves, and canned peaches on the dining room table. After Grandpa had prayed, Grandma poured the coffee.

Pearl smiled at her father. Both knew that he would make a remark later about the weak Low German coffee. " 'Might as well be tea,' he'll say," she thought.

Then to her grandmother, Pearl said, "I just love your fancy flowered china. It's so delicate. I like to hear the ring of the cup in the saucer."

"What she means is that we use the big, heavy farmer cups for everyday. The good set of china you gave Katherine for a wedding present we're saving." 138

"*Ja*," said Grandma and passed the *Zwieback*.

"I remember when I helped you roll the balls of dough for the *Zwieback* when I was little. First the big ball, then the little ball on top of that. I had a hard time making the little ball stay on top of the big ball," said Pearl, laughing.

"*Ja*," said Grandma and passed the groundcherry preserves.

Pearl summoned courage to broach the purpose for their visit: "Grandma, we were wondering if you could come over and stay with Marian for a few days now that the Academy has started. She has the chicken pox and can't go to anyone's house."

"Oh, *meine Marichen*."

"See, Daddy's school starts tomorrow. Ruth starts first grade tomorrow in town, and Cal and I are at the Academy."

"Oh, my, *alle zum Schule*."

"Yes, and . . ."

Grandpa cleared his throat. "John, do you remember last July Fourth when you and Katherine brought a freezer of sherbet for Grandma's 79th birthday?"

"Yes, we were all here. Rev. Derk Tieszen and his wife were here too."

"Well, that was LAST year. Anna is now more than 80 years old and she cannot do that kind of work anymore, taking care of children."

"You know, Grandma, it's hard for me to remember that you are 80 years old, because you look so much younger than that," said Morgan, honestly.

"*Ja, danke schön*."

Pearl helped Grandma clear the table. Then, as Pearl and Morgan were preparing to leave, Grandma handed Pearl a bag of Zwieback and groundcherry preserves. "*Für die Madchen. Es ist gut zu essen.*"

Thank you, Grandma. They love groundcherry jam."

Morgan and Pearl rode silently in their '34 Chevy into the setting sun. As they approached the Wiens farm, Morgan asked, "Shall we stop and ask Aunt Eva to come?"

"She has Arvel at home, and she helped me do the washing just two weeks ago. I hate to ask her again so soon."

"Well, I guess we'll just have to paddle our own canoe," he said, sighing dejectedly.

"Let's try Bertha—Bertha Walter. She's looking for a job. Maybe she can do it," said Pearl, hopefully.

Sunday, September 12, 1937

Pearl had a visitor this evening. Cal also went along. I am home alone with the little children. If Ma only were here.

Monday, September 13, 1937

Cal and I shocked cane after school. Marian is staying at Paul L.'s this week during the day. Evelyn came along from Academy to help Pearl after school.

Tuesday, September 14, 1937

D. E. Mendel is cutting cane and corn for me. The hybred corn is very tall but has not much corn on. My open pollinated corn is better. I got Herman Haupt to shock corn for me. He wants $2 a day.

Thursday, September 16, 1937

Everybody in school. Ruth bawled quite a bit this morning. Did not want to go to school. She does not like school in town.
Marian likes staying at Paul L.'s during the day.
Pearl got 99% on an American history test.
Sent car payment of $13.57.

Friday, September 17, 1937

Got warrant for attending county teachers' meeting — $5.05.

Saturday, September 18, 1937

Sowed 13 acres rye in southwest field with Jake Walter's team. Grasshoppers ate about 2 drills wide on early rye field.

Sunday, September 19, 1937

No church today because of Sunday School convention in Spink Co. We did not go to any other church because our car did not work. Abe Wiens family visited here in afternoon and took Marian along for the week.

Monday, September 20, 1937

County teachers' institute held at Freeman College Gym. Woodburn of Spearfish Normal was conductor. I was elected president of Hutchinson County Teachers' Association and delegate to SDEA convention in Sioux Falls in November.
Woodburn and I went to the movies in Freeman in the evening.

Tuesday, September 21, 1937

J. F. Hines, State Sup. of Public Instruction, spoke at teachers' institute. Jones, a very dynamic character, conducted the singing. Had an art demonstration, and Emily Parker, county home extension agent, spoke on hot lunches.

Adeline Kleinsasser came back from Spink to help us.
Joe L. Hofer bought a young ram for $15.

Friday, September 24, 1937

Children drove with our car today and took Glanzers along.
Had our first Young Citizens League program at #51. Theme
was Autumn. The children need more practice.
Wind blew most of our cane and corn shocks over. Had first
killing frost.

Saturday, September 25, 1937

Cal and I hauled 3 1/2 loads of cane shocks to barn. The wind
had blown most of them over. Was told cane should stay out 6
weeks to dry but ours was out only 3 weeks.

Sunday, September 26, 1937

Church was very cold this morning because stove was not set up.
Roan cow, Pauline, broke her horn in the barn. Cal retrieved
it. He wants to make a bugle out of it.
Went to Bethesda Church C. E. program in evening because
Adeline was on the program. Stopped at Abe Wienses to get Marian
but they were not at home.

Monday, September 27, 1937

I am having vacation from school this week. Sowed rye with
our horses because Nelly is over her sleeping sickness.
Went to Wienses in afternoon to get father-in-law's potato plow
and my little daughter, Marian, who had been there over a week.

"Guess what, Daddy!" exclaimed Marian as they were driving
home. "The trailer got loose."
"Whose trailer? When?"
"Uncle Abe's trailer. We were taking some pigs to Yankton."
"How did it happen?"
"Uncle Abe said the bolt came out of the hitch. I saw it first.
I was in the back seat watching the trailer out the back window.
It was going back and forth across the road."
"Did you tell Uncle Abe?"
"No, I just watched it."
"Well, when you see something like that, you should tell."
"You mean tattle?"
"That's not tattling. That's avoiding danger. It's your responsibility to tell when something is not right."
"I told him when we LOST the trailer."

"Well, that was good."

"Yeah, I saw the trailer going backwards, away from us, zig zagging across the road."

"Did you lose any pigs?"

"No, Aunt Eva said it was a miracle the pigs didn't get away. What's a miracle?"

"A miracle is divine intervention."

"What's davine invention?"

"That's when something bad could happen but God doesn't let it happen."

"Did we ever have a miracle?"

"Well, yes. But we've had the other kind too – accidents. We've had bad things happen, bad accidents."

"What bad accidents did we have?"

"When Mother died and Baby Katherine died. Those were bad accidents. What else happened when you stayed with Abe and Eva?"

"They bought me a dress."

"Really?"

"Yeah, after Uncle Abe sold the pigs we went to a store and they bought me a dress."

"Well, that's nice. What color is it?"

"Brown, so it doesn't get dirty right away, Aunt Eva said."

Tuesday, September 28, 1937

Re-seeded rye the grasshoppers had eaten. At some places they ate 4 to 6 drills wide. After school Cal, Pearl and I re-shocked some cane and tied the shocks so they couldn't fall over again. Herded cattle along the section line. Have very little pasture.

Wednesday, September 29, 1937

Picked corn and got wood ready for winter fuel. Corn better than it's been for a number of years. Started taking down section line fence on southwest field. I want to plow it up so snow does not lodge on the road and so not so much land is wasted.

Thursday, September 30, 1937

After school we dug 30 bu. potatoes with Grandpa's plow. Walter children helped us. Have a lot of trouble with cattle getting out. There is not enough feed. I don't want to turn them on the rye field yet, but I might have to.

Friday, October 1, 1937

Rained just enough to prevent field work, so we sorted potatoes. Some are quite big. Marian and Adeline helped.

"I'll pick out the baby potatoes," Marian offered.

"Put them in the pail," instructed Adeline, lifting Marian to the wagon box filled with golden brown potatoes. "But don't throw them in. Be gentle. Just drop them in so they don't get bruised."

"I like the little ones."

"Sure, they're cute. We can boil 'em in their jackets and eat 'em with cream," offered Adeline.

"Or fry them with onions and eggs. That's the way I like 'em," said Morgan.

"I like the little potatoes in soup," piped up Marian.

"Reminds me. We should make a big kettle of soup. Gets better every day it sits on the back of the range," suggested Morgan. "Look at these beauties! We ought to get a good price for these in town."

"Who would buy them?"

"Schambers or K & K. But they have to be uniform in size, clean, and have no rotten or bruised spots."

"Look at this funny one. It looks like a Teddy bear," remarked Marian, holding up a bear-shaped potato. "And here's a snowman."

"Worst thing about potatoes is peeling 'em," Adeline mused.

"Don't need to be peeled. Cook 'em with the peelings on," instructed Morgan. "That's the best part anyway. That's where the vitamins are."

"Peels in mashed potatoes?" protested Adeline.

"Well, maybe not in MASHED potatoes. But in fried potatoes, the peelings would be just fine. Just like when we fry apples, the peelings just cook up."

"We'll see."

"Honey, don't wipe your fingers on your dress after handling each potato. That's what makes your dresses so dirty! Just wait 'til we go up to the house to wash your hands before dinner," instructed Morgan.

"But they feel so dirty."

"Dirt never hurt anyone. Adeline, are we gonna have boiled or fried potatoes for dinner?"

"I'm sick of potatoes already."

"Well, I'm not. Just brush clean some of those little ones and boil 'em in their jackets. Potatoes and fresh cream. And maybe some dill pickles that Aunt Katherine made for us! That'd make a good dinner."

Saturday, October 2, 1937

Fixed the hog barn so we could put pullets in. After supper all helped carry pullets.

143

"I hate to carry chickens! They peck!" complained Ruth.

"Everybody's gotta help. You and Marian don't have to go into the brooder house. Just stand by the door and we'll hand the pullets to you," instructed Morgan.

"What if we drop them?"

"Just don't drop them! Just carry one in each hand. And if it gets away, it won't break. It'll find its way back to the brooder house tomorrow."

"Yuk! It stinks in there," protested Marian, standing by the door.

"That's just Black Leaf 40 and creosote on the roosts," said Pearl.

"AND manure!"

"Waddaya 'spect? They're chickens!" explained Cal. "They never had a WPA toilet built for them."

"Here," said their father, handing Ruth an up-side-down white Leghorn pullet by its feet. "Hang on. Here's another one for the other hand."

"Hold still!" Ruth screamed at the chickens.

"And here's one for you, Marian. Hold it with both hands. You only have to carry one. But be careful. Don't drop it!"

Cautiously the family made its way through the chilly night air. Morgan led the way across the farm yard holding the kerosene lantern in one hand and four pullets by their feet in the other hand. "Uh oh, we forgot to lock up Lucky so he won't bark and scare the chickens. You do that before your next trip, Cal."

"He prob'ly wonders what's going on."

"Prob'ly thinks somebody's stealin' chickens," said Adeline.

"Well, it's been done, and in this community too. Someone from our church, in fact," said Morgan.

"Who? Someone I know?" asked Adeline.

"I won't say, but he had to go before the whole church on a Sunday morning and confess."

"Really? I'll bet that was embarrassing!"

"Embarrassing isn't the word for it. HUMILIATING, that's what it was. But I think he learned his lesson. Hope so, anyway."

"Why would anyone do that?"

"For cash. You can always sell chickens, just like eggs and cream. Trouble was he tried to sell 'em to Ed P. Hofer and Ed knew this family didn't raise Leghorns. This guy hadn't culled the chickens at all, just brought in the general run – good laying hens and roosters all together. Brought whatever he could pick off the roosts. So Ed P.'s suspicions were confirmed," explained Morgan.

"I heard someone in our chicken house once," said Ruth.

"When was that?"

144

"Last summer. One night I had to get up to pee and heard the chickens crowing like somebody was after them."

"That could have been a fox or a coon. The dog should have barked. If you hear anything like that again, be sure to wake me up!"

"What'll you do, shoot 'em with your shotgun?"

"No, but I might fire into the night sky and let the noise scare 'em off."

Sunday, October 3, 1937

From church we all went to Peter G. Hofer's place for dinner and stayed for supper. Nephew Peter G., Jr., and his Mrs. were there too. Had a very nice visit.

The children went over to the Wollmans for a while. The Wollman boys are some pretty good athletes.

"What are you so mad about?" Morgan asked Pearl as they were driving out of Peter G. Hofer's yard.

"I just get so embarrassed!" she confessed.

"Whatever for?"

"Somebody invites us for dinner and we stay for supper too," Pearl explained.

"Well, they invited us to stay."

"Sure, when we don't leave and it's choring time, they're gonna ask us if we wanna stay for supper."

"Listen, my sister Mary is gonna tell me if they are going to church or have other company coming. People try to help out the best way they can, and you ought to be thankful."

"I am, it's just that I think we shouldn't assume we've been invited for two meals on Sunday."

"I bet you had a heavy date on for tonight. That's why you're so mad! You must've missed your date," Cal realized.

"Oh, you guys! You're just awful!" Pearl cried in the back seat.

Monday, October 4, 1937

Pearl stayed home from school. She and Adeline picked one load of corn. The pullets laid 5 eggs.

"Look, five eggs! We got five little eggs from the pullet barn," exclaimed Marian as she and Ruth showed Pearl their cache in their straw-lined tin syrup pail.

"Can we have these for breakfast tomorrow? We want to eat these baby eggs," said Ruth.

"Okay, but you're gonna have to get up when we call you the first time tomorrow. Otherwise there won't be time to fry your eggs."

"We promise," said Ruth.

"Promise you'll let me comb your hair without crying too?"

"You pull too hard!"

"I can't get through the snarls in your long hair without pulling. Either promise not to cry or we'll take you to the barber and get you a boy's hair cut."

"I don't care. Just stop pulling. Ma never pulled my hair."

"Mother was home all day. I have to get everybody else ready for school and myself too," explained Pearl.

Wednesday, October 6, 1937

Went to South Church to hear a Rev. Underwood, a very fluent speaker. The church was packed. We stood outside in the hall with many others.

Friday, October 8, 1937

Children got home late from school because Academy had a baseball game with Marion H. S., and Paul Glanzer was on the Academy team.

Cal and I unloaded a load of cornstalks and a load of corn after school. Also picked some seed corn. It certainly takes long to do all the work after school.

Saturday, October 9, 1937

Pearl, Cal and I picked 35 bu. corn while Adeline was home with the girls. Marie Walter was here to help too.

"Okay, here's a list of the Saturday work we have to do today," said Adeline to her young helpers. "Wash the floors, dust, fill lamps with kerosene, wash chimneys, bake bread, sweep the sidewalk. Who wants to do what?"

"I wanna bake bread," said Marian.

"You can help with that but I think I'd better bake the bread," said Adeline.

"I like to clean up," said Marie. "I'll wash the floors and the kids can help by dusting before I sweep."

"Might be better to dust after broom sweeping," advised Adeline.

"I'd rather put kerosene in the lamps than dust," said Ruth.

"Why don't we fill the lamps and wash the chimneys first? Then, if we spill some kerosene, we can clean it up."

"Marian, why don't you sweep the sidewalk so the menfolks don't track in any more mud than we already have in the house? I have to start the bread dough right away 'cause we're out of bread. Dough oughta be ready to make *Roll Kuchen* by dinner."

As Marian stepped outside with the broom, she could hear the "bang, bang, bang" of hard, ripe ears of field corn being thrown against the bang board extension on the wagon box. The "giddy-yap" directions of her father to his team of horses rang through the crisp fall air. "I wish I could help pick corn instead of sweeping the sidewalk. Maybe I could drive the horses," Marian thought and dropped the broom and ran to the fence to watch for the pickers on their return trip. Meanwhile she collected fallen leaves. Pretty leaves – yellow and orange – all different shapes and sizes. Soon she had more than she could hold.

"Marian? Yoo-hoo, where are you?" Adeline called from the porch.

"I'll pretend I didn't hear," Marian thought.

"Marian," scolded Adeline as she approached the little girl whose hands gripped the leaves tightly, "you must answer me when I call! What are you doing here? I thought you were supposed to sweep the sidewalk."

"I wanted to drive the horses and help with corn picking instead."

"You're too little to drive the horses. Besides, they don't need a driver. Your Daddy tells them when to go and when to stop. And they obey him!"

"What's the problem?" called Morgan as the wagon and pickers approached.

"I wanna help you and Cal and Pearl pick corn," cried Marian.

"Sorry, Honey, that's too dangerous. You might get run over by the horses," said Cal. "But, tell you what, I'm thirsty. Could you bring me a jug of water?"

"Yeah, you can be our water boy," suggested Morgan. "Just bring it to the fence and we'll look for you with the jug when we come around again."

That night, everybody went to town, including Marie and Adeline. On the way, Morgan asked, "Waddaya all need?"

"Shoes," answered Pearl for the group. "I think we all need shoes."

"Okay, you can all go to K & K's and get your shoes," said Morgan, magnanimously.

"Me too?" asked Marie, incredulously.

"Sure, you worked today, didn't you? Everybody who worked today gets shoes."

"How'll we pay for them?" asked Pearl.

"Put it on the bill. Our ship is gonna come in one of these days."

"Wow! I can't believe it! Is he serious? I haven't had a new pair of shoes in ages. I just wear hand-me-downs from my sisters," said Marie.

"When Dad says something, he means it," confirmed Pearl.

They all traipsed into K & K's general store triumphantly and proceeded to the shoe department. There were just enough empty chairs for them, since one was occupied by Justina, someone they knew who went to the Salem K. M. B. Church.

"Well, well," remarked Amelia Dewald, the clerk, as she approached the expectant females sitting in a row. "What's your pleasure?"

"We're all getting new shoes," announced Ruth. "Daddy said so."

"Wonderful! What kind did you have in mind?"

"Something practical, I think. Oxfords, brown Oxfords. Daddy would want us to get shoes that would be durable, that would take the wear and tear," explained Pearl to the little ones.

"Brown Oxfords is a good choice, then."

"I'm gonna take real good care of mine," said Marie.

"The best way is to keep them polished. And never polish over dirt. Scrape off all the mud and dirt with a table knife, nothing too sharp, then wipe the shoe with a damp cloth, and polish them," Amelia directed them.

"Reminds me!" shouted Adeline. "One thing that wasn't on our list of things to do today was polishing all the shoes for Sunday. Well, we'll have new shoes to wear, and we can polish Cal's and Uncle Morgan's shoes tonight when we get back, as a thank-you."

"Hmmm, looks to me like I gotta get me a job at Morgan's too," mused Justina to Amelia.

"You want me to add this to your account?" Amelia asked Pearl when she saw no cash or check forthcoming.

"Please. Dad said our ship was going to come in pretty soon."

Sunday, October 10, 1937
Mission Fest in our church. Rev. Peter J. Stahl and Rev. Jacob B. preached in the morning, Rev. Jacob A. Tieszen in the afternoon, and C. E. program in the evening. Collection for missions was over $200.

Monday, October 11, 1937
Pearl stayed home from school to pick a load of corn with Adeline. Marian at the Walters.

I have had the cattle on the rye field for over a week. Hope they don't do too much damage.

Tuesday, October 12, 1937
Had to pull the car with a team to get it started this morning. Took Marian to Joe L.'s and got 10 gal. gas. After school Joe Hofer had to push my car to get it started. He broke the rear bumper

on both sides. I had Andrew Schaefer charge the battery. It was all run down.

Friday, October 15, 1937
Cal stayed home from school to help Adeline pick a load of corn.

Saturday, October 16, 1937
Snowed nearly all day except when it rained. Cut some tires for fuel. The yard is very muddy. This weather is good for the rye but not for the corn and cane still out.

Wednesday, October 20, 1937
Cal and Pearl both stayed home to finish husking corn. Walter family came too to help us. We still have half our cane out and also the corn fodder.

Friday, October 22, 1937
Car trouble again — starter, flat tire, and radiator frozen. Got to school ten minutes to 9, so the children were all late after driving to Freeman.

"I don't want to go in late," cried Ruth.

"You have to go in. You can't stay in the car. We're all late already and you're just making us later," scolded Pearl.

"I hate to go in late. Everybody turns around and makes fun of me for coming late."

"Just tell Miss Henley we had car trouble. She'll understand."

"Okay," said Ruth, reluctantly, and walked slowly to the front door of Freeman Independent School. When she opened the glass-paned door, the halls were quiet and empty. All the children were already in their rooms with the doors closed. She went down the hall to her room with "Grades 1 and 2, Miss Bess Henley" printed on a placard above the door. Ruth hesitated. She did not want to turn the door knob.

As she hesitated, Superintendent E. L. Holgate came around the corner. "What's the matter, Kiddie? Why aren't you in your room?"

"I came late and I'm scared to go in," she explained.

"Well, now, we can't have that. Come, I'll go with you," he said, taking her hand and leading her to Miss Henley's desk. "I found this little girl in the hall. She belong here?"

"Yes, take your seat, Ruth. You're late, but we were just getting started with reading. Take out your reader. Thank you, Mr. Holgate."

Suddenly Ruth burst into tears. "What's the matter?" asked Miss Henley.

149

"My lunch pail! I forgot my lunch in the car!"

"Well, maybe your sister or brother will find it and bring it to you. If not, I'll share my lunch with you."

As Ruth wiped away her tears with the back of her hand, Mr. Holgate entered the room again and said, as he approached Ruth's desk, "This your lunch? Your brother said you forgot your lunch in the car." Smiling, she took it from him.

"Say 'thank you' to Mr. Holgate and put your lunch pail in the back of the room with the others."

"Thank you," Ruth said and found room for her pail among the other tin syrup pails standing like shining sentinels.

"Now, class," sighed Miss Henley, "maybe we can get down to business. Mary Lou, begin reading on page 11, please."

Saturday, October 23, 1937

Jake Walter brought us a Buffalo Carp from the James River. It was fat and real good. The state did some fishing and sold them for 3 1/2cents per lb.

Sunday, October 24, 1937

All in church but Pearl, who stayed home to herd cattle in the corn field and study (she claims).

I went to the Gym to hear Prof. E. G. Kaufman of Bethel College preach on Titus in Crete.

Monday, October 25, 1937

After school I took Marian to Dentist Wollman to have one of her teeth pulled because she complains of a toothache. He wanted to inject to deaden the pain but she would not let him do it. We went home without the tooth pulled.

Tuesday, October 26, 1937

County nurse, Miss Leona Tuegen, in #51 today to test the children. Deloris Hofer has one bad eye, her left.

The county health unit is planning to have a clinic at our school to vaccinate for smallpox and diphtheria. It seems quite a few are interested in vaccination.

Wednesday, October 27, 1937

Miss Josephine Zehnpfennig, Co. Sup. of Schools, visited #51 today. In the evening she, Rose Perman, Miss Ludeman and I went to Yankton concerning SDEA. We might organize into regions. I spoke on the work of the state legislature concerning school legislation.

Friday, October 29, 1937
Hired Marvin Hofer to build the fire at school and sweep the floor for 25¢ per week. The stove is a slow starter but holds heat well once it is started. The boys track in a lot of mud.

Tuesday, November 2, 1937
Took 7th and 8th graders to County Court House for court session. Pete Waltner sued an insurance company and won.

Wednesday, November 3, 1937
Had Marian vaccinated by Dr. Payne, county doctor from Tripp. There were 27 other children in the clinic in our school basement.

"I got vaccinated today," Marian announced to Pearl.

"Did it hurt?"

"Yeah! I cried!" confessed the little girl.

"What were you vaccinated against?"

"I don't know. What was I vaccinated against, Daddy?"

"Smallpox and diphtheria," he answered.

"Box and theory," she repeated.

"Well, that's a good idea, 'cause one of my classmates died of diphtheria."

"Today?"

"No, when I was in the fifth grade and going to our country school. It was Warren Thomas."

"Yeah, I remember they quarantined us and the school," said Cal. "County nurses came out to check us over real good and take our temperatures before we could open the school. They had nailed a big sign on the school house door that said QUARANTINED."

"Will I die of . . . .?" Marian asked Pearl.

"Diphtheria. No, that's why you got a vaccination, to prevent you from getting it."

"I was vaccinated against diphtheria too," said Morgan.

"Today? You mean you were never vaccinated before?"

"Nope."

Thursday, November 4, 1937
Cal played basketball after school so we got home after sundown. Children complained of stiff arms in school.

Friday, November 5, 1937
Got my warrant for teaching. Paid $27.14 on car, gave Adeline $5., paid Julius Albrecht $10, paid Bob Wipf $3.92, and the College Bookshop $4.

Charged nearly a ton of Montana coal at Farmers' Lumber Yard—$9.25.

Sunday, November 7, 1937
After church we went to John L.'s for dinner and supper. John and I had a meeting at the College concerning school problems.

After choring we visited Grandpa and Grandma Tieszen. They were glad to see us.

Monday, November 8, 1937
Took a trailer load of old shingles to school to use for kindling, using Paul L.'s trailer. When I took the trailer back, Lizzie gave us a dressed goose. Had part of it for supper. It was real good.

Cal took Adeline to her uncle, Jake F. Walter. She wants to go to Chicago.

Tuesday, November 9, 1937
Dr. Payne was around checking up on vaccinations. He claims Sam's, Marvin's, and Luella's didn't catch. They are supposed to go to some other school to be revaccinated. Marian's caught.

Thursday, November 11, 1937
Marian stayed with Mrs. Paul L. Her smallpox vaccination is inflamed.

The children came home very late from school. They were having class basketball tournaments and Cal played center on the freshman team. Not much time to do chores.

Friday, November 12, 1937
Lizzie made Marian a petticoat.

Driving Marvin's bicycle, Irvin Hofer hit Andrew Nachtigal with the handle bar of the bike and knocked Andrew's tooth loose and cut his lip badly.

Saturday, November 13, 1937
Snowing this morning and very strong wind. Cal and I put up a fence on the east 80. We moved the fence so it won't block snow on the road. Plan to plant alfalfa there next spring.

Went to Marion after 5 to have radiator cleaned out and had supper at Grandpa's.

Sunday, November 14, 1937
Very cold. Were all at home. Mrs. Dr. Derk Tieszen is to be buried today. She was his second wife, Kathryn Schartner. His first wife, Mary Kleinsasser, died before Katherine and I were married.

Monday, November 15, 1937

Adeline still in Chicago. Marian staying with Mrs. P. P. She likes it there.

"What did you do at P. P.'s today?" Pearl asked as the children were driving home from Freeman after school.

"I played in the front room by the pillars."

"Did Aunt Anna say it was all right?"

"Yes, for a while. Then she called me into the dining room where she was mending socks in front of the window. It was nice and warm in there. We listened to the radio a while and I looked at magazines. She let me cut out some pictures."

"Did you help her any?"

"I helped her pair up socks and fold farmer handkerchiefs."

"Did she give you any ice cream? I bet you had ice cream!" said Ruth.

"No, but we made cookies together and she gave me some. Here's one in my pocket for you. She said I should give it to you."

"I wish I could stay there instead of going to school," complained Ruth as she bit into her sour cream cookie.

"Everybody has his own work to do. You used to stay home with Mother, helping her. Now your work is to go to school and Marian's work is to play," explained Pearl.

"Work is to play? I never heard of that! That's dumb!"

Thursday, November 18, 1937

Had 2 inquiries about rams from my ad in the ARGUS LEADER. Most people want older rams.

Friday, November 19, 1937

Set up our hard coal burner at home. It will be more comfortable now. It was very cold this last week.

Finished exams today. Some very low grades again and some good ones.

Saturday, November 20, 1937

Johnny and Mary Klein came down from Spink. Mary is remodeling some clothing for the children. She made a dandy coat for Ruth from an old wool coat of mine by turning the fabric inside out. It is very warm. She also made dresses for the girls out of Katherine's old dresses.

Sunday, November 21, 1937

Left Ruth and Marian at Tiahrts and went to the opening session of SDEA's 55th annual convention in Sioux Falls. Main event was the unveiling of statue of Gen. Beadle. Beadle's daughter was here from California for the celebration. Next year is the centennial of Beadle's birth. His statue will be placed in the Hall of Fame in Washington, DC. He is the first educator to be so honored.

Monday, November 22, 1937
Johnny and I went to Sioux Falls for SDEA. Dr. A. J. Stoddard, Sup. of Denver Public Schools, was the main speaker. He pictured American schools and the American scene. He spoke again in the afternoon before the History Club but they had it in such a small room we had to go to the gallery.

Sup. J. F. Hines spoke to the general assembly in the evening. Rabbi Goldstein of Omaha spoke at Hickory Stick Banquet on "Representative Americans" at the Cataract Hotel.

Tuesday, November 23, 1937
Johnny and I drove home each night from Sioux Falls. Dr. Thomas Cole of the U. of Washington spoke to the general assembly in the morning. Heard Rabbi Goldstein again at luncheon speak on "The Book and the Sword."

Attended History Round Table. Kraushaar discussed Indian service and Dr. Norton of Augustana College discussed "War Clouds on the Old World." He really makes you think.

Wednesday, November 24, 1937
Last day of SDEA. Over 4,000 teachers registered. Prof. Culp of Aberdeen Normal and Dr. Dawson of Washington, DC, were speakers.

Had lunch in a restaurant and then went to a gift show, including Ted Shawn and his dancers.

Had big supper at John J. B.'s on way home. Stayed to visit a while.

Thursday, November 25, 1937 (Thanksgiving)
Went claims adjusting for Mennonite Aid Plan. Allowed Jake M. Waldner $15 on his windmill.

Saturday, November 27, 1937
Cal and I burned Russian thistles and hauled straw to the house for banking around the foundation.

Sunday, November 28, 1937
All in church. Invited for dinner and supper to Joe J. Hofer's near Stanley Corner. Had duck and goose and all the trimmings.

Monday, November 29, 1937

Pearl is staying home with Marian. I am sorry it has to be done that way.

"I can't do it all—field work, house work, taking care of the kids, and going to school at the same time. It's just humanly impossible," cried Pearl.

"But you were getting such good grades—a 99 in history. I don't understand it," said Morgan.

"That's just the point. I can't continue to get good grades if I don't have time to study.

I thought maybe Mary would stay, but she went back to Spink with Johnny. Did you pay her anything for re-making those clothes for the girls?"

"No, I thought she did that because she wanted to."

"Sure she wanted to, but you know she needs a steady job, just like Adeline does. They can't work for just room and board and an occasional gift."

"I'd like to pay them regular wages, but you know we just don't have the money. I gave Johnny the can of cream when he was here. Thought he'd share the check with Mary."

"Well, maybe he did but he also bought us a box of Delicious apples. So you know he didn't have much left out of that cream check. I'm worried about Marian too, being farmed out to so many different relatives—Aunt Eva, Aunt Anna, Lizzie, P. P.'s, Joe L.'s."

"I thought she was getting along all right. You know, she hasn't been stuttering like she did before Mother died. And she's learning a lot too."

"She's learning some things she shouldn't be learning."

"Really?"

"Yeah, especially from the little boys."

"Oh! Well, maybe you can stay out for the winter quarter and then go back in the spring."

Tuesday, November 30, 1937

We all went to see the College play, "The Life Eternal," a Catholic play. Nephew Jerome was in it. Well done. They had a big crowd. Took in some $90 besides the student tickets.

Wednesday, December 1, 1937

Ruth and I went to Freeman H. S. in the evening to see their operetta. It was poorly done, just a practice for the students, I suppose.

Thursday, December 2, 1937

Got a card from Adeline. She wants some money. It seems she cannot make expenses in Chicago.

Friday, December 3, 1937

The wind tore down two wings on our windmill wheel. I suppose a rod or nut got loose first.

Saturday, December 4, 1937

Much colder. Ground is frozen. Jakie Waldner came to help us get water into the barn. Jake dug open the old hydrant and a trench but had trouble connecting the 18 foot pipe I bought.

Paid balance on Katherine's funeral at Burial Assoc. meeting in Viborg. (Got $45.80 check for per diem, mileage and director's salary.) Got home at 1 a.m. Sunday. Very cold driving.

Sunday, December 5, 1937

Did not go to church in morning. For dinner and supper at Paul L.'s for goose and trimmings. From Paul's place we went to Silver Lake M. B. Church for program by Sunnyside Bible Academy. Heard 3 talks and a variety of songs.

The parlor was nice and warm when we got home.

"Brr, I'm cold," Marian chattered through her teeth in the front seat.

"We're almost home. It won't be long and you'll be nice and warm. I can see the red coals glowing in the hard coal burner," said Morgan as he turned into their driveway.

"I can see the red too. Hurry up! I can't wait to get in the house," Ruth shuddered as she huddled closer to her Dad in the front seat.

"I'll race you to the house," challenged Marian, opening the car door as soon as the car had come to a stop in the garage.

"Okay!" Ruth took up the challenge but slipped on the icy ground and fell, crying, "You pushed me."

"I did not!" replied Marian.

"Quiet, both of you!" commanded Morgan, opening the front door. Past him rushed the two little girls through the dining room and into the parlor. They tore their woolen parka hoods from their heads and threw their coats onto the nearest chair.

"Oooh! It's so cozy warm in here," said Marian, running up to the chrome-plated stove.

"Look, you can see little blue flames above the red coals," said Ruth.

"Careful so you don't burn yourselves. Don't touch those isinglass windows. Those blue flames mean it's very hot. You can pull a wooden chair up to the stove and warm your toes on the fenders before going to bed. But first hang up your coats," instructed Morgan, lighting the Aladdin lamp on the library table.

"I can't reach that high," complained Marian.

"Okay, give me your coat and I'll hang it up for you," said Morgan, standing in front of the hall tree. "Ruth, give me yours too. I'll get your pajamas and after your toes are warm you can get ready for bed."

Marian and Ruth removed their shoes and sat together on an oak chair, resting their stockinged toes on the chromium-plated stove fender. "Look," said Ruth, pointing. "You can see fairies dancing above the coals."

"I don't see them."

"Then you must be blind."

Monday, December 6, 1937
Ran out of gas this morning on the way to school. Someone stole our gas at the Silver Lake Church last night. Hope it was a traveler on the highway who needed it worse than we did.

"Do you know any boys who roam around church yards stealing gas?" asked Morgan after Cal had returned with a can full of gas from Joe L.'s pump.

"No, but it would be easy to do. Just siphon it out with a rubber hose."

Tuesday, December 7, 1937
Regular old time blizzard with drifting all day. If there had been more snow, the roads would be blocked.

Joe P. Glanzer gave us a talk in school on trapping and handling furs. He had skunks, civits, weasels, minks, muskrats, raccoons and a badger.

Thursday, December 9, 1937
Windmill is not repaired yet. Cattle and horses have no water. We did chores after supper.

Friday, December 10, 1937
Our horses followed Walter's horses into Philip Mensch's alfalfa hay. He came up to my school mad. He wants to be paid for the hay. Our cattle were gone in the evening looking for water. Ben Schrag was here to fix the windmill, but he did not tighten one wing.

Saturday, December 11, 1937

Finally started the windmill. It pumped all day. Got hard and soft coal and paid $20 on account. Bought second hand stock tank for $3 from Bob Wipf. Paid blacksmith shop $2 for fixing bumper. Sold $4.52 worth of cream @ 38¢ per lb. butterfat. Gave it to Pearl.

Sunday, December 12, 1937

Had supper at John L.'s and heard several good plays over his radio afterwards. John L. and Mrs. and Joe L. and Mrs. are going to Parkston on Tuesday for Soil Conservation banquet.

Tuesday, December 14, 1937

College Founders Day. Pearl went down to help with the cooking, so Marian was in school with me. She likes it in my school.

In the evening we all went to the College Gym to see pictures of Palestine and hear Dr. Heerstrom speak on Christian education. The hall was packed.

Mr. and Mrs. Henry Tiahrt were here. Mrs. Tiahrt said she was not satisfied that we did not bring Marian up there so Pearl could go to school.

Wednesday, December 15, 1937

Pearl and Cal went to hear Herrstrom at the Gym again. He spoke on the three kings that abdicated for love: Adam, Jesus and Edward. He did not think very highly of Mrs. Simpson, they said.

Thursday, December 16, 1937

John J. B.'s brought us 3 kinds of sausages and pork chops and stayed for supper. We all went to the Gym. Herrstrom spoke on Communism. He made some very strong statements about the Russian government.

Friday, December 17, 1937

Herrstrom spoke on "The Coming World War." He pictured some of the future implements of war. The Japanese have a torpedo regulated by one man. The meetings are well attended. Many people have to stand.

Saturday, December 18, 1937

Had annual church meeting. Jacob B. claims he cannot preach and teach school at the same time. He wants more money. I was secretary of the meeting and was elected a regular teacher. Two women — Sarah B. Hofer and Mrs. Paul Decker — were also elected. The levy is again $15 per family.

Tuesday, December 21, 1937

Had Pearl watch my school while I went to Viborg in the afternoon. I was re-elected board member of Burial Assoc. Got an extension on my land loan. Must pay $250 by March 1, 1938.

"If you don't behave yourselves, I'm not going to let you put up this Christmas tree!" declared the substitute teacher, Pearl, to the twenty pupils, many of whom were just a few years her junior.

"Aw, Teach, really?" asked Marvin.

"Yeah, really! I brought our artificial tree and ornaments from home just so you could have a tree in school. But if you aren't going to appreciate it, I'll just fold up the branches and take it back home!"

"Aw, that would be a shame, wouldn't it, Fellas? Not to have a scrawny little tree like that?" asked Irvin.

"C'mon, you guys, be nice," pleaded Luella. "Behave yourselves, or you'll be in Dutch with Morgan tomorrow!"

"Okay, we'll behave. But we want to decide where the ornaments go," bargained Sam.

"These are all precious ornaments. Very delicate. They belonged to my mother," said Pearl.

"I thought your mother was so religious that she didn't allow you to have a tree," replied Florence.

"She didn't, the last couple of years, until we begged so hard that she relented. But she kept these ornaments safe and sound, even when we couldn't have a tree."

"I'd say the angel should go right over here, on the side," said Sam, teasing.

"No, Dummy, the angel goes on top!" exclaimed Florence.

"I thought the star went on top!" said Sam.

"The angel on top!" shouted some partisans.

"The star on top!" shouted others.

After a vote, the angel won top placement.

"I think it would be better if we let the older girls decorate the tree while the boys practiced their parts for the program," suggested Alice.

"Yeah," shouted a chorus of girls.

"How can we do that without the girls? Our plays have both boys and girls in the cast," said Sam.

"Well, you practice 'Twas the Night Before Christmas' while we put up the tree and then we'll all practice our plays."

"That sounds like a good compromise," said Pearl, trying to regain control. "Okay, the older girls over here. You guys look over your parts and listen to Sam's recitation. And let's have the little ones

159

make paper chains. I'll need some help with the little ones. Alice, will you help me cut the construction paper and get out the paste?"

Sighing with relief when all were finally occupied, Pearl thought, "I don't see how Pa puts up with this crowd every day. No wonder he took off for Viborg."

Wednesday, December 22, 1937

Have our Christmas tree up in school. Solomon was very close to getting a licking today for jumping through the window yesterday while Pearl was in charge.

Thursday, December 23, 1937

Pearl wrapped individual Christmas presents for my pupils 'til 2:30 a.m. I am getting quite a few Christmas cards. Speaker A. C. Miller of Kennebec and Karl Mundt of Madison wrote.

Friday, December 24, 1937

Had a little Christmas program at school. Gave pen and pencil set to all boys and ties to three biggest boys. Gave handkerchief sets to all girls. Have ten boys and ten girls. Let school out at 3 p.m. Got necktie from Sam, pair of socks and handkerchief from Rosa and Pauline and a box of cherry chocolates from the Glanzers. Marian got a necklace from Mary Glanzer and a ball from Florence. Had church program in the evening.

Saturday, December 25, 1937

All in church this morning. Went to Jacob L.'s for dinner, supper and evening. All Jacob L. Hofer, Sr.'s sons, daughters and mates were there, even Smokey Joe and Viola from Onida. I got a nice pocket knife from Mr. Hofer, Sr. Ruth and Marian got dresses, socks and hair ribbons.

"How's come we got invited to the Hofer Family celebration this year? We're not in their family," observed Ruth, clutching her gifts as the Kleinsasser family drove the few miles south on Highway 81 to their home.

"We're not in their IMMEDIATE family," answered her father, "but we're related. Mrs. Jake L., Sr., is my oldest sister, Elizabeth, and I am her baby brother. You remember when she came to stay with us in the summer after Mother died?"

"Yes, she brought peppermint drops."

"Well, she did that because we are part of the family."

"Maybe they felt sorry for us," offered Pearl. "Maybe they thought we'd be lonesome for Mother this Christmas and needed a little cheering up."

"Maybe they think we're orphans, like Gladys and Sammy Hofer," said Cal.

"We're not orphans!" insisted Ruth. "We still have Pa."

"Miss Loewen says sometimes the word is used to apply to persons who have lost only one parent. So don't be surprised if someone refers to you as an orphan someday," said Pearl in her best schoolmarm tone.

"When did she say that?" asked Cal.

"She wrote it on my theme. You know, the one I wrote about Ma's death and got only a B- for."

"Well, well, you learn something new every day!" said Morgan.

Sunday, December 26, 1937

Not in church this morning. Thawed out pipe and started windmill. Went to Grandpa and Grandma Tieszen in the evening after visiting Tiahrts in the afternoon. The children sang songs and said their pieces.

Tuesday, December 28, 1937

Johnny Klein was here helping Cal haul straw to pack the water tank. I gave John a dollar for helping. In the evening we menfolks went to town. Cal and I saw "The Passion Play" at the movie theatre. What was shown was good, but not much was shown. John had a date.

Wednesday, December 29, 1937

Johnny helped Cal manure barns and haul straw. I gave him use of the car for helping.

Grandpa and John Tieszen were here. They put in two windows in the chicken barn and closed up the middle door.

Friday, December 31, 1937

Herbert Hoffman was observing in #51 from the College methods class.

In church for old year's end. When we got home I had a call from John J. K. Stahl to come to Freeman. His father had died at age 84. Went to Viborg together and John bought the funeral, suit and all, for $112.83.

1938
Political Alienation

Saturday, February 5, 1938
Finally bought a diary. Paid John A. Wipf $5 on radio. Still owe $17.50 on $30 radio. It belonged to Jacob L. Hofer, Sr. I bought it with Battery B and A, complete.

Sunday, February 13, 1938
Visited Jake L.'s for supper and evening.

As Morgan and his small daughters entered their warm parlor after the visit, he walked directly to his newly-purchased battery radio and turned it on.

"And now it's time to sing 'Heavenly Sunshine'," said Fuller.

"Okay, now, everybody sing," directed Morgan, while his daughters sang:

"Heavenly sunshine, heavenly sunshine,

Flooding my soul with glory divine;

Heavenly sunshine, heavenly sunshine,

Hallelujah! Jesus is mine."

Saturday, February 19, 1938
County teachers' meeting in Olivet. Harkness of Aberdeen Normal spoke on speech instruction, Mosby of Irene on Russia, and a woman doctor from Pierre on children's health in school.

Tuesday, February 22, 1938
Got $5 warrant for attending teachers' meeting. My birthday. Born 1896. Had school 'til noon. Children gave me a birthday party in the afternoon. Had a short program on George Washington and a big feed—sandwiches, cake and ice cream.

"Mr. Kleinsasser, will you tell us something about what school was like for you when you were little?"

"Well, I was thinking about my first school experiences while you were presenting the program and how different they were from what you enjoy today.

"I was the youngest of nine surviving children and we lived where I live now with my family three miles north of Freeman. Before I was old enough to attend school, the schoolhouse stood on our yard. I used to go over to the school to listen to the recitations, much as my little daughter Marian does when she comes to visit our school. When I lost interest, I would raise my hand to ask permission to be excused. When the teacher gave permission, I would run home. Later the school was moved one mile north on land set aside by law for a school. It was called Sunshine, District #26. It's closed now because we don't have enough pupils to keep it open.

"I liked school. One day I was supposed to stay home to herd cattle and sheep, but I sneaked off and ran to school. Even in those days there was a compulsory school law. Another day when I was supposed to be herding sheep, I stopped at the school but there were no children there. The teacher, according to law, was there to keep the schoolhouse open. But the law seemingly did not require children to be there. So the teacher probably stayed until one o'clock and then went home to do his farm work.

"This incident really impressed me, because while I wanted to go to school so badly but had to herd sheep instead, this teacher was getting paid just to sit in the schoolhouse and read. Most children stopped going to school after the sixth grade."

"Did you have any pets when you were a boy?" asked LaVerne.

"Yes, like most boys, I had a pony and a dog. The pony was named Bay and the dog Dash. Bay was a good pal of mine and even knew a few tricks. He had a habit of stopping short and bracing his front feet, so I sometimes slid off over his neck. Then I

Morgan on Bay

163

would have to look for a large rock to stand on so I could mount him again.

"Whether I rode my pony or walked, Dash was always along. He was a mixed breed, including some bull dog. He was a good protector. One time there was such a heavy rain that the water rushed down the ravine that ran through our land. To get the sheep home, we had to cross the ravine. With the help of my pony and Dash, all the sheep got home safely. My pony had to swim across with me on her back."

"Any other pets?" asked Sam, who wanted to keep the teacher talking so as to avoid an assignment.

"Yes, I had a Poland China pig that became a pet. He followed me all over the yard."

"How did you decide to become a teacher?" asked Rosa.

"Well, I attended Freeman Academy because my father wanted to support the local institution. I took up the Normal course to become a teacher and graduated in 1917. I went to farming the home place after I married but couldn't make any money at it. I went back to college, finished the two-year Normal course in 1933 and started teaching again."

"How's come you got into politics?" asked LeRoy.

"I looked at what was going on up in Pierre, and I decided I could do as well as any other lawmaker up there. I was particularly interested in school legislation. I wanted to improve the public education system in South Dakota."

"Did you do it?" asked Deloris.

"Not yet. It's pretty hard to get anything accomplished in your first term. I thought there should be a minimum salary for teachers, but we had to fund the Old Age Pension first in order to get matching funds from the federal government, and few legislators wanted to levy any more taxes."

"Why was that?"

"Because most voters don't want to pay more taxes, especially during a Depression. We just couldn't find a painless tax. And those interests that have the money, such as Homestake Mine and investment companies that have gotten a lot of land through farm foreclosures, have good lobbyists and they can prevent a tax on their property."

"Are you gonna run again?"

"Yes, I plan to. Gimini Christmas! You kept me talking a long time. It's time to clean up the party and get ready to go home. I really appreciate the party. It's the first time a school has given me a birthday party. Thank you, all of you!"

Friday, February 25, 1938

Pearl and Cal went to a rollerskating party. Cal went to get LaVerna Waltner but got stuck in a snow bank taking her home.

Saturday, February 26, 1938

Thawed all day. Took chains off the car wheels. Paid bills with my school check: Gelfand's – $4.88 in full; Standard Service – $2.98; Schamber's – groceries, $4.47; Preheim for hard coal – $8.50. Bought a 10 pound carp from Matt Kleinsasser for 80¢.

Circulated petitions for Karl Mundt of Madison and Harlan Bushfield of Miller. Mundt is running for Congress and Bushfield for Governor on the Republican ticket.

Atty. John C. Graber will represent me on trespassing charge filed by Mensch. He sued Jake Walter and me for $20 each. Seems to me the damage our horses did to his alfalfa hay is a half ton at the most.

"Grandpa would roll over in his grave if he knew I was being sued. 'Talk it out. That's the right way. Mennonites don't go to court', he'd say."

"You're not suing Mensch. He's suing you," Cal reminded him. "What alternative do you have but to defend yourself if you are sued?"

"That's just it! Mensch is so unreasonable about it!"

"Well, you know our livestock was getting out a lot. When did it happen, anyway?"

"Last year, before Christmas. After the blizzard when the windmill froze up and there was no water being pumped. They just took off with Jake Walter's horses and walked over to Mensch's alfalfa field and started eating from the stack."

"I'll bet Jake's stomach ulcers are acting up again!"

"Has Max said anything about it?"

"No."

"Mensch came up to District #51 during school time, just furious. Made an awful spectacle. Scared the children. He demanded I pay him for the hay they ate. Said my livestock were always out."

"Well, he's got a point there."

"He can stay home all day and mend his fences, but I have other things to do. I'd like my fences to be in good repair too, I'd like the windmill to pump all the time, and I'd like my animals to be well behaved too, but. . . ."

"Do you have a good lawyer?"

"Yeah, J. C. Graber."

"A Mennonite defending a Mennonite."

"He thinks Mensch will settle for less out of court."

165

"I hope it doesn't go to trial," said Pearl, hovering over the stove. "My Academy civics class visited the county court when Waltner was fighting that insurance company. They ask you all kinds of questions. It could be very embarrassing if they get evidence about our livestock getting out all the time."

Sunday, February 27, 1938
After church went with Ed C. Graber to look at Silver Lake and the slough and ditches. We want to plat the land and then make a drive to get a dam across so the water will run into Silver Lake.

Monday, February 28, 1938
Pearl started to school again after being home for the winter quarter. I do not know how she will get along. She has a lot of ambition. We have nobody working for us now.

Tuesday, March 1, 1938
Jacob P. Hofer came to school to tell me he is not satisfied with Solomon's progress.

"I admit I am more interested in the subject matter the upper grades are studying, but I try to give the same amount of time to each grade level," Morgan explained.

"But don't you think the little ones should have more time since they're just starting out?"

"It's a matter of practice with the primary grades. They need a lot of repetition. Maybe you and your Mrs. could listen to him read at home."

"He doesn't like to read for us."

"Does he see you read? Do you take a daily paper?"

"We take the COURIER and read the Bible."

"Maybe you could tell him some Bible stories, like 'Joseph and the Coat of Many Colors' and have him tell it back to you."

"He's backward. He doesn't talk much at home."

"I'll try to give him more time, but I cannot shortchange the others. I have twenty pupils in seven grades and as many subjects." Then, rising to shake Mr. Hofer's hand, Morgan said, "I'm glad you came in, Jake. Recess time is over. I've got to call the children in from the playground."

Mr. Hofer put on his cap and walked toward the door. "I see you got your little girl here too. That means you got 21 scholars."

"Not really. She entertains herself or the upper grade girls take care of her."

"If the upper grades can take care of her, maybe they can help Solomon too."

"That's not a bad idea! We'll try some of that," said Morgan, pulling on the bell rope to call the children from recess. As the children scraped the mud off their shoes and filed in to hang up their coats in the cloak room, he took Luella Schmeichel aside. "Luella, you're a good helper. When you finish your civics lesson, will you practice with Solomon? He needs some help with his reading and spelling."

"Sure, if he'll work with me. He's pretty shy."

"Don't pressure him. Just be kind and maybe he'll open up." Then, turning to the seventh graders, Morgan said, "I heard over the radio last night that the revolution in Spain is still in progress and that Japan is fighting an undeclared war in China. I want you to find Spain, Japan and China on the world map. Then I want you to find out what they're fighting about. Does anybody have a daily newspaper at home?"

"We do," said Marvin and Moses simultaneously.

"See if you can find any articles about those trouble spots. Those of you who have radios at home, listen for news about the war in Spain and the war in China. Today you can read background on Spain and China in the encyclopedia. Ask yourselves: Why is a little country like Japan going against a giant like China?"

Wednesday, March 2, 1938
Marian stayed at Joe L.'s for the day. She likes it there.

"You can play in the bay window," said Annie, Mrs. Joe L. Hofer, to Marian and her son Harvey as she cared for the baby, Delmar.

"I wish we had big window sills like this at home," said Marian, climbing up to the sunlit ledge.

"It's old fashioned," said Harvey, dismissing her wish.

"Yeah, but it's nice and warm and big enough to sit in and draw or color."

"It's where your great grandparents used to live—the Isaac Tschetters—your Daddy's grandpa and grandma. It's a house like they had in Russia," explained Annie as she kneaded her bread dough, "but I'd rather have a new house instead of a combination house and barn."

"Yeah, sometimes it stinks!" exclaimed Harvey.

"Sure saves on heat, though," said Annie. "Having the animals on the other side of the wall keeps the house a lot warmer. And we don't have to go far to milk the cows on cold and stormy nights."

Combination house and barn

"Wish we had our own gas pump too. You must be rich to have your own gas," said Marian.

Laughing, Annie said, "We're not rich. Joe has a little business selling Archer gas and oil on the side. Your Daddy buys here sometimes."

"I know. Maybe if we had a gas pump we wouldn't be running out of gas all the time."

"You'd still have to remember to put it in," mused Harvey, drawing a car in his Big Chief tablet.

After school, when the older children and Morgan had picked up Marian at Joe L.'s, Morgan asked her, "Well, what did you learn today?"

She thought a moment. Then she said, "That your grandpa and grandma used to live where Harvey lives now."

"That's right! Grandpa and Grandma Tschetter! And my mother, your grandmother, spent her first winter there with three little babies."

"THREE?" asked Cal.

"Well, Anna, Mrs. Joe M., was the only real baby. She had been born on the *Mosel*, crossing the Atlantic in May of 1879. But Elizabeth, Mrs. Jake L., and Paul, your Uncle P. P., were still small. Elizabeth was three and Paul two."

"So Grandma went home to her mother for the winter with three small children?" asked Pearl, amazed.

"You see, Father had just constructed a sod house south of where our horse barn is now and there was no stove in it, so it got awfully cold for small children. So she and the children spent the winter in that warmer combination house and barn."

"Yeah, the cows in the barn helped keep the kids in the house warm," chuckled Cal.

"There's another interesting story about Mother visiting her mother there. Like most young married women, she wanted to visit her mother one hot summer day. So two oxen were hitched to the wagon and Mother and the three children were put in the wagon. Mother directed the oxen with a *haw* and a *gee* (*gee* for right and *haw* for left). A rope was leading back from one ox's horn. Everything went well until they came to a lake on Johnny Gross's land. The oxen were hot and thirsty, so they just walked into the lake with the wagon and Mother and the three children in it. Brother Paul . . ."

"You mean Uncle P. P.?"

"Yes. Brother Paul says he remembers the water coming into the wagon box."

"How old would he have been then?"

"Old enough to remember. So it was probably not the first summer they homesteaded but a little later."

"What happened then?" asked Marian.

"When the oxen got cooled off, they walked out and took Mother and the children to their destination.

"How far would that have been—from the homestead to her parents?"

"The same distance it is today between our place and Joe L.'s place, but she wouldn't have been going on roads. It would have been cross country, about 3 miles."

Thursday, March 3, 1938
Our radio is quite busy after we come home from school. We charged the A battery once. Still have the same B batteries.

Saturday, March 5, 1938
Jake Walter and I went in to see Atty. J. C. Graber about Mensch's suit against us. Mensch's attorney, Wm. Metzger of Olivet, talked him into settling for $5 from each of us. Our horses didn't do that much damage, but it's better to settle that way.

"I think we got off pretty cheap," murmured Jake as the pair emerged from the law office.

"I'm glad the case didn't go to trial. Father would be pleased with the outcome. He didn't believe Mennonites should be litigious," said Morgan as he swung out of his diagonal parking place on Freeman's Main Street.

"Yeah, but when you're dealing with *nicht unsrege* or *Fremde*, they don't always feel the same way. They wanna get whatever they can."

"Metzger must have told Mensch I didn't have much money anyway. He knows my finances. He's chairman of the County Republican Party."

"Most of the money goes to the lawyers anyway."

"That's what Father always said. 'Settle without lawyers', he'd say. I had an idea once to study law, but Father objected. J. W. and P. P. too. He didn't want any of his sons to be lawyers. That's why J. W. and P. P. both became preachers."

Tuesday, March 8, 1938

Had 2 lambs today. The buck triplets born yesterday are in good shape. Fed the sheep cane and alfalfa all winter, with corn fodder that still had some corn on. We did not lose any sheep this winter.

Max is here visiting Cal. It is 9:30 and Pearl is still washing dishes. Ruth is drying.

Friday, March 11, 1938

Heard Norman Thomas, the Socialist, talk over the radio on the sharecropper question.

Just heard that Germany took over Austria without a fight. German troops marched in at noon. Hitler has control of his own country now. What next? I'm glad our people are out of there!

Sunday, March 12, 1938

Heard Adolph Hitler speak from Gratz, Austria. He spoke of a united German people. Not a fluent speaker but forceful.

Monday, March 14, 1938

Pearl stayed home from school to wash clothes and bake bread. She already is a good baker.

Tuesday, March 15, 1938

Was 20 min. late to school because the brake was stuck and we could not use the car. I walked to Jake Walter and he took me to school. Carl Schmeichel took me home in the evening. We released the locked brake and put on the chains because roads are very muddy. Got through with our chores at 11 p.m.

Wednesday, March 16, 1938

Practiced spelling and declam pieces most of the day. Pupils representing our school in spelling will be: Alice Nachtigal and Irvin Hofer, 7 & 8; Rosa Hofer and Luella Schmeichel, 5 & 6; Melvin and Selma Glanzer, 3 & 4; Deloris and Pauline Hofer, 1 & 2.

Thursday, March 17, 1938

Lineman, the county agent, and Fred Bender were here to take me to a Soil Conservation meeting at Summit #51. Lineman explained the new farm program. People are not very well pleased with it.

Sunday, March 20, 1938

Children went to church this morning. Sam Stahl came over for dinner with the children. Had C. E. in the evening. Cal sang in a quartet with Sam, Erwin Gross and Paul Glanzer. It was a fair program. 13 out of 14 numbers were delivered without substitution.

Monday, March 21, 1938

The county is graveling the road past Joe L.'s place. In school the children practiced running, jumping and ball throwing for rally day.

Hitler is now in complete control of Germany.

Tuesday, March 22, 1938

Elizabeth Kautz and Alice Walter taught for me since I went to a Republican meeting in Mitchell with Leon Weier, Turner Co. Rep., and his wife. Legislative members had a meeting and luncheon @ 35¢ at the Masonic Temple.

Cal was home seeding Burbank wheat on plowed land.

Wednesday, March 23, 1938

Practiced spelling and speaking in school. I even have to force the children to run and jump. They do not care to enter anything.

Thursday, March 24, 1938

School only in the forenoon. Many of the children wanted to go to Iva Kleinsasser's funeral, which was held in the Gym. Big crowd. Six girls were pall bearers. She died of blood poisoning, which started from an infected boil on her neck.

Cal started sowing Durham wheat this morning. We are drilling the wheat into the cornfield without discing in order to retain moisture.

A. C. Kaufman at Park Lane mill said he would pay same price for Durham as for Burbank. He wants to use it for cracking.

Friday, March 25, 1938

Had regional elimination spelling, speaking and athletic contests in our school. Got only one placing in declam – Sam Hofer, 1st in 7th & 8th grade. Got 6 places out of 8 in spelling.

Saturday, March 26, 1938

Got my petition from John L. and sent it to Olivet. He had 85 signers. Gus Freitag of Kaylor entered the race late and will oppose me in the primary for State Rep. Hutchinson Co. lost one seat in the House because of declining population.

Metzger & Bill Schenk will fight it out for States Attorney. Henry Gross & Wm. Tschetter are the candidates for County Judge.

Sunday, March 27, 1938

Taught Sunday School. Went to John J. B.'s for dinner and supper. In the evening we went to Bethesda Church for a program by pupils in the evening Bible school at Silver Lake Church. It was well delivered. Road crew started work on Highway 81.

Thursday, March 31, 1938

7th and 8th graders are working furiously on their book reports and essays required by County Sup.

Friday, April 1, 1938

Sam Hofer came along with me from school so he could go to the Academy play with us. "Campus Quarantine" was fairly well done for Academy people.

Pearl had a date with Benny Gross of Sully Co. He is a College student. She did not get home 'til midnight.

Saturday, April 2, 1938

Took six 7th & 8th graders from my school to the College for Campus Day. They had contests in ciphering, spelling, Bible and declamation in the forenoon and athletic contests in the afternoon. They also furnished a free lunch. Schools from Turner and Hutchinson Counties participated. My students placed as follows: Alice Nachtigal, 1st in oral spelling and Bible; Sam Hofer, 2nd in humorous reading; Florence Hofer, 2nd in ball throw and high jump; Ruth Schmeichel, 3rd in ball throw and 4th in oral spelling.

Monday, April 4, 1938

Joe P. Glanzer told me that Mary and Aaron sang over WNAX.

Ed Maendl, Cal & I went to Parkston for a meeting concerning the road leading past our place on the south. Hornbeck of the State Highway Commission was there and the District Engineer, Sparks. It seems that our road will not be built unless the county builds it.

Tuesday, April 5, 1938

Heard that County GOP Chairman Metzger tried to get Johnson out against me in the primary. Did not succeed so he got Gus Freitag to run. Metzger did not like my bill to divide the state north and south for Congressional districts. He said we had nothing in common with the voters west of the Missouri River. The real reason is, I think, that Karl Mundt and Francis Case would have to run against each other in the primary. Mundt was the biggest vote getter in the last election and they do not want to take a chance the Democrats could get in. I proposed the legislation because of the lopsided districts. There are 507,000 people east of the river and 167,000 people west of the river. In effect, Rapid City can elect the Congressman from the west district.

Wednesday, April 6, 1938

I am reading ANNA KARENINA. Tolstoy says about drinking, "The first glass sticks in the throat, the second flies down like a hawk, but after the third they're like tiny birds."

Cold and plenty of snow piled up. Gov. Jensen got stuck near Andrew Aman's place and stayed overnight. He was on his way to speak to the Lion's Club in Freeman.

Freeman P. S. was not open because of snow so Ruth came to my school. She likes country school.

Thursday, April 7, 1938

I ordered 2,000 blotter cards for campaign purposes. They cost $3.50 for 2,000. I'll have to fight it out with Freitag.

Our cows were not home when we got home. They finally appeared in Jake Walter's field.

Saturday, April 9, 1938

Took my contestants to Olivet for county contests. Sam Hofer got second on his piece. He was also elected secretary of the YCL.

Had two calves today. The purebred roan cow had a roan bull calf and the Jersey cow had a red bull calf. We now have three cows to milk.

Did some electioneering in town tonight. Met quite a few from Kaylor, Tripp, and Parkston at the contest in Olivet. I know Freitag will not get all the votes in that territory.

Sunday, April 10, 1938
All in church but Marian, who is at Tiahrts.
Docked the tails and castrated male lambs this afternoon. We have 24 lambs.

Monday, April 11, 1938
Had a bid to speak at Hickory Stick meeting in Tripp but got the letter in the mail at 5:30 and the dinner was to start at 6:45, so I did not start out.

Good Friday, April 15, 1938
Pearl and I went to Sioux Falls to get repairs for the car. Tiahrt boys replaced the muffler for me. Rained all the way home. Was so muddy we could not drive in by our mail box. Had to walk home. I carried Marian and Pearl carried the cat which Marian had gotten at Tiahrts.

Tuesday, April 19, 1938
Mary Klein started working for us. She will work 'til Academy is out. It will be better for Marian than tramping around.
Pearl and Esther Tiahrt went away with Benny Gross and Johnny Klein. Esther sang a solo over WNAX.
Mary and the children and I visited Mrs. Jacob L. Hofer, Sr. She is very sick with diabetes.

Thursday, April 21, 1938
Atty. Wm. Schenk of Tripp came to see me. I told him about the line-up Metzger, his opponent, has with Freitag, my opponent. Metzger wants to butcher one of us and he doesn't care who it is, just so he gets his job. We agreed Schenk would work for me in Tripp and I'd work for him in Freeman.

Saturday, April 23, 1938
Did some heavy campaigning in Menno. Dave Wipf said Freitag should get 2/3 of the votes out of Menno.
Some voters objected to my introducing school bills in the last session, especially the minimum salary for teachers and the 9 month school year.
Got my Soil Conservation check – $227.01.

Monday, April 25, 1938

Finished exams in school. I have 3 more days of school this week and then another later for review and final exams for the 7th and 8th graders. It would be better to have 9 months of school.

Tuesday, April 26, 1938

Children finished their drawings and I put them on composition wood. Made out the report cards for lower grades. I let all pass in lower grades. Some have poor grades but it is hard to keep anybody back in such a large school.

When I said I was going to town in the evening, Cal went upstairs to change clothes. I did not know he wanted to go along. He fell asleep and slept until I came home and woke him up. The girls thought I had taken him along.

"Somebody phoned for you and I told them you went to town," laughed Mary.

"Who was it?"

"I don't know."

"Male or female?"

"Male. He didn't say who he was and I didn't ask him. Didn't recognize his voice either."

"He might not have given his name if you had asked."

"I know. Too many rubber neckers on the line."

"We have about fourteen on Line 6 now. When you turn the crank, you can hear at least three or four receivers go up."

Wednesday, April 27, 1938

School picnic. Got 5 gal. ice cream from Co-op Creamery and put Pearl in charge while I went to Parkston to campaign. Saw Peckham on the street but didn't go into his office 'cause he said if the Republicans vote, they should vote for a real Republican, Freitag. I guess he thinks Republicans don't want to improve education. I expect to carry Parkston and vicinity. Made some very good contacts.

Thursday, April 28, 1938

Went to Olivet to have some absentee ballots mailed out. Before leaving Freeman I stopped at law offices of Gross and Graber. They told me to go to Metzger and call off our fight. I told them, "Nothing doing."

When I got to the county seat, Metzger called to me three different times to come to his law office. We finally made a truce that he would not work against me if I don't work against him. But I don't trust him anymore.

Had a long talk with Bill Schenk. He is sending out a circular letter answering Metzger's charges that Schenk spent twice the amount of money in two years in office that Metzger spent in four years in office. Schenk spent an average of $1374 per year for office expense and mileage whereas Metzger says he spent an average of only $687 per year.

Schenk is charging Metzger with seeking two offices at once, that of Parole Officer for SD and States Attorney for Hutchinson Co. I hope Metzger gets the best beating of his life. It will get him off his high horse.

Friday, April 29, 1938

Campaigned in Kaylor, Olivet and Menno. Had a long talk with Dave Wipf. Metzger is traveling the story in Olivet that I would be another J. J. Wipf, meaning that if I lose in the primary I will turn against the Republicans in the general election.

Gov. LaFollette is speaking in Madison, Wisconsin, tonight outlining the new party. I hope it is successful.

Saturday, April 30, 1938

Campaigned in Parkston and Dimock. Henry Rempher claims to be neutral, but Peckham has put in some work against me. Dentist E. R. Doering of Parkston is working in my behalf. He thinks the minimum salary for a country school teacher should be $75 per month, and a country school with all eight grades should employ two teachers. He also thinks minimum for grade teachers in city schools should be $100 per month and for high school teachers $150. Educated people know the value of education.

Sunday, May 1, 1938

All in church this morning. Mary's cousin, John Hofer, who lives near James River, fell from a horse and broke his neck. We visited there and Mary stayed for the funeral.

Plan to go to bed early to be ready for the last day of campaigning tomorrow.

Pearl went on a date with Benny Gross.

Monday, May 2, 1938

Campaigned in Freeman, Olivet, Menno, Tripp, Parkston and in Oak Hollow, Kulm, Beardsley and Susquehanna Townships. Got very sleepy going home. Election will be a very close contest.

Tuesday, May 3, 1938 Election Day

Tried to haul in some voters, but it's quite a job. Our Mennonite people do not have any interest. The Koerners and Amans bring their women folks while the Hutterische, *as a rule, have a hard time bringing themselves.*

We are getting the returns in Freeman very fast because the ballot was short.

I got beat by Freitag by 44 votes. Schenk got beat by Metzger. Only about 2,000 votes were cast.

In District I, there was a contest for County Commissioner, so they turned out a large vote. That was one reason Freitag beat me.

Wednesday, May 4, 1938

Had a bad night. Couldn't sleep well. The election actually affected me. It is not easy to lose. It makes one sick in the stomach. Politics is quite a game. A whispering campaign is hard to oppose. Someone started the rumor that I had said I could win without the Koerners, Amans and Mehlhafs. It is a lie but that is all right with some guys in a campaign.

I hauled manure today.

Evelyn came along with Pearl after school to help with housework. Ruth stayed at P.P.'s because she and Jean want to go to a play at the high school. Ruth likes plays a lot.

Thursday, May 5, 1938

Election effects are passing over. I went to town today to have a wisdom tooth extracted by Dr. Mike Wollman. The root broke off so he had to dig around quite a while to get it out. He charged me 75¢ for the job and gave me pills to relieve the pain if it gets too severe.

Friday, May 6, 1938

I dragged thistle field in order to plow it. Pearl is in town working on the Junior-Senior banquet.

Hauled rocks after school.

As Morgan threw the rocks into the wagon, he thought, "This one's for Freitag; this one's for Metzger. . . .Some of these rocks have been rollin' along so long they're all smoothed down. No rough edges left. Ground swellin' and heavin'. Buried for a while, then surfacin' again. Been here for ages. We move 'em around a little, but they're still here. I picked rocks here with Mother and Father. Big granite boulders."

Saturday, May 7, 1938

Cal and I raked and burned Russian thistles.

"How's come they're called RUSSIAN thistles?" asked Cal as he and his Pa watched carefully the dried thistles blazing, spitting and crackling.

"Because they really came from Russia. They are not native to the prairie. They were first noticed in Bon Homme County around 1874."

"Isn't that when the first colony was established?"

"Yep, that's it.

"So these pests were brought here by the HUTTERITES?"

"It's possible. But remember that Turkey Red Wheat was also brought from Russia by the Mennonites."

"We don't grow Turkey Red around here."

"No, it's too cold here. That grows best in Kansas."

"How can thistles spread like they do?"

"A thistle has a tremendous supply of seeds, about 20,000 over one large globe. And it loses its seeds over several months since some are loosely attached and others are practically buried in the stems and branches. Some thistles can even grow up from these branches if they get covered by drifting soil at fence rows."

Went to town with Mary and the little girls. Pearl attended and Mary cooked for the Junior-Senior Banquet. They came home after midnight.

Atty. H. L. Gross gave me the official count in the election. Officially Freitag beat me by only one vote, 1156 to 1155. The tally showed an error made in the poll book in Kulm Township so 43 votes cast for Freitag were thrown out by the canvassing board. It was clear that the intention of the voters was to vote for Freitag. The election judges of Kulm Township came to Olivet with the total figures but had no tally account. Because of this technicality the 43 votes were thrown out. So, technically, I got beat by one vote.

Sunday, May 8, 1938

Taught Sunday School. At Jake L.'s for dinner and supper. Went to Ortmans to see about renting an Allis Chalmers tractor. He said my neighbor Sam Schmidt has it 'til about May 20.

Visited Grandpa Tieszen in the evening.

"It's for the best, John," said his father-in-law. "It's God's will. It's too hard for the children at home when you're in Pierre."

"But they're getting older. They can assume more responsibility."

"Too many things can go wrong during the winter months. I remember Katherine crying over the frozen windmill pipes when you were in Pierre in '37."

"She was in the family way then," Morgan explained.

"*Ja.*"

Tuesday, May 10, 1938

I took Mr. and Mrs. Jim Prins and two of their four children to Sioux Valley Hospital. One of the boys had broken his leg years ago and was still troubled by it. Seems as though Jim could find nobody who would take them up. He promised to work for me for three days.

I learned about their problem when I was campaigning. You always learn about people's troubles when you ask for their vote.

While in Sioux Falls I stopped at the S.D. Wool Buyers. They pay 13¢ per lb. for wool now and 3-5¢ more later, depending on grade. Native wool is supposed to bring 17-19¢. Mr. Groenwald wanted me to buy wool for them in the Freeman community but I do not believe I can do the job justice so I sent him to Joe L. or Joe P. Glanzer.

Wednesday, May 11, 1938

Joe P. started to plow for me with his new John Deere tractor. He wants $1.10 per acre for plowing and 5¢ more for dragging. We will plant Minnesota #13, 3 kernels to the hill.

John Pettis, our new county agent, was here taking up a lot of my time. He has hybred seed corn he wants me to try.

Thursday, May 12, 1938

J. J. Mendel editorialized in the COURIER about my defeat: "The official count gives J. P. Kleinsasser 1155 votes and Freitag 1156. Kleinsasser lost by one vote. This will make many feel bad because they did not vote but were for Kleinsasser. So many figure one vote means little and stay home. It does not help a candidate to be for him unless you vote for him."

Friday, May 13, 1938

Spoke on school finance at a PTA meeting 4 mi. east of Bridgewater on Highway 16. Paul E. Hofer was chairman. They gave me $1.50 for travel expenses. This is the first money I ever got for speaking, as far as I can remember.

"Well, I appreciate being asked to speak on school finance here in McCook County. It's good to know there are some people actually interested in it. Usually I am asked to speak on how a bill becomes a law.

"I'm sorry you couldn't vote for me on May 3. As Paul said, I actually lost the election in large part, I think, because I was too interested in the schools. Some of my fellow Republicans smeared me by saying I wasn't a true Republican. I thought good schools were a non-partisan issue. That's why I introduced the bill which became law in the last session to take the election of County Superintendent of Schools out of politics, so the County Superintendent can now run on a non-partisan ballot, like the County Judge.

"As you know, like the rest of the nation, we have a serious problem funding education at all levels in South Dakota. And, because I am a farmer like most of you, you don't have to tell me the reason. The extended drought has forced many of our families to seek public assistance, depleting the aid funds of some counties. At the close of 1934, 39% of our state's population was on federal relief rolls. No other state had a higher percentage of population on relief than we did. 71% of all state banks had closed between 1920 and 1934, wiping out many a man's savings and resulting in widespread tax delinquencies with the counties holding tax deeds to millions of acres.

"As a result, the total indebtedness of South Dakota school districts was $17 million. Half the districts were operating on a registered warrant basis and many teachers were unable to cash their salary warrants.

"There was some improvement with the infusion of federal dollars into South Dakota, enabling aid to unemployed teachers, aid to school districts, part-time jobs for college students and loans to school districts so they could pay back-salaries of teachers. Some of our citizens were actually able to pay taxes to the local units of government which provide for schools.

"The South Dakota Education Association has been working on a long-range plan to improve the quality of education in our state. These are some of the items in the plan:

"1. *Nine-month term.* On the 16th of this month I will return to Summit #51 to begin reviewing with my 7th and 8th graders for their final county examination. They will have been out of school for about a month at that time. An extra month of instruction would do them more good. The younger children, especially, forget too much over the long summer vacation, and they cannot help too much in the fields anyway.

"2. *Larger units of administration.* We have far too many small enrollment schools since the birth rate has been declining and since so many people have moved from the state during the Depression. Before this decade is out, if present trends continue, we will have lost 50,000 people. With more cars available, we could save money by consolidating schools and transporting children to a neighboring school. My home district, Sunshine #26, had only four grade pupils this year, so our school board is paying their tuition to attend the Freeman Independent Public School.

"3. *State support for a minimum program of education.* We need an equalization of educational opportunity and that can best be achieved by state support on a per-pupil basis to districts with a tax base too small to support their schools. Eventually we must shift the burden of support from the local district to the state. Our counties and school districts are too unequal in population and wealth to depend upon local funding. Some counties have many, many acres of public lands from which they derive no tax income.

"In 1935 the state legislature took a giant leap forward with the enactment of the gross income tax. 50% was to go to common schools and 45% to be distributed to elementary and secondary schools on a per-pupil basis, about $10 for each school-age child in the state. In no case was a district to receive more from that source than it raised by a levy on property. That was to be distributed by the Commissioner of School and Public Lands along with the permanent school fund income, which amounted to a little over $3 per pupil. The remaining 5% of the tax went to elementary districts in distress, with 75¢ of the dollar to go toward salaries and 25¢ for other expenses. Of course, schools which wanted this help had to apply for it.

"A property relief act was also passed in 1935 to replace the gross income tax. It included a net income tax and a sales tax.

"When I was in the legislature last year we revised the formula for distribution so that of the amount going to the districts, 20% was to go to distressed schools and 80% to the other school districts. You may remember that it was called the Eighty Per Cent Fund, allotted to the districts on a per-pupil basis. Then we reduced the property tax levy in each school district accordingly. We also restored the state levy which had been removed in 1933. Now some are talking about abolishing it again in a special session.

"This may be more than you wanted to know about school finance, but since you're paying the bill one way or another, you should know some of the problems and the ramifications.

"I also tried to set a minimum salary for teachers. As the Depression eases we are going to find it difficult to get good teachers unless we can pay them a living wage. I had 20 scholars in 7 grades this year and taught for $55 a month. I could not feed my family on that, as you know. I have to farm in order to teach and teach in order to farm. And there are many more like me. I know my students are being short-changed, but I am doing the best I can. In the years to come we are going to have to pay more to attract and retain good teachers or our young people will not be prepared for adulthood."

Paul E. stepped to the front of the room. "Morgan, on behalf of the PTA, I thank you for coming out tonight and giving us such a thorough presentation. I know it is corn planting time and you probably left a field to come here. I smell the coffee, and the ladies have laid out a spread of sandwiches and cake. Why don't we have lunch now and then we can go into our question period later?"

"Suits me! I didn't have time to eat supper tonight, and I've been smelling that coffee for the last ten minutes."

"Okay, folks, get some lunch and then we'll come together again in 15 minutes for a discussion," said Paul, dismissing the audience.

"Morgan!" called Joe Wurtz. "I wanted to ask you, how can we get our people out to vote? Why, we may as well have stayed in Russia if they don't take their citizenship any more seriously than that!"

"You said it, Joe. It's very discouraging. I went around, registered folks, offered them rides to the polls, took them absentee ballot applications. They just seem apathetic. But when it comes to complaining about politics and politicians, they're good at that!"

"I wish I could've voted for you. You know, I think you should run for Congress, in a larger district. You're better known in parts of Turner County and McCook County than you are in western Hutchinson County," said Joe.

"Thanks for your vote of confidence. But running for Congress is out. I learned that in the last election. There's too much territory to cover in our Congressional District—half the state. But you're right about Hutchinson County. When I first was elected State Representative, we had two representatives and I ran only in the eastern half. But because of declining population in our county, we lost a representative and I had to run in the whole county. I live two miles from Turner County and not much more than that from McCook County, so many people who supported my candidacy could not vote for me.

"Morgan, here, have a sandwich! I know you always enjoy something good to eat," called out a plump lady from behind the serving table.

Sunday, May 15, 1938

I chaired the C. E. meeting in our church in the evening. Rev. Alfred Waltner spoke on Mennonite mission fields. We conduct work in Montana, Oklahoma, Arizona, India and China.

Thursday, May 19, 1938

This is the fourth day this week that it has rained. Small grain crops look very good. The rye pasture is just wonderful. We are milking five cows now. We should get some hogs to take care of the skimmed milk. We're feeding it to calves and chickens now. The chickens like it clabbered.

Sunday, May 22, 1938

Heard Dr. J. E. Hartzler speak on "Unfinished Temples" at the Gym tonight—on things we aim to do but can't accomplish. He said it is better to aim high and miss than aim low and hit.

Sunday, May 29, 1938

Our coal-fired brooder house got too hot overnight and around 50 chicks smothered. We had bought 185 chicks from Fensel at $5.50 per hundred. We hatched 240 chicks with our own incubator.

Went to the Tieszen homestead for Grandpa and Grandma's 50th wedding anniversary. Wish Katherine could have been there. 33 children, mates and grandchildren were present.

L to R, top row: Cal and Pearl Kleinsasser. Bottom row: Marian and Ruth Kleinsasser.

As the Kleinsasser family drove into the long driveway of the Jacob P. Tieszen homestead, three miles west of Marion, they passed a large machine shed where Uncle Abe Tieszen, who now lived on the place with his family, carefully stored his implements. "That's where we got the potato plow," Marian reminded her father.

Cars were parked all over the farm yard, and boys were darting in and out of the cars, standing on running boards, trying out the steering mechanisms, lifting the hoods to examine the engines or turning on a car radio to see if it really worked.

The women folks were carrying food to the long tables set up on the lawn under the tall elm trees. The tables consisted of thin boards laid over sawhorses and were covered with oil cloth. And what a bounty there was laid on them – fried chicken, baked ham, potato salad with home-made boiled dressing, deviled eggs (which Pearl had fixed), *Zwieback, Pluma Moos, Obstkrapflen, Pepar Krut*-flavored string beans. And coffee and lemonade to go with the fruit pies.

"Come over here and see the flowers Aunt Bertha has," said Cousin Arpah. "See, she has poppies, peonies, bridal wreath already blooming."

"I wish the mulberries were ripe. They have the longest mulberries I have ever seen – at least an inch long!" said Ruth.

"We have June berries and loganberries too, but they're not ripe yet either," said Darlene, who lived there.

Rev. Derk Tieszen, almost blind, said a prayer before dinner, blessing the food and the family assembled. After the feasting there was a brief program of Scripture reading, a meditation on the significance of the event, reminiscences of times past, and a prayer for good health and faithfulness.

David J. R. Hofer, a teacher who had married the youngest Tieszen daughter, Susannah, gave an historical sketch. He said Jacob P. Tieszen and Anna Kliewer had both been born in South Russia but came to America in 1874 on the ship, *Cimbria.* They were married on May 27, 1888, the year of the Great Blizzard in South Dakota, when many people had lost their lives. Four boys in the East Freeman community had perished trying to walk home from school. The Tieszens had nine children: George, Marie (Mrs. Jake Tiahrt), Jake, Anna (Mrs. Henry Tiahrt), Katherine (Mrs. John Kleinsasser), John, Eva (Mrs. Abe Wiens), Abe, and Susannah (Mrs. Dave J. R. Hofer). All of the children except Katherine were still living. They had, to date, 31 living grandchildren.

In closing, greetings were read from Kliewer relatives in California.

Monday, May 30, 1938 Memorial Day

Cal went fishing with the Wiens family while the girls and I went to Freeman for the Memorial Day celebration. Rev. J. E. Hartzler spoke on "America, Coming or Going?" He reviewed civilization from the Egyptians forward to the modern world. He said Jesus was the center of the drama because He put the individual above the institution.

In the evening we went to the Baptists (KMB Church). Jake Hofer from California is preaching there. We have lost so many South Dakota people to California that they are starting to come back and convert us now.

Tuesday, May 31, 1938

John L. and I went to Parker for a Soil Conservation meeting. They discussed the crop insurance program for wheat. Sounds good. We get hail once or twice every three years on this farm.

Wednesday, June 1, 1938

Went to town to get staples for fencing and other supplies. Saw quite a few sympathizers. It is too late now. The election is over.

We planted Cal's cane, low prussic acid, for his 4-H project. I planted 4 rows low prussic variety and 10 rows of Vaconia.

Thursday, June 2, 1938

Took a case of Leghorn eggs to Fensel to pay off our bill. We are all caught up now. Chicks are doing fairly well.

Cultivated potatoes with the corn cultivator.

Organized a sorghum and corn 4-H club at our place. I am supposed to be the leader. Cal was elected vice president. Eleven boys and Pettis were present. Pettis brought samples of varieties for all.

Friday, June 3, 1938

Rained during the night so I locked up the sheep and trimmed the manure and dirty wool off to prepare them for shearing.

Cal and Mary went to town. I gave them the cream.

Saturday, June 4, 1938

Mary went back to Spink with Prof. D. S. Wipf and took Marian and Ruth along for two weeks' vacation.

Cal had some barley ground for horse feed and mixed some of it with bran for calf feed (300 lbs. barley to 100 lbs. bran).

Sunday, June 5, 1938

Five of my 4-H club boys, including Cal, went to camp at Swan Lake. I took them to the Meridian station from where they drove with Pettis.

Had 8th grade graduation at Olivet. Alice Nachtigal was the third highest in the county. Nachtigals went with Pearl and me. Our car got a vapor lock in Olivet, so we had quite a time starting it.

Wednesday, June 8, 1938

Cal home from Swan Lake. He placed third in a weed judging contest and cut his toe while swimming.

Thursday, June 9, 1938

Cal started cultivating corn this morning but broke the rods that held the seat up. They had been cracked before. I rode to town with John Pfeiffer, the mail carrier, and sent Ries out to weld the piece. He has a handy welding outfit on a trailer.

Rode with Hugo Haar to Sioux Falls to get my car. They repaired the fenders for $18.50. Two months ago a different guy gave me an estimate of $24.50.

Bought Cal a jacket, shirt and socks. On the way home I stopped at John J.B.'s. Sister Katherine gave us 23 ducklings.

Friday, June 10, 1938

Pearl and I went to town. Got $4.50 for cream and $5.70 for eggs.

Saturday, June 11, 1938

Hauled 3 loads of alfalfa hay home, two with 3 slings to a rack. Pearl leveled the loads because Cal was cultivating.

Paul L.'s brought 7 started goslings which Lizzie had hatched from our eggs.

Pearl and Cal went to town in the evening while I stayed home. It was quite lonesome because the little girls are at J. W.'s in Spink.

Sunday, June 12, 1938

Taught Sunday School. Jacob B. preached. P. P. Tschetter is to be here beginning next Sunday for a series of revival meetings in our church. Jake L. and I went to a Catholic picnic north of Highway 16 where Emil Loriks spoke. When we got back to Jake L.'s, John L. and the boys were there with crabs they had caught at Gottlieb Schmeichel's place. Had a good time eating.

Johnny Klein came back from Kansas. He said no jobs are to be gotten down there because the rust is damaging the wheat. So he'll work for us.

Monday, June 13, 1938

Johnny started shearing sheep. One sheep died while he was shearing it. Apparently it choked to death. I sheared after I finished cutting alfalfa, and John went cultivating.

Tuesday, June 14, 1938

Cultivator seat that Ries welded for $2.50 broke down entirely.

Cal and I turned the raked alfalfa at noon. It was quite wet. Finished shearing sheep. We got two bags full from 28 sheep.

Wednesday, June 15, 1938

Pearl and I went to the Co-op Creamery picnic. Emil Loriks was the main speaker. Mr. Olson from State College spoke on pasturing and quality cream. He said all their cattle that bloated did so between 7 and 8 in the evening.

Saturday, June 18, 1938

Went to Sioux Falls to get Adeline. She had sent a card saying she'd arrive at noon on the Rock Island Line. I could not find her. From Sioux Falls I went to Viborg for a Burial Assoc. meeting.

Sunday, June 19, 1938

Did not go to church this morning since I got home from Viborg at 1:15 a.m. Cal and I went to the ball game in town in the afternoon.

Morgan on Freeman Academy ball team, 1915-16, in front of Old College building. Morgan kneels, far right, without cap.

Turning to his son as they sat on the plank seats behind the umpire, Morgan said, "Baseball was my game. I played third base for the Academy, and Paul L. and I organized what we called the Silver Lake Team. I was the manager. I remember one game with Dolton when we shut 'em out 6 to 0. Paul L. was the pitcher. We even had uniforms – gray with colored trim. Each member bought his own equipment."

"How'd you get from game to game?" asked Cal.

"By horse and buggy."

"Why'd you break up?"

"Father was opposed to my playing baseball, especially on Sunday. One time he hid my ball and glove. It rained that night and since he had hidden them in an old tank, my glove got soaked."

"Did you stop then?"

"Not really. I played regularly even after I was married. I remember we had a game near Dolton just a few days after your mother and I were married. Two of us outfielders collided while trying to catch a ball. My eyes were black and blue for a few days!"

"Did Ma make you quit playing?"

"No, but she didn't like it too much. Some of the other fellows' wives made them quit, though. Lizzie for one. She told Paul L. he was a married man now and should pay more attention to his family obligations. So the team gradually broke up."

"Were you good at it?"

"I had enough speed then to catch quite a few fly balls. Not like now."

Monday, June 20, 1938

Adeline came back from Chicago. I guess she could not make a go of it there. Or maybe she came back for romantic reasons. She went away with John P. Hofer tonight.

Ruth and Marian are still at J.W.'s. So now I have two of his children at my place while he has two of mine. Mine don't eat as much yet.

Cal sprayed the potatoes with arsenate of lead. The little girls weren't here to pick off the bugs.

Tuesday, June 21, 1938

Our white cow, daughter of Pauline, had a roan bull calf last night. We now have seven calves, all bulls.

John cultivated while Cal repaired the garden gate and made other repairs. Pearl was getting mad about calves getting into the garden.

I went to our school election at #26. Sam Schmidt was elected clerk. We decided to send our grade pupils to Freeman school again and let the high school-age students decide between the Academy or Freeman H. S. We are to get $6 per mo. for transportation.

Wednesday, June 22, 1938

Pearl is 18 years old today. Took wool to Sioux Falls with Fensel. Fleeces averaged 12 1/2 lbs. Got $45.76 advance.

Bought white paint for Cal. He wants to paint the tires.

Thursday, June 23, 1938

Rev. P. P. Tschetter came over for a visit. He will conclude his two weeks' revival in our church on Sunday. He was using Joe A.'s car.

In the afternoon Cal and I went to Olivet for the field day on Rames' farm. His corn and cane are much better than mine are. There were 3 speakers from State College. One was a weed expert.

Got the final grades for my seven 7th & 8th graders. We averaged excellent in the county.

Tornado northeast of Tripp demolished three farms.

Saturday, June 25, 1938

Went with John L., Jake L., Jr., and Paul E. to Mitchell to hear a Waters from Wisconsin. The speech did not amount to much. He damned the AAA and the Roosevelt Administration. Met Oscar Fosheim, Democratic candidate for Governor. I had quite a visit with him. He bought me a piece of pie and a cup of coffee. Came back after dark. We all had supper at Paul E.'s. Annie is a good cook. She made beef stew and noodles.

Sunday, June 26, 1938

I was in church alone this morning to take the Lord's Supper. We all went to church in the afternoon and evening. It was Rev. P. P. Tschetter's last meeting here. He is now going to Beadle and Spink.

Monday, June 27, 1938

Cal is running the tractor for Sam Mendel and Johnny is pitching hay for Joe P. Glanzer. I replanted cane because the cut worms got so much of it. #51 school board met and gave me a contract for $70 a mo. for 8 mos.

Thursday, June 30, 1938

Cal did not go out to cultivate corn 'til 5 p.m. because of the heat.

We have 50 tame ducks and 2 wild ones. They went into the oats field so we could not find them for a while.

Shook mulberries to eat with cream and sugar.

"Who planted your mulberry trees?" Johnny asked Morgan at the table.

"Your grandfather, Paul Kleinsasser, did when he homesteaded. They brought mulberry seeds and other seeds – like cucumber and watermelon seeds – along from Russia. A lot of mulberries grew in

189

the southern part of Russia, where they came from. They raised silk worms, too, on the leaves."

"Do you have any mulberry trees up in Spink County?" asked Cal.

"None left. They all died out in the drought."

"We could give you some little trees," offered Morgan. "There are little ones coming up all over, wherever the birds stop.

"It's too late to plant them now. Maybe next spring," said Johnny.

"Someone told me it's better to let the birds do the planting. When did your folks move up there, anyway?" asked Cal.

"Before you were born. In 1919. Land was very cheap at that time, I heard. Before we moved, we used to live in the northwest corner of this section; did you know that?"

"Yeah, Pa told me that—where the plum trees are now."

"People who went to Sully County bought as much as seven quarters of land from the sale of one or two quarters in Hutchinson County," said Morgan. "That was before the World War, prices were up, and some Mennonites were worried that there wouldn't be any more farm land for them to buy in South Dakota. They wanted to stay close to their people. Father mortgaged this farm to give J. W. and others a start in Beadle or Spink. Then, when the Depression set in, a lot of people lost their land."

Saturday, July 2, 1938
Pearl canned a half box of Bing cherries. I got a 12 lb. lug for $1.59.

Sunday, July 3, 1938
We all visited the grandparents this afternoon. Most of Katherine's brothers and sisters were there. Had a big supper. Dave J. R. was there from Minnesota. He wants to sell me some red barn paint for $1.20 per gal.

Heard Mr. LeTourneau, an implement manufacturer from Peoria, Illinois, speak at the Gym on four bankruptcies: physical, financial, moral and spiritual.

Monday, July 4, 1938
Pearl and the little girls went to Henry Tiahrts to do the washing. Marian fell on the sidewalk and cracked her head.

"Buddy had a rope tied across the gate and I didn't see it," wailed Marian, as Pearl picked her up off the concrete.

"Is that true, Vernon?" demanded Aunt Anna.

"Naw, it was just a little string. I expected her to break it when she ran through the gate."

"I don't understand why you're always causing trouble," said his sister, Esther.

"Well, it's bleeding. We can't stop the bleeding by blaming. I think we better take her to a doctor. Where's the nearest doctor?" asked Pearl.

"That would be Dr. Kaufman on Main Street in Marion. But I'd better phone him first and make sure he's there because it's the Fourth," said Anna, rushing to the wall phone. "Central? Get me Dr. Kaufman, please."

"Here's a wet towel," offered Esther. "I'll hold it over the cut to stop the bleeding."

"Dr. Kaufman was home. He said to come right in. He'll meet you in his office next door. We'll finish the washing, won't we, Ruthie?" coaxed Aunt Anna.

"I wanna go along. I wanna hold her," Ruth wailed.

"Cry baby!" teased Buddy.

"Be quiet, Buddy! You've made enough trouble for one day already," Esther scolded.

"Big fuss about a little bump!"

"She's got a hole in her head and it's bleeding! Her brains could come out!" shouted Ruth. "You're a big bully!"

"Are my brains coming out?" Marian asked Esther as they moved cautiously to the '34 Chevy.

"No, it's just a cut. But we should probably have it stitched up," said Esther as Pearl pulled out of the Tiahrt farm and crossed the Vermillion River bridge.

"What a way to spend a holiday! I would rather be at the union church picnic at Swan Lake."

"How ya doin', Marian?" asked Esther.

"It's starting to hurt. Do you see any brains yet?"

"No, not yet. Not even much blood. That's 'cause you're sitting up."

"Will it hurt when the doctor sews me up?"

"He'll probably deaden the pain before he takes the stitches."

"Here we are," said Pearl, turning into the doctor's driveway.

"Oh, it's the doctor that has the little deers in his front yard!" exclaimed Marian.

"DEER, not deers, little DEER," emphasized Pearl.

Inside Dr. Kaufman's office Marian was relieved to see the kindly doctor with jet black hair. "We'll have to shave a small area around the wound before we can sew it up. We can't have your golden curls getting in the way," he said. "How old are you, Marian?"

"Almost five!"

"Well! You're a big girl already. Soon you'll be going to school."

"I go to school with my Daddy sometimes. I go to his school, where he teaches."

191

"Ah, yes." Then, turning to Pearl, he said, "It's just about a year since your mother died, isn't it?

"It'll be a year this Sunday."

"Well, the first year is always the hardest," said Dr. Kaufman.

Laughing nervously through a cracking voice, Pearl said, "My Dad says the FIRST HUNDRED YEARS are always the hardest!"

"He takes the long view."

"How's your sister Ruth?"

"Okay. She wanted to come along but we persuaded her to stay back and help with the washing."

"I delivered her in the middle of a snow storm – in January, I believe it was. Couldn't get home for three days."

"That's why Ma had such good care, I guess," said Pearl.

After the cut was stitched up, Dr. Kaufman said to Marian, "You've been a very good patient. How would you like to take one of these figurines?"

"You mean one of these deers?"

"DEER, not deers," repeated Pearl.

"Thank you," said Marian, clutching a tiny doe.

Tuesday, July 5, 1938

Jake Walter was cutting grain when I got up at 4:45 this morning. Seems to be ambitious. Awful hot for horses. In the last two days of cutting we used up 50 lbs. of Mexican twine.

Wednesday, July 6, 1938

Raised binder to cut rye about 12 inches high. Rye straw is hard to cut, too rank.

Daisy hurt her frog and went lame in the afternoon. I had to get a horse from Jake Walter so I could cut 'til evening.

Cal wanted to go to a 4-H club meeting at P.P.'s. Because I had to return Jake's horse and get another one for tomorrow, I told Cal to come right home after the meeting. He got peeved at that and went to bed instead.

Joe L. said I could use one of his horses.

Thursday, July 7, 1938

Cal and I tried to lead Joe L.'s horse behind the car but she would not follow. So Cal had to ride her home.

Saturday, July 9, 1938

Grasshoppers are in the rye fields by the millions and have done a lot of damage. They eat the kernels in the dough stage.

Mrs. Henry Tiahrt, Edna, Esther and Buddy were here at noon. A year ago today Doc. Ernest took Katherine to the hospital in Sioux Falls.

Sunday, July 10, 1938
Just a year ago today at 1:30 a.m. that Katherine died.

Cal, Marian and I went to Marion to have Dr. Kaufman take a clamp out of Marian's scalp. Her sore is healing.

Pearl, Cal & Johnny went to a show in Freeman.

Some people were even cutting grain today.

Wednesday, July 13, 1938
Johnny shocked barley in the forenoon and rye in the afternoon. He says grasshoppers ate even the twine.

Pearl was over at Walters where they have a new baby boy named Carney Ray.

Friday, July 15, 1938
Boys finished shocking today while I cultivated cane. The flies just torment the horses. Creepers very bad. Ground is dry and hard. Hoppers are now attacking the cane. We celebrated the end of shocking by buying 3 quarts of ice cream.

Sunday, July 17, 1938
Dr. Pardee of the U. of S. D. spoke to the Welfare Committee at the College. He is in sympathy with denominational schools, especially the junior colleges. FJC is accredited by the University.

Monday, July 18, 1938
Cal and I are pitching bundles at Jake L.'s machine. Cal helps me, or, rather, I help him. Joe's rye bundles are very heavy.

Tuesday, July 19, 1938
Threshed rye and Ceres wheat at Joe L.'s Our horse Daisy was home this morning. She tore her halter rope.

Am pasturing six head of cattle at Sam Mendel's place. We are completely out of pasture and have been feeding ground barley.

Wednesday, July 20, 1938
Threshed Burbank wheat at Paul L.'s. Went straight to bed when I got home. Feel quite tired.

Thursday, July 21, 1938
Threshed barley and oats at Paul L.'s. Johnny is going home tomorrow. He worked here 11 days. I still owe him $8.30.

Friday, July 22, 1938
Marian and I took Johnny to Stanley Corner to hitchhike home.

As they neared their destination, Johnny turned to Marian sitting between him and Morgan and said, "I'm sorry I'll miss your birthday on Sunday. How old will you be?"
"Five."
"Seems like you're old enough to give ME a present for your birthday."
"Give YOU a present? People with birthdays are supposed to get the presents."
"No need to buy anything. How about singing my favorite song?"
"Oh, I can do that!" And she did.
"Oh, Johnny, Oh, Johnny,
How you can love.
Oh, Johnny, Oh, Johnny,
Heavens above.
You make my glad heart jump with joy,
And when you're near me, dear me, ..."

Got a letter from the Federal Land Bank. They are beginning to check up on income and expenses.
Threshed some real good oats at Jake L.'s. Cal is still pitching. He seems to like it.

Sunday, July 24, 1938
Very few people in church today. The KMB's had baptism in the creek. Had dinner and supper at John J. B.'s. Cal took the car to town and Pearl went away with a Stahl boy. It surely is lonesome here without Katherine.

Wednesday, August 3, 1938
Finished threshing at John L.'s and moved the machine here at noon. Threshed one truck load of rye when the belt tore. Boys got a new feeder belt, put it on, and in a few revolutions the feeder shaft broke. Got a new one that a Preheim had ordered for his machine. Expect to be going tomorrow.

Thursday, August 4, 1938
Finished threshing one field of rye, all the barley and started on the oats. At 6 p.m. the feeder shaft broke again. Machine must be wearing out. We've been threshing 16 days now.
Pearl has a lot of helpers: Sister Katherine, Eva, Anna Tiahrt, Mrs. Jake L., Jr. and Marjorie, and Clara & Marie Walter.

Friday, August 5, 1938

Boys repaired machine 'til noon. Had shaft welded in Parker for $5. John L. pitched for his boys who went with Cal and Pettis to Brookings for a livestock judging school.

Saturday, August 6, 1938

Finished threshing at 2:30 p.m. Our crew: Jake L., Jr., engineer; Paul L., separator man; Sam Ratzlaff, Art Adrian, Roland and Jakie Hofer, Harry and James Clancy and Jesse Dillon of Pond Creek, Oklahoma. Cal and I were grain men.

Had an 8 gal. keg of beer furnished by the boss of the machine. Some of the boys had too much, especially James.

Sunday, August 7, 1938

Did not go to church. Oklahoma boys left for North Dakota and Cal left for Black Hills 4-H camp.

Monday, August 8, 1938

Started to fence up stubble field so we can turn livestock in. Pearl helped.

Thursday, August 11, 1938

Cal wrote both Pearl and me from Camp Judson near Rapid City. He wrote Pearl that he's glad she sent so many quilts along.

I marked lambs and sorted out rams. Ruth helped.

Brought my cattle back from Sam Mendel's pasture. Paid him $4.55 for 23 days or a dollar a head per month.

Saturday, August 13, 1938

Cal washed and polished the car. It was extremely hot. Corn is gone for grain and now is burning up as feed.

Sunday, August 14, 1938

Rev. Alfred Waltner preached on Christian education, especially for FJC. Joe P. Glanzer and I are to go around collecting for the College next Wednesday.

Visited grandparents in the afternoon. They had attended the General Conference in Canada. Bethesda Church joined the Conference in 1897. Hutterthal Church has not joined yet.

Monday, August 15, 1938

Went to Yankton with George M. Hofer, who trucked 4 head of cattle for me. Netted $118.56.

Tuesday, August 16, 1938

Had car overhauled for $27. Had steering device fixed and piston rings put in.

Oklahoma boys came back after working in North Dakota only 4 days.

Wednesday, August 17, 1938

Prof. Ben P. Waltner and I were out collecting for the College among Hutterthal Church members. We got $25 in cash and $19 in pledges.

As they drove along the country road, Morgan asked, "Well, Ben, how do you like being president?"

"I'm not really president, John. I'm just acting president."

"You're putting on a pretty good act, then," said Morgan, laughing.

"The hardest part is raising the money, of course."

"When is Johnny Unruh coming back?"

"After he finishes his graduate study, in March of next year. That's the understanding. I'd rather be teaching biology or animal husbandry or raising bees on my farm. By the way, how is Calvin's 4-H project coming?"

"Both Pearl and Cal have livestock projects. And Cal is on the livestock judging team. He aims to represent our county at the State Fair."

"I'd like to bring my Animal Husbandry Class out to see your stock this fall."

"You may come out to look at it, but I won't be home. I'll be teaching again at Joe P. Glanzer's school."

"Well, if we can't use your farm as a demonstration project for animal husbandry, maybe we can get you to be a critic teacher for College practice teachers. I'll tell my sister Caroline about you."

Thursday, August 18, 1938

After digging 40 bu. potatoes the Oklahoma boys took James to Yankton to leave for home. Jesse is working for John L. and Harry came back to our place.

We had a 4-H meeting here tonight.

"Now you kids will have to stay out of the dining room and be quiet while the meeting is going on," insisted Pearl.

"Why? Why can't we be where the people are?" asked Ruth.

"Because you're not old enough to be in the club yet."

"Where do we have to stay?"

"You can stay in the kitchen."

196

"But it's dark in there."

"I'll give you a kerosene lamp and you can draw or color at the table. Now hurry up! A car just turned into the driveway. And don't go peeking through the curtains at who comes either. You can have refreshments with us afterwards," said Pearl, closing the door behind her.

Reluctantly Ruth and Marian opened their box of crayons and started drawing on used wrapping paper which had been flattened and stored. Through the door they could hear people arriving. First was John Pettis, the county agent, who had the farthest to drive. "Looks like we're finally going to get this club off the ground!" Pettis said.

"We called everyone to remind them, so we should have a good turnout," said Pearl.

The little girls were listening through the keyhole. "That's Melvin Hofer, I think," said Ruth as she heard Cal greet the newcomer.

"And Roland and Jakie," said Marian.

"That's Marvin now."

After the pledge of allegiance to the American flag and the 4-H pledge, the president called the meeting to order.

"One of my lambs died this morning," said Cal.

"Did you find out why?" asked Pettis.

"No. Looks like he ate something that poisoned him."

In the kitchen Marian spied a large gray book on the shelf. With the aid of a chair she reached it and brought the heavy tome to the table. She opened it to colorful illustrations. "Look, here's a map of the United States."

"That's no map, Dummy," laughed Ruth. "That's a side of beef with all the cuts marked. This is Mother's cook book."

"Oh! I wonder what's in that can on the shelf."

"Seer-up, I bet. Let's see."

Soon the girls were licking cane syrup off their fingers and wiping them on their dresses. Suddenly the door opened and Pearl stormed in. "I wondered why it was so quiet in here! Look at your dresses! Now you wash up and go straight to bed!"

"But you said we could have refreshments with the 4-H club," protested Ruth.

"You've already had your refreshments. March!"

With heads held low they proceeded through the dining room and the club meeting. Their exit was marked by peals of laughter from the 4-Hers.

Sunday, August 28, 1938

Katherine and I would have been married 19 years today.

Went to a Republican rally in Yankton in the afternoon. Gurney, Mundt, Bushfield, and Hammerquist spoke.

Monday, August 29, 1938
Started school at #51. I have 22 pupils, 11 girls and 11 boys in 7 grades. Have 5 first graders and no sixth graders.
Cal is plowing and Harry Clancy is painting the barn.

Tuesday, August 30, 1938
Cal took a trailer load of sheep to the county fair. Another one of his lambs died. Marian fell down the barn steps.

"What were you doing up in the hay mow, anyway?" asked Pearl, picking Marian up.

"I was throwing hay down for the sheep," she answered, wiping her tears with the back of her hands.

"Where does it hurt?"

"On my seat."

"You'll probably be all right then. I've told you a hundred times you have to be careful on those steps. The new hay makes them very slippery."

"What were you doing by the barn so you could hear me?"

"I was bringing Harry some lunch."

"Do you like Harry?"

"Of course. I like everybody."

"Does he like you?"

"I don't know. You'll have to ask him. Now, I've got to go back to the house and watch so the kerosene stove doesn't flare up. You coming too?"

"No, I wanna talk to Harry."

"Okay, but don't get paint on your dress!" instructed Pearl as she ran to the house.

Marian walked around to the west side of the horse barn where Harry was applying white paint to the barn trim. "Hi!" she said, sneaking around the corner of the barn.

"Hi! You startled me. What are you up to today?"

"I fell down the steps in the barn."

"I heard you cry. We're lucky Pearl was here or I would have gotten paint all over your dress picking you up. You have to be careful on those steps!"

"Where do you live?"

"Oklahoma. Pond Creek, Oklahoma."

"Where's that?"

198

"It's south of here, thataway," motioning with his dripping brush. "If you went to Freeman but kept going, you'd hit Nebraska, then Kansas, and then Oklahoma."

"How'd you get here?"

"My brother James and I – you remember him – James and Jesse Dillon, we all followed the harvest north. We went to Kansas first, worked in the wheat fields there, shocking and pitching bundles. Then we went to Nebraska, did the same thing there. Then we came here to South Dakota and got jobs on the thrashing crew your Dad and Cal pitched for. Worked here about 20 days. Remember when the thrashing machine was here and you and Ruth played in the grain in the trailer?"

"Yeah."

"We went up north, to North Dakota. But the crop was so bad we only got work for four days."

"Then what'd you do?"

"We thought about going on to Montana, but we decided to come back here instead."

"How's come?"

"Well, we like the cookin' here," he said, smiling broadly.

Friday, September 2, 1938

Went to Tripp this morning for teachers' institute. Took some pupils along to the fair. Stayed for evening program and fireworks. Got total of $23 premium money for sheep, both in 4-H and open class.

Saturday, September 3, 1938

At teachers' institute. Karl Mundt spoke. Prof. Harkness discussed visual education. Couldn't see because machine wouldn't work. Left Tripp about 5 p.m. and brought back a trailer load of sheep.

Monday, September 5, 1938

Cal and Ruth went to Freeman to school, Cal at Academy and Ruth at public school. Pearl is home cooking. Harry is plowing.

Tuesday, September 6, 1938

Max started at Freeman H. S. We had given him the first-year books that Cal used and had enrolled him in Academy, but I guess Jake couldn't come up with the tuition.

Wednesday, September 7, 1938

We are driving with our car this week, taking Walters and Glanzers along. Glanzers drive on alternate weeks. Walters are to pay $2.50 apiece per mo.

Sold 11 doz. eggs @ 19¢. Bought 12 lb. box of prune plums for 75¢.
Took my plow lays to town to be sharpened, but the blacksmith
shops were closed. They had reached an agreement not to work after
6 p.m.
Eddie Maendl came to have his 1930 Model A Ford insured for
$125 in the Mennonite Aid Plan.

Friday, September 9, 1938
Bon Homme Colony bought four yearling rams from me for $15
apiece. I paid Harry $10 and Joe L. $30 on gas account. Deposited
$10 in bank and bought a shirt for $1.35 and a red tie for 85¢.

Sunday, September 11, 1938
Harry and Cal went to the Bon Homme Colony with Harry's car.

"Were they serious when they invited us to come for church?"
asked Harry.

"Yeah, but their services are awful long. Sometimes they go on
for three hours, all in German."

"Well, I wouldn't be able to understand that."

"And the sermon is read out of an old collection of sermons
handed down from the olden days. So it's hard to stay awake. The
singing is real draggy too."

"Well, I'm glad you told them we'd come for dinner instead,"
Harry chuckled.

"Yeah, should be good. They might even have some wine or
beer. Depends."

As Harry's gray coupe approached the colony, it raised a cloud
of dust. Curious children dressed as miniature peasants appeared
as out of nowhere. Little boys with black cotton trousers and white
shirts came running, and little girls with tiny braids covered by
polka-dotted *Ticheles* poked their heads out of family apartments
to gaze at the strange outsiders. As Cal and Harry emerged from
the coupe, Cal asked the nearest boy, "*Wo ist deiner Prediger?*"

"*Er ist jetzt beim Schulhaus.*"

Turning to Harry, Cal translated. "He says the preacher is still
at the schoolhouse, where they hold church. The preacher is the
head of the colony. Let's walk up there."

They proceeded to a small, white clapboard structure with an
iron bell in its tower. Harry remarked, "I'm amazed to see so many
stone buildings out here on the prairie."

"Those are the first structures they made in 1874, when they
came from Russia. Bon Homme was the first Hutterite colony
established in the new world."

The preacher, Joseph Wurz, emerged through the door and extended his hand in welcome. *"Grüsse Gott."*

Cal introduced himself and his companion and explained their mission. "When your sheep boss bought some rams from us this week, he invited us to visit your colony. Harry here is from Oklahoma, and he's never seen a Hutterite colony."

"Welcome! We're always glad to show and explain our way of life. Too bad you didn't get here in time for worship. But dinner should be ready soon, and you're welcome to join us." Harry and Cal smiled and followed the preacher, who led them to a large dining hall where the men were already seated on wooden benches at long tables. *"Hier, setzen sie."* Across the hall sat the women. Children were not to be seen.

"Danke schön," said Cal.

After the preacher pronounced a prayer of thanks for the food, large bowls of steaming chicken noodle soup were placed on the tables by adult versions of the girls Harry had earlier seen peeking out of doorways. "They must be hot," Harry said to Cal, under his breath, taking in their long, dark, gathered skirts and aprons with blouses and weskits worn above. Dark scarves topped their braids.

There was little spirited conversation at the meal, just a subdued tone of informal cordiality and familiarity. Across the table Cal recognized some of the young men who had accompanied the "Sheep Boss" to Morgan's farm a few days before. They nodded mutual greetings.

After the noodle soup came steaming bowls of *Rindfleisch, Sauerkraut, Kartoffel Knödel und Pluma Moos.* Many helpings later another prayer of thanks was said and the men staggered to the door under their heavy loads. Older men were drawn to couches in private apartments. Younger men gathered under a large boxelder tree and began to pick their teeth with sharpened match sticks, sucking a few remaining tasty morsels out of the spaces between their teeth.

The Hutterites were curious about Harry's car, about Oklahoma, about the harvests he had worked on his way north to North Dakota. "We have colonies in Montana and Canada that we hope to visit before winter sets in," said Mike Waldner.

"How many colonies are there in South Dakota now?" asked Cal.

"Well, there's Jamesville near Utica and New Elm Spring near Ethan and Rockport near Alexandria," answered Daniel Wipf.

"Rockport. Isn't that where the C. O.'s were from that were persecuted at Alcatraz prison during the World War?" asked Cal.

"Yes, the Hofer brothers. They refused to wear the Army uniform."

"My sister Pearl read about them in her Mennonite History class at Freeman Academy," said Cal.

"Looks like we could have another war. Could be bad for us here. There's a lot of anti-German feeling going around. Lord knows, we're not for Hitler. That's the kind of militarism we were fleeing when we left Europe in the first place," explained David Decker.

On the way back to Cal's home, Harry had further questions. "How do they distribute the money among the families?"

"They don't. There is no private property, except for some clothes and household items. They believe that God's way is to hold all in common."

"Women too?"

"NO! Each person's needs are met and each person has a job or responsibility to the community. Did you see that old man cutting bread?"

"Yes."

"He's the *Brotschneider*. That's his job. He can't do field work any more, so he has a job to suit him."

"What do the women and children do?"

"Women cook and clean in shifts. They garden and can. Children go to school and take care of younger children in the *Kindergarten*."

"Sounds like a very orderly society."

"You might even say rigid. It's too structured for me. I need more freedom. I wouldn't want a boss telling me what to do all the time."

"But don't you have a boss now—your Dad—telling you what to do?"

"Yep, too much of the time. That's why I know I wouldn't like it all the time."

"They seem to be worried about another war."

"During the World War there was so much hostility toward them that some of their cattle were rounded up and shipped to Yankton to be sold to buy Victory Bonds. Some colonies closed down and moved to Canada."

"How many people are there in a colony?"

"About a hundred—counting men, women and children. When they get any bigger than that, a group splits off into a daughter colony and establishes itself somewhere else. There's no problem finding land in South Dakota. Plenty of land is still available, especially ranch land in large tracts."

"How do they get the money to buy land when many people are being forced off the land by foreclosure?"

"They are affected like everybody else is, but because they are so tight and have an economy of scale with lots of diversification, they usually make out better than individual farmers. They're usually smart enough to buy good land and locate near water, such as the James River or Wolf Creek."

"I can see why other farmers would resent them buying up land," said Harry.

"Yeah, that's a problem. And they stick to themselves and use the German language. That makes people suspicious. They also buy wholesale and that angers the local retailers."

Wednesday, September 14, 1938

Cal is 15 today and in Huron at the State Fair representing the county on the 4-H livestock judging team.

Harry is plowing. Adeline came back to work, so Pearl is going back to school.

Sunday, September 18, 1938

Pearl, Adeline, John P. Stahl and John P. Hofer left at 7 a.m. for Beadle and Spink.

Cal, Ruth, Marian and I went to Abe Wienses but they weren't home. Went to George Tieszens for the afternoon and stopped at Henry Tiahrts. It is sometimes hard to get a meal at the Low Germans.

Monday, September 19, 1938

Adeline and Pearl got back at 1:30 a.m.

Had first frost of season. James Clancy and another boy from Oklahoma came up today. They cut down some dead trees to pay for their supper.

Saturday, September 24, 1938

Have three hired men from Oklahoma working on foundation for new tank house. Bought 200 lbs. Pride of the Rockies wheat flour for $5.25. Pearl and Adeline have been doing a lot of baking.

"Get me a sifter of flour, Ruth," directed Adeline as the young girl entered the kitchen.

"Can't reach it. The flour is down too far in the barrel."

"Take a look," said Adeline.

Ruth lifted the tightly fitting cover from the metal barrel and peered in. "Why, it's almost full. Daddy musta got a hundred pounds of flour."

"No, if he'd only gotten a hundred pounds, you still wouldn't be able to reach it. He got two hundred pounds."

"Wow! Where are the flour sacks? I wanna see the patterns."

"They're out in the pantry in the dirty wash, but they still need to be opened. If you bring them here, I'll get you started so you can pull the stitches out."

"Then will you make me a new dress?"

"Not today. We have too much Saturday work to do today, but when I get time, I will."

Ruth brought the flour sacks into the kitchen. "There's one blue flowered pattern and one red one."

"Which color do you like the best?"

"I like the blue."

"Okay, then, Marian will get the red one."

"Let's supprise her. She likes supprises!"

"Okay, but now I need some help kneading the flour into the dough. Wash your hands and help me. We got to get this bread rising in time for dinner. We're out of bread and we got three more men to cook for today."

Roswell Bottum of Sioux Falls was here to sound me out on a special legislative session. He wants to keep Gov. Jensen from calling it. I agree and will write Jensen.

Germany might march into Czechoslovakia. All of Europe is roused up ready to go to war.

Thursday, September 29, 1938
Hitler, Chamberlain, Mussolini and Daladier had a conference today. They want to settle the Sudetenland dispute.

Saturday, October 1, 1938
Cal, Pearl and I sang in our church choir at the Sunday School convention in Bridgewater. Our singing was bad because we did not have a piano and we could not hear the pump organ.
Brother J. W. and family stayed here overnight.

"Well, well, well, look who's here!" said Rev. J. W. Kleinsasser as he entered the homestead after the service and greeted his nieces and nephew with a hand shake and a hug. His gray felt hat had its familiar three dents in the high crown. "Is my Adeline taking good care of you all?" he asked, giving his daughter a bear hug.

"Just fine!" said Cal. "Don't we all look pretty well fed?"

"Sure do! You must've had a pretty good potato crop this year," he said, chuckling.

Rev. J. W. Kleinsasser

"You used to live here?" asked Ruth.

"Sure did, where the plum and chokecherry trees are now. Still getting any fruit off those trees?"

"Not much. It's been too dry. Just enough plums to bring home in my pockets, usually. O'course, I sample quite a few when I'm working in that part of the field," Morgan laughed.

Sunday, October 2, 1938

Attended S. S. convention in afternoon and evening. Had supper at George M. and Maggie's. Had to sit on bleachers in Bridgewater gym. Have a back ache as a result.

Wednesday, October 5, 1938

Miriam Glanzer went to Yankton for Pancake Day one day before exams. Mrs. Joe L. took Deloris to Yankton to have her glasses checked. It seemed to me that pancakes also had something to do with it.

John P. Hofer took Adeline to John J. B.'s so Aunt Katherine could take care of her while she recuperates from infected wisdom tooth. Pearl has to stay home from school to cook for the Oklahoma boys who are picking corn. Poor Pearl!

Thursday, October 6, 1938

Signed papers for wheat loan at Federal Land Bank in Freeman. Intend to use wheat loan money to pay 1936 taxes and half of 1937 taxes.

Friday, October 7, 1938

I was elected to the local Soil Conservation Committee. Harry Clancy and Jesse Dillon left for Minnesota to husk corn.

Tuesday, October 11, 1938

Went to Mitchell for a Soil Conservation meeting and stayed for a Democratic rally.

Wednesday, October 12, 1938

Pearl went to Academy play practice in the evening although she's been out of school for a week due to Adeline's illness.

Friday, October 14, 1938

Had Republican rally at #51. Candidate for States Attorney, Metzger, was the main speaker. His subject was the WPA sanitary privies in relation to soil conservation. He read the directions for the toilet and then poked fun at them. He said people should check up on their Soil Conservation committeemen. He charged committeemen with increasing their acreage while reducing others' acreage.

All county candidates were present, including Freitag.

Saturday, October 15, 1938

John P. Hofer took Adeline to Beadle Co. They are supposed to have an engagement party tonight.

John L., Paul L., Jake L., Cal and I went to Mitchell with my car to hear Sec. of Agriculture Henry Wallace speak. There was quite a crowd. The speech was broadcast over WNAX. Cal and I shook hands with Wallace. I talked to Emil Loriks and Oscar Fosheim.

Sunday, October 16, 1938

I was working on report cards this morning. Pearl and Marian went to Spink Co. with John P. Stahl for John and Adeline's engagement party.

Cal and I went to John L.'s for supper. John gave Cal a haircut. Then went to Leon Weier about Burial Assoc. matters.

The cows did not get milked tonight. Pearl is not home at midnight.

Monday, October 17, 1938

Pearl came home from Spink at 5 a.m. Marian stayed there with Adeline.

The WPA toilet gang did some more work at the school. They cut a door into the horse barn so it can be used as a car shed.

Pearl went to play practice in the evening while Ruth stayed at P. P.'s.

Went to Republican rally at Clayton. I had the honor to introduce Earl Hammerquist of Farmingdale, candidate for Commissioner of School and Public Lands, who was the main speaker. They tell me I gave him a good send off. He made a good speech and garnered many votes, I think. He stayed overnight with us.

Tuesday, October 18, 1938
After breakfast with us, Earl Hammerquist left for Chester. They are to have a caravan campaign in Lake Co., Karl Mundt's home county.

I got up at 4:30, looked for the cows with a lantern, but could not find them.

Thursday, October 20, 1938
Heard Sen. Bulow speak in Freeman after supper. He did not make much of a speech. Other candidates were on the platform but none spoke.

Friday, October 21, 1938
Cal, Ruth and I saw "The Plainsmen" movie in Freeman. It is a S. D. pioneer story. Got my school warrant – $63.

Saturday, October 22, 1938
Snowed this morning. Paid John A. Wipf $5 on radio, Julius Albrecht $4.25 for repair of armature on Chevy. Bought bu. apples for $1 and a half bu. tomatoes for 50¢.

Sunday, October 23, 1938
In church this afternoon and evening for Mission Fest. In the afternoon Rev. David Tieszen, Peter Stahl and Abe Duerksen spoke. Tieszen is related to Katherine. In the evening David Schultz spoke. The collection was $153, less than last year although we had a better harvest this year.

Monday, October 24, 1938
Max, John L. and Roland, and Cal and I went to a Republican rally in Menno. Bushfield and Gurney and Miss Olive Ringsrud, candidate for Secretary of State, spoke. County candidates were introduced. Had a big crowd. Atty. J. C. Graber is now chairman of the county GOP.

Someone visited us while we were away.

"How do you know?" asked Morgan.

"Cause when I got home from play practice, the dishes had been washed and the floor swept." 207

"Oh, I thought you and Ruth managed to clean up before you went to Freeman."

"No, I just made it in time for practice. Miss Loewen has a fit if anyone is late."

"Well, it was prob'ly Sister Katherine."

"I hope do. She wouldn't be shocked if she saw our dirty dishes on the table and spread the word all over Kingdom Come."

"People who place more value on washed dishes than on an education – we don't have to worry about their opinion," Morgan asserted.

"It's kinda spooky wondering who was here – anybody walking in. You know, I think we ought to get a key for the front door and lock up when we leave," suggested Pearl.

"What? We'd have to get at least four keys for people coming and going at all hours. And then we'd have to worry about people forgetting or losing their keys and being locked out. No, we're not going to start that. We've never had keys for our doors. Don't believe in 'em. Besides, people couldn't get in to do the dishes!"

"But tramps could be sleeping here when we get home," said Pearl, apprehensively.

"Look, my father and mother lived on this place when Indians still roamed around occasionally and they never locked a door!"

"I know! Grandma told me about an Indian who just walked in the door. The only way to communicate with him was to give him a slice of bread with jelly on it, she said."

"We often had 'men of the road' stop for a meal because one would leave a message for another such as a stone on top of a fence post, meaning this was a good place to get a meal. Mother never let anybody go away hungry. Even gypsies would come by and play their instruments and dance in exchange for food."

"But gypsies steal. What if gypsies came by while we were gone and walked into the house and took something?"

"We don't have anything of value in this house that someone might want to steal. If they need food or something like that more than we need it, they're welcome to it."

Thursday, October 27, 1938

I am keeping the girl pupils in at recess for a whole week – all 11 of them – because they did not act properly on the school ground during the noon hour.

"Miriam says you're not being fair to the girls 'cause the boys were just as bad," said Joe P. as he stopped at the school the next morning.

208

"I can discipline only for what I see or know. And through the window I heard the girls daring the boys to open their *Schlitzes* if the girls pulled down their pants," said Morgan.

"What I heard was that the boys dared them first," offered Joe P.

"That could well be, but I heard the girls taunting them, and I expect better behavior from the girls than that!"

"I agree. We can't have that going on in school. And they're going to get it worse at home!" vowed Joe P.

"I wish I could be with them on the playground all the time. But with 22 children in 7 grades, I need to catch my breath during recess once in a while or prepare for the next period."

Friday, October 28, 1938

Cal, Joe L., John L., Jake L. and I went to Menno to hear Oscar Fosheim, Dem. candidate for Gov. He gave me a few good compliments – something about being one of the progressive Republicans in the legislature. We had lunch together after his talk. I suppose I will get criticized for doing it.

Sunday, October 30, 1938

We got up at 10:30 this morning. I wanted to see whether Cal and Pearl would wake up alone. I gave it up at 10:30. We, of course, were not in church.

In the afternoon the Henry Tiahrt family came over.

Monday, October 31, 1938

Children had a YCL program in school on the Halloween theme. Moses Glanzer is president. After the program they served sandwiches, cake, potato salad and fruit nectar. Lower grades made Halloween pictures.

Got a statement of account from Federal Land Bank. $1,344.96 in back interest and principal was due Oct. 25. How I will make these payments, I do not know.

Wednesday, November 2, 1938

Leo Temmy, Rep. candidate for Atty. Gen. of Huron, was in Freeman to give a political talk. He did quite a bit of knocking the farm program, particularly the slogan, "Cost of production plus a fair profit for the farmer." If that law were ever allowed to materialize, it would be all right. But I am afraid it is just another slogan.

Thursday, November 3, 1938

Today was the National Corn Huskers Bee at Dell Rapids, 22 mi. north of Sioux Falls. There were 21 huskers from 12 states. Ted Balko of Redwood Falls, Minn. was the winner and got $100. There was an immense crowd estimated at 137,000. Good display of machinery, hybred corn, etc. Long lines at eating stands. Pearl and I went along to Sioux Falls with Tiahrts, then by train to Dell Rapids field. Someone stole $21 from Henry Tiahrt soon after we got on the field. Paid 50¢ for round trip train ticket. Spent 5¢ on the field and had 40¢ supper in Sioux Falls at the Motor Mart.

Had no school today. Max helped Cal do the chores.

Friday, November 4, 1938

Marian came back from Spink with Adeline and John P. Hofer. Then Adeline and John went to Olivet to get a marriage license.

Saturday, November 5, 1938

Wedding party practiced at church in the evening. Johnny, Jake and Paul Kleinsasser are staying here overnight.

Sunday, November 6, 1938

At 2 p.m. Adeline and John were married at our church by J. W. Went home to do chores and then to Joe A.'s for wedding supper. Then about 8 o'clock we had a peanuts, apples and cake lunch. Had a fair program.

J. W. has turned into a strong Republican. Maybe he has a job promised.

Tuesday, November 8, 1938

Election Day. A fair vote is turning out. I voted after school. Did not vote a straight ticket.

Went to town after school. Had a tally meeting in City Hall. We got all the returns from the 35 precincts in the county.

Wednesday, November 9, 1938

Got home at 2 a.m. Republicans happy, Democrats in dumps. Republicans won every major position in S. D.: Bushfield, Gov.; Olive Ringsrud, Sec. of State; Mundt, U. S. Rep.; Gurney, Sen. Mundt and Gurney were both defeated two years ago. Only Democrat who won in our county was Ed Weidenbach, auditor.

Thursday, November 10, 1938

Acting Pres. Ben P. Waltner came to my school to discuss making me a critic teacher and using my school as a laboratory for College Normal students.

Friday, November 11, 1938

Had a short Armistice Day program. It is just 20 years since the end of the World War, a totally useless war. Thank God a second world war has been averted. Our people have suffered enough from the anti-German hysteria of the World War.

The Academy presented their play, "The Family Doctor." Pearl played the role of Hannah, the doctor's housekeeper. It was well presented. Alfred Nachtigal played the role of a business man. After the play Pearl brought home the "props" for the girls to eat. They especially enjoyed the stuffed olives.

Sunday, November 13, 1938

Had C. E. at our church in evening. Rev. P. R. Schroeder spoke on the evils of tobacco and alcohol. He stated the Boy's Contract with the Brown Diabolus:

"If only you will let me have cigarettes, I agree:
1. To pay out $5,000 in 50 years.
2. To carry around a spasmodically beating heart.
3. To invite hardened arteries.
4. To impair oxygen-carrying power of blood.
5. To exhale foul breath.
6. To practice filthy habit of spitting.
7. To run risk of cancer of mouth.
8. To display stained teeth.
9. To cut down athletic ability.
10. To lower productive efficiency.
11. To shorten life expectancy by 7 years.
12. To accept duller brain.
13. To deaden moral & spiritual power.
14. To become pitiful slave to ceaseless craving from which I shall have only one chance in 100 to escape."

Tuesday, November 15, 1938

Had meeting with Marie Waldner, librarian, and Joe Graber to plan a solicitation of alumni for College library. We divided the alumni up according to church affiliation, if possible.

Wednesday, November 16, 1938

Just heard a broadcast from Catholic University concerning the Jewish persecution in Germany. The Germans under Hitler are depriving the Jews of their property and civil rights.

Thursday, November 17, 1938

County nurses came to school to work with the children. Most of the children had made good gains. Miss Kopel complimented them.

Friday, November 18, 1938

Amos Tschetter gave an interesting talk at the College on his trip to Europe. The Jews are being driven out of Germany. Their property is being confiscated. The U. S. might let them enter our country.

Saturday, November 19, 1938

Paid Aid Plan insurance $4.52. Bought hat for $3.75. Had teeth cleaned for $1 and paid Dr. Wollman $10 on account. Paid White Eagle $2 for gas.

Cal hooked to a solid rock while plowing and broke one of the lay points.

Benny Gross from Sully was here looking for Pearl. She was in town with Cal.

Sunday, November 20, 1938

P. P.'s borrowed a team of horses, Bullet and Nelly.

Pearl went away with Benny Gross and is not home at 11:45. Girls and I had some sauce before they went to bed. I'm ready too. Graded papers all evening. It is raining now.

Monday, November 21, 1938

SDEA Convention in Mitchell. Bradley Young of Mitchell, Adam Pressler of Selby and I are on a legislative committee. In the morning we heard Dr. Sutton of Atlanta, Georgia, speak on character and education.

Tuesday, November 22, 1938

At SDEA. 3600 people attending. I am sampling books from publishers. Really enjoy looking at the books.

Bishop Oxnam of Omaha spoke in evening. A sure fire speaker, very powerful.

Wednesday, November 23, 1938

Last day of SDEA. Program rather light. Packed house. A few outstanding numbers: Janice Porter, a singer; a whistler and a juggler.

I was on the nominating committee today.

Got a few more books to sample.

Not much of a program for the Rural Division. Miss Zehnpfennig is chairman for 1940.

Thursday, November 24, 1938 Thanksgiving.

Home today. Had duck and dressing for dinner. I read, listened to radio and corrected papers all day.

Max was here to play Ping Pong in the evening.

Some strange calves are here now.

Friday, November 25, 1938

Had school today. Max and Cal hauled straw around the water tank for insulation.

Had Thanksgiving program at school during YCL period.

Took cream to town after school. Sells for 25c per lb. butterfat.

Car developed bad knock because it loses oil.

I deposited $169.02 in bank to pay taxes.

Saturday, November 26, 1938

Cal, Max and I worked all day in sheep barn fixing up a good feeding rack with 2x4's. Graded papers all evening. Paul Decker came looking for his calves.

Sunday, November 27, 1938

Taught class on "Thou shalt not steal."

Heard Father Coughlin over the radio from Detroit. He criticized the Russian Jews. Said Nazism comes from Communism. Newspapers and radio are attacking him, and he was defending himself.

Monday, November 28, 1938

Saw Miss Caroline Waltner at College about the practice teachers. She intends to send two shifts up, one in forenoon and other in afternoon. Four teachers are to be in each group.

I received 20 textbooks and workbooks for inspection from publishers displaying at SDEA.

Tuesday, November 29, 1938

8 practice teachers came out.

Cal took his first shave tonight. He had to let them grow a while in order to find them, that is, after putting on the lather.

Wednesday, November 30, 1938

LeRoy Graber does not seem to be getting along very well as music director in my school. Must make a change. Della Graber does good job teaching art and primary reading.

Thursday, December 1, 1938

Paul Hofer is now the music director. Co. Sup. visited school this afternoon. She told me to give Vivian Hofer extra work in Reading as she gets done too soon.

Went to town at noon with one group of practice teachers to see the feed loan representative, but he was not there. Went back with other group of teachers.

Children now have their play supervised and have longer class periods.

Friday, December 2, 1938

Very interesting having all the practice teachers. We are making a drive to sell the most Christmas seals per capita in our group, the over 20 group (big group). They are to help eradicate tuberculosis.

Saturday, December 3, 1938

Beautiful weather. Because our car is still in repair shop, we used Richard Waltner's car to drive to Leon Weier, who took us to Viborg for last Board meeting before annual meeting of the Burial Assoc. I got check for $63 (per diem, mileage & salary as director).

Sunday, December 4, 1938

In the afternoon we went to the Gym to hear the College broadcast by remote control over WNAX. Exactly 100 people were involved with the performance. Pearl and Cal both sang.

Monday, December 5, 1938

Miss Caroline Waltner observed the practice teachers today. She was not satisfied with the physical surroundings, so the girls are washing the windows and seats.

Pearl sold a ram, #77, to J. B. Hill of Mitchell. He is to go on a farm near Vermillion. Pearl is a good sales girl.

Tuesday, December 6, 1938

Rode home with one of the practice teachers, Leonard Preheim. I get home much earlier that way. Cal came home when the sun had already set.

Wednesday, December 7, 1938

Pearl bought a coat from Shriver and Johnson in Sioux Falls for $13.

George Tieszen was here for a ram. I had traded with him.

Cal came home quite late. They were practicing for Founders' Day at College.

Cows have very little milk, but the pullets laid 13 eggs today.

Thursday, December 8, 1938
Warm enough for children to play outside at recess. Miss Edelman, one of the practice teachers, took the primary grades to the basement to play and sing with them. They enjoyed "Here We Go 'Round the Mulberry Bush."

Bertha Walter came over to do the housework for Pearl but we overslept so Pearl stayed home and they both did the washing and other housework. I paid Bertha 50¢.

Cal is supposed to give a report on his trip to the Conservation camp in the Black Hills but he's looking for an excuse to get out of it.

Joe S. Glanzer was in school taking measurements to build a book case.

Saturday, December 10, 1938
Marian and I went to Olivet for teachers' meeting. She wanted some picture books. She got them. Her favorite is FERDINAND THE BULL by Munro Leaf. Ferdinand must be a Mennonite because he does not like to fight.

Sup. of Public Instruction I. D. Weeks spoke.

Bought a suit from Schamber's for Cal for $18, including two shirts. He sold two rams to Ed Schumacher of Parkston. Got $27 for the two.

Sunday, December 11, 1938
After church we went to Tiahrts for dinner and supper. Even had ice cream. Went home, did the chores and then went to Freeman to hear the East Freeman Band and Village Choir. They charged 15¢ admission. They want to establish a fund for some deserving student.

Alfred Nachtigal was one of six who gave his speech over WNAX concerning T. B. and the sale of Christmas seals. Hope he wins first prize of $70.

Monday, December 12, 1938
John and Adeline came over. They might take the Jersey cow for what I owe her in labor. I owe her $35.

Tuesday, December 13, 1938
Cal brought some sweeping compound to school from Wipf Bros. Pearl went to the Gym with Johnny Stahl. Sunnyside Bible Academy is giving a cantata with Ed Crum as director.

Wednesday, December 14, 1938

Called off school so practice teachers could go to College Founders Day celebration. I also was there all day and evening. Saw Mrs. Louis Linscheid, Katherine's cousin. Linscheid is the preacher at Bethany Church now.

College gave very good pageant, "There is Room," with Prof. Gerhard Toews directing. 120 voices involved. Cal and Pearl both sang in the chorus, Cal baritone and Pearl soprano.

Thursday, December 15, 1938

Cal gave his report at the county 4-H banquet. Atty. H. L. Gross gave a talk on juvenile delinquency. Not so good. Missed the subject.

I substituted for Amos Kleinsasser. How bad mine was, I do not know.

Marian and Ruth stayed with Jake Walter family during the evening.

"I wanna hold Carney Ray," said Ruth, after the girls had taken off their wraps.

"No, I wanna hold him!" insisted Marian.

"You'll both get your turn to hold the baby," said Mrs. Walter.

Lily Rose and Leona Jane, Carney Ray's little sisters, were themselves sitting in the rocker before the kitchen stove, rocking their brother.

"Did you have supper?" asked Mrs. Walter.

"No, Pearl didn't make supper because they all went to the banquet," said Ruth.

"Well, then, you can eat here. Set two more places, Bertha."

"Where do you want to sit, beside Marie or Max?" asked Bertha.

"I want Ruth to sit by me," cried Lily Rose.

"And I want Marian to sit by me," cried Leona Jane.

"All right! We got plenty of room on this side of the table. We'll just squeeze in two more plates. You can all sit on the bench," said Mrs. Walter, gathering Carney Ray in her arms.

"Wish we had a baby brother," said Ruth.

"Well, maybe you will have, one day," said their hostess.

Friday, December 16, 1938

John and Adeline came for the Jersey cow. I gave it to Adeline partly for back wages and the rest for a wedding present.

Saturday, December 17, 1938

Went to Sioux Falls with Eddie Maendl instead of going to our annual church meeting. Bought some dresses for Ruth and Marian and also some articles of clothing for Cal and myself.

216

Johnny Klein came down from Huron where he is attending Huron College. He has two weeks of Christmas vacation.

Five different people were here to look at the 5 bull calves we have advertised for sale. No sales.

Sunday, December 18, 1938

Home all day but went to Gym in evening to hear Rev. Smucker of Bethel College. He is a very interesting speaker. Makes his sermons too short.

Monday, December 19, 1938

Had Marian with me at school. Practice teachers are still at it.

Tuesday, December 20, 1938

Practice teachers took over the school this afternoon while I went to the annual meeting of the Burial Assoc. in Viborg. We adopted new by-laws making it a cooperative but we want an opinion from the Atty. Gen. about cutting out proxy voting.

Took a ride in a new Plymouth, one of those high-wheeled ones with plenty of clearance.

Heard Rev. Smucker again at the Gym. His topic was "The Lord's Prayer."

Wednesday, December 21, 1938

Practice teachers put up our artificial Christmas tree this morning. Children made decorations for it. Marian was along.

After school she and I went to Tiahrts to pick up the nuts they had ordered from Kliewer relatives in California, but they had already brought the nuts down. We got 21 lbs. almonds and walnuts at 21¢ per lb. Marian stayed at Tiahrts.

Bought other Christmas goods at Gelfand's.

Thursday, December 22, 1938

Cal went to town to see a basketball game between Bethel College of Kansas and FJC. Freeman got badly beaten.

Ruth and I wrapped Christmas presents for the school children and practice teachers.

Friday, December 23, 1938

Morning practice teachers left at 10:15 after our little program. They had a program at the College.

Arnold Graber, a graduate of the State School for the Blind at Gary, gave us a very interesting talk about the work there. He wrote in Braille for most of the children.

I gave the practice teachers each a box of candy and the children a package of nuts and fruit and a book. I got 3 neckties.

Bethel College played Nettleton Commercial College of Sioux Falls. Nettleton had four Indians on their team. Bethel won 40 to 32.

Saturday, December 24, 1938

Deposited my Soil Conservation check for $210.21.

Had Christmas program in church. Pearl sang in the choir, and Ruth and Marian said pieces in English. Little girls got a dollar from Joe P. Glanzer.

Afterwards Pearl, Johnny Klein, Mary Klein and John P. Stahl went to Catholic mass in Marion. Mary came down from Spink and Johnny has been working here during his Christmas vacation.

Sunday, December 25, 1938

Very beautiful day. All in church. For dinner we went to Peter G. Hofer, Sr. About 5 p.m. we came home, did chores and then went to Jacob L. Hofer, Sr.'s for their family Christmas. Marian got a toy drum and Ruth a checkered dress.

"Let's play Christmas program!" urged Vivian.

"I'll play my drum," volunteered Marian.

"No, I mean a church program. We can't have a drum in church. We can't have a tree either. No Christmas trees in church, only in school," said Lorraine.

"Why?" asked Merlin.

"Because Christmas trees are a pagan custom!" retorted Deloris.

"What's pagan?" asked Harvey.

"Heathen! What people did before they got converted."

"Oh."

First the Hofer children lined up all the chairs they could find in their grandparents' apartment for the congregation to sit in. Then they pulled blankets off beds to wrap around Mary and Joseph, who were played alternately by all willing participants. Harvey wanted to use his brother Delmar as the Baby Jesus, but Deloris said he might get hurt. So Vivian's new Christmas doll was commandeered instead.

The "Wise Men" brought fruit and nuts from the kitchen and everybody ended the program by sitting in a circle and eating. Finally, they were treated to angel food cake which Evelyn had decorated with colored sugar sprinkles.

Monday, December 26, 1938

Much colder today. Some snow and a fierce wind. All we need is more snow to have a perfect old time blizzard. We were all glad to stay in the house today.

"It's snowing in the bedroom!" shouted Ruth as she awoke in the northwest corner bedroom.

"What's the problem?" asked Morgan as he stumbled out of his bedroom, dressed only in long underwear.

"Look, you can see tiny specks of snow. They're blowing in through the window," said Ruth, waking Marian, who had the feather tick pulled over her head.

"I thought you and I did a better job than that of puttying those storm windows! Pull down the shades. That might help keep out some of the cold; then come out in the parlor where it's nice and warm. You may get dressed in front of the stove."

Ruth picked up her pile of clothes and then dumped them next to the hard coal burner. "Oooh! That feels good! Where's everybody else?"

"They're all a bunch of sleepy heads this morning. They're staying under the feather ticks."

Peeling an orange and dropping the peels into the coal bucket, Ruth asked, "How's come Joe P. Glanzer gave me a dollar?"

"I don't know. Maybe he likes you."

"Does he like Marian too?"

"Sure, he likes all of us. He's a friend of ours. What are you going to do with your dollar?"

"I don't know. Buy something, I guess."

"I have a proposition for you. If you lend it to me, I'll pay you interest."

"What's interest?"

"Interest is money paid for the use of money. Can you say that? Interest is money paid for the use of money."

"Interest is money paid for the use of money," repeated Ruth.

"If I give you a nickel for letting me use your money this week, I'll be paying you interest for your dollar. Then at the end of the week you'll have your dollar plus five cents."

"Okay, you can use my dollar, but I want my nickel first."

"It's a deal," said Morgan, shaking Ruth's hand and getting a nickel for her out of his change collection on the upright piano.

Tuesday, December 27, 1938

Back in school but no practice teachers.

Lillian Waldner was here to investigate going to Freeman College but she could not make the right connections. She works in a cafe in Huron. John P. Stahl took Lillian to Stanley Corner to catch a ride back to Huron. Mary and Johnny Klein went along to Stanley Corner for the ride.

Went to grandparents in the evening. They gave Pearl, Cal and me a dollar each and 50¢ each to the little girls. Cal gave Grandma a foot stool he had made in Shop, so Cal got another dollar.

"Let me sit on it," begged Marian.

"Grandpa wants to put his feet on it," said Pearl.

"That's all right. I can put my feet up tomorrow. You sit on it now, *Marichen*," said the white-haired gentleman.

Marian picked up the smooth oak stool by the two handles carved on each side and carried it to a spot directly opposite Grandpa Tieszen. She sat on it. After a few moments she got up, rubbed her hands over the blue striped velvet-covered cushion set in the center and sat on it again. "It feels good," she explained to Grandpa, who was watching her antics. Soon she and Ruth moved to the Jenny Lind-style maple daybed.

"How did you make it?" Grandpa asked Cal.

"It was a Shop project at school – manual training."

"Ahhh! It is good handiwork! Who is your teacher?"

"Professor Albert Schwartz."

"Well, it is very nice work. What do you plan to take up in school?"

"I don't know. I like a lot of things – agriculture, mechanics."

"He's more mechanically inclined than I am," said Morgan. "He's studying German too."

"I'm glad to hear that! We have to keep our Mother tongue alive. It hurts me so when the young people cannot understand their grandparents."

"Sometimes the grandparents have to make an effort to learn the new language too," said Morgan. "In Russia, they say, our people did not know, on the average, more than 7 words of Russian."

"*Ja.* I tell Grandma she should try to speak English, but it is very hard for her."

"My mother never really learned English. And when they lived in Russia, she never learned Russian," said Morgan. "She depended on Father to conduct the business affairs, and she pretty much stayed at home and took care of household matters," said Morgan.

"I thought you said she was a midwife," interjected Pearl.

"She was, but only among our people. We lived only with *Hutterische* people. There was no one else around – like English people here – who needed her help."

"She didn't help Low Germans – Mother's people?" asked Pearl.

"Distances were much greater then, going by oxcart or horse and buggy. Ten miles east of our place would have been a great distance, particularly if you were unfamiliar with the people through church or family ties."

"*Ja*, we didn't really know much about the *Hutterische* people here or in the Old Country. We lived in different villages there," said Grandpa.

"It really took the College to break down barriers among the different groups. When young people started going to class together or playing ball together, a lot of suspicion or hostility started easing," said Morgan.

"Were you and Mother among the first to marry across ethnic lines?" asked Cal.

"No, there were others before us, but it still was not too common when we got married."

"Well, I wouldn't say it is common today," interrupted Pearl. "And there's still some bad feeling between the groups."

Meanwhile Marian and Ruth were sitting on either side of Grandma on the daybed, listening in on the conversation. Marian ran her fingers over the spool-like arms. Ruth ran her fingers along the pieces of the crazy patchwork quilt thrown over the daybed. And Grandma periodically pulled each girl's skirt down to cover her knees. "Tsk, tsk, tsk," she said, shaking her head.

Wednesday, December 28, 1938

Had our Silver Lake Telephone Co. meeting. I was elected secretary. The new levy will be $4 per year.

Mary, Pearl and Bertha butchered 6 ducks and 6 geese.

Thursday, December 29, 1938

Pearl and Mary canned 29 half gallon jars of ducks and geese.

Sent $11.20 to the Co. Sup. from sale of Christmas seals. We aim to win a prize.

Friday, December 30, 1938

County agent was in our school to give a speech on 4-H club work. He showed the watch that Albert Preheim won for first place in the state handicraft competition. Cal was elected secretary of the new handicraft club.

Saturday, December 31, 1938

Went to church for New Year's Eve program but got there too late because we came home from town too late. Saw the New Year in.

1939
War Clouds Looming

Sunday, January 1, 1939

Weather very warm — 50 degrees at 2:30 p.m. We were not in church this morning. Mary Klein started working for us on December 27, 1938. She wants at least $10 per mo.

Monday, January 2, 1939

I had no school because Gov. Jensen declared it a legal holiday. Took Johnny to Stanley Corner to catch a ride back to Huron.

Tuesday, January 3, 1939

Practice teachers are back. They are teaching most of the classes now. Looking over lesson plans keeps me busy.

Thursday, January 5, 1939

Sent check to Fed. Reserve bank for $77.70 on my wheat loan. I bought back my Durham wheat because I can get more for it here than the loan amounted to. A. T. Kaufman at Park Lane said he can pay as much for Durham as for Burbank.

Friday, January 6, 1939

Miss Caroline Waltner came out to school with the practice teachers to investigate. She is more pleased now than at the beginning. Her brother, Prof. Ben Waltner, came out to get her.

Saturday, January 7, 1939

Got toothbrushes from Co. Sup. Paid Mary $2.

Sunday, January 8, 1939

Grandpa and Grandma Tieszen and the Wiens family came with father-in-law's new Plymouth. It is the high variety with plenty of clearance. They stayed for supper and the evening.

Thursday, January 12, 1939

Horses accidentally turned the water hydrant open, which drained all the water out of the supply tank. I started the windmill when I came home from school to replenish the water.

Over KELO I heard Sec. Harold Ickes and Frank Gannett discuss whether newspapers are free. Ickes claimed they are not and Gannett said absolutely yes.

Friday, January 13, 1939

Joe S. Glanzer visited school while four of the practice teachers were teaching. He seemed satisfied. Herb Hoffman applied to teach my school next year.

Monday, January 16, 1939

Tried to start our car this morning by pulling with one horse, but it did not work. Glanzers then started it by pulling with their car. I drove to our church where the water started boiling. Along came the practice teachers. I told them to start school without me. I stopped at Joe L.'s. Joe thawed out the radiator and put in 2 1/2 gal. Polar Bear anti-freeze solution. Got to school at 10:30.

Made out application for a social security card.

Tuesday, January 17, 1939

Last day for practice teachers. Each one gave a speech. I think they learned quite a bit. There certainly was a big difference between their first and last weeks. Miss Waltner is pleased with their progress, too.

Wednesday, January 18, 1939

No practice teachers. It seems queer to go back to all that mess of work without any help. My beginners will miss their teachers.

I waited at school for the children to get back from FJC. It got quite late to do chores. Weather permits us to feed the cattle and horses their cane outside. They clean it up very well.

Thursday, January 19, 1939

Having January thaw.

The 4-Hers want to put on a play.

Heard discussion of "isms" in America over the radio. Also Sen. Hamilton Fish of New York talked against this "mad preparedness for war."

Friday, January 20, 1939

Marian was sick this morning. Ruth wanted to stay home too. Claimed she was sick.

Mary complains that the day is too long home alone with Marian. She is lonesome and homesick.

Kept Clarence and Harvey in from recess because they don't study their spelling.

Saturday, January 21, 1939

Dan Merk and Henry Ewert here looking at bulls for sale. I suppose my price is too high. I asked $55 for one, roans $45, youngest $40.

Cal sold a rooster and two Leghorn hens @ 8¢ per lb., and two heavy hens @ 13¢ per lb. for total of $2.05.

Sunday, January 22, 1939

Mary went to Sioux Falls with John P. Stahl. Jacob M. Hofer is bringing his cattle and horses over to water. His windmill won't work.

Tuesday, January 24, 1939

Mary and Marian spent the day at Adeline's and then came to my school to get a ride home.

At the Gym we heard a Rev. Weiss from the Sioux Falls Mission. He played an accordion and a xylophone.

Rep. Freitag's picture was in the paper. He was appointed to the Appropriations and Education committees. It's ironic.

Wednesday, January 25, 1939

At 9:30 p.m. we heard on radio the report of the prize fight between Joe Louis and John Henry Lewis. Joe knocked out John Henry after two minutes of terrific boxing. The match netted Joe $34,000 and John Henry $15,000.

Thursday, January 26, 1939

The girls organized a clothing 4-H club here tonight. Mary is to be leader and Pearl was elected president. Cal brought the girls out from town and took them back. Solomon Wollman was along. Cal and Solomon are pretty good pals.

Sunday, January 29, 1939

After church Peter G.'s Dave, Emma and Lydia were here. Pearl went away with Pete Hofer and two others. Willie Tschetter came for Lydia, and Melvin Hofer for Emma. John Stahl is here for Mary.

Tuesday, January 31, 1939

Sinclair Lewis is in Sioux Falls today for his play, "Angela is 22" or something like that. I would have liked to see it, but Cal wanted to see Freeman H. S. play the Yankton College freshmen. Freeman won the county tournament and must think they are some players to want to meet Yankton College.

Wednesday, February 1, 1939

Snow storm today. Carl Schmeichel came for his children at noon and took Paul L.'s along. John Nachtigal came with a wagon to help his Andrew home. I drove his horse to Joe L.'s but could not go farther, so stayed overnight.

Joe is sick with rheumatism but at 9 p.m. we went out to start his light plant. Joe got it started.

Thursday, February 2, 1939

Feels good to be home today. Snow is piled up in yards and ditches. The children came up to Joe L.'s for me.

Mary went away with John Stahl. I think they went to see cousin Emma Hofer at the colony. Emma teaches the colony school, but there are no colony people there.

Saturday, February 4, 1939

In the evening Max, Cal and I saw "Robin Hood" at the movies. Cost me 31¢ and Cal 16¢.

Sunday, February 5, 1939

Pearl wanted to go to Freeman tonight to see "Robin Hood" and to Marion tomorrow rollerskating. She has now changed her mind about going tonight.

Monday, February 6, 1939

Pearl went away with somebody. It seems Elizabeth Walter and Stella Harnisch were also along. I told Pearl not to go to a roller skating party at Marion. I hope she obeyed me because those parties are certainly not good places to go for entertainment.

Tuesday, February 7, 1939

Extremely cold. Max came over tonight to play Ping Pong. There is not much studying going on.

A few people are losing sheep with a lambing disease. It seems the ewes carrying two lambs are the ones affected.

Wednesday, February 8, 1939

Ripped the gears in our car this morning on coldest day of winter. Mary has a cold and Marian is taking capsules for her tonsilitis.

My Social Security number is 504-05-9914. Some people are opposed to the social security idea.

Thursday, February 9, 1939

Bertha and Max Walter are staying here tonight. Storm is raging. Made ice cream. Repair bill for car was $20.

Friday, February 10, 1939

Called school off. Tried to call students through Bridgewater but could not get anybody. Phoned KSOO to have them broadcast closing over radio.

Max and Bertha here all day. Bertha went home in evening but Max stayed. Made more ice cream.

Saturday, February 11, 1939

Calvin wanted to go to Freeman again tonight. I did not permit him to go, so he got quite mad. He slammed the door and went upstairs. I suppose he went to bed. Max walked home.

Sunday, February 12, 1939

All in church. I taught class. Children went to Walters in the afternoon. Max and Cal made ice cream again tonight.

Heard a story about a Father and Son Banquet. The boy wanted to go, but the father said, "We'll go next year." The next year the boy got ready to go, but the father had forgotten about it and came home too late to go. He promised the boy, "We'll go next year."

Six months later the boy was hit by an auto and after some time died. When the Father and Son Banquet came up again, the father went alone. He went to the boy's room and found two faded tickets that should have been used the year before.

Tuesday, February 14, 1939

Got a Valentine from Vivian Hofer. Heard that Amanda Harnisch's school burned. It was an old, condemned school. The chimney started burning. I hope they consolidate a few of those 5 and 6-pupil schools.

Wednesday, February 15, 1939

Most of the children are paying for their pictures. A photographer was around some time ago taking pictures. He made 13 of each one. The 12 were to sell for 50¢, 6 for 35¢, and 3 for 20¢. I see now how they can make a go of it. So far only 2 brought some pictures back, and 13 bought all the pictures.

Pearl went to a College play with Pete Hofer, and Mary went with John Stahl. Cal also wanted the car. Claims he has a date.

Thursday, February 16, 1939

In the evening Pearl and I went to the movies. They showed "Mary Carey's Chickens" by Kate Wiggins. It was fairly good.

Had farewell party at Jake Walter's. They are moving south of town. The children will certainly miss them. Edwin Maendl will move on the place.

Saturday, February 18, 1939

Our school sold the most Christmas seals in the county. We received a book and a "True Vue" picture slide machine for visual education. I got six films with the machine.

Monday, February 20, 1939

Could hardly get the car out of the shed. The ground was so icy that the horses could not get a foot hold. Car froze up again. John L. took me to school. Was 30 minutes late. The children already had school started. Paul L. came up to school with his car and I took his car home.

Tuesday, February 21, 1939

I used Paul L.'s car to get to school. Quite a few of the children are out of school with the flu.

Wednesday, February 22, 1939

This is my birthday. The children had a program and party. They brought all the eats. In the evening we had another party organized by Mary, it seems. P. P.'s, Peter G.'s, John J. B.'s, and John and Adeline were here. It was a complete surprise to me. Adeline stayed here overnight to help Mary clean up.

Cal lost a $14.90 check from the Wool Growers' Assoc. which I had endorsed. I hope somebody does not cash it.

Thursday, February 23, 1939

Mrs. Paul L. is still very much concerned about the looks of her daughter, Vivian. She fell on the ice and opened up a cheek wound caused by a sheep buck knocking her down and stabbing her with his horn.

Pearl stayed in town. The debaters will be at FJC tomorrow.

Cal, Mary and Adeline went to Freeman to see Theodore Tschetter, Joe D.'s 14-year-old boy, who died of pneumonia and heart trouble.

Adam Pressler of Selby wrote concerning school legislation and I answered right away.

Friday, February 24, 1939

FJC had a debate tournament. Ten schools were represented. Pearl was down all day to help cook for the debaters. Cal is listening in on the debates.

Saturday, February 25, 1939

Had first live lamb this morning. The ewe had two but one was dead. Got some sheep mineral from Park Lane.

Sunday, February 26, 1939
Jacob B. was sick so Jacob L. Hofer, Sr., was the preacher. He talked on Revelations.

Monday, February 27, 1939
Nine out of 22 children absent. Soil Conservation committee is using our school basement for sign up.

Tuesday, February 28, 1939
Called off school for the week because the children have the flu.
Cleaned out two box stalls to use for lambing. Loaded up a load of corn from horse barn. Mice ate a lot.
Jacob M. Walter family moved to the C. P. Dickman farm south of town.

Thursday, March 2, 1939
Purebred white cow had twin heifer calves, both red—a great event.

Saturday, March 4, 1939
Veterinarian Saner came to clean the white cow. Charged $3. Twins seem to be all right.

Monday, March 6, 1939
In the evening we all went to the movies to see Shirley Temple in "Heidi."

Riding home in the Chevy after the movie, Marian asked, "Where was Heidi's mother?"

"She died."

"Where was her Daddy?"

"He died too. She was an orphan. That's why she went to live with her grandfather," explained Pearl.

"I liked the part where Heidi taught Klara, the little crippled girl, how to walk," said Ruth. Then, after a pause, "I wish I could have a goat like Snowball."

"We have lambs. Pretty soon there will be lots of little white lambs for you to play with," said Morgan.

"And bottle feed?"

"Prob'ly. We usually have to feed some with the bottle," said Morgan.

"I thought it was amazing that everything turned out happy for everybody in the end," noted Pearl.

"Yeah, there were no villains," said Cal.

"Except for the snooty housekeeper at Klara's house," said Pearl.

That night Morgan heard Marian calling out in her sleep, "Where are you, Mommy? Where are you?"

Thursday, March 9, 1939

Mary went to Adeline's to help her get settled in their new location. John P. and Adeline moved into Sam J. Hofer's house. Sam sold out and moved to Omaha. Adeline had been living with her in-laws, Joe A. Hofers.

The Federal Land Bank had a meeting in town. They fed some 600 people. The town was crowded.

Friday, March 10, 1939

Marian was in my school today. There is plenty of mud on the school ground and a big percentage of it gets hauled into the school room.

Sunday, March 12, 1939

Heard men's chorus from North and South churches sing in Gym tonight. It was some really good singing. Prof. Crum of Sunnyside Bible Academy gave a piano solo.

Thursday, March 16, 1939

Mary was not home again this morning so Marian went to school with me.

Had meeting at Park Lane Feeds concerning the Poultry Show and 4-H club work. First National Bank will furnish money for 4-Hers to buy chicks and feed. The money is to be paid back in six months.

Friday, March 17, 1939

Weather warmer during day. Children are practicing athletics and spelling for the contests.

John R.'s children broke their buggy wheel when they drove away from school. Florence rode home on horseback as fast as the horse could run. She is quite a tomboy.

Saturday, March 18, 1939

I manured the barn while Cal and Mary papered the upstairs rooms and Pearl ironed. Paid Finer $6.59 for paper.

Monday, March 20, 1939

Pearl stayed home from school. She and Mary calcimined the dining room and tore the linoleum out of the dining room and put it in the kitchen. Those girls would change a lot of things if they had the money.

Tuesday, March 21, 1939

Pearl stayed home to help Mary. In the evening Pearl and Cal went to Freeman for a rollerskating party at the College.

Wednesday, March 22, 1939

Bill Schultz, a refugee from Poland, is working for us at a dollar a day except on Saturday. He won't work on Saturdays.

Started sowing Thatcher wheat. Sowed 10 acres in cornstalks. We are not discing the ground. We put the drill down as deep as we can.

The temperature was 80 degrees. Too hot for horses.

Friday, March 24, 1939

Had field day at my school with five other schools. Six of my pupils, grades 2-8, placed first in spelling, written and oral. Deloris Hofer won 1st in declam, grade 3.

Saturday, March 25, 1939

County agent took Cal to Yankton to speak over WNAX on a 4-H program. He has a nice radio voice.

Tuesday, March 28, 1939

Got warrant from #26 for transportation of Ruth to town school. Bought 3 gal. harness oil @ 45¢ and case of puffed wheat (24 packages) @ $2.25.

Saturday, April 1, 1939

Took contestants to county contest in Olivet.

Cal brought home the dresser he had made in Shop.

Sold 45 doz. eggs @ 13¢.

Bronc had peppy male colt. Put iodine on its navel. Horse that John Gross brought up to sub for Bronc is no good. No power. Gross wanted $20 for it. Borrowed a horse instead from Joe L. Cal rode it home. Paid Joe L. $16.28 for gas, oil, and kerosene. (Acct. pd. in full)

Ed Maendl will plow for me at 90¢ per acre.

Tuesday, April 4, 1939

Ferd Walter and Kurt Kleinsasser laid a Congoleum printed rug in the dining room. Cost $18.

Wednesday, April 5, 1939

Mrs. Abe Wiens phoned that Ortman called them saying we could rent his AC tractor. Cal went to get it and Max delivered the students. Cal is plowing the southwest corner rye field. Joe L. brought 50 gal. gasoline.

Friday, April 7, 1939

Cal and I bought a sow with 8 pigs from Ben Spies in Luverne, Minn. for 4-H work. Paid $40.

Sunday, April 9, 1939

Easter Sunday. After dinner at Abe Wiens we saw oil drilling outfit at the Albrecht farm. Isaac Tieszen leased the land. They are down 216 ft., making 15-inch hole. Visited grandparents in evening.

Monday, April 10, 1939

Had Easter Monday services at church but I was teaching. Ruth had school but there were no classes at College. Cal dragged with the tractor.

Wednesday, April 12, 1939

Got 40 signers on a petition to refer the four-year Normal School law to the people in the next election. Mr. Purchl of Burke, a member of the Board of Regents, is interested in it.

The Haars would not sign for business reasons. Ed Preheim, Mgr. of College Gas and Oil Station, did not sign either. Spike Walter at K & K first did not care to sign but eventually did although he said he would vote in favor of a four year term.

Thursday, April 13, 1939

Bill Schultz had to re-sow one field of barley. He had set the drill at 1 1/4 bu. when it should have been 2 bu. to acre. So in re-sowing he went opposite to the direction first sowed. He was upset at his mistake, but it could not be helped.

Saturday, April 15, 1939

Planted 2 bu. seed potatoes. Little girls helped.

Sunday, April 16, 1939

Cal and Pearl started catechism and Bible instruction at church on Sunday afternoons with Jacob B. They are using the 1934 version done by Rev. P. P. Tschetter and Rev. P. R. Schroeder.

Monday, April 17, 1939

Last day of school at #51. Took 3 1/2 gal. chocolate ice cream to the picnic. Children brought sandwiches, Jello, cake, bars and potato salad. No one went away hungry. When Joe Math, Joe P. and Joe S. Glanzer came for the children, we gave them each a dish of ice cream.

Tuesday, April 18, 1939
First day home from teaching. I bedded the sheep and made a creep for the pigs. Cal hauled rocks after school.

One young ewe had a lamb out in the field and just left it there. I went to look for it and found the little creature walking along the woven wire fence. Some sheep are too dumb to be mothers!

Wednesday, April 19, 1939
Sowed 83 lbs. crested wheat. Bullet went so fast that the reins hurt my hands holding her back.

I was invited to a party at the College. All the High School, College and critic teachers were there. We had a very enjoyable time playing old-fashioned parlor games like Spin the Bottle.

Thursday, April 20, 1939
Girls' 4-H club had a basket social at Adeline's. Had more baskets than boys. Baskets sold from $1.50 to 25¢. Girls were very disappointed. Cal took Shirley Kleinsasser and John Stahl took the rest of the girls from town to Adeline's place.

"They're selling Pearl's basket! Hurry up and get in here!" Adeline called to Peter A. Hofer as he drove up in his coupe to what had been his grandmother's house.

"What do you mean? Basket of what?" asked the young man.

"The 4-H club is having a basket social with an auctioneer and everything. The baskets are going too cheap."

Peter stepped into the large living room which had been transformed into a party atmosphere with crepe paper streamers hanging from the ceiling. "Come on in, young man," said Leo Link, the auctioneer. "I got a dandy basket here for you. It's in the shape of a keg of beer – very clever. Might even have a bottle of beer in it!" he said, winking.

"Ha! Pearl's so naive she doesn't even know how to spell *Hamm's*. She's got just one *m* in it," laughed the worldly-wise fellow.

"I have a bid of 75 cents on this unique basket. Now, that's a steal! Won't you give me a dollar? It's for a good cause – the club!"

"One dollar," Peter bid.

"One dollar! Now that's more like it!" Pearl kept her head down as as not to reveal herself as the basketmaker.

"Peter must be interested in this basket," thought his cousin, John P. Hofer, the host. "I bid one and a quarter!" said John.

"One fifty!" said Peter.

"One seventy five?" asked Leo of John.

"Nope, too steep for me."

"Well, then, it's yours for one fifty," said the ebullient auctioneer, handing it over to Peter.

Later, sitting in Peter's coupe and munching on their sandwiches, Pearl asked, "Why did you buy my basket?"

"I took pity on the maker. I figured anybody who couldn't spell *Hamm's* needed a lot of sympathy."

"Oh, you. . . . You're such a kidder!"

Friday, April 21, 1939

Dug grave for Mrs. Peter Waldner, M. S. Six others were helping but Jake M. Hofer and John M. S. didn't do much. I'm afraid I hurt my back.

Went to the Waldner home at night for a little service. Jacob B. preached.

Saturday, April 22, 1939

Was pall bearer for Mrs. Waldner's funeral. She was buried by the county. Eisenbrey was the undertaker.

Sunday, April 23, 1939

John P. Stahl took Mary home to Spink because Rebekah Basle fell down the cellar and got hurt. Marian hurt her knee so I stayed home from church with her. My back hurts very much. I will have to see a bone setter.

Monday, April 24, 1939

Am quite sick today. Went to Tieszen Clinic in Marion to see Dr. Joe Tieszen. He tried to set my back but it did not help any. It just hurt some more. I must have the flu.

Sheep and cattle are on the winter rye field. It is not growing very fast. Had very little rain.

Tuesday, April 25, 1939

Home all day, in bed most of the time. Sent Cal to town for medicine. Did not help much. I don't think it's the right stuff.

Pearl went to Sioux Falls on their "sneak day." Came home at 1 a.m.

Wednesday, April 26, 1939

Have a real case of flu. Signed up for wheat insurance—$23.96 on 21 1/2 acres.

Cal took me to Doc Ernest in evening. Charged me $2.50 for medicine and consultation. Forgot the medicine downtown, so Cal had to go back for it.

Friday, April 28, 1939

Still sick in bed with flu.

Young people had amateur contest at Frank F. Walter house. Amos Walter got first prize on his Joe Louis-Max Schmeling fight imitation.

Saturday, April 29, 1939

Benny Gross took Pearl to the Junior-Senior Banquet. She wore a blue formal gown with a corsage.

Marian got badly sunburned while she and Cal were hauling rocks.

Sunday, April 30, 1939

Pearl went with Benny Gross to the Salem KMB Church to hear Negroes from the Baptist church in Sioux Falls sing. I am still sick.

Monday, May 1, 1939

Took Cal and Ruth to school and had another check-up. Doctor said I was not over the flu. I could have told him that.

Delivered my test papers to the Co. Sup. Court was in session. Schenk had a case with Shandorff of Mitchell about a wrecked truck.

Tuesday, May 2, 1939

Cal and Reuben Stahl went to Lake Charles to fish but could not because of rain. That must have been the only place it rained. We had just a light sprinkle.

Wednesday, May 3, 1939

Hauled straw away from chicken barn. I play out very soon. Cal helped me after school.

Helmuth Schnaidt was here to check on the wheat. We either have to reseal now, deliver the wheat May 31st, or buy the wheat back from the government. I intend to buy mine back.

Pearl took Marian to Home Ec. class to demonstrate child development.

Got a letter from Prchal that we do not have enough signatures to refer the 4-year Normal law.

Friday, May 5, 1939

Despite my bad back I took five of my students to rally day in Tripp. None of them placed. Some of my smart guys didn't even go.

Melvin Ratzlaff from #98 got first in Class B high jump. His sister Lillian won second place.

Monday, May 8, 1939

Ben Janke was on a drunk because it was his birthday and that must be celebrated, he said.

Prof. Foley of State College gave a talk on poultry at the Gym. He had been at the Poultry Congress in Cleveland.

Tuesday, May 9, 1939

Joe L. was here to plow up a little sod with his AC tractor, but it is so dry that it does a poor job.

Wednesday, May 10, 1939

Senior Class Day at Academy. Pearl read a paper on "Who's Who." She will not graduate because she lost two quarters of work staying home to do housework and take care of Marian.

Thursday, May 11, 1939

Children had a 4-H picnic at Lake Charles. Cal and Reuben Stahl caught 2 bullheads.

I planted white corn. Sent another filled petition to Prchal. Still have severe backache.

Friday, May 12, 1939

Had another lamb this morning. The lambs have come very scattered this year.

Planted hybred corn that Cal got from county agent. Planted Pioneer 352 nearest to east fence so we can watch its progress.

Saturday, May 13, 1939

I think Dr. Joe Tieszen got my back set this time. In the afternoon Herb Koerner and Cal tried to shear sheep and did not seem to know how, so I sheared and hurt my back worse than ever.

Pearl ran a knife into her hand. Put iodine on sore but has quite a bit of pain.

Sunday, May 14, 1939

Jacob B. preached on "Mother's Day." Girls wore white carnations they ordered through Chas. Preheim.

Went to Marion to see Dr. Joe Tieszen but he said he could not fix my back alone.

Monday, May 15, 1939

Beautiful day but my back must be out of joint now. Got Auch to shear sheep. He charges 15¢ per sheep using hand shear. One ewe (#73) had a ram lamb, so we did not shear her.

Tuesday, May 16, 1939

Got questions that 7th and 8th graders will write on. I have 6 this year. Moses Glanzer and Rosa Hofer have not handed in all their book reports.

Friday, May 19, 1939

Finished tests. I think they are quite hard. Language test had questions on material not to be taught this year.

Tuesday, May 23, 1939

Pearl and Home Planning Group decorated the Gym for Alumni Banquet. About 140 attended. Atty. William Schenk of Tripp spoke.

On the way home from the banquet, Morgan said, "The Gym looked really nice, Pearl. Where did you get all the flowers?"

"Oh, we bummed them wherever we could. Spirea we got from Mrs. Louis Linscheid."

"She's Mother's cousin, you know."

"I know. That's why I thought I could ask her. Some tulips we got from Marie Waldner."

"She's a friend of mine, you know."

"I know. Lilacs we got from Mrs. Johnny D. Unruh."

"Well, it surely looked nice. You must have inherited some of your mother's artistic ability."

"Hope so."

Saturday, May 27, 1939

Went to Milltown for 4-H picnic but the grounds were too wet to have it. Caught 20 fish, though. Jake L. speared a few carps. Voss, the game warden, took all the black bass away from Jake, who thought he had caught crappies.

Sunday, May 28, 1939

Pearl and Cal went to catechism in the afternoon. In the evening we went to the Salem KMB Church for a musical program. Ran out of gas a half mile from home. Carried Marian most of way on my back.

Monday, May 29, 1939

Went to church for Pentecost Monday. Rev. Martens, a refugee from Russia, spoke. He had some hair-raising experiences. Maybe we are in for something as bad or worse.

Got an extension on my Fed. Land Bank loan to Sept.

Planted sweet corn, pop corn, Navy beans, and low acid cane. Cal planted a half bu. seed potatoes from Chas. Preheim — 3 varieties — and sunflower seeds.

Got 350 started Leghorn chicks from Fensel @ 6¢.

Tuesday, May 30, 1939

Planted Sooner milo and rolled up the corn planting wire. Our chicks are sick. Lost 25 so far.

Thursday, June 1, 1939

Abe Olfert of Marion was here demonstrating a gas iron with an air pump. Paid down $2. He wants $3.25 more if we keep the iron.

Cal went to town to help Pettis set up for poultry judging school tomorrow.

Friday, June 2, 1939

Cal and Pearl went to poultry judging event. Cal took some of our chickens to judge.

I plowed the old straw pile land in the pasture and part of the lake bed with sulky. Also the lake in alfalfa field.

Christ Saner was here to vaccinate the horses but I am short of money so we did not do it. He vaccinated Cal's 4-H pigs for $2.56 (8 pigs).

Sunday, June 4, 1939

Had no church this morning because Preacher Mike Hofer was ordained in the Bridgewater church.

Went to Olivet for county graduation. Ruth Schmeichel and Marvin Hofer went along. Florence Hofer got "bucky" and did not go. My eighth graders all passed.

Monday, June 5, 1939

Had birthday supper at Tiahrts for Arnold's 23rd birthday. Had spring chicken. Grandparents were there.

Wednesday, June 7, 1939

John J. B.'s got hailed out.

Thursday, June 8, 1939

Still losing chickens. Pearl was in town but did not find the cause from hatchery men. Fensel did not interest himself and Jake T. Gross was not home.

Friday, June 9, 1939

Exceedingly dry. Cannot get much of a crop. Hot in afternoon. Lost 19 chicks today. Lost 100+ so far.

Saturday, June 10, 1939

Got spray for chicks and some medicine for their water. They must have gotten moldy feed.

Took Ruth to Dr. Wollman. She had two teeth filled. She made a big fuss about it. He had to freeze the gums so he could work on her teeth. She was very much afraid.

Monday, June 12, 1939

Northern District Conference is being held at the South Church. Brother J. W., Rebekah, John, Paul and Elizabeth are all here from Spink.

John L. was here to measure my fields for compliance. I may be long in wheat. Could sow 32.9 and he checked 32.1. Too close for good health. I am 10 acres long in Soil Conservation acres.

Wednesday, June 14, 1939

Rained an inch last night. Lightning killed a young horse at Jake L.'s. We allowed him $90 damage in Aid Plan. They allowed me $8 damage to hog house and big barn.

Dipped Cal's pigs with lime sulphur dip.

Thursday, June 15, 1939

Marian had her tonsils removed by Doc Ernest this morning. Mrs. Hildegard Schmidt was the nurse. Ruth was along and watched part of the time until she told Ernest, "You're gonna kill her!" Marian stayed at P. P.'s afterwards, but I brought her home in the evening.

Pearl was canning Leghorn roosters because they are worth only 5¢ per lb.

"What would you like for supper?" asked Pearl.

"My throat hurts," answered Marian.

"Did you eat at P. P.'s?"

"I had Jello and ice cream. They said I could eat all the ice cream I wanted."

"Maybe we can get Cal to bring you some ice cream later tonight. If we had a Frigidaire like P. P.'s do, we could have ice cream and Jello anytime we wanted it."

"Why don't we?"

"We live too far from the high line. They live close to town and the high line goes right past their place."

238

"Yeah, but Joe L.'s and Paul L.'s have electric lights, and they live farther from town than we do," said Ruth.

"Well, Joe L. has a light plant and Paul L. has a Windcharger."

"Why don't we have a windcharger?" asked Ruth.

"Because it costs money."

Friday, June 16, 1939
Cal started cutting alfalfa. Very thin stand. I raked with Bullet and Bronc. They went so fast, I had to hold them back. Arms ached from holding the lines.

Saturday, June 17, 1939
Iky Tschetter came over at 11:30 p.m. and we sat up visiting 'til 1 a.m.

Sunday, June 18, 1939
Did not go to church. Iky Tschetter was here from Beadle for the night. He says their crops look better than ours.

Children are picking mulberries. Marian is also outside. Her throat seems to be healing.

Monday, June 19, 1939
Cal helped paint the outside of the church. He painted some of the highest places. Says he does not want to be a painter.

Pearl and I hauled 4 loads of hay. That's all we got from 12 acres. Last year we got 17 loads.

Tuesday, June 20, 1939
At school election Mrs. Sam Schmidt acted as clerk because Sam was working on the road. Alfred Hofer nominated his father for treasurer. He was elected. We decided to have no school and send the grade children to some other school. Transportation allowance for each child will be $4 per mo. High school pupils are permitted to attend the school they prefer, either Freeman Academy or some public high school.

Wednesday, June 21, 1939
Co-op Creamery picnic today. I helped dish out ice cream. We gave 3 small dips and cookies. Ice cream was so hard that we had to let it melt a little before we could get it out of the tubs.

Thursday, June 22, 1939
Pearl is 19 years old. The girls were at Jake Waldner's for mulberries. They got only enough to make pies.

Went to Henry Tiahrts in evening. Had ice cream. Henry nearly hailed out. He wants some cattle to pasture his fields.

Friday, June 23, 1939

Lillian Waldner is here from Beadle. She helped Pearl in forenoon and then went to P. P.'s in afternoon to visit.

Cal set up a barrel with a faucet at the windmill to heat water with sunpower for shower bathing.

"I don't want anybody messing with my shower," Cal announced.

"Can't we take showers too?" asked Ruth.

"You kids are still little enough to take baths in the tub. I don't want the water to be all used up when I get home from working in the field all day. I need enough water to get the dust and grime off," he insisted.

"Okay, nobody's gonna touch your shower," said Pearl.

"I guess that means we won't have to wash his back anymore," observed Ruth.

"Well, he's gonna need more soap. And his hair will be stiff from washing it in well water. He'll be glad to get back to bathing in rain water soon enough," said Pearl.

Sunday, June 25, 1939

Children all in church. Cal and Pearl had catechism in afternoon. I read THE COUNTRY GENTLEMAN from cover to cover.

Monday, June 26, 1939

Rained about an inch at 1 p.m. Went out plowing with the sulky after supper. Plowed ends of corn fields and one patch of lake bed. Quit plowing at 8:30 and pulled weeds.

Paul L. called that I am supposed to come to their school board meeting tomorrow night.

Tuesday, June 27, 1939

We all went to Paul's. Summit #51 offered me a contract of $65 per mo. but I refused to sign. I want $70, what I had last year.

Had another good rain between midnight and 1 a.m. while we were still at Paul L.'s. Lizzie had prepared a midnight lunch of steak and macaroni. On the way home we slipped off the grade near our mailbox. Cal carried Marian on his back and stepped on a piece of glass. He cut his foot badly.

"Okay, kids, it's time to get up. The sun is beating down already," Morgan emphasized.

"I'm sleepy. We got home too late last night," moaned Ruth.

"You can take a nap later. After breakfast I want you kids to pick up every piece of glass and every nail you can find in the yard. Cal cut himself on a piece of glass sticking up in the road and there is absolutely no excuse for it. I'll give you a nickel for every can of glass and nails you pick up."

"How big a can?" asked Ruth. "A gallon can or a cream can?"

"I mean a little can like pork 'n beans come in. About a 2-cup can," explained Morgan. "You can line 'em up at the end of the day and I'll pay you. You've got to prove you did it. Then you can dump the contents down the toilet hole."

"Okay!" exclaimed Ruth and began shaking Marian awake. "C'mon, Honey, we're gonna make us some money today!"

Wednesday, June 28, 1939

Took Pearl to town to catch a ride to Swan Lake 4-H camp. Cal did not go this year.

Went to town in evening to buy 80 ft. of rope for hay mow. Paid $4.60 for rope and 85¢ for pulley.

Thursday, June 29, 1939

Had a little rain. Repaired fence so cattle have to stay on rye field. There is practically nothing for them to eat. We are very short on pasture. Sooner milo is making very slow growth.

Went to Paul L.'s to sign contract to teach #51 again at reduced salary of $65 per mo. on an 8 month basis. I know there were others after the job. They claim they don't have the money.

Friday, June 30, 1939

Started cutting with binder again, barley and oats. We set the reel way down so we can get about 3/4 of the grain. Started on volunteer rye. It is very poor stuff, too thin. Grasshoppers are doing much damage.

Saturday, July 1, 1939

Cut barley and oats. Very poor crop. We have some of the poorest fields in the community. We plowed our land late last fall and it dried out too much.

Cal still goes lame from the glass he stepped on, but he can shock up the bundles as fast as the binder drops them.

Pearl came home from Swan Lake camp.

Sunday, July 2, 1939

Had ice cream party at Eddie Maendl's. Plenty of good ice cream. Cal had a date, probably with Shirley.

Monday, July 3, 1939

Sprinkled a little this morning. It will be a scorcher today. Finished cutting rye patch and started on Thatcher wheat. The wheat is the only field this year that is any good at all.

Tuesday, July 4, 1939

Pearl went to Sioux Falls with Alfred Tschetter. About 7 p.m. a big storm came up from the west. It threw our hay rack off the wheels. Did not rain much, though. We couldn't find the ducks for some time. Eight were out during the rain. Fifteen were with the chicks in the brooder house.

Wanted to celebrate the Fourth by making ice cream with Maendl's freezer, but they were using it.

Wednesday, July 5, 1939

Finished cutting wheat by p.m. lunch time. Tried to cut a little of the barley in the southwest field. There are very few heads and it is very short. I think I will abandon the field and use it for pasture.

Turned the cows out on the Sudan grass back of the house. Cut some early sown Sudan with the binder.

We used up only 50 lbs. of binder twine on all of our grain this year.

After Cal went to town I took a shower bath at the windmill. I take one nearly every evening now. He used an old gasoline barrel and you can still smell the gasoline.

Prof. and Mrs. Gerhard Toews were here soliciting students for FJC and Academy.

Thursday, July 6, 1939

Cal is cultivating Sooner milo for first time. I took the canvases off the binder. Our binder platform is worn out. It will have to be replaced for next year.

Friday, July 7, 1939

Had a wonderful rain last night. Must have been 1 1/4 to 1 1/2 inches. Couldn't cultivate so Cal went fishing with Alfred Hofer. They caught about 30 fish.

We started fencing up the last-sown Sudan grass for pasture. Rye pasture is all gone. Sheep don't have enough.

Saturday, July 8, 1939

Raked and hauled home the oat hay. It had gotten several rains. Some of the oats had threshed out. Very dusty.

In the afternoon I went to Gerhard Lang to have my back set in place. He charged me 50¢.

I signed up for parity payment on wheat and sent the papers to Parkston. Acreage planted, 31.6
1939 allotment, 32.9; normal yield, 12.5 bu.
Rate of payment, $1.37; gross farm payment, $45.07.

Sunday, July 9, 1939

Two years ago Katherine was taken to McKennan Hospital, from which she did not return alive.

Pearl and Cal are still taking catechism on Sunday afternoons.

For supper we went to Abe Wiens. Had young chicken, new potatoes, string beans, cake, etc.

Monday, July 10, 1939

Pearl and I worked on two fences so sheep would not get out.

Ben Ratzlaff was here to tell us we will start threshing tomorrow at Pete Ratzlaff's place.

Tuesday, July 11, 1939

Cal and I pitched at machine today. We had four racks. It was very hot. Got so heated that I had headache all afternoon and evening. I am taking salt tablets.

Went to John J. B's to ask whether we can have some help. Sister Kathcrine will help us with cooking for threshers.

Wednesday, July 12, 1939

I took Cal to Pete Ratzlaff to pitch. Henry Ratzlaff and Irvin Ratzlaff will each run a bundle rack. I can't take it.

Thursday, July 13, 1939

Very hot. Finished threshing at Pete Ratzlaff. Moved to Jacob C. Schmidt before a.m. lunch and finished after p.m. lunch. Moved to my place and threshed three bundle loads of oats in one hour. Blew the straw into the hay mow of horse barn. Cal will not pitch here but will help elevate the grain.

Pearl went to get Sister Katherine to help with cooking. We give dinner and afternoon lunch. Breakfast and supper are to be eaten at home.

Friday, July 14, 1939

Sprinkled a little but we started threshing soon after. Got 150 bu. oats, 75 bu. barley, 144 bu. wheat and 8 bu. rye. A very poor crop, but I cannot help it any this year. Will try to raise a better crop next year.

I had the wheat on corn ground. It averaged 4 1/2 bu. One field of oats on corn ground was fair. The other field of oats on spring plowing was very poor. Barley on plowed ground was very poor. Will try the wheat on plowed ground and oats on corn ground for next year.

Machine moved to Ben Ratzlaff after finishing here. Cal is pitching for me. After supper Cal cultivated cane 'til he could not see the rows.

Sunday, July 16, 1939

All in church. I taught class. Pearl and Cal had catechism in p.m.

I worked all afternoon on map study for C. E. program in evening. It did not go over very well, but the total program went over anyhow.

Monday, July 17, 1939

Cal is pitching at Ben Ratzlaff's. We furnish one team and rack.

I cleaned up the grain by the straw piles to use for chicken feed. The machine is getting old, so it leaks at a few places.

Tuesday, July 18, 1939

Threshing at Irvin Ratzlaff near Silver Lake School. Grain is much better there than here.

Moved fence. Took out middle fence on east 80. Intend to put one right on the property line this fall.

Wednesday, July 19, 1939

Cal is pitching at Henry Ratzlaff's for me. Am moving fence straight south of horse barn so livestock can be turned into different fields without much driving.

Got Abe Wiens' spray pump to spray our late potatoes with Red River compound. It surely fixes the blister beetles and bugs. Grasshoppers die also if they eat it.

Friday, July 21, 1939

Pete Ratzlaff lost a cow from cane this morning. I phoned up the rendering works for him.

Ed Maendl's hired boy borrowed my rake this morning and broke it.

Started cutting Sudan grass. In low spots it is very good, but rest is practically all dried up.

Saturday, July 22, 1939

Broke mower pitman cutting weeds on section line.

Bought sweet corn from a Yankton boy @ 10¢ doz.

My niece, Mrs. Jacob D. Wollman, gave us 16 ducks. We now have 68 ducks.
244

Wrote county committee that I want to seal my wheat and want an adjustment on the wheat insurance.

Sunday, July 23, 1939
Got to church late this morning so did not teach my class. Pearl and Cal had catechism in the afternoon. In the evening we went to see the grandparents. They were not home, so we went to see Mrs. Mary Tiahrt and Harry. They were not home, so we went to John J. B.'s. They were not at home either, but we waited until they got home from the Dolton church. Sister Katherine fixed a midnight lunch.

Monday, July 24, 1939
This is Marian's birthday. She is six years old.
Cal cleaned up and reorganized the blacksmith shop in the garage in the forenoon. In the afternoon he started to cultivate Sooner milo. Creeping jinnies have hurt it.
Adeline and John came over for a visit. We got some ice and made ice cream at Ed Maendl's to celebrate Marian's birthday. Adeline and John went over there with us.

Tuesday, July 25, 1939
Mr. and Mrs. Jacob L. Hofer, Sr., came over for a visit. I spent quite a bit of time with them. Sister Elizabeth brought us a big crock of pickles.
Pearl and the girls were in Freeman for a canning demonstration.
County Agent Pettis came to check my cane test plot. He hoed some out to thin it.
Had threshing settling up party at Ben Ratzlaff's in the evening. They served ice cream and soda crackers. Cal and the team earned $12.85 more than our labor. Our threshing bill was $14.70. I paid down $4.70 and have a balance due of $10.

Wednesday, July 26, 1939
Our cattle were out this morning. Found them at Ed Maendl's. Went to town in evening. Pearl was on a date with Alfred Tschetter.

Thursday, July 27, 1939
Cleaned chicken barn and painted roosts with oil. Also cleaned debris out of hole by water hydrant in chicken barn. We have rats in our chicken barn.
Raymond Howe and his wife, a Kliewer girl, were here from Shafter, California.

245

Friday, July 28, 1939

Reuben Stahl and Cal are hauling stones from the rye field which we intend to plow. Helped the boys move a few big rocks with the stone boat.

"Too bad we don't have my mother here to help us," Morgan said to the boys.

"Grandma Kleinsasser?" asked Cal.

"Sure! She was a big help! She was, what you might call, pleasingly plump. And when a big boulder had to be dug out of the ground she would sit on a timber or crowbar while Father would loosen the rock."

Cal laughed uproariously.

"Of course, we were none of us underweight. She fed us all pretty well. Meat, potatoes and bread. That was a pretty steady diet."

"How's come we never get done pickin' rocks?" asked Reuben.

"They just keep workin' their way up. Every time it freezes and thaws, more come up. The rain exposes them, and plowing turns 'em up," said Cal.

"Yeah, we prob'ly raised a better crop of stones this year than grain," remarked Morgan, adjusting the log chain around a boulder. "Some of these rock piles date from when Father homesteaded. We used to have little rock piles all over the farm. We've consolidated some of them over the years or thrown 'em in the lake. But when it's dry, like this year, the lake is the best place to raise a crop."

"Why can't you use them in building, like they do out East?" asked Reuben.

"They're too smooth and round for a foundation by themselves. You have to pour concrete around them," answered Cal.

"In the East they use rocks for fences but I don't like permanent fences. I like to move my fences and plow up the fence rows – plow the top soil that's blown up to the fence into the field again," said Morgan.

Saturday, July 29, 1939

Had crabs for breakfast and "bullets" for dinner.

Went crabbing again in the afternoon in the Vermillion R. at Henry Tiahrt's using young Jake L.'s net. Did not catch many, but the ones we got were much bigger. Girls went along to visit Tiahrts. Velma Howe from California came along back with us. In the evening the children all went to town. I stayed home to eat crabs.

Sunday, July 30, 1939

Did not go to church. Took some crabs to John L. and asked him to take my place at the College Welfare Committee.

Had Kliewer Family reunion at Sherman Park in Sioux Falls. It was quite a gathering. Raymond Howe is a good entertainer.

Monday, July 31, 1939

Up at 5 a.m. Hot weather continues with no rain.

Bought sack of sugar for $5 and two lugs of apricots. Pearl cooked some field corn since we do not have any sweet corn. Got my parity payment on wheat—$45.07.

Tuesday, August 1, 1939

Got Ortman's tractor and P. P.'s plow but the tractor developed a knock so we did not use it. Picked rocks.

Pearl canned field corn. It is good if picked young.

Wednesday, August 2, 1939

Went claims adjusting for Aid Plan at Joe K. Kleinsasser. We allowed him $9 for wind damage to garage and corn crib. He is to replace the shingles on the house to determine cost of damage.

Thursday, August 3, 1939

Helped Abe Wiens fill silo. He filled an upright yesterday and a pit silo today.

Pettis was here practicing with 4-H demonstration teams and judging team.

Ortman came to fix his tractor. A bearing had worn out.

Friday, August 4, 1939

Cal plowed 11 hrs. with Ortman's tractor and P. P.'s plow.

Made change on south end barn driveway. Some of the pigs crawled underneath the wire and hurt their backs.

Bought a box of peaches @ 83¢ and 2 boxes apricots @ 89¢. There is a little fruit war going on.

In the evening we went to grandparents. Ray Howe showed moving pictures he had taken of Boulder Dam, Bad Lands, Black Hills, etc.

Saturday, August 5, 1939

Three-teated white cow had a dark roan heifer calf.

Saw Prof. P. F. Quiring in town. He is painting his house. He was my Academy teacher in 1917.

Cal plowed 11 hours again.

Sunday, August 6, 1939

Went to Tieszen church this morning. Rev. Alfred Waltner baptized 30 people. Had big crowd.

Pearl and Cal went to catechism in afternoon.
For supper we went to Adeline's. Pearl and Cal both went away
with Alfred Tschetter.

Tuesday, August 8, 1939
Rented a plow from Ortman because P. P. needed his.
Cal is working out a 4-H demonstration with Noah Mendel hav-
ing to do with dipping sheep.

Thursday, August 10, 1939
Pettis caponized some of our roosters at a 4-H club meeting
and then took Cal, Pearl and Irene Kleinsasser to Gross Hatchery
to practice poultry judging.
Sold 3 rams to Jamesville Colony for $55.

Friday, August 11, 1939
Cut corn with binder after making several adjustments to binder.
Paid John A. Wipf $5 on radio account.

Saturday, August 12, 1939
Rained last night. Cal tried to plow but got stuck so he shocked
corn. I started cutting low acid cane in lake bottom south of barn.

Sunday, August 13, 1939
All in church. Paid Joe K. $7.50 for my church dues.
Pearl and Cal at catechism in afternoon.

As Hutterthal's young people gathered in the first three pews on the men's side of the wooden frame church building, a hot afternoon breeze blew across the stubble field and through the screened window. The preacher, Jacob B. Hofer, stood before his reluctant charges and said, "Let us bow for prayer."

All heads bowed and Jacob B. proceeded: "Our Heavenly Father, we thank thee for the opportunity of coming before thy throne of grace this afternoon. We thank thee for the manifold blessings thou hast bestowed upon us, for health and strength. Now be with each and every one of us as we open God's Word. Speak to our hearts that we might learn of thy plan of salvation for our lives. We pray all this in the name of Jesus Christ, the Author and Finisher of our faith. Amen. Now, who studied his lesson for today?"

All heads remained bowed.

"Nobody?"

"Well, I read it over once, but I can't say I STUDIED it," said Pearl.

"Did you at least READ it, Cal?"

"No, I can't say I did."

"Well, we'll have to read it here then. Who knows where our lesson for today begins?"

"Chapter Six, Church Discipline," answered Melvin.

"That's right. Page 66. Read the first question, Marjorie."

" 'If a brother or sister of the church should fall into sin, how should such a one be dealt with?' "

"Read the answer, Evelyn."

" 'We are to restore such a one in the spirit of meekness'."

"Yes. What does meekness mean?" There was no answer. "Pearl?"

"Not being proud."

"All right. How could somebody be proud about another brother or sister falling into sin?"

"Well, if you were glad they got caught and you didn't."

"All right. Can you give an example?"

"Well, if somebody got caught stealing chickens, you shouldn't lord it over him.

"Even if you know he committed a sin?"

"Yes."

"What are the scriptural references for this?"

"Galatians 6:1 and Matthew 18:15."

"Read Galatians 6:1, Cal."

"Okay." Cal fumbled around, looking for Galatians.

"It's before Ephesians."

"Right. Galatians 6:1. 'Brethren, if a man is overtaken in any trespass, you who are spiritual should restore him in a spirit of meekness. Look to your self, lest you too be tempted.' "

"What does that mean?"

"Well, it's sorta like the Golden Rule. Treat the offender as you would like to be treated."

"That's a good way to put it, Cal."

"And the other reference – Matthew 18:15. Read it, Evelyn."

" 'If your brother sins against you, go and tell him his fault, between him and you alone. If he listens to you, you have gained your brother'."

"And what if he doesn't listen to you?"

"Then 'take one or two others along, that every word may be confirmed by the evidence of two or three witnesses'."

"But, what if the offender refuses admonition and persists in living in sin?"

"Then tell it to the church."

"And if he refuses to listen to the church?"

" 'Let him be to you as a Gentile or a tax collector.' "

"Meaning?"

"Put him outside of the church."

"But if he repents? Read II Corinthians 2:6 and 7, Melvin. That's after I Corinthians."

Laughter all around. "I know. 'Sufficient to such a man is the punishment, which was inflicted by many; we must all the more forgive, and comfort him.'"

"Yes. What does it mean to repent?"

"To be truly sorry for what you have done, to turn around and not do it again," said Pearl.

"Yes. Praise the Lord for the victory over sin which we have through our Lord Jesus. Is there any discussion?"

"If somebody comes before the church, then, does that mean that he didn't receive correction from the two or three who admonished him?" asked Pearl.

"Not necessarily. He may have been reproved by his parents and the minister but felt he wanted to make a full confession before the brotherhood."

"If he was forgiven by those he offended, why should he come before the whole church who may not know anything about it?" she persisted.

"Maybe it was a burden weighing on his heart and he felt he should humble himself and make a full confession. Any other questions? No? Well, then I'll let you go early today since it's so hot. Be sure to read your lesson for next Sunday on 'The Destiny of Man.' Let us bow for closing prayer. Evelyn, will you lead us in prayer, please?"

"Let's say the Lord's Prayer. 'Our Father, who art in heaven....'"

Went to John L.'s in evening. We had ice cream, cake and Jello.

Monday, August 14, 1939

Cal's pigs were at Maendl's place. We tried to drive them home at noon, but they always wanted to go back. I got so tired out that we gave up driving them home.

Went to town and bought one lug pears, $1.19; one lug peaches, 79¢; 3 lugs overripe apricots, $1.50. Pearl is making jam.

Tuesday, August 15, 1939

Dug out rocks on a strip of sod close to section line. Cut thistles with mower in order to plow. Cal and I plowed total of 11 hrs.

Saturday, August 19, 1939

Pearson was here to look at Bullet. I wanted $125. He said it would take two like that to bring $125. I asked him whether he could use her for $100 and he said not.

Cal caponized some roosters for Maendl. He got 10¢ each, which I think is too much. I told him to charge 5¢.

Sunday, August 20, 1939

Got up too late to go to church. I am reading ABRAHAM LINCOLN, BOY AND MAN by James Morgan. Got it from the Freeman Public Library last night.

Cal and Pearl went to catechism in afternoon. We all were in church in the evening. Rev. Jacob A. Tieszen is holding revival meetings in our church all week.

Pearl went up to Rev. D. W. Tschetter's with Alfred for supper.

Our supper consisted of a whole watermelon which Cal bought from Josh Tschetter.

Monday, August 21, 1939

Mrs. Art Adrian was here looking for their cows at noon. We found them in our corn field. They had been in the Sooner milo. After dinner Cal and I fenced between our cane and Adrian's land.

Tuesday, August 22, 1939

County agent was here to plat the cane field. After dinner we all went to Yankton for a poultry and egg judging event. Pearl, Cal, and P. P.'s Irene are on the team.

Wednesday, August 23, 1939

Cal caponized more cockerels for Maendl. He charges a nickel now.

I went to Sioux Empire Fair with Mr. and Mrs. Pettis. The children went to the revival meeting at church.

Friday, August 25, 1939

Got my wheat allotment for 1940 — 39.9 acres. I have 228 acres of cropland total.

Pearl is still making jam.

Had 4-H meeting at Pete Ratzlaff's after revival meeting.

Saturday, August 26, 1939

My oldest sister, Mrs. Jacob L. Hofer, Sr., is very sick with diabetes. It is affecting her eyes.

Sunday, August 27, 1939

All in church in morning. Cal and Pearl had catechism in afternoon. Calvin and several others in the class answered the altar call tonight at the revival. It was the last night of Tieszen's preaching.

Monday, August 28, 1939

Cal and I got the sheep and pigs ready to take to the county fair tomorrow morning. I had a load of feed ground at Park Lane. They were 720 lbs. short. One of the guys claimed a sack got stuck in the spout. They have been short several times. I am afraid the boys need watching.

Tuesday, August 29, 1939

Cal and I took livestock to the fair. I took 11 sheep and Cal took 5 Duroc pigs. He won champion gilt and champion litter in 4-H plus 4 blue ribbons, 2 for boars and 2 for gilts. My winnings in open class were $25.50. Cal's in 4-H were $19.50.

Pearl entered canned goods, breads and poultry.

Ed Maendl took a trailer load of hogs and sheep over to Tripp. A wheel came off his trailer. I came home with him and milked 4 cows after midnight.

Wednesday, August 30, 1939

Pearl and I were the only ones home this morning. Cal stayed at Tripp with the livestock and the little girls are at P. P.'s.

Thursday, August 31, 1939

Biggest crowd today at fair. Gate receipts were $1600.

Got our prize money. Cal got an additional $2 for his Durocs in open class and $5.50 in Handicrafts on his dresser.

Friday, September 1, 1939

Slept in the cattle barn at fair last night. Packed all the things for Girls' 4-H. Cal's dresser will go to the State Fair, also the 4 Duroc pigs. Sold a ram to Solomon Tiede for $15.

Saturday, September 2, 1939

Cal paid $15 on his note for the sow. I paid off my threshing bill ($10). Paid K & K $5 on account and Ellwein & Dewald $4.74 on account (in full).

Tuesday, September 5, 1939

Pearl, Cal and I are all in Huron at the State Fair. Showed hogs all forenoon. Cal got a blue and three reds on four pigs. The

252

DAKOTA FARMER photographer took pictures of Cal and his winning pigs.

We ate at the 4-H camp most of the time. J. Robert Kleinsasser is the mess sergeant.

Wednesday, September 6, 1939

Ed Maendl was milking our cows when I got up this morning. He thought I was still in Huron.

Thursday, September 7, 1939

Cal and Pearl rode home from the State Fair with A. T. Kaufman. Sold two rams to Jamesville Colony for $37.50.

Friday, September 8, 1939

Went to Huron this morning with Roland Haar to bring back the livestock in his truck. Bought 3 dresses each for Ruth and Marian and a pair of Oxford gray trousers for myself ($3.98).

Saturday, September 9, 1939

Saw motorcycle and auto races at fair. Pearl and Cal were at church in afternoon to practice for the baptism tomorrow.

Sunday, September 10, 1939

Pearl and Calvin were baptized in our church in the forenoon. Albert Ewert, a missionary to China, spoke in the afternoon and Rev. Louis Linscheid preached in the evening. There were 12 in the baptism class.

Monday, September 11, 1939

My school started today. I have 20 pupils. Pearl and Cal started at the Academy. Ruth and Marian attend Freeman Public School. Marian is a first grader. Weather very hot and dry. Temperature hovers around 100. After 3 p.m. the schoolroom is almost unbearable. There is no pasture for the cattle and the corn is drying up fast.

Thursday, September 14, 1939

Cal is 16 years old today. He was arrested for speeding. Might be fined. They claim he was racing on Main Street with Solomon Wollman.

Took out wheat insurance on 12 acres winter wheat and 27 acres spring wheat.

Friday, September 15, 1939

Missed the College corporation meeting because of Burial Assoc. meeting in Viborg. Cal and I got home about 1 a.m. Cal was my driver because I get sleepy when driving.

Sunday, September 17, 1939

Pearl went to Yankton in the afternoon with Rev. D. W. Tschetters. Alfred is taking up the pre-medical course at Yankton College.

At C. E. in the evening Pres. J. D. Unruh gave a very well thought out speech on Christian education.

Pearl went away with Pete Hofer, I think. She is not home yet at 11:45.

Monday, September 18, 1939

After 7 p.m. Cal and I went to see Elias Kleinsasser, small court justice. Cal is accused of racing on Main Street.

"Town Marshal Paul Groves clocked 'im goin' fifty miles per hour between the College and the Co-op Gas and Oil," said Finer.

"I can't believe our '34 Chevy can reach that speed within a couple of blocks!" protested Morgan. "I was about ready to trade in that car."

"Well, that's what Paul said. And it's not the first time, either. People have been complainin' to me about them racin'."

"Pretty hard for me to believe," said Morgan, shaking his head. On the way home Morgan broke the silence. "Is it possible you were going fifty miles per hour?"

"It's possible."

"Why, that's terrible. That would be an awful thing to have on your record."

"I think I better plead guilty and pay the $25 fine. Solomon is."

"Well, it'll have to come out of your bank account."

"I'll pay the fine," said Cal.

Wednesday, September 20, 1939

Broke the rear axle on the car. Joe Louis knocked out Pastor in the 11th round.

Sunday, September 24, 1939

Took Lord's Supper in church this morning. Pearl went away with Peter Hofer and Cal got sick in the afternoon, so I had to do the chores alone.

Monday, September 25, 1939

The children were all sick this morning, so I went to school alone. Started snowing this morning.

Tuesday, September 26, 1939

Ruth and Marian are still sick. Andrew Schaefer came to my school with a '37 Chevy Sedan to trade me for my '34 Chevy. I offered him $250 to boot as it stands or $275 and four new tires. The cane was all covered with snow this morning, but it did not freeze.

Wednesday, September 27, 1939

Drove to Parkston to the Teachers' Institute with the '37 Chevy. Dr. Art Briese was the main speaker. He put on an impersonation of an Englishman visiting America. He fooled most of us. He certainly fooled me.

Paul Glanzer and I went to the Corn Palace at Mitchell afterwards. Saw the 5:45 show. Paul Whiteman led the orchestra. I saw how they broadcast those cigarette programs.

Thursday, September 28, 1939

Signed up for my wheat sealing loan. Will use the money to pay taxes. It will amount to about $94.

Cul und I took our car back to Schaefer. It does not steer well, has a bad clutch, and uses oil.

Around midnight Johnny Klein knocked on the door and woke me up. He came back from the Corn Palace with John Stahl.

Friday, September 29, 1939

Johnny went along with the children to the College.

Sam Mendel is putting up a windmill on a well that Jacob L. Hofer, Sr., drilled about 50 years ago. The pipes and rods are in good shape. He is pumping water with the tractor now.

Marian got very sick tonight. We gave her Ex-Lax, castor oil, and some other stomach medicine.

Johnny and Cal went away – to a literary society meeting, they said.

Saturday, September 30, 1939

Had an Aid Plan meeting at Bethany Church. Elected delegates to the general meeting in Mt. Lake, Minn.

Marian got quite sick so I called Doc Ernest to examine her. He thinks it might be appendicitis.

Sunday, October 1, 1939

Did not go to church this morning. Marian is quite sick. Mary Klein is staying here. Doc Ernest came out towards evening.

Monday, October 2, 1939

Everybody in school but Marian. John R. Hofer lost 5 cows on cane today. It was second growth, frost bitten cane. We had our cattle on low acid cane, also frost bitten.

Doc Ernest was out again. He thinks Marian has kidney trouble. Got some medicine for her and a tonic for both girls called vitrate by Upjohn.

Jake Walter's horses were on the section line today. They had come all the way up from the C. P. Dickman farm south of town where Walters moved.

Wednesday, October 4, 1939

Marian went back to school. She feels quite a bit better. Mary went to her sister Adeline.

We had a health clinic at school. Three other schools came to be examined by the county nurse.

Sunday, October 8, 1939

Had Sunday School convention in Bridgewater. Had dinner at Paul E.'s and supper at Joe Pullman's. I was nominated for chairman but lost to Rev. Jacob B. Brother J. W. was elected secretary.

Monday, October 9, 1939

Clarence Hofer of Beadle stayed here overnight. He has a rheumatism that draws his joints out of place.

Glanzers want to drive their car to College all this month so Joe P. can use their car next month buying furs.

Paid Schaefer $25 on car. Still owe him $200.

Thursday, October 12, 1939

Pearl came home from school at noon to do the washing. She is also selling the STAR, the College paper, and ads in it. She wants to get the prize for selling the most.

Cal and Benny Tschetter took some girls to the Marion H. S. play. Benny stayed here overnight.

Saturday, October 14, 1939

Ground was frozen this morning, so could not start sowing wheat 'til noon. Sowed 12 acres by nightfall.

Dug 10 bu. potatoes with Grandpa's plow. Had preacher's boys out to help as well as Benny Tschetter. Paid Benny one dollar and the boys 25¢ apiece.

Wednesday, October 18, 1939
Shot a pheasant after school. Saw many in the morning but the season is open only in the afternoon.

We are closing school at 3:30 now and taking just a half hour for the noon hour.

Friday, October 20, 1939
Cal sold his sow to Morrell Packing Plant. She weighed 435 lbs. and brought $6.05 cwt.

Went to SDEA in Sioux Falls. Heard Miss Enslow, author, talk on THE LITTLE SCHOOL IN THE FOOTHILLS.

Roomed with Earl Hammerquist at the Cataract Hotel. Sen. Vandenburg spoke on his experiences in Europe. Afterwards Earl and I saw the movie, "Young Lincoln." It was good.

Saturday, October 21, 1939
Dr. Joseph Roemer of Tenn. spoke. He said, "Education may be the salvation of democracy." Got a few textbooks from publishing representatives.

Sunday, October 22, 1939
Shot 7 pheasants. Stopped in at young Peter G. Jacob L. figures on taking a trip to California with Pete. Jake has relatives there.

Monday, October 23, 1939
We are having pheasants almost every meal. We skin them to save time. Unloaded Sooner milo bundles into granary since we have no grain to fill it.

Cal and Benny took some girls to Menno for a play. It is hard on the gas.

The Watkins man sold me a bottle of linament and some cold pills for $1.05.

Wednesday, October 25, 1939
FJC Student Assoc. is having the STAR party tonight. Pearl's side won. She sold more subscriptions alone than all of the other side. She won the prize.

I am playing ball with the children in school.

Sunday, October 29, 1939

Abe Wiens offered me a job to teach their school next year. Cal and Benny used our car to go to the Salem KMB Church. Pearl was home for once.

Monday, October 30, 1939

John P. Gross phoned that our sheep got out on the section line and went into his rye field.

Children went to Freeman H. S. for "Stunt Night" to raise money for the town library.

Thursday, November 2, 1939

Pearl stayed home to do the washing but could not get the Maytag started. Alice Wipf of Onida is staying here. Pearl had left the car switch on last night, so Glanzers had to push our car to get it started.

Saturday, November 4, 1939

Boys started fencing, but the ground is extremely hard for post hole digging. You have to water the ground to dig. Prospects for a crop next year are bad.

Paid over $100 taxes. SW quarter, $58.54; W half, $32.18. Personal, $10.10.

Sunday, November 5, 1939

Could not get car started so we did not go to church. Pulled car with team to start it and drove it to Schaefer's Garage. He worked on it for an hour and could not make it go. He gave me his car so we could go to John J. B.'s for dinner and supper.

Sold Bullet to Pearson for $65.

Friday, November 10, 1939

Academy had their play, "The Family Upstairs." Pearl played Emma Heller, the mother. They had a big crowd.

Sunday, November 12, 1939

Went to Bethesda Church for a program by FJC. When we got home John J. B.'s and two colony men, Jacob and John Mendel from Canada, were here. Missionary Vogt from China had spoken in our church.

Monday, November 13, 1939

Colony boys came to my school. After school I took them to visit various relatives. Had supper at Derby's. Then Editor J. J. Mendel and Brother P. P. went along with us to the Jamesville

Colony near Utica, where we left the boys. I had two glasses of colony wine. I think the boys were looking for wives.

Tuesday, November 14, 1939
My pocket watch stopped in school so I did not let the pupils out 'til 4:40.

Friday, November 17, 1939
After school I went to town with Paul L. and stayed for the 4-H banquet. Bought a coat each for Ruth and Marian. Ruth's was $4.25 and Marian's $2.75.

We served 138 people. Pearl got a medal for canning and Cal got the Wilson medal for best in livestock. My club members all completed their projects.

Sunday, November 19, 1939
Took Cal to chiropractor Emil Tiesen. Cal hurt his knee yesterday trying to dig post holes in the hard ground. Tiesen said it was just a bruise.

Tiesen was at Wagner in the afternoon. They are still hoping for oil.

Monday, November 20, 1939
I bought a bat for the pupils to play ball at school. They enjoy playing kitten ball.

Ruth enjoys listening to radio plays, especially "Lux Presents." They will give one of George Bernard Shaw's plays next week.

Pearl and Cal are studying for quarter tests.

Wednesday, November 22, 1939
Cal came home after his tests and fixed the plow, which broke yesterday. He plowed SW corner field and disced the Sooner milo field. I burned weeds after school.

Thursday, November 23, 1939
Mrs. Josephine Zehnpfennig Williams, Co. Sup., visited school with her deputy, Miss Ella Schaal of Tripp. Miss Schaal is a very nice looking young lady.

Friday, November 24, 1939
Pearl and Cal are finishing their Academy exams. Cal is making some fair grades. Pearl could do better if she did not spend so much time writing letters.

Saturday, November 25, 1939

I went to see Miss Waltner at the College about the practice teachers. I want a change and think I'll get it.

Sunday, November 26, 1939

Alice Wipf came along last night. She went with Pearl and Cal to hear THE MESSIAH sung at the Gym tonight by the Community Chorus.

Monday, November 27, 1939

Practice teachers came up to school. They are Alice Wipf of Onida, Orpha Schrag of Freeman, Evelyn Perryman of Sioux Falls, and Jeanette Huber of Freeman.

Moses Glanzer said he does not have time to build the fire for me at school in the morning, so I got his brother Aaron to do it for me.

Picked up Joe Stucky who was walking on the way to town. He said I should come out for Co. Commissioner.

Pearl and Cal went to Marion to roller skate. It is just too bad [sic].

Tuesday, November 28, 1939

After school I went to Olivet for a Crop Improvement Assoc. meeting. We plan to have a banquet in Freeman on Dec. 7. I am responsible for putting on the feed. Plan to have a few professors from the State College there.

I ordered some pamphlets from CAPPER'S FARMER: "Plains Land Management" and "New System of Farming" for 5¢.

THE DAKOTA FARMER printed a pasture program that would give steady pasture throughout the summer and allow the permanent pasture to rest and reseed itself:
Apr. 15-June 1 — Rye sown preferably the last of Aug. or early Sept.
June 1-July 10 — A mixture of 1 bu. oats, 1 bu. barley & 1/2 bu. rye sown as early as possible in spring.
July 10-Sept. 10 — Sudan grass sown May 20 to June 1.
Sept. 10-Oct. 15 — Stubble and meadow aftermath or rape. (Rape is not suited for milk cows.)
Oct. 15-Nov. 15 — Fall rye.

Wednesday, November 29, 1939

I am taking practice teachers to my school with my car. Weather is still wonderful. Cal will drag thistles and possibly plow after school.

Thursday, November 30, 1939

Thanksgiving Day. Ruth, Marian and I were in church. Jake I. Walter preached a good sermon. For dinner and supper we were at Jake L. Hofer, Sr. 260

Jake L., Jr. and Peter G., Jr. and their wives came back from California about 6:15 p.m. They said some people are sorry they left S. D. for Calif.

Heard Sen. Bulow in Freeman in evening. He spoke on the Arms Embargo bill, Hitler, etc. He said why people voted for the Arms Embargo repeal = profit, propaganda.

John L. and I asked the Dorcas Society to serve the meal for our Crop Improvement Assoc. banquet on Dec. 7.

Taxpayers' League will have a meeting in Menno tomorrow.

Friday, December 1, 1939

Prof. D. S. Wipf was here for the three-teated cow. He is to pay me $1.50 per week for use of the cow, he to furnish the feed.

Luella Thomas observed all day in school.

Got a $7.74 refund on gas from state. Sent $3.50 to Spiegel for what they say I owe them for quilts Pearl ordered.

Saturday, December 2, 1939

Got a load of hard coal (1760 lbs) for $14.30 with Stolp's trailer. Paid Gottlieb Schmeichel $5 for triple loaf of wood he is to bring.

Went to Yankton to see Atty. Clark about Burial Assoc. affairs. Bought 2 pr. silk stockings for Pearl, a top coat for me at $15, a top coat for Cal at $12 at Hub. Clothing Store (Gurney).

Tuesday, December 5, 1939

Still beautiful weather so children play outside. Prof. John Congdon, chemistry teacher at the College, visited our school all forenoon and gave a talk about science.

Pearl and Cal are going to church choir practice. They are getting ready for Christmas.

Saw Dan Merk. He said the doctor told him to feed his sows wheat germ oil if they do not come into heat.

Thursday, December 7, 1939

Had our Crop Improvement banquet. Weather is best it's been in 50 years. Had baked ham dinner. College quartet sang and David Wollman played his harmonica and guitar. Professors A. M. Eberle and Clarence Shanley of Brookings spoke.

Sunday, December 10, 1939

Karl Mundt gave a non-political talk on world affairs at the South Church. He makes a forceful speaker.

Monday, December 11, 1939

Got up real early but wasted a lot of time downtown rounding up the practice teachers.

Tuesday, December 12, 1939

Very windy. Water supply tank is full but we cannot stop the windmill. A real dust storm.

Wrage and Wirt of Parker came up to my school to buy a ewe for 4-H club work. I let the practice teachers take care of the school while I went home with them and sold the ewe for $27.50.

Wednesday, December 13, 1939

All four practice teachers are doing good work. I would not mind if we had them all winter.

Thursday, December 14, 1939

College Founders' Day, so the practice teachers did not come out. Went to pageant in the evening put on by the College.

Friday, December 15, 1939

Went to basketball game between Dakota Wesleyan of Mitchell and FJC. The score was overwhelmingly in favor of Mitchell, 60 to 30.

Saturday, December 16, 1939

Cal and I went to annual church meeting. Cal put in his bid ($69.24 per annum) for janitor. Joe K. had the low bid of $64.75 and got the job.

We decided to have one English service per month (the first Sun. of month). Raised church levy for unmarried boys. It is to be 1/3 of the family levy of $15 or $5. I was elected secretary of the Mennonite Aid Plan.

Tuesday, December 19, 1939

I was elected secretary of the Burial Assoc. board. From Viborg I went to Menno where I spoke to Atty. Ulmer in support of nephew Dave M. Hofer's bid for Dolton mail carrier. He said whoever gets the majority of precinct committee men and women to endorse him will get Ulmer's endorsement.

Wednesday, December 20, 1939

Co-op Creamery paid out $10,000 in dividends. Ours was only $13.

Last day for practice teachers. I bought each a box of handkerchiefs and a box of candy.

I bought Christmas presents for my pupils: older boys a pocket knife and girls a box of handkerchiefs. Three smaller boys got a necktie. I was afraid they would get hurt if I gave them a pocket knife.

Saturday, December 23, 1939

All in town in evening. Bought Christmas dresses for the girls and a $3.98 pair of shoes for myself.

Spoke to a few about coming out for Co. Sup. of Schools. Got some encouragement. Heard that Huebner of Menno might be a candidate. Atty. Henry L. Gross will again be a candidate for Co. Judge.

Sunday, December 24, 1939

Got up too late to go to church. Cold but no snow.

Heard a Christmas program from Rome broadcast from the North American College. Also heard a man speaking from Berlin at 6:15 p.m. It was 1:15, Christmas Day, in Berlin.

Had Christmas program in church. Marian gave a German piece, Ruth a piece in English ("Why Do Bells on Christmas Ring?") Pearl and Cal were in the choir. They had to move the pulpit to accommodate everyone in the choir. Later the choir came to our place caroling. I recognized Johnny Klein as they sang at my window.

"Let's stop at Morgan's first," suggested Johnny.

"He'll still be up. If you want to surprise him, you'll have to catch him at the end of the tour. He'll be asleep by then, most likely," said Cal.

"Okay, we'll go to Jacob P. Maendl's first, then west and north toward Bridgewater, east to Dolton and then back south toward Freeman," said Jac. Mendel, their director.

The Hutterthal choir, bundled up against the cold, piled into cars and headed toward the Jacob Maendl farm southwest of the church. Through the window they could see the older couple sitting at the kitchen table, reading the Bible by kerosene lamp.

"*Stille Nacht, Heilige Nacht*" the choir sang below their window. Mrs. Maendl paused in her reading, her hands folded over the Bible. A black flowered shawl covered her white hair.

When the choir had finished, Mrs. Maendl opened her door. "*Kommst herein*," she said.

"Thank you, but we're just starting out," said Jac.

"*Willst Kendy hob'n?*"

"Yeah!" came the chorus.

She passed among the carolers a bowl of peppermint candy. "*Fröhliche Weinachten!*" she said.

263

Back in the car, Pearl said, "She is the sweetest lady! She makes the best dill pickles, too. She makes some for us every summer."

"I know! She makes some for us too," said Grace, the preacher's daughter.

The carolers made their rounds, alternately freezing their toes and fingers, warming up under horsehide blankets. Near midnight, as they approached John J. B.'s near Dolton, Johnny Klein said, "I'll bet Aunt Katherine will have something warm for us."

"At midnight?" asked Grace.

"Sure, she's prepared many a midnight lunch for us," said Pearl.

After singing "We Three Kings" and "O Come, All Ye Faithful," the choir was invited into the large and warm farm kitchen. "What do I smell?" asked Johnny as he hugged his aunt.

"I believe it's *Fleisch Wurst!*" suggested Pearl.

"You're right. I got sandwiches and cocoa for all of you. Come on in!"

As the group drove south on Highway 81 to Morgan's farm, there was hardly any traffic. Only an occasional kerosene or gas lamp was to be seen through a farmhouse window. "I'm sorry there was no snow this Christmas," said Grace. "Christmas is always more romantic with snow."

"Yeah, but we'd be tracking up everybody's house with snow on our galoshes," practical Pearl reminded her.

"Not to mention the danger of getting stuck!" said Johnny.

"We do have the moonlight, though," said Grace.

As they turned into Morgan's farmyard, only the glow of red coals in the hard coal burner could be seen through the parlor windows. "Everybody's asleep, even Pa," said Pearl.

"Let's go around to his bedroom window," said Johnny.

"Watch out so you don't stumble over the snow fencing," cautioned Cal. The group quietly made its way to the north side of the house protected by an embankment of packed straw. "Careful you don't snag your silk hose," cautioned Pearl to Grace.

"Quiet! Let's wake him up by caroling, not jabbering!" scolded Johnny.

Jac. Mendel led in singing "O, Little Town of Bethlehem." Suddenly two little faces appeared in the window west of Morgan's window. "We woke up Ruth and Marian," said Pearl, waving to her sisters.

After the choir sang "Joy to the World," Morgan appeared at the window in his pajamas. "Come to the front door and I'll give you some fruit and nuts." As the choir assembled around the entrance, Morgan started pitching apples, oranges and walnuts at individuals. "Here, catch!" he said. Then, seeing oranges elude grasps, he chided, "Some of you should have brought your catcher's mitts!"

Ruth and Marian in their pajamas watched the merriment. "Can we have an orange too?" asked Marian.

"Sure! Catch!" And Morgan sent an orange flying to each of them.

Pearl, shivering in the cold, decided to leave the carolers at this point to warm up before the parlor stove with its isinglass windows and then to climb into bed between her two little sisters. Cal and Johnny would continue to the end of the choir's tour.

Monday, December 25, 1939

Christmas Day. Beautiful day – no snow. After church we went to John J. B.'s for dinner and supper. Had Christmas gathering at Jake L.'s. All the children and partners were there except Smokey Joe and Viola of Onida. I got a Sheaffer pen and ink stand from my nephew, Paul L., in the gift exchange.

Tuesday, December 26, 1939

Had school. In the evening we went to grandparents. Benny Tschetter was along. Ruth and Marian got 50¢ for saying their pieces and the rest of us, including Benny, got $1.

Wednesday, December 27, 1939

Butchered 46 ducks. Took 16 to the Freeman locker. People helping Pearl were Sister Katherine, Little Katherine, Mrs. Jake L. and daughter Marjorie, Mr. & Mrs. Abe P. Tieszen, Mrs. John L., Benny Tschetter, Johnny and Paul Kleinsasser.

Thursday, December 28, 1939

Much colder. Took 6 ducks to Morfeld Meat Market. Got credit for 36 lbs. at 12¢ per lb.

Mrs. Paul L. and Mrs. Abe Wiens helped Pearl can ducks.

Had telephone meeting. Paid my dues for 1940 ($4.20). I was elected secretary.

Saturday, December 30, 1939

No water for cattle. Windmill pumped for a while, then quit. Took Johnny Klein to Stanley Corner to catch a ride back home.

Sunday, December 31, 1939

Had Sunday School election during the S. S. hour. I was elected teacher of Class 7, a men's class. Joe K. and Sarah B., teachers of the youngest children, had been elected at the annual meeting. We have four women's classes, all taught by men.

Had Watch Night Service in evening and a shower for Jacob B.

"It'll be like a pound party or a housewarming. But you know Jacob B. has a large family and a small salary," said Paul E. as he informed individual members of the congregation of the planned shower. "Let's keep it a secret. Anything that might be damaged by freezing, such as eggs or jars of fruit and vegetables, can be stored in the baby room 'til after the service. I'll keep him out of there."

After the customary conclusion to the Watch Night Service, in which Joe K. read the names of all who had died during the year and asked, "Who will be the first one in the new decade?" the members filed out of the church. First came the children, row by row. Then came the men folks and after them the women folks. Slowly they made their way to the four-wheeled trailer that had gradually been filling with one-hundred-pound bags of "Pride of the Rockies" flour, graham flour, Holly beet sugar, cases of canned goods, Butternut coffee, Morton salt, gunny sacks of potatoes, carrots and beets. The eggs and glass-preserved fruits and vegetables were brought from the "baby room," which served also as the minister's prayer room and cloak room.

As the minister's family gathered with awe and gratitude near the trailer, Paul E. prayed for a blessing on the food and for guidance in the new year.

Rev. Jacob B. Hofer, their pastor, responded. "Sometimes I thought I couldn't go on, being both a rural school teacher and your preacher. But God has given the strength. And we thank you for this generous outpouring of gifts. May God richly reward you."

Shaking Jacob B.'s hand, Morgan said, "I know how you feel. Many's the time I figured I couldn't make it without Katherine, teaching school and farming at the same time. But, somehow, with everybody's help, we manage."

"With GOD'S help, Morgan, GOD'S help."

1940
Running and Losing

Tuesday, January 2, 1940

Waited in the dark at my school for Cal to come with the car. He tried to get Julius Albrecht to fix it. We got home at 6:30. I went to town after supper. Tried to get Bill Schultz to do chores for us, but he won't come out. Bill is badly spoiled by relief.

Marian showed me how Miss Bess Henley, her teacher, wrote the change in the decade from 1939 to 1940 on the blackboard.

Wednesday, January 3, 1940

Ben Schrag and Pete Schmidt fixed our well. Some of the rods were torn off, so we had no water for two days. Gave the chickens cistern water. An Unruh boy who works with Schrag was hurt at our place. A large hook fell on his head and he had to have eight stitches taken.

Friday, January 5, 1940

Had AAA meeting. They showed two pictures: "The Plow that Broke the Sod" and "The River."

Saturday, January 6, 1940

I helped Pearl with housework in the forenoon. Prof. D. S. Wipf brought the three-teated cow back. He had used her for five weeks.

Saw H. L. Gross about my candidacy for Co. Sup. He said the Olivet group will be for me. Some think Effie Carlson will come out.

Thursday, January 11, 1940

Windmill is fixed and strong wind is blowing from northwest, so mill is pumping today. Big tank and two smaller ones are now full.

Sarah Hofer fell while playing in the school basement and hurt her head. I took her home after treating the cut.

Saturday, January 13, 1940

I went with Jake L. to a DeKalb Hybrid Seed Corn meeting in Sioux Falls. Got the Aid Plan secretary books from D. J. Mendel. I put announcement of my candidacy in Tripp, Menno and Parkston papers. Had pork roast from the locker.

Tuesday, January 23, 1940

Harvey and Clarence, second graders, certainly comprehend the stories they read and can tell the stories clearly. Vivian is the best oral reader but doesn't get the thought as well. I gave the boys each a dime for telling their stories so well.

Thursday, January 25, 1940

Cal and I saw the county basketball tournament. Freeman beat Menno 31 to 18 and won the championship.

Saturday, January 27, 1940

Circulated my petition.

Joe Stucky said Huebner would run well in Tripp. He found just one man against Huebner. Thinks Menno is 50-50 for Huebner and Parkston to be my stronghold, next to Freeman.

Thursday, February 1, 1940

At school officers' meeting in Menno, the Co. Sup. told board members to give Huebner a hand when he came into the room. Of course, the people did.

Saturday, February 3, 1940

Had long talk with H. L. Gross. He said I should favor the deputy, Ella Schaal, for my deputy to get the Tripp vote.

Got more signers on my petition.

Tuesday, February 6, 1940

Francis Smidt wrote that I should see Richard Schamber. I hope I can get the help of the Lutherans and other denominational schools for my candidacy.

Wednesday, February 7, 1940

Two more candidates out for Co. Sup. — Roger Carlson of Menno and Bernice Newell north of Scotland. We are going into the primary now for sure. I hope Huebner can be eliminated as it seems he will be my toughest opponent. J. C. Graber thinks I'll have no trouble in the primary.

Thursday, February 8, 1940

Got the suit from Spike Walter that I had ordered — 2 pr. trousers ($36.50), 7 button vest. Coat, chest 44 1/2 in., length, 30 in.; pants, inseam, 30 in., waist, 42 in.

Friday, February 9, 1940

AAA met at #51. Payments will be less this year.

Saturday, February 10, 1940

Got haircut from Leon Gering. Had 1,000 campaign cards printed at COURIER for $3.25.

Had teachers' meeting in Olivet. Nearly all present. #51 won the prize in medium-size school and also high in county for sale of Christmas seals. Won same last year. We got a basketball and two boxes of candy.

Sunday, February 11, 1940

Church was filled this morning. It thawed all morning. I taught class.

I took the girls to see "Young Lincoln" at Freeman. I had seen it at SDEA so I knew it was suitable.

Monday, February 12, 1940

Ernest Schamber came out and we went to Clayton and Olivet to see a number of Lutherans about my candidacy.

Tuesday, February 13, 1940

Ernest Schamber and I went to Beardsley for a AAA meeting at Kulm and German Townships. He introduced me to quite a few people. Saw Tiede, who is running for State Rep. He said Parkston sentiment is in my favor.

Wednesday, February 14, 1940

Had children make a Valentine for their ma and pa. After school Ernest Schamber and I went to Mettler School north of Menno and then to Kaylor. Big crowd at Kaylor.

Thursday, February 15, 1940

After school I went to Susquehanna and Liberty Township meetings held in Parkston. Met quite a few people. Jacob Lindeman took some of my cards to pass out.

Friday, February 16, 1940

After school Schamber and John Aman and I went to Tripp. I did not get to talk to many people because they had a minstrel show. Wm. Schenk thinks I will have a good chance because Miss Schaal is too young.

Cal and Benny simonized the car.

Saturday, February 17, 1940

John Nachtigal and I went to Olivet and Menno campaigning. I need 106-264 signers on my petitions.

Saw Miss Schaal and offered her the deputyship if she does not file her petition.

Sunday, February 18, 1940
Had an interesting discussion in Sunday School. Some of the old timers think Sunday School should be more "preaching" and less discussion. They did not have Sunday School in Russia because German and Bible were taught in the common schools, which were run by the Mennonites or Hutterites, as the case may be. Brother J. W. was the first to start Sunday School in this country among our people.

A group of men had a jack rabbit roundup around Wolf Creek. They got 478 rabbits which sold for 15 1/2 cents each. Apparently we have an oversupply when the skunk population drops.

Monday, February 19, 1940
Cal is fixing the spotlight on the Chevy. He wants to do more jack rabbit hunting.

Tuesday, February 20, 1940
Joe P. Glanzer, Paul L. and I went to Parkston for their Mid-Winter Fair. Joe bought 2 beavers on the way over, one for $12 and the other for $12.50.

Had a good meeting. Met many voters. Banker Winter said he would support only a woman for the job.

Wednesday, February 21, 1940
Had sign-up for the Soil Conservation program in my school. Got quite a few signers on my petition. Went to Parkston campaigning after school. It seems I should get a good vote out of Parkston. Prof. Eberle of the State College was there to speak.

Thursday, February 22, 1940
My birthday. Had a little program after recess on the George Washington theme. AAA is having sign-up at my school and I am meeting a large number of prospective voters.

Friday, February 23, 1940
I did not have school. I went visiting other teachers and did a little campaigning on the side. Saw Mrs. Tripp, the county nurse, and told her about the Joshua R. M. Hofer case. She said she would investigate. Roger Carlson and Wilbur Ackerman think Miss Schaal will get the highest vote in the county.

Saturday, February 24, 1940

Short of feed. Out of alfalfa. Bought 10 bu. corn and 3 bags egg mash.

Our school got a large amount of surplus commodities: apples, pears, oatmeal, onions, wheat flour, beans, raisins.

I heard Dr. Payne said he thought Miss Schaal could not run the office of Sup.

Monday, February 26, 1940

Gave each of the children a pear at noon from the Surplus Commodity Administration.

Got an invitation from Henry Ripp of Dimock to come to a dairy meeting at their co-op cheese factory tomorrow.

Tuesday, February 27, 1940

Pearl has finished her Academy course and will stay home for the spring quarter.

Joe P. Glanzer went with me to Dimock for the cheese meeting where I gave a little talk. Joe bought a beaver from Guericke.

Wednesday, February 28, 1940

Pearl is practicing for a speech contest to be held at Augustana Academy in Canton.

Our feed is almost gone. Cal is a good feeder, but he uses up too much feed.

Friday, March 1, 1940

Had two visiting teachers – Anna Wollman and Katie Hofer. They seemed to enjoy our work.

Jonath Waltner and I went to the Crop Improvement Assoc. in Olivet. I am on the committee. I dealt out more campaign cards. Emanuel Frier said he thought Miss Schaal was too young for the job.

Saturday, March 2, 1940

Pearl did not win yesterday but learned by being in the contest.

"What did the critics say about your oration?" Morgan asked.

"Here are the criticisms," she said, handing a sheaf of papers to her father.

"Let's see what we can learn from the experience," he said and read:

" 'Went to stage with handkerchief in hand!' Exclamation point! I guess that's *verboten*. Well, we learned something. 'Made a good appearance.' Well, that's good, except for the appearance of the handkerchief, I guess. 'Had not learned to project sound – was difficult to hear.' We'll have to let you call the hogs a little more often. 'Unfortunate choice of oration.' What does that mean? I thought you wrote it yourself."

"No, it was in the category of 'Committed Oratory,' not 'Original Oratory.'"

"Well, that was your mistake right there. You can't give other people's orations as well as you can give your own. Whose was it, anyway?"

"It was by Joseph Connolly of the School of Mines on 'The Need for Vocational Education'. Miss Loewen suggested it to me."

"'Statistics are never interesting.' True, unless you're one of the statistics. 'Audience restless. Pretty and sweet.'"

"Isn't that nice?" Pearl said, sarcastically.

"That's called faint praise. 'Pretty and sweet but not an orator. She should tell a story, not give an oration.'" Well, what does that tell you?"

"Not to enter any more speech contests!"

"Not necessarily. Could mean to enter in the 'Dramatic Reading' category instead of Oratory. They don't have 'Story Telling', do they?"

"No."

"What does it tell you about what you ought to take up in college?"

"I don't know."

"Probably means you should prepare to be an elementary school teacher and not run for Congress."

Sunday, March 3, 1940

Visited Abe Wienses. They have a new son named Dennis Ray.

Monday, March 4, 1940

John J. B.'s came to visit. Kids wanted to go rollerskating but I did not permit them. They went to Freeman instead to hear a preacher, a Rev. Fast, who had been in South America.

Thursday, March 7, 1940

Pearl is teaching for me today. I went to the Fed. Land Bank meeting. They passed a resolution that anyone delinquent in payments cannot serve on the Board.

Friday, March 8, 1940

Went to Parkston for AAA meeting. Wallace, Farley and Roosevelt spoke over the radio. A couple girls sang cowboy songs. Did quite a bit of campaigning. Phil Lichter said he'd pass out my cards in Tripp.

Saturday, March 9, 1940

I pulled one of Marian's teeth.

"I don't want my tooth pulled," cried Marian, running into her bedroom and slamming the door behind her.

"C'mon out. It won't hurt," said Morgan, holding the pair of chrome-plated pliers which he had unwrapped from their burgundy flannel square covering.

"Yes, it will! It always does!" she protested.

"You should let Daddy pull your tooth. I always do," said Ruth, sanctimoniously.

"Liar. You run even faster," Cal reminded her under his breath.

"Why not let it fall out? It's loose and will come out by itself if I wiggle it," pleaded Marian.

"That's just the point. You've got your hand in your mouth all the time wiggling your tooth. That's the way to get germs. And I don't want you going to town with your hand in your mouth," said Pearl.

"Who's going to town?" asked Marian, through the door.

"We are, if you let us pull your tooth."

"Yeah, you're holding us up. We might get late to the show if you don't get it over with!" said Ruth.

Slowly Marian opened the door. Morgan took her by the hand and sat her down in his desk chair. "Okay, now, it's going to be over in a second. Just lean back on my arm." He grasped her head firmly in his left arm. "Open up wide. Okay, I got it!" he said, showing her the tiny tooth. "Now we can go to town."

And the gallery of siblings applauded.

Sunday, March 10, 1940

I stayed in bed with a cold while Cal chored 'til 10:30. Marian came home from church with sore eyes and Pearl went to town to get medicine.

Cal moved the radio into the parlor. We should have done it months ago. We would have saved quite a bit of coal if we had.

Monday, March 11, 1940

Marian has pink eye and Pearl is home. She cried quite a bit last night. Maybe the medicine is too strong or I put too much in. I am worried.

Lambs are coming, of all nights. Glanzers got stuck in a snow bank. The girls came in to warm up. Ruth stayed in town with Aunt Emma. Storm is raging.

John R.'s Irvin died after an illness of a few hours. He was an Academy sophomore and had been my student.

Friday, March 15, 1940
Marian opened her eyes this morning. She can see as well as ever.

"Good morning, Honey. How are you feeling this morning?" Morgan asked his youngest.

"Fine," said Marian as she began to rub the encrusted brown medicine from her eyes.

"Don't rub too hard, Honey."

"I can see!"

"Come out into the parlor so I can get a better look at your eyes," said Morgan, leading her from her bedroom.

"Where's Ruth?"

"She's staying with Virginia and Aunt Emma. Come over to the window and open your eyes as wide as you can. Do you still have any pain?"

"No, they feel good."

"They look good too! Thank God!"

Pearl entered the warm parlor with a tray of cereal bowls. "Good morning! You're up early," she said.

"I can see again."

"It's a miracle!"

"Can I go back to school today?"

"No, it's awfully cold out. You and I will stay home where it's warm and cozy."

"I'd rather go to school. I can read again."

"You'll stay home today. Pearl and you can read together," said Morgan. "We don't want to take any more chances. You should be ready to go back on Monday. Let's eat, Pearl."

"Where's Cal?" asked Marian.

"He's finishing the milking. He'll be in in a few minutes. But we got to eat now or I'll be late for school. Now, let's pray." As they gathered around the library table near the hard coal burner, Morgan said, "Heavenly Father, we thank thee for the night's rest and for the food thou hast provided. We thank thee, too, that Marian's sight has been restored. In Jesus' name, we pray. Amen."

Cal broke through the double doors. "Hey! Look who's up!" And he swooped Marian out of her chair and into his arms.

"I can see again, just as good as before," she said.

"Well, I'll be! That's swell!"

Saturday, March 16, 1940

After Irvin Hofer's funeral I went to town campaigning and gave my signed petitions to Ed Weidenbach to file at the court house on Monday.

Sunday, March 17, 1940

Thawing. Two ewes had triplets this afternoon. One was born dead.

Cal took the car to the Tieszen Church. The Academy Mixed Glee Club is to sing there.

Monday, March 18, 1940

Marian went back to school. She was one of the six high in her school with her reading, "Kitty."

Pearl brought home the dressing table she made in Shop.

"Oh, it's so pretty! Did you make it all by yourself?" asked Ruth.

"Yes, I did. From buying the lumber to painting and sanding. Here, you grab hold and help me carry it into our bedroom."

"Where you gonna put it?"

"In the northwest corner, so I'll have light from both the west and the north when I'm putting on my make-up."

"Can I use it too sometimes?"

"If you're careful. I don't want it to get any nicks and scratches because I'm going to show it at the Fair this fall."

Soon the blue kidney-shaped dressing table was placed in the bedroom corner. "All I need yet is to design a metal contraption to hang the skirt on so I can open the skirt and use the vanity drawer in the middle."

"Where's the bench?"

"It's still in the idea stage down at the Shop. I bought an old adjustable piano stool at an auction sale. I'm going to buy a round mirror to hang on the wall too."

"A matching blue ruffle around the mirror would be nice," suggested Ruth.

"No, I don't like dust catchers around mirrors."

On the mirrored tray Pearl placed her Lady Esther cold cream and facial powder, a bottle of Evening in Paris perfume and her Tangee lipstick. Then, as a crowning touch, she placed her glass violet corsage in the upper left hand corner. "Perfect!" she proclaimed.

Wednesday, March 20, 1940

Had Boys' 4-H Handicraft club here. Cal is to be the leader. Five other boys came. They are interested in making things out of tin foil.

275

Friday, March 22, 1940

Good Friday. All in church in morning. Girls went to Eddie Maendl's in the afternoon while Cal and I did the chores, which are taking longer to do with the lambs coming.

I am reading Sandburg's LINCOLN; THE PRAIRIE YEARS. Cal is reading KNIGHTS OF THE RANGE by Zane Grey.

Saturday, March 23, 1940

Marked most of the lambs with an ear notcher.

Cal and I went to town in the evening. Did a little campaigning. Spike Walter told me someone from Wittenberg Township told him that Wittenberg will vote for me if I don't talk out of turn.

Sunday, March 24, 1940

Easter Sunday. Bronc had a colt by the straw pile during the night.

Monday, March 25, 1940

Mr. & Mrs. D. D. Glanzer and baby Wesley visited school today. They said they enjoyed it.

Cal stayed home from school but did very little outside work. He wrote a theme on Boulder Dam.

Friday, March 29, 1940

Had our regional spelling and declam events at my school. Aaron Glanzer won in Grade 5 & 6 declam. Vivian Hofer, Melvin and Selma Glanzer, and Luella Schmeichel won in spelling.

Reuben Stahl and Ernst Harder, an exchange student from Paraguay, came home with Cal. Harder's family fled Ukraine in 1924 and Germany in 1935.

Saturday, March 30, 1940

Cal's sow had 17 pigs last night, 14 live ones. He and Reuben took turns getting up every two hours to put them to the nipple.

Had a larger campaign poster printed. Posted them in Olivet and Tripp. Expect a fair vote out of Tripp.

Sunday, March 31, 1940

Girls and I went to Salem KMB Church for ordination of John S. Mendel and Edwin F. Walter. Took 4 of Cal's pigs to John J. B. because his sow had only 2 pigs.

Monday, April 1, 1940

After school I distributed larger campaign poster in Menno. Atty. Ulmer said he and his wife will vote for me. Dentist Glanzer said

I helped his profession when I was in the legislature, so he will help me.

Went to town board. Saw Dave Wipf but could not have a talk. Coops and Metzger promised not to fight me, but I don't expect any help. Metzger said either Schaal, Huebner or I will be eliminated in the primary and both Carlson and Newell.

Tuesday, April 2, 1940

Hitched up the young colt. He did not bother at all.

We seem to have enough moisture now. Turned the sheep out on rye field even though there is not much for them to eat. They get a change and exercise. Ewes are still lambing.

Paul Math Hofer's horseman, Jake Diede, took quite a few of my campaign cards and will work for me in Menno.

Saturday, April 6, 1940

Sowing oats today. Took Pearl to a 4-H club meeting. Marian and Ruth stayed at E. L. Holgate's. Holgate is the Public School sup. and Mrs. Holgate is 4-H club leader.

Campaigned in Parkston. I still expect a big vote out of Parkston. Sam Dekker said Hy. Rempher was not for me. He is still mad that I did not recommend his son for a job without seeing him. He may do me some harm. It seems the Democrats are for me in Parkston. Luckily, I got the Sup. office on the non-partisan ballot. Got home at 2 a.m.

Monday, April 8, 1940

Campaigned in Menno after school. Went to Olivet after dark to a Weed Control Board meeting. I got very sleepy coming home.

Saw the Tschetter Colony boss. He does not want to let the colony people vote. I would like to have their votes.

State Attorney General Leo Temmy ruled that those colonists who had returned to S. D. in 1936 after living in Canada about 18 years are not qualified to vote in this election because they have not lived here five years. Metzger had asked for a ruling on their case. They left for Canada during the World War because of persecution.

Wednesday, April 10, 1940

Germany took over Denmark without a fight. They are now going into Norway. Norway seems to be resisting a little.

Thursday, April 11, 1940

Cal went back to school after being home to sow grain for 3 days. I went dragging after school. Daisy did not want to pull. She might have a colt tonight.

Saturday, April 13, 1940

Vivian won the county spelling contest for Grades 1 & 2, both oral and written. A sow had a litter of 7 pigs. Daisy had a pretty mare colt.

Wednesday, April 17, 1940

Campaigned in Kaylor. Found more people against a woman sup. than at any other place in the county.

Thursday, April 18, 1940

Heard that Miss Schaal is making a house to house campaign in my area.

Friday, April 19, 1940

Delivered absentee ballot applications. I will get all the votes I can.

Saturday, April 20, 1940

Drove toward Dimock all day. I am trying to see all the school board members of all the districts. Am getting a lot of encouragement from farm people. Was rather disappointed in Dimock, a Catholic area. One cannot tell much about an election. The Ripp boys (hog breeders) belong to that church.

Wudel in the lumber yard said Huebner would make a strong run in Parkston. He thinks Miss Schaal won't even make a showing.

Sunday, April 21, 1940

Got sleepy on way home from campaigning last night. Got home at 1:30 a.m. and went to barn to let a lamb suck. One of the ewes I got from Pitts in Alexandria had a lamb.

Monday, April 22, 1940

Drawing for placement on the ballot will be: Carlson, Newell, Huebner, Kleinsasser, Schaal.

Tuesday, April 23, 1940

Got a cut that the ARGUS LEADER had of me. Might use it for publicity in the newspapers. Got surplus commodities for school.

Wednesday, April 24, 1940

Pearl forgot to let the sheep out, so they look sick. Seem to have pneumonia. Cal stayed in town to work on their Junior-Senior banquet.

Thursday, April 25, 1940

Roads very muddy. Should have a good alfalfa crop this year. Losing some lambs. We have been feeding some poor ground alfalfa. Pigs doing fine.

Jake Diede was here overnight with Paul Math's horse to breed Daisy. At 2 o'clock he called for Paul's truck to take him home because the horse got sick.

Friday, April 26, 1940

School picnic. Bought 3 gal. ice cream. 7th and 8th graders will write their final exams May 23 & 24.

Saw pictures of our India mission station at our church. A Tieszen is preaching.

Saturday, April 27, 1940

Electioneered in Parkston all day and evening. Wanted to get into Starr Township but the rain stopped me. Put my ad and picture in the Parkston paper.

Sunday, April 28, 1940

Many lakes are full. Some crops may drown out. Sheep are on the rye field.

Monday, April 29, 1940

Campaigned in Menno all day and evening. Put my ad in Menno paper. Saw Huebner. He said somebody had said he was definitely against parochial schools. He indirectly blamed me for saying so. Huebner expects 90% of the Menno votes to go to him and Carlson.

Got $59.80 check for expenses while re-evaluating for Aid Plan.

Wednesday, May 1, 1940

Campaigned in Tripp. Miss Schaal will lose many votes there if I can see the lay of the land. Huebner will get quite a few too, I believe. I would judge the votes will run Kleinsasser, Schaal, Huebner, Newell and Carlson.

Thursday, May 2, 1940

Ed Weidenbach and I went north of Freeman to gather absentee votes. Got 9 all evening. It is a slow process.

Friday, May 3, 1940

Campaigned in Starr and Cross Plains Townships. I believe the person who will canvass that community will have it. Met Ella Schaal several times. Bernice Newell was out there also.

Saturday, May 4, 1940

Had Rally Day in Tripp. I was one of the judges. In the afternoon the YCL Chorus sang. Campaigned a little in Tripp, then in Oak Hollow, and then in Parkston. Carlson, Huebner and Newell were also there. Some Democrats said they would support me.

Sunday, May 5, 1940

Did not teach Sunday School class because I was not prepared.

Monday, May 6, 1940

Campaigned in Parkston and Dimock and in Cross Plains, Starr and Susquehanna Townships. I expect a fair vote out of the townships where I campaigned.

Tuesday, May 7, 1940

Election Day. Hauled in votes from Silver Lake and Grand View Townships.

Wednesday, May 8, 1940

Am home after election and glad the thing is over. It is hard work to campaign in the whole county. Ella Schaal and I will battle it out in the fall.

Saturday, May 11, 1940

Shelter belt crew is here planting trees. They get them in the ground in a hurry. Cal and Reuben planted shrubs and Chinese elms around the house.

Marian went to Sally Kleinsasser's house for the weekend.

"I'm glad the decision has come down to you and Ella Schaal. I'm sure you'll be able to beat her in the general election," said Wanda to Morgan as she took Marian's overnight bag at the back door.

"Well, I'm not so sure about that. That young lady has a lot of vote-getting power. And it's not just her pretty face, either."

"She certainly has a lot of spunk. She campaigned on our street several times," said Wanda.

"She wanted to make sure she hit the areas where I was well known. And, of course, she's had the experience of being deputy to Miss Zehnpfennig, now Mrs. Williams," added Morgan, "so she was confident. Well, it's hard to compete with an attractive single woman who has no family responsibilities. I think I may have too many irons in the fire."

"We'll be glad to help out by having Marian stay here with Sally. They always have such a good time together that she's no bother at all."

"I appreciate that." Then, calling to the front room where the girls were playing with Shirley Temple paper dolls, Morgan said, "Good bye! And eat so you don't have to eat when you get home!"

"Oh, Daddy, stop teasing!"

Monday, May 13, 1940

Pentecost Monday. Had Lord's Supper. About 70 members were present. Had fish dinner and supper at Jake L.'s. Boys went crabbing but got only two pails full.

"Well, Morgan, I think you're gonna have your hands full with that pretty lady from Tripp next fall," said Jake L. to his Uncle Morgan.

"Listen, Jake, even though you're my age, you better treat your uncle with a more respect than that!"

"I'm just tellin' you what I think. A pretty lady like that is going to get a lot of votes out."

"I know. She's got more energy than I've got too. Seems like that's what the kids go for in school too – somebody who can play with them and make school fun."

"Did you see that article in the ARGUS today that said Iowa school boards are lookin' for teachers with 'oomph'? I thought that would be in favor of my Evelyn and Marjorie."

"Yeah! I could hardly believe what I read – the State Department of Public Instruction putting out a bulletin that says since children have no choice in attending school, the boards should give them teachers who are attractive, love their work and can make school life happy."

"They cost less too!"

"Sure, you can get a young, inexperienced teacher for a few bucks less than an experienced one," said Morgan morosely. "But that's what you're getting: beauty, youth, and less experience and stability."

Tuesday, May 14, 1940

Dragged the Sudan grass field. We just drilled the Sudan into the winter wheat field. Wheat is nearly gone.

Cal came home from school at 3 p.m. and started plowing with Ortman's tractor.

Wednesday, May 15, 1940
Went claims adjusting for Aid Plan. There was a strong hail storm Sunday night in places. Awful early for the hail season to start. Cal plowed 14 1/2 hrs.

Thursday, May 16, 1940
Cal finishing final exams and plowing. I dragged and started planting corn.

Friday, May 17, 1940
Ruth and Marian had their school picnic at Freeman. Pearl and Cal had theirs at Milltown. Bought 2 bu. seed corn from Wipf Bros. that Jonath Graber had brought in.

Saturday, May 18, 1940
Planted DeKalb hybrid seed corn I bought from Jake L. Cal plowed 7 1/2 hrs. Desperately need rain. Have had none since week before election.

Thursday, May 23, 1940
7th and 8th graders started writing their finals.

Sunday, May 26, 1940
Went to Gym where they are training vacation Bible school teachers.

Thursday, May 30, 1940
Memorial Day. Freeman had a program but Cal and I sheared sheep. It is hard on my back.

Monday, June 3, 1940
No rain yet. Very hot. Ruth and Marian started Bible school at #51. Kathryn, Evelyn and Margaret Hofer teach.

Tuesday, June 4, 1940
Heavy rain last night, the first in a month.

Wednesday, June 5, 1940
Pearl and Cal went to Swan Lake 4-H camp. Ruth and Marian are staying at Paul L.'s. I plowed weeds under. I made wieners, rolls, cheese and coffee for supper.

Thursday, June 6, 1940

Pauline, the bell cow, had a calf prematurely. It is very weak and small. Fed it with a bottle tonight. Set 3 hens with duck eggs. Am home alone. Ruth and Marian moved from Paul L.'s to John J. B.'s.

Friday, June 7, 1940

Got Ruth and Marian about 1 p.m. They brought a kitten back from Paul L.'s.

Saturday, June 8, 1940

Pearl and Cal came back from 4-H camp. Both were elected camp chiefs. It is an honor, but hard work too. They had to enforce regulations, have bed check, etc.

Monday, June 10, 1940

Bought a hay rake from father-in-law for one dollar. Visited precinct committee men and women about the Republican organization meeting tomorrow.

Pearl did the washing all day and then went rollerskating with Peter Hofer without any supper.

Saturday, June 15, 1940

Cal cultivating corn. Not a very good crop. Most of it came up after the rain. Creepers are taking over. We fenced a small area of the oat field for the horses because they like oat feed. Rye is too hard. The girls are herding cattle on the section line. Pearl went to the beauty parlor in the afternoon to have her hair fixed.

Tuesday, June 18, 1940

School meeting at #26. Board decided to leave it up to a vote of the parents of school age children whether we would have school or not. High school age children may attend Freeman Academy if they desire.

Cal got stuck with the tractor and it took 3 horses to pull it out.

Saturday, June 22, 1940

Jake Diede, the horse man, brought Pearl a birthday cake on her 20th birthday. Heavy wind and rain last night flattened some grain.

Sunday, June 23, 1940

Heard a broadcast from Philadelphia concerning the Republican convention. They will be using television to transmit pictures to New York.

Tuesday, June 25, 1940

Borrowed a duck foot cultivator from Jake Fast to work on weed control near the section line. Raked the prairie hay along the section line. Some of it is under water from Saturday's rain. Cal duckfooted shelter belt.

Thursday, June 27, 1940

Pettis came for the 4-H Handicraft club meeting here. He spliced my hay rope as a demonstration to the boys. They also learned how to make rope from twine.

Friday, June 28, 1940

Wendell Wilkie of New York and McNary of Oregon were nominated by the Republicans for Pres. and Vice Pres.

Wednesday, July 3, 1940

Wormed the lambs and some of the old ewes with capsules. I had them locked up a few days before.

Friday, July 5, 1940

John P. Stahl and Mary Kleinsasser were here. They are to get married next week and want to have a party at Rev. Peter J. Stahl's place. Grasshoppers are getting into the oat field. Girls are picking string beans and shaking mulberries.

Thursday, July 11, 1940

Started for Spink Co. at 1:30 p.m. for Mary and John's wedding.

"I can't imagine how Mary could plan a wedding in the middle of the week and in the middle of harvest," complained Morgan as the family set out for the Doland-area farm of his brother Jake W.

"They had to plan the wedding during Johnny's vacation. He works for the Decatur Cartage Co. in Chicago," said Pearl.

"And the harvest hasn't started yet up in Spink County. They're always a little behind us up North," said Cal.

"Hold your horses!" scolded Morgan as Cal accelerated the '37 Chevy once they got on to Highway 81.

"We have to be there by 4 o'clock for the rehearsal," said Pearl, encouraging Cal's speed.

"What's a rehearsal?" asked Marian.

"It's a practice. We'll go through the motions of the wedding ceremony before it actually begins."

"Will I practice dropping the flowers?" asked Marian.

"I don't know if you'll actually scatter the petals along the aisle, but Mary will tell you where to walk and stand, when to sit, and so on."

"What color will my dress be?" asked Marian.

"White, with tiny pleats, like Mary's dress."

Soon they passed Bridgewater. Morgan remarked on the potential grain crops, the weeds, what looked like hail or wind damage. "Look at that Leafy Spurge! How can people in good conscience let that stuff spread? It's practically all over the field!"

Next came Emery, then Alexandria, which was the cue for Ruth to say, "Let's sing 'Alexander's Rag Time Band'!"

"Okay, everybody sing:
'C'mon along, c'mon along, Alexander's Ragtime Band.
C'mon along, c'mon along, it's the best band in the land.
You can play a bugle call like you never heard before. . . .' "

Soon the Kleinsasser family was driving through Mitchell, home of the Corn Palace. After what seemed like an interminable wait, they came to Huron, in Beadle County. "If J. W. had moved to Beadle, we'd be there now."

"Why'd he move to Spink?"

"Cheap land. But there's still plenty of Hutters in Beadle County. And they're movin' into the city of Huron too," answered Morgan.

"Sounds like *urine*. I hate when people pronounce it that way. It's named after the Indian tribe, the Hurons, and should be pronounced properly," announced Pearl.

"Yes, ma'am," said her father.

Over gravel and dirt roads they drove until they found the Emmanuel Mennonite Church in the middle of the treeless plain, where the Rev. J. W. Kleinsasser was the minister. Most of the wedding party was standing on the concrete slab in front of the church, waiting for the Hutchinson County contingent to arrive. As Morgan eased his body out of the front seat of his automobile, he said to Mary, who had rushed toward him, "Well, we almost made it on time! It's just a few minutes after 4."

"I knew you wouldn't be EARLY, Uncle Morgan," said Mary, smiling through her tears and hugging him.

"I imagine Cal had the accelerator down to the floor boards a couple of times," mused the groom.

Soon the bride and her father had gathered the wedding party in the church for the rehearsal. Meanwhile Morgan walked in the surrounding fields, looking over the crops. "It's even drier up here than at home," he observed, "and the native grasses seem different. The rolling hills are nice but there's more danger of erosion."

Between the end of the rehearsal and the ceremony at eight o'clock, Morgan and his family relaxed at J. W.'s farm. "That's the biggest barn I ever saw," said Cal, as he turned into the driveway.

"You'd have to have a good hay crop to fill that hay mow," Morgan agreed.

285

While the young female cousins fussed with dresses and hair-dos upstairs and the young male cousins did chores and sat on car fenders to chat, Morgan and J. W. sat in the parlor. "Well, Morgan, it's three years since Katherine died," said J. W. "Is the passage of time helping to heal the wound any?"

"Yep. It's a little easier now. I miss her terribly, but I don't think about her night and day anymore."

"Anybody else in the picture? You're still a young man, you know, and the girls need a mother."

"No, I haven't thought about it much. Katherine was quite a lady. I think it would be hard to find someone to take her place."

"There isn't anybody who could take her place, and nobody should. But there are nice women who could be good help-mates to you," said the pastor and brother.

"I think Pearl and Cal would resent a stepmother. They're pretty strong-minded individuals, and I'm afraid I know where they got it from. There would just be too many fights."

"Wouldn't they appreciate some help around home?"

"Oh, sure, but not from a stepmother," said Morgan, emphatically, ending the conversation, when Aunt Rebekah entered the room to announce that the sandwiches were ready.

"We'll just have a light supper because there'll be lunch after the wedding at church," she said.

Because there was not enough room for all to sit at the table, those present went in traditional order to fill their plates. The men first, then the children, and finally the women served themselves ham salad sandwiches, potato salad and pickles. "You children can sit out on the back porch," instructed Cousin Adeline, who was helping her mother in the kitchen. "I'll bring you each a glass of nectar."

"Let's sit on the second step and make a table out of the porch," suggested Ruth as she shooed the kittens from the sun-drenched steps.

"Look how far you can see from here," said Marian, standing on tip toes and looking westward into the now-declining reddish sun. "You can see the crick where Uncle J. W. took me crabbing."

"C'mon in to get dressed for the wedding," called Pearl to the girls.

Upstairs Mary and Adeline were curling their hair with curling irons heated over the chimney of a kerosene-burning lamp. "Ooh, that stinks like burning feathers," grimaced Marian.

"Lucky you, with your naturally curly hair, you don't have to curl your hair," said Adeline.

"Okay, you have to be very careful now not to get your dress dirty. When you're ready, I want you to go downstairs and sit in the parlor with Daddy and Uncle J. W.," Pearl instructed Marian.

"Well, well, well, look who's here, and so pretty too," said Uncle Jake as Marian entered the parlor shyly.

"Come here and sit on my lap," Morgan invited.

"Pearl said she was not supposed to get mussed up," announced Ruth.

"Okay, just sit there, then, and practice being good in church. But, whatever you do, obey me," laughed Morgan.

"It won't be long before we have to leave for the church," said Uncle J. W. "My, how the young people fuss about their weddings nowadays. Didn't use to be that way, remember? Used to just have a wedding during the worship service on Sunday. All these fancy clothes now, satins and lace. You can hardly tell a Mennonite from a worldly person!"

Soon the wedding party and the family assembled at the church. The sun had not yet set, but a stillness had fallen over the prairie. Meadowlarks perched atop fence posts provided the prelude. It was for Morgan his favorite time of day, when he loved to go tramping through fields.

Kleinsasser-Stahl wedding party. L. to R.: Sam Stahl, Lillian Waldner, Barbara Stahl, John P. Stahl, Mary Kleinsasser, Mary Ruth Gross, Marian Kleinsasser, Jake W. Kleinsasser, Jr., Pearl Kleinsasser, John J. Kleinsasser.

Marian was instructed to carry her flower basket to the front of the church where Uncle J. W. stood. During the sermon Marian got to sit on a little Sunday School chair. But nobody said she couldn't turn around during the sermon, so she turned occasionally, looking for Daddy and smiling when she spied someone else in the congregation she knew.

At the reception in the church basement there was a lunch of more ham salad sandwiches and wedding cake. As the gifts were opened, jokes were made about many of them. The bride got the lion's share of the gifts, although they would be living in a tiny apartment with a Murphy bed.

When it came time for the bride and groom to set off from the church on their honeymoon, exiting the church basement became impossible. Local rowdies decided the couple could not leave until some in the shivaree party had been served coffee and cake, giving others in the group the necessary time to let the air out of the coupe's tires and decorate the car with old shoes and tin cans.

"Please let me get out," pleaded Mary. "I have to go."

"Go? Go where?" they asked, incredulously.

"You know! I have to go or I'll have an accident."

"Well, maybe five dollars will be enough to let you out," said the captain of the shivaree band.

"Here's your five dollars," said Johnny, flinging a five-dollar bill at them. "Now get out!"

Saturday, July 13, 1940

Cut oats all day. Pretty good crop but creepers and weeds too. Grasshoppers are gaining advantage.

Saturday, July 20, 1940

I cut alfalfa 'til 9 p.m., then raked it 'til 1:30 a.m. Pearl and Cal got home from town at 2 a.m.

Sunday, July 21, 1940

All in church. Had C. E. in the evening. I gave an object lesson on gossip with five boys helping me. The story had changed considerably by the time it was told by the last boy.

Tuesday, July 23, 1940

Barn is practically full of hay. We have not had so much hay in a long time. Cal started threshing today. Corn is firing. Can't expect much corn. Sprayed potatoes for blister beetles.

Saturday, July 27, 1940

Started threshing here. Cal and I are taking care of the grain. Clara Walter is helping Pearl. Took grain to Park Lane to grind. They claim the Golden Rustproof oats is too hard to grind.

Friday, August 2, 1940

Pearl and Marilyn Wollman, the dentist's daughter, went to Brookings for a 4-H Roundup. Wind blew half our windmill head down.

Tuesday, August 6, 1940

Pearl went to Black Hills with 4-H girls from Bon Homme and Charles Mix Counties. I brought Marie Walter up to help us while Pearl is gone. We are pulling cockleburrs out of corn fields.

Thursday, August 15, 1940

Figured up hours and bushels for threshing. We threshed here 31 hrs. Cal pitched a total of 186 hrs., so our pitching is all paid.

1204 bu. oats   @ 3¢ 36.12
290 bu. rye   @ 5¢ 14.50
204 bu. barley @ 3¢   6.12
*   Total $75.64*

Sunday, August 18, 1940

Boys had 4-H club meeting here after church. They painted signs for the parade at the county fair. Cal's sign says RAISE A LITTER OF 14 PIGS. Cal got his pigs ready to take to the Sioux Empire Fair.

Monday, August 19, 1940

Pete Ratzlaff accidentally drove over one of Cal's boars and broke its leg. Cal won 1st and 2nd boar, 1st and 2nd gilt, and 1 for litter at Sioux Empire Fair.

Tuesday, August 27, 1940

Cal got 5 blues on his 5 pigs at the Hutchinson Co. Fair. We got all the placings in Shropshire sheep. In open class Duroc show, Cal got 1st and 3rd places in boar, 1st & 2nd in gilt, 1st get of sire and 1st produce of dam.

Wednesday, August 28, 1940

Pearl went to College for Young People's Retreat but attended only one session. She went to town in the evening to practice her demonstration with Marilyn Wollman. They are demonstrating use of low-cost homemade cleaning supplies.

Friday, August 30, 1940

Cal got $11.65 in 4-H and $6. in open competition. I got $10.75 on sheep. Hutchinson Co. premiums are not high enough.

Wednesday, September 4, 1940

Cal and Pearl are at the State Fair. Cal got 4th and 5th place boar, 4th and 5th place gilt, 3rd for young herd, 3rd for get of sire and 2nd for produce of dam.

Friday, September 6, 1940
Pearl and Cal went to school. Pearl is in her first year of college and Cal his last year of academy work.

Saturday, September 7, 1940
Got some small Russian watermelons from John J.B.'s.

"Just load 'em up, boys," Morgan said to his nephews. "You can put 'em in the trunk or in the back seat. But put 'em on the floor of the back seat in case I have to stop short."

"It's kinda hard to find room here," said Ted, looking at the junk, including a log chain, in the trunk.

"Do the best you can; do the best you can. Thank you very kindly, Sister," said Morgan to his youngest and favorite sister.

"It was a very good year for melons. Lots of rain. I've been making watermelon pickle out of some of them—not the sweet kind but the Russian kind—in big crocks."

"How's come you're not teaching this year, Uncle Morgan?" asked Sam.

"Well, Sam, I'll tell you. I'm in a tough race for County Superintendent of Schools. I intend to win, and it just takes too much time away from campaigning if I have to teach on top of farming."

Monday, September 9, 1940
Had my picture taken in Parkston. Went to Republican Barbecue at Lake Mitchell with Hy. Rempher.

Tuesday, September 24, 1940
In Sioux Falls I had 2 cuts made, one for a small card and one for a bigger card. Also had stickers printed: KLEINSASSER FOR SUPERINTENDENT.

Wednesday, September 25, 1940
Very dry. No grass for livestock. Cattle and horses are eating straw. Bought sheep mineral and mineralized block salt.

Sunday, September 29, 1940
Went to Wittenberg Church in morning with Prof. D. S. Wipf, who preached there. Then to John S. Mendel's church in forenoon and Ohio Synod Lutheran Church in afternoon. Went with Wipf, Joe Stern and Seydel to see Atty. Wm Schenck. They want to get Coops and Metzger off the conscription board.

Tuesday, October 1, 1940

Showed 2 Shropshire rams at Huron show and sale. They're too small. They brought only $20 and $28. Highest sold for $68. Shot 10 pheasants on the way home after 4 p.m. Cal and I both have licenses.

Wednesday, October 2, 1940

Campaigned in Freeman all day. Put up big cards and stickers in all the business places. Had good reception everywhere. Shot 5 pheasants after 4 p.m.

Thursday, October 3, 1940

Campaigned in Menno and Parkston. Had fairly good reception. Will have an ad in the movies. Shot 3 pheasants. Ernest Schamber was with me to help with Lutheran contacts.

Tuesday, October 8, 1940

Went to Fed. Land Bank meeting. Made good political contacts. The bank representatives have a new plan of paying according to crop production.

Thursday, October 10, 1940

Ella Schaal's cards were up in Freeman today. I suppose she was in town.

Sunday, October 13, 1940

Nobody went to church in morning. Went to Evelyn and Arnold Hofer's wedding in the afternoon. It was a real wedding. Had some of the best eats. Even had beer.

Tuesday, October 15, 1940

Poor crowd in Menno for the Democratic rally. It was a rather weak speech for Oscar Fosheim, candidate for Gov. He told the story of the little boy selling kittens; the punch line is:

"You're right, Mister, they were Republican kittens a couple weeks ago when you bought one. But these are Democratic kittens now because their eyes have been opened."

Thursday, October 17, 1940

Electioneered in Parkston. Saw Titus Pope in Susquehanna and Henry Ripp in Cross Plains. Went to a Lutheran church supper in Parkston, where I saw Jake Lindeman. He promised to go with me to Milltown and Foster on Wed.

Friday, October 18, 1940

Went to Kaylor with Hy. Gross and Ernest Schamber for Republican rally.

Saturday, October 19, 1940

Children dug potatoes, Cal plowed and I went to Menno campaigning. Marian got sick.

Sunday, October 20, 1940

All in church for Mission fest. Marian got sick.

Monday, October 21, 1940

Pearl stayed home with Marian, who has a bad stomach. Sam Dekker traveled with me in Clayton Township. Had dinner at Emil Tschetter's (Peter G.'s Barbara).

Tuesday, October 22, 1940

Traveled in Wolf Creek and Clayton with Sam Dekker. He did me a world of good with the Sterns and his other relatives. Had dinner at Robert Stern's place. Had Republican rally at Freeman.

Wednesday, October 23, 1940

Traveled in Foster and Milltown with Jake Lindeman of Parkston. Had good results. Should get a big vote out of those townships. Was at a Catholic bazaar in Parkston. Got home at 2 a.m. very tired and sleepy.

Thursday, October 25, 1940

Cal and I went to a rally in Tripp. Contacts were not any too good. That is Schaal territory.

Saturday, October 26, 1940

Bill Schenk said Huebner was for Schaal because I was too tough on him in the primary. Made some good contacts in the evening. Got home at 1:30 a.m.

Monday, October 28, 1940

Nick Boehmer of Susquehanna was supposed to campaign with me but he was picking corn. Was in Parkston for a while. Then went to the Catholic church in Dimock for a bazaar. Saw quite a few there. Schaal was there too. She got too big a hand when she was called on by the chairman. Henry Ripp introduced me to quite a few people. I stayed at Sam Dekker's overnight.

Tuesday, October 29, 1940

Ripp and I campaigned in Starr, Liberty and Cross Plains. Old man Gottlieb Metzger is working against me in Cross Plains.

Wednesday, October 30, 1940

Muddy roads. Saw a few people on the way to Tripp.

Thursday, October 31, 1940

Worked in Kaylor a little. Was at a rally in Olivet. Very few present. Stayed overnight at Tripp with Pete Hofer. Saw some of the Friers.

Friday, November 1, 1940

Campaigned with Emanuel Frier in Kulm, German and Fair. Did not see so many but had good reception mostly. Stayed overnight with Jake Heth.

Saturday, November 2, 1940

Campaigned in Oak Hollow, Capital and Wittenberg with Heth. Good reception, especially in Capital. Was in Menno in the evening.

Sunday, November 3, 1940

All in church in morning. I taught class. Went to Engbrecht church in the evening.

Monday, November 4, 1940

Went to Menno to hear Karl Mundt. Worked a little in Menno. It looks bad for me in Menno. Bulow spoke at Freeman for the Democrats. He had a good reception.

Tuesday, November 5, 1940

Election Day. Hauled some votes in Freeman and Grand View Township. Jacob M. Wollman and I got 6 votes from people who were confined due to illness. It takes about a half hour per vote.

Wednesday, November 6, 1940

Lost by one vote.

Thursday, November 7, 1940

Got Soil Conservation check for $198.47. $100 was assigned to First National Bank.

Sunday, November 10, 1940
Snowing and blowing. Tried to put some of the chickens into the barn. Cal carried the ducks into the horse barn. They would not walk a step. We put all the sheep in the back shed.

Monday, November 11, 1940
Big blizzard. Roads are all blocked. Nobody is in school. The wind blows the snow in at every crack.

Tuesday, November 12, 1940
Blizzard is letting up. Joe Math Hofer lost 27 turkeys and Paul Waldner lost 400. They both were insured in the Aid Plan. Hundreds of pheasants froze to death (or rather, suffocated). Nobody in school.

Wednesday, November 13, 1940
Children went to school. Barns are full of snow. I worked on the storm windows.

Thursday, November 14, 1940
Signed up for the new variable plan at the Fed. Land Bank. I pay 1/3 of all corn and small grain crops produced, 1/2 of the alfalfa and $75 cash for farmstead and pasture.

College gave "Little Shepherd of Kingdom Come." It was well rendered.

Saturday, November 16, 1940
Fairly warm today. Went to Parkston for 4-H banquet. Cal was chairman. Pearl received a plaque from WNAX. She is 20 and will be out of club work next year. She will also receive a trip to Chicago for the 4-H Club Congress and the International Livestock Show.

Saturday, November 30, 1940
Pearl left by train from Marion for Chicago. I gave her $6. Her trip is to be free. Snowed and drifted all forenoon.

Johnny Klein is here from Huron College. He uses our car to date Gladys Hofer, Sammy's sister.

Monday, December 2, 1940
Paul Kleinsasser is picking corn here. I pay him 6¢ per bu. Most of the time I am working in the house since Pearl is in Chicago.

Tuesday, December 3, 1940
Took a barrow to John J. B.'s to butcher. Joe J. Hofer and Mr. & Mrs. Joe K. Hofer helped. Got 9 gal. lard. After I got the children from school we went back to John J.B.'s for supper.

Gritz Wurst, Fleisch Wurst, Leber Wurst, Greiten Schmaltz. Pork chops, cracklings. Smoked hams yet to come. The abundance, the aromas are almost overwhelming, Morgan thought, as he entered his sister's kitchen.

"I asked Skip Walter once for *Gritz,* and he brought out white hominy grits. 'That's not what I want,' I said, 'I want *Gritz!*' " reported Morgan.

"Buckwheat groats is what the English call it. Russian Jews call it kasha," said Cal.

"Whatever they call it, I like it!" emphasized Morgan. "Reminds me of what Dan Schmeichel used to say: 'I don't care what you call me, so long as you don't call me too late for breakfast.' "

"Gritz sausage is my favorite," said Ruth, examining the ample buffet on the dining room table.

"You can take an assortment for your locker, Morgan," said Aunt Katherine.

"If they make it to the locker before we eat 'em all up!" interjected Cal.

"How do you make Gritz, anyhow? Couldn't a person just make it in a frying pan on top of the stove without putting it in casings?"

"Sure, you could, but the flavors might not be blended as well."

"I wanna get your recipes for *Gastel* and *Nukele* too sometime," said Morgan.

"Doesn't Pearl make them?"

"Sure, but she's in Chicago."

"Okay, but let's eat now!" call Aunt Katherine.

After Uncle Johnny asked the blessing in German, the two families dug in with relish. "I bet Pearl isn't eating this well in Chicago," said Cal.

Wednesday, December 4, 1940

Took hog meat and sausage to the locker. At the Freeman Poultry and Grain Show I saw Rep. Bishop, McPherson Co. State Rep. He said I'd have a good chance to get a job working for the legislature.

Went to Viborg for Burial Assoc. meeting. I was elected secretary.

Friday, December 6, 1940

Went to the U. at Vermillion with Rep. Gunderson. Met quite a few senators and reps. We were called on stage by Pres. Weeks and introduced to the student body.

Heard correspondent Elmer Davis, met him later and sat with him at the dinner table.

We were shown around all the buildings and treated royally. Saw a basketball game between U. of Nebraska and U. of S. D. S. D. won 40 to 39, with two overtimes.

Saturday, December 7, 1940

Worked on driveway with 4-horse scraper. Pearl came home from Chicago. She had a lot to talk about.

Tuesday, December 10, 1940

Home all day writing letters to Reps. about a job in Pierre. Cooked Navy bean soup for dinner. I need to soak the beans overnight first from now on.

Sunday, December 15, 1940

Our church decided to join the Northern District Conference and the General Conference of the Mennonite Church.

Monday, December 16, 1940

Had planned to go to Parkston with John L. today but it blew too much. Thought the roads might get blocked. I cooked vegetable soup while I was reading. Got letters from some State Reps. I had written.

Tuesday, December 17, 1940

Went to Viborg with George Erickson for the Burial Assoc. meeting. George and I were re-elected. There was some opposition to me. They wanted to get Chris Jensen on the board. In the nomination ballot I won 43-18.

Thursday, December 19, 1940

Had Rockford Borman type some letters for me. I wrote each of the Reps. I am a candidate for 1st assistant bill clerk in the House. Pearl spoke to the YWCA at the College about her trip to Chicago.

Friday, December 20, 1940

Went to Parkston to see Rep. Gottlieb Tiede and Sen. Tiede. Also saw Hy. Rempher. Rep. Tiede and Rempher will help me, I believe, but Sen. Tiede wants to be President Pro Tem, so he is paddling his own canoe. He is sponsoring a girl from Douglas Co. as page. Wm Ackerman and Ted Koenig are also looking for jobs. Pearl gave a party for her 4-H club girls at Sup. Holgate's home.

Saturday, December 21, 1940

Marked and clipped sheep all day. Some have so much wool in their face that they cannot see.

All went to town in evening. Pearl wanted more money than the cream amounted to, so she bawled after she got home from town.

"I hope you didn't get too many big ideas when you were in the Windy City," said Morgan, watching his eldest cry.

"Big ideas? I just want to be able to buy a pair of stockings when I need them."

"If you didn't wear silk stockings all the time, you wouldn't go through so many pairs."

"I'm not going to wear heavy cotton stockings and look like an old woman!"

"Well, then, you have the alternatives of not using so much cream in cooking or milking more cows so you have more cream to sell."

"I don't use much cream in cooking."

"Let's think back to what we had this week with cream in it."

"Well, there was creamed beef, creamed beans, cream in the mashed potatoes, creamed carrots, creamed onions. Maybe I AM using too much cream," she conceded.

"We could drink skimmed milk, too, instead of whole milk."

"No, that's where I draw the line! I will not let the girls drink skimmed milk!"

"Okay, then, let's try first by cutting down on the use of cream in cooking, much as I hate the idea," said Morgan, "at least 'til another cow comes fresh."

Sunday, December 22, 1940

Cal used our car for a date. I had to give him a dollar because he was out. He spends quite a bit.

Monday, December 23, 1940

Children are home from school for Christmas vacation. Pearl did the washing and the girls picked up corn cobs in the hog barn. Cal manured the horse barn and hauled straw.

Some of our sheep are going blind.

Tuesday, December 24, 1940

Cal and I marked sheep and I worked on pedigrees. Repaired granary so snow doesn't blow in.

Went to our Christmas program at church. Pearl sang in the choir, and Ruth and Marian each said a piece in English. I helped deal out Christmas packages.

Wednesday, December 25, 1940

After church we went to John J. B.'s for dinner. In the evening we went to Jake L.'s for their family gathering. I got a good pair of gloves from John L.

Thursday, December 26, 1940

Went to Tiahrts for dinner. Saw Rep. Moore of McCook. I might go along with him and Odell to Pierre on Jan. 2.

Visited grandparents after dinner and went to Bethesda Church in the evening. Rev. Kroeker from the Silver Lake Church gave a report concerning the Civilian Public Service camps to be established for conscientious objectors to war. The Mennonite Central Committee is sponsoring them. We will have to support the boys there. The government will not.

Saturday, December 28, 1940

All four of our horses got out. We found them at Peter Waldner, M. S. Chris Saner came to look at the sheep. They have some kind of eye disease. Cal and I saw Jimmy Stewart in "Mr. Smith Goes to Washington." It was quite true to life.

Sunday, December 29, 1940

Heard Roosevelt speak over the radio. He said very little. He favors sending all possible aid to England.

Monday, December 30, 1940

Sen. Wheeler of Montana, an isolationist, spoke over the radio against our preparedness for war.

1941
Hailed Out

Thursday, January 2, 1941

Met Reps. Bishop, Moore and Odell at Stanley Corner for a ride to Pierre.

Saturday, January 4, 1941

Got a job as First Assistant Clerk in the House. At the final count I had no opposition, so I got all the votes. Walt Matson of Huron is Chief Clerk. Effie Peterson of Parker is Second Assistant Clerk and Pearl King of Faith is Chief Enrolling Clerk. I am staying with Sen. Buehler of Hanson Co. until I get a permanent place.

Friday, January 10, 1941

I check the JOURNAL every day for errors. I have plenty to learn. The House is still establishing its rules. Wrote home.

Sunday, January 12, 1941

Went to Catholic church. Father McGuire gave a good sermon but the rest I did not understand. I was invited after a good hint to a beaver supper at Piner's home, where I got a room. Olive Ringsrud, Secretary of State, also was there. The beaver tasted good.

Monday, January 13, 1941

Did not start Session 'til 8 p.m. so Reps. had a chance to get back from the weekend. Did a little routine work and then had some horse play about roses that disappeared from the Speaker's desk. I am staying with Leon Weier at Piner's home.

Wednesday, January 15, 1941

Chamber of Commerce put on a Dutch lunch. Had liver sausage, ham, pickles, bread, potato chips and beer.

State Historical Society met. Doane Robinson, who has been a member for 40 years, was present.

John C. Graber came up for a S. D. Cement Plant meeting. He is on the Commission.

Have not had a letter from home in 3 days.

Saturday, January 18, 1941

Had midnight session. Started at 12:01 and adjourned at 12:28. Passed 2 bills. Went home with Sen. Olsen of Viborg. Started at 7:30 a.m. and got home at 3 p.m. Road very icy south of Mitchell. Piner gave me 2 beavers.

"BEAVER!?" exclaimed Pearl.

"Yes, beaver. We're going to prepare it and have it for supper."

"But I never HEARD of eating beaver," she protested.

"Well, I had it up at Piner's, and it was good."

"I wouldn't know how to BEGIN preparing it."

"It's all butchered. All we have to do is cut it up and cook it slowly with salt, onions and water."

"I'm not TOUCHING it. You can cook it if you want to."

"All right, then, I'll cook it," said Morgan.

"And you can EAT it too!"

"Fine. I'll do that."

Morgan had his fill of beaver that night and nailed two beaver tails to the door frame of the garage to commemorate the event. It was several days before the "gamey" smell left the house.

Monday, January 20, 1941

Started for Pierre at 2, got here at 7, and had Session at 8 p.m. Got first check today—$101.50—payment for 14 days. Sent $25 to Schaefer for car, $20 to Kean Adjusting Co. in Sioux Falls for hospital bill for Mrs. Kleinsasser. The bill was 3 1/2 years old.

Wednesday, January 22, 1941

Went to Farm Island Camp for Dutch lunch supper. The Isaak Walton League put on a good feed there for 50¢. Some of the boys got into poker games. Quite a bit of money was in circulation.

Sunday, January 26, 1941

Ralph Hilgren of the ARGUS LEADER spoke on "Freedom of the Press" at the Methodist Church. Heard new definition of a lie: gross exaggeration.

Tuesday, January 28, 1941

Had joint session with Senate to hear Gov. Bushfield stress need to reduce sales tax by one cent and eliminate net income tax.

Wednesday, January 29, 1941

Theodor Brock from Narvik, Norway, spoke in the Auditorium on conditions during the German invasion of Norway. He escaped

*and is speaking in the interest of Norwegian relief. Had Legislative
Dance, but I went to my room and read READER'S DIGEST instead.*

Thursday, January 30, 1941
*Cal sold 5 ewes to M. F. Morton of Bassett, Nebr., for $100.
I hope his check is good. Bought Cal 2 shirts and ties to match
for $6 total and a snow suit for Ruth @ $4.*

Monday, February 3, 1941
*Saw Pres. J. D. Unruh at College. Father-in-law gave a bond
to the College for $100, interest $2, to be used for Pearl's tuition,
which is $105.*
Paul L. is using some of our locker space for his beef.

Wednesday, February 5, 1941
*Sent Pearl a dress, kid gloves and pillow cases and a snow suit
for Marian. Morton's check was good.*

Thursday, February 6, 1941
*A driver's license law was discussed by some lawyers in the
House chamber during the evening.*

Friday, February 7, 1941
*Had breakfast at Piner's for 25¢. Gunderson had pages pass
out cigars since he became grandpa. Secretary of State Olive Ringsrud
will have an open house at her apartment from 8 to 12 p.m. to mark
her birthday.*

Sunday, February 9, 1941
*Went to Methodist Church twice. Visited with people in St.
Charles Hotel lobby in the afternoon. Dr. Edge of Dakota Wesleyan
was the speaker at the Methodist Church.*

Monday, February 10, 1941
*Got 2nd paycheck – $152.25. Had 18 roll calls today. Adjourned
at 10:07. Had 68 pages of copy. Met with Fish and Game Commission regarding fishing in James River and putting dam across the
river near Wolf Creek.*

Wednesday, February 12, 1941
*Session recessed at 3 p.m. for a Lincoln Day celebration. Rep.
O. H. Hove, a Colman minister, said his faith in God made Lincoln
great. The chorus from Pierre Indian School sang. An Indian preacher,
Ben Brave of McLaughlin, led in prayer. I took him out for lunch*

later and learned quite a bit about Indians, including that most Indian men pluck their beards.

Saw N. E. Steele, former lobbyist for SDEA. I miss him here. He's teaching at Aberdeen Normal now.

Got letter from home. Marian has measles and Pearl is staying home with her.

Wednesday, February 19, 1941

The REA has many representatives in Pierre. There are some bills in committee on Power and Power Development. The REA is making rapid progress in S. D.

Friday, February 21, 1941

Reps. must have been very tired today. They voted like a group of lower grade school children. It was pitiful sometimes. Got through with only House bills and one Senate bill. Drove home with Hilgren and 3 secretaries. From Stanley Corner I rode south with a trucker from Yankton.

"What did you bring us this time from Pierre?" asked Ruth, hugging her Daddy as he came in the door.

"Open my satchel and see. I'm tired. I walked home all the way from the highway," he said, removing his overcoat and hanging it on the hall tree.

Carefully Ruth and Marian unlatched Morgan's suitcase and lifted the cover. They found magazines, newspapers, stationery, and paper clips. "Is this what you brought us, paper clips?" asked Marian.

"There's something else in there. Keep looking," he said, pouring himself a cup of coffee from the pot on the range.

The girls kept looking until they found, wrapped in tissue paper and nestled in a corner, two small birch bark canoes. "Oh, they're Indian canoes!" shouted Ruth.

"Yep, just like the Indians use. Met an Indian in Pierre, name of Ben Brave."

"Does he wear feathers?"

"No, not at the State House. But he probably has a head dress at home, on the reservation."

"What's a reservation?"

"It's where the Indians live. The government set aside some land for them, mostly land good for hunting and fishing, because that's what they like to do."

"No good farm land?"

"No, they don't like to farm."

302

"I thought the Indians taught the Pilgrims how to plant corn by putting a fish in the hole with the seed," remembered Ruth.

"You're right! I don't know. It's a mystery to me. Maybe the Indians on the East Coast liked farming better than those in South Dakota do, or maybe our Indians realized before we did that Dakota land isn't as good for farming as eastern land is."

"Rev. Brave said he might be able to get me a peace pipe and a tobacco pouch."

"There's an Indian that's a PREACHER?" asked Ruth.

"Yes, they practice religion, and part of their ceremony is passing the peace pipe."

"Are you gonna smoke it?"

"No, I thought I'd give it to Dr. Unruh for the College museum. An historic peace church like ours should have a peace pipe from the Sioux Indians of South Dakota."

"Pearl says Indians used to roam around here when Grandpa and Grandma Kleinsasser came from Russia. Grandma told her!"

"Even later than that. Yeah, we probably took their land. I'm sure Grandpa never thought of it like that at the time. I know Grandpa did not like it when roving bands of horse thieves in Russia came and took his horses!"

"They stole Grandpa's horses?"

"Yes. Our people had common pastures in the village of Johannesruh. The horses were pastured during the night by a hired herdsman. Often the horses were stolen from different villages. One night eight horses were stolen from the Johannesruh pasture. The herdsman claimed he knew nothing about it. Father believed that our herdsman himself belonged to a band of thieves and that it was his turn to give up horses that night. It was never proven but certain suspicious actions of the herdsman led Grandpa and others to believe it."

Saturday, February 22, 1941

Graber came with his portable grinder to grind alfalfa and Sooner milo for us. Cost $6.50

Went to Menno looking for a cream separator. John Mendel in the Gamble store has a remodeled Mellotte with a new bowl for $55. Dave Wipf has a second hand DeLaval for $25 in trade for mine.

Sunday, February 23, 1941

Now Ruth has the measles. Did not go to church. Slept 'til 10 and had a big dinner at noon. Waited for Ralph Hilgren at Stanley Corner for one hour to get a ride back to Pierre. It was snowing. Got here at 8 p.m.

Monday, February 24, 1941

House met at 2 p.m. with a light calendar and the Senate met at 8 p.m. Senate sessions are not very interesting.

Tuesday, February 25, 1941

House met at 2. In the evening we were all invited to Room 120, where they had plenty of food: 3 kinds of olives, veal loaf, sausage, bologna, smoked herring, pickled herring, American cheese, brick cheese and shrimp. For drinks we had Coca Cola, coffee, 3 kegs of beer, and some even drank whiskey.

HB273, the 9 month school bill, passed 40 to 33.

Wednesday, February 26, 1941

House reconsidered HB 273 54-21 and later moved to postpone indefinitely any action on the bill.

Rep. Tiede is being put on the spot. He was called to the Governor's office and told how to vote. First he was against reduction of the one cent sales tax but now seems to have changed his mind.

Thursday, February 27, 1941

Had Third House in the evening. Hilgren organized the show. I played the role of Motley, Matson played Sorenson. Hilgren took A. C. Miller's part and Cadell acted Miss Ringsrud's part.

Monday, March 3, 1941

Senate killed the Good Friday bill. It was amended to cut out Good Friday and that, of course, killed the bill.

Wednesday, March 5, 1941

We have 34 bills up for final passage. SB77, the tax bill, is reported out DO PASS. I had 123 pages of the JOURNAL to check.

Thursday, March 6, 1941

Just heard that Gutzum Borglum, the Mount Rushmore sculptor, died in Chicago.

I had 163 pages of JOURNAL copy.

Friday, March 7, 1941

Constitutional officers put on a Dutch lunch at 5:30. Worked 'til 3:30 a.m., March 8, when Session adjourned. SB46 took up all the time. Could not agree on the liquor question. Had 196 pages of JOURNAL copy.

Saturday, March 8, 1941

Drove to Stanley Corner with Kemper of Sioux Falls and to Freeman with Paul D. Hofer.

Went to AAA meeting in Parkston with Pete Ratzlaff. Had a good crowd. Roosevelt, Wallace and Wickard spoke over the radio.

Sunday, March 9, 1941

Not in church. Cal got stuck on the section line.

We now have 5 lambs. Bill Schultz, our hired man, says the first one came March 6.

Bill and I played checkers.

Monday, March 10, 1941

Bill left with the school children this morning. He sat in the trunk. I paid him $10 for January and $15 for February. The ewes are in very good condition. Bill did a good job feeding. The rabbits ate most of the trees in the shelter belt.

Tuesday, March 11, 1941

Went to town with Pearl, who is practice teaching. Insured Joe E. Hofer's summer kitchen in the Aid Plan.

Saw 3 basketball games: Emery vs. Yankton, Scotland vs. East Freeman, College vs. Olivet. Yankton, Scotland and College won.

Thursday, March 13, 1941

Had 3 lambs last night. Two were very cold this morning so I brought them to the house to warm up. They are not very strong.

It is 5 minutes to 6 and the children are not home from school yet.

Friday, March 14, 1941

I am very sick with a cold. Milked the cows this morning in great misery. There is a Crop Improvement meeting in Olivet but I am too sick to go.

Saturday, March 15, 1941

My cold is much better. Helped Cal manure the barn.

Got 2 good ewe lambs from #190 ewe. We put grease on her last summer on account of the flies. She looks like a show sheep.

Pearl had her 4-H club meeting in town. She has charge of a young girls' group.

Sunday, March 16, 1941

Rev. Ed Duerksen of North Dakota preached on the Mary and Martha story and making use of our opportunities. Also explained how the Northern District Conference works.

Ordered car license. Cost $8.50.
Gave College Chapel talk on legislative work. Made it too long.
Saw Marian and Sally shopping at Red and White.

"What in the Sam Hill are you girls doing downtown at 9:30 in the morning? I thought I just dropped you off at school a half hour ago, Marian."

"We're buying groceries for Miss Henley," Marian answered. "She hurt her leg and can't walk to the store."

"Does Mr. Holgate know you are on this mission?"

"Yes," said Sally. "We met him in the hall and showed him Miss Henley's note."

"Well, go ahead and buy your groceries. Then I'll take you back to school."

Soon each girl was carrying a small paper bag of groceries to the '37 Chevy parked diagonally in front of Red and White. "Sit in front. I've got too much paraphernalia in the back." Marian slid in next to her father. She was used to having her knees bruised by the gear shift. Sally might not be.

Morgan backed out of the parking space and made a U-turn at the intersection, waving to Walt Bruun, the Creamery man; Wilmer Fensel, the Hatchery man; and Adolph Waltner, the Banker. As he turned east off Main Street and headed toward the Public School, Marian pointed out Dr. M. M. Hofer's house and Sally pointed out Clarice Schmidt's grandparents' house. Morgan pulled into the oval drive in front of the school and parked.

"You don't have to go in with us," said Marian, dreading he might.

"I want to see Miss Henley," he said.

Morgan opened the door for the grocery shoppers and they all entered the room. Twenty small heads turned to gawk. Miss Henley limped to the rear of the room. "Sorry about your fall, Miss Henley," said Morgan. "Do you need anything else?"

"No, thank you, Mr. Kleinsasser; this is fine, if the girls got everything on the list."

"If you need anything else, transportation or anything like that, just let us know."

"That's very kind, Mr. Kleinsasser. Class, this is John Kleinsasser, Marian's father. He's a farmer. He helps us get our meat and eggs and bread. But he's also a politician and a teacher. He's helped make laws at the State Capitol."

"Good morning, Class. The name John Kleinsasser can be confusing. I'm John P. Kleinsasser. Sally's father is John *A.* Kleinsasser. I'm sure you know he's a mail carrier." Then, turning to Miss Henley, he announced, "I'm on my way to the College Chapel to give a speech on legislation affecting education. If you like, I would be happy sometime to tell your scholars how a bill becomes a law, the simplified version, of course."

Thursday, March 20, 1941
Still quite a bit of snow in piles. Fields very muddy. No field work has been done.

Friday, March 21, 1941
Oiling harnesses. Ducks and geese are going north. We have quite a few lakes, but none of the birds seem to settle on our lakes.

Saturday, March 22, 1941
Cal wanted to go to town tonight but he got stuck in the yard. That discouraged him from going.
Alma Waldner helped Pearl with housework.

Sunday, March 23, 1941
Not in church. Had 4 lambs this morning, 2 sets of twins. One of the mothers, #161, did not have a lamb last year.

Monday, March 24, 1941
Had meeting in Freeman regarding the REA.

Tuesday, March 25, 1941
Alfred Thomas was here for a visit.
Read in the paper that Ivan Johnson, once secretary to Gov. Jensen, was sentenced to a year in prison for making false reports as a tax collector. He failed to remit state net income tax returns.

Wednesday, March 26, 1941
Veterinarian Matter from Vermillion tested our cattle for tuberculosis. Wheat is priced at 77 to 78¢ per bu.

Thursday, March 27, 1941
Saw a large flock of wild geese on our rye field west of house. Worked all day on the yard. I get tired slugging around in the mud.

Friday, March 28, 1941
One sow had 14 pigs, one dead.
Marian was in Menno at the county spelling contest for town schools. She did not win but she must be a fair speller to represent the Freeman school in her grade.

"What word did you fall down on?" asked her father.

"Read."

"Red?"

"Read, past tense of *to read.*"

"Didn't you ask them to use it in a sentence?"

"Yes, but I still misspelled it."

"Well, we'll have to work with the TRUE BLUE SPELLER more. How did you get there?"

"Miss Johnson, the third and fourth grade teacher, drove her car."

"You mean that black '39 Ford?" asked Cal, who was doing his homework at the dining room table.

"Yeah."

"What kind of driver is she?"

"Jerky. She steps on the gas and then lets up on the gas all the time. All the way to Menno she did that."

Saturday, March 29, 1941

Another sow had pigs, 16.

I have a sow that has no milk. I must have overfed her yesterday. So I fed the pigs with a formula from Dr. Clark: 1 pt. cow's milk, 1 pt. lime water, 1/4 pt. cream, 1/8 lb. sugar.

Also gave the sow an enema with 1 qt. lukewarm soft water, 1 level teaspoon salt, 1 level teaspoon baking soda.

Sunday, March 30, 1941

Pearl went to Avon Mennonite Church to sing with a College group. I went to Canistota to get medicine for the sow. Had dinner at John J. B.'s.

Cal went away in the evening with Mike Stahl and Pearl went with Pete Hofer.

Thursday, April 3, 1941

Saw wild geese near Highway 81. They seemed tame.

Tried our Gallaway cream separator. The cream tested 36% butterfat this morning. Eggs bring 19¢ and cream 32¢ per lb. butterfat.

Sold 50 bu. wheat to Conrad Ellwein @ 80¢ per bu.

Saturday, April 5, 1941

Alma Waldner here helping Pearl. Cal is greasing the drill. I traded a setting hen for an old disc from Jacob P. Maendl, which I am fixing on. It is only 7 ft. wide but is better than none if I can make it work.

Sold a load of rye at 42¢ per bu. Ed Walz was here to check the sealed grain and he advised me to sell the rye because it had gotten wet in the granary.

Sunday, April 6, 1941

Pearl took our car to drive some of the College Chorus to Worthing and Hurley to sing. The rest of us were home.

Monday, April 7, 1941

Went to town with the children to work on repairing the back end of the hay rack at Farmer's Blacksmith Shop. Got some repair parts of an old wagon from Jake M. Walter.

Tuesday, April 8, 1941

Cal went to Sioux Falls on senior sneak day. Marie Waldner went with the class as chaperone.

Pearl got stuck in the yard with the car so I had to pull her out with the horses.

I tried to manure the barn but Nelly got balky, so she broke a brace on the spreader.

Wednesday, April 9, 1941

Pearl, Ruth and Marian stayed in town overnight. Cal came home from Sioux Falls sometime in the morning.

#56 ewe disowns one of her twin lambs. Last year she disowned 2 of her triplets. I made an extra pen for her in the barn. The yard is a quagmire.

Thursday, April 10, 1941

Girls came home. It rained some more. Have not sown any grain.

Fixed harness because Daisy tore hers yesterday. Burned out car battery cable.

Friday, April 11, 1941

Good Friday. Went to church in forenoon and John J. B.'s for dinner. Got some bedding that Sister Katherine had repaired for us. I gave her some more money for the ticking, etc.

Saturday, April 12, 1941

John J. B.'s John is helping Pearl plant garden. Paid him $1.

Bought Waconia cane from Ben Fast for 8¢ per shock. Cattle seem to like it. Cane field is wet. Loaded only 8 or 9 shocks per load.

Sunday, April 13, 1941

Home all day. Rained last night and several times during the day. Docked lambs' tails and lost one a short time after docking. Cal went away with John J. B.'s Johnny and Orphan Sammy.

Went out to look at my alfalfa. The low places are still black and possibly dead. I had cut it three times in low places and grazed it with sheep last fall.

Pearl is home for a change tonight.

Monday, April 14, 1941

Easter Monday. Sent insurance payment ($2.25) to State Accident Assoc., Brookings; and National Benefit Assoc., Mitchell ($1).

Went to College for musical program forenoon, afternoon and evening. The churches gave the program in the forenoon, the High School and Academy in the afternoon, and the College Choir in the evening.

There was a tornado at Henry, Mike and Philip Schopperts last night.

Tuesday, April 15, 1941

Dragged the shelter belt and sowed Thatcher wheat. Horses did not have much power. It is still quite wet, but many farmers are in fields with tractors.

Cal went to a sow litter 4-H club meeting at Noah Mendel's place and came home a little before midnight.

Saturday, April 19, 1941

Marie Walter is helping Pearl. Cleaned discs on drill and manured barn. There is no alfalfa for sheep.

Sunday, April 20, 1941

Not in church. Very muddy. Sun shone a few times.

Wednesday, April 23, 1941

Bronc had a colt. Borrowed a horse from Joe L. He wants it back when he gets a hired man.

Thursday, April 24, 1941

Cal is home from school sowing barley in the northwest field. I hurt my hip and went to Emil Tiesen for help.

Friday, April 25, 1941

John J. B.'s Johnny brought one of their horses down at noon to work here. We had to take Joe L.'s back at noon. Johnny sowed 5 acres crested wheat with oats and some sweet clover. Cal started discing with Ben Ratzlaff's tractor.

I wanted to go to Sioux Falls to hear Sen. Burton Wheeler, Democrat of Montana, speak in opposition to our war involvement, but I couldn't get there. Blaine Simmons of the America First Committee sponsored him.

Saturday, April 26, 1941

Cal disced with Ben Ratzlaff's tractor this morning until Ben needed it.

Had an inner spring mattress made out of one of our old wire bed springs for $14. Should be good for my back.

Sunday, April 27, 1941

Went to Bethany Church this morning to hear the College Choir. Went to Grandpa and Grandma Tieszen in the afternoon and to College in the evening to hear Dr. Rood speak.

Monday, April 28, 1941

I went to Emil Tiesen again concerning my hip. It still pains but I think it is in place now.

Cal planted shrubs around the house after school.

I went to Freeman to hear Dr. Rood lecture on war as seen through the Bible, but the children stayed home.

Tuesday, April 29, 1941

Have a sick sheep. Seems to be pneumonia. George Pietz of Tripp bought a litter of 4 pigs for $35 for his boy to use for 4-H club work. He paid $5 down.

Wednesday, April 30, 1941

Took John J. B.'s horse back with Butcher Miller's trailer and got a flat.

Thursday, May 1, 1941

The sheep with pneumonia died.

Sowed alfalfa with drill. Mixed alfalfa with oats and sowed a little brome grass with alfalfa. Set the drill at 1 bu. oats per acre. Mixed 2 gal. brome and 3 1/2 to 4 gal. alfalfa seed per drill full.

Friday, May 2, 1941

Started sowing sweet clover with endgate seeder. Bred Bronc and Nelly to John A. Wollman's horse.

Saturday, May 3, 1941

Signed up for REA lights. Joe L. was getting the signatures. It seems the line will go on Highway 81 and then branch off.

Pearl went to a 4-H club meeting in the afternoon. She was barely home when Cal took the car to his Junior-Senior banquet.

Sunday, May 4, 1941

Heard Dr. Rood in the evening. Ruth accepted Christ as her personal Savior. Quite a few took a stand. All the preachers were on the platform.

Monday, May 5, 1941

All went to Jake W. Gross for sow litter club. Boys are Cal, Jake Gross, Roland, Jake and Raymond Hofer; Noah Mendel, Amos Mendel and Melvin Ratzlaff.

Ruth and Cal will be in the purebred sheep club along with the sow litter club.

Tuesday, May 6, 1941

Sunshine today. Went to John M. Schrag's sale. Orlando bought most of the good machinery.

Got a load of cane from Dr. Isaac Tieszen's land.

Took 7 head of cattle to Paul Decker to pasture: 1 white cow, 3 part roan purebred heifers, 1 tan heifer, 2 small red heifers.

Wednesday, May 7, 1941

John L. and I went with H. Schnaidt to a AAA meeting in Yankton concerning agriculture in the defense program.

Friday, May 9, 1941

Shelter belt men replaced trees that had died out. Starting from west in north field, rows are: caragana, oak replanted to ash, ash, ash, hackberry to American elm, American elm, cottonwood, cottonwood, Chinese elm to box elder, lilac to plum.

South of barn, from west: caragana to lilac, Chinese elm to boxelder, cottonwood, cottonwood, American elm, hackberry to American elm, ash, ash, oak to ash, Russian olive to plum.

Started plowing patch north of house for potatoes.

Saturday, May 10, 1941

Alma Waldner was helping Pearl 'til Paul Decker came for her. We planted potatoes after making rows with the corn planter.

Made fence straight north of boxelder tree to fence in the trees and potatoes. I raked Russian thistles in the afternoon. Cal transplanted some caragana bushes that were pretty well leafed out.

Sunday, May 11, 1941

Herded sheep on Sooner milo this morning while the children went to church. All went to John L.'s for dinner. Cal and Pearl went away in the evening.

Wednesday, May 14, 1941

John J. B.'s John picked rocks on Sooner milo field while I fenced. Hot! Planted apple, plum and cherry trees.

Thursday, May 15, 1941

George Pietz came back to trade a boar pig for a gilt. We had made a mistake when we sold him the litter for club work.

Friday, May 16, 1941

John plowed with Ben Fast's tractor 11 hrs.

I dragged in afternoon. Harrow cart axle broke so I walked it 'til Cal came home from school. It is hard for me to walk in loose plowed ground.

Wednesday, May 21, 1941

I went to Parkston with John L. for meeting concerning referendum on wheat marketing quotas.

Thursday, May 22, 1941

Ascension Day. Pearl and Cal had their last school exams while Ruth and Marian had their school picnic. Cal washed the car and pruned fruit trees. Pearl went away with Pete Hofer without even setting up the cream separator.

Friday, May 23, 1941

Pearl went to College picnic in the morning while Cal planted corn. Cal and I helped Carl Schmeichel repair telephone line until 3 o'clock, when Cal went to the picnic.

I went with Pres. J. D. Unruh and J. J. Mendel to see Dave P. Gross and A. R. Wollman on account of the College Endowment Plan. FJC has a $40,000 drive on.

S. D. poet-laureate Badger Clark spoke at Freeman H. S. tonight.

Sunday, May 25, 1941

All in church but Cal. Jacob B. and I will be delegates to Northern District Conference in Butterfield, Minn. Went to Peter G.'s for dinner. Dave filled out his draft questionnaire.

Monday, May 26, 1941

Cal and Pearl went to College for Alumni Day Athletics in the afternoon. Cal, Pearl and I went to Alumni Banquet in the evening while Ruth and Marian stayed at Eddie Maendl's place. I paid $1 for my plate. Alumni decided to buy an electric Singer sewing machine for the Home Ec. class.

Pearl graduated with honors from the One Year Normal course and Cal from the Academy. Dr. Smucker of Bethel College was the banquet speaker.

Tuesday, May 27, 1941

Went to graduation exercises at the College.
Roosevelt gave his fireside chat. He wants to give England help.

Thursday, May 29, 1941

Edgar Hofer was here from Bridgewater to deal on a Farmall tractor, H model, equipped. He wants $1020.

Friday, May 30, 1941

Cal plowed with Ortman's tractor 'til bolts tore off in tractor wheel. Chris Saner vaccinated 27 pigs for $9.

Saturday, May 31, 1941

Wheat marketing quota election today. Only 66 voted from Grand View and Wolf Creek Townships. Vote was 44 for, 22 against. John L., George I. Walter and I were on the committee.

Sunday, June 1, 1941

Dry and hot. Corn is not all coming. Worms do much damage. Heard that the wheat quota carried the nation 4 to 1.

Monday, June 2, 1941

Silver Lake MB Church had a Young People's Conference with Rev. Bestvater of Tabor College in Kansas as speaker. Girls went in morning, and I went with them in the afternoon and evening.

Tuesday, June 3, 1941

Cal plowed, I hauled rocks and Eli Hofer started shearing sheep. We have 55 to shear.

Wednesday, June 4, 1941

Went to town in evening. Had a meeting concerning control of Leafy Spurge. Pettis, John L. and I were elected to meet with the county commissioners to buy sprayer.

Thursday, June 5, 1941
Ruth and Marian in Bible school.
Cal started cutting alfalfa.

Saturday, June 7, 1941
Went to Northern District Conf. at Butterfield, Minn, with Pres. Unruh at 1 p.m. Got there 5:45 p.m. John C. Mueller and Adolph Preheim were along.

Sunday, June 8, 1941
Pres. Unruh is chief speaker at Conf. His topic is the Holy Spirit.

Tuesday, June 10, 1941
Am staying with J. John Frieszen. He and his wife taught at FJC from 1914 to 1916 and again from 1923 to 1929. Strawberries are ripe.

Wednesday, June 11, 1941
Brought home strawberries from Frieszens and Rudolph Linscheid. Paid nothing for all the time we were in Butterfield.

Thursday, June 12, 1941
Helped Pearl with strawberries. Wanted to put some in locker in boxes, but Bill Morfeld said they had to be in closed containers like a fruit jar or ice cream container.

Friday, June 13, 1941
Ruth and Marian were in the Bible School program at Silver Lake Church.

Saturday, June 14, 1941
Doc Ernest and I took Marian to Sioux Valley Hospital for appendicitis attack. Dr. Regan did not operate. He is not sure what it is.

"Maybe I ate too many strawberries," Marian theorized from her hospital bed.

"I don't think so, but, then again, maybe you did. I remember once you got convulsions when you ate too much sweet corn. But you were a lot younger then," said her father.

"Maybe those strawberry seeds got stuck in my appendix. Aunt Anna said that can happen with mulberry seeds. What did the doctor say?"

"Dr. Regan? He examined you and couldn't find the problem. He wasn't going to cut into you if he wasn't sure you had appendicitis. He said the appendix was there for a purpose and if it wasn't inflamed, you'd be all right."

The nurse in a well-starched uniform entered the hospital room with a cup of beef broth and a glass tube sticking out of it, prompting Marian to ask, "What am I supposed to do with this?"

"Drink it through the straw."

"Is this the hospital where Mother and Baby Katherine died?" asked Marian between sips, after the nurse had left.

"No, this is Sioux Valley. Mother and the baby were at McKennan."

Doc Ernest came into the room and said, "We want you to stay here overnight for observation. If you're all right tomorrow, you'll be able to go home."

"Will I have to stay here alone?" she asked.

"You won't be alone. There are nurses and doctors all over this hospital. We'll see you tomorrow," said her father.

"Tell Ruth that I'm drinking broth through a glass tube."

"Okay, Honey, I'll tell her. She'll be jealous that you get to lie around all day while she has to work."

Sunday, June 15, 1941
Went to Sioux Falls with Abe Wiens and brought Marian home from the hospital. We stopped at the airport for a while to watch the planes. Cal went to 4-H camp at Lake Herman.

Monday, June 16, 1941
I turned alfalfa hay over with Herman Mensch's side delivery rake. It is hot and windy.

Robert Stern, Mr. Brown and some helpers are staking out the road south of our place to grade it.

Tuesday, June 17, 1941
Put up alfalfa. Paul Heuneman came around so we had him pitch hay. He stayed for dinner.

Had school election. Sam Schmidt was re-elected. Only 2 at meeting.

Wednesday, June 18, 1941
Cal came home from camp at 6 p.m. so we finished the alfalfa stack.

Thursday, June 19, 1941
Tiahrt boys came to take Pearl to Sioux Falls to shop for Elmer's wedding. She bought a dress for $6.95 and shoes for $3.50.

316

Friday, June 20, 1941
Bought a used double row McDeering cultivator for $5 from Edgar Hofer in Bridgewater.

Sunday, June 22, 1941
Pearl is 21 years old today. All in church this morning. Jacob B. is gone so Joe J. read a chapter and gave a little sermon.
Elmer Tiahrt and Huldah Gortmacher were married.

On the way home from the wedding, Ruth said, "Huldah was so pretty. She always has the fanciest clothes – lace and furs and everything."

"She's nice and friendly too. Every time Elmer brought her to Grandpa's church, she smiled at me."

"I think Elmer is nicer since he's been going with her."

"Yeah, he was mean to me once when I was staying at Tiahrts."

"Why, what did he do?" asked Morgan.

"He said whoever didn't work shouldn't eat. Said it was in the Bible."

"Oh, he was just kidding," laughed Morgan.

"No, I think he meant it. I told him I couldn't work as hard as he did but I was helping Aunt Anna in the kitchen."

Tuesday, June 24, 1941
In the evening we all went to town to see Gunderson of Yankton show Conservation pictures on wild life.

Thursday, June 26, 1941
Took in the Freeman Lumber Co. program. They gave away over 100 prizes. Had big crowd.

Friday, June 27, 1941
Our big red twin heifer had a red heifer calf while pasturing at Paul Decker's.
We sprayed the potatoes, half with Red River Valley and other half with arsenate of lead. There are 4 varieties of bugs.

Saturday, June 28, 1941
Butchered a yearling sheep and put meat in locker.
De-tailed 4 lambs we had overlooked.
Rained an inch last night. Have some water in lakes now.

Sunday, June 29, 1941
Roads very muddy. Home all day. Sudan is making good progress. Pearl & Cal went away in the evening.

317

Monday, June 30, 1941

Too wet to cultivate so we weeded in shelter belt. Tried to rent a tractor from Ortman but all are in use.

Tuesday, July 1, 1941

Brought 3 of our cattle home from Paul Decker's pasture. He is running out of pasture too.

Wednesday, July 2, 1941

Cool weather. Only around 65 degrees. Some are cutting rye and Burbank wheat but ours is still green.

Thursday, July 4, 1941

Went crabbing with Harvey Wiens around 2 o'clock. Caught a gunny sack full. Highest temperature was 83.

Saturday, July 5, 1941

Bought a sack of ration balancer from Ed P. Hofer. He said cream stations are getting particular with sour cream. Several cans were rejected recently.

Sunday, July 6, 1941

Gave a report on the North District Conference in church this morning. Went to Paul E.'s for dinner and supper. Annie gave us 4 Leghorn roosters and a nest of duck eggs. Marian stayed at Paul E.'s for a little vacation.

Monday, July 7, 1941

Sent wheat loan money to Commodity Credit Corp. in Minneapolis.

Shook mulberries so Pearl could make jam. We now have 8 gal.

"I'm getting sick and tired of steering this jam," said Ruth, standing on a kitchen chair in front of the bubbling kettle of mulberry and rhubarb jam on the kerosene stove.

"*Stirring*, not *steering*. Keep the wooden spoon down on the bottom of the kettle so the jam doesn't scorch!" instructed Pearl, as she sorted the twigs, bird droppings, leaves and green fruit out of still more mulberries on the oilcloth-covered kitchen table.

"It's getting hot here and the jam is gonna burn me pretty soon. It's starting to bubble hard."

"We'll start counting when it comes to a rolling boil. If you don't want to stir, you can have my job of sorting mulberries."

318

Ruth was silent for a moment. Then she remembered Marian. "Marian should be home to do this too. She always gets out of work. When is she coming home, anyway?"

"On Sunday. Maybe you can go up there then for a little vacation."

"Really?"

"If you help me this week." Ruth sighed and kept on stirring.

Wednesday, July 9, 1941

Pearl and Cal went to town in the evening for the drawing but they got there too late. So they could not get the pitch fork we had won.

At 11:30 p.m. it began to hail.

Thursday, July 10, 1941

Our crop was totally destroyed last night. I went adjusting for the Aid Plan with Jake M. and A. R. M. Hofer.

Friday, July 11, 1941

Adjusted losses all day. Brought cattle home from Decker's. Cal and Pearl fenced up one barley field for cattle and sheep.

Hail insurance adjuster, Schaefer of Delmont, gave me 100% loss on wheat, oats, barley and rye. He deferred payment on the corn.

Saturday, July 12, 1941

Cal is working for Mike Stahl. Paid Emil Tiesen $6 on account.

Sunday, July 13, 1941

All in church. Taught girls' S. S. class. Peter G.'s were here. Cal is to work for them after a week from Monday. Marian came home from Paul E.'s and Ruth went up there. Paid church dues of $7.50.

Monday, July 14, 1941

There is a carnival in Freeman but we are not there. Adjusted for Aid Plan all day.

Wednesday, July 16, 1941

Mrs. Jacob L. Hofer, Sr., is in Sacred Heart Hospital in Yankton. Went to three farmers looking for a Milking Shorthorn bull. P. P.'s Irene is helping Pearl.

Monday, July 21, 1941

Cal has been working at Mike Stahl's but will go to Peter G.'s tomorrow. I am helping P. P. thresh. It is 105 degrees.

Sister Elizabeth died this morning.

"My oldest sister. The first one in the family to go. Born in South Russia. Came here on the boat when she wasn't even three years old. Lived on this place 'til she married Jacob L. She was always good to Mother. Helped take care of the younger children.

"Only reached age 65. Diabetes took her. She liked her peppermint drops. Katherine's parents in their eighties already. Wonder what that means for our family.

"She worked hard all her life 'til young Jake L. married, and she and Jake L., Senior got the apartment in the big house. Annie was good to her.

"She helped us when Katherine died. She wasn't too spry then.

"Said she wished sometimes she had died young, before she could sin. She was burdened by a sense of sin. Why? She was such a good woman."

Wednesday, July 23, 1941

Threshed at P. P.'s in forenoon and went to funeral in afternoon. Jac I. Walter, Jake Adrian and P. P. Tschetter preached.

Mrs. Joe M., Mrs. John S. Waldner, Mr. and Mrs. J. W., Lillian and Edwin Waldner and a few others were here from Beadle and Spink. We gathered at Jake L.'s after the funeral.

Thursday, July 24, 1941

Got bull from D. D. Glanzer. He bred red polled cow and red twin heifer.

Got a load of barley (73 bu.) from P. P. and took it to Park Lane to be ground for feed.

Friday, July 25, 1941

Traded in old cream separator on a new McDeering stainless steel separator. Paid $65 cash.

Saturday, July 26, 1941

Loaded up all the rye bundles I had cut before the hail. It was not quite one load.

Hail insurance adjustor gave me 85% loss on 35 acres of corn ($297.50). Earliest corn seems to have the most damage.

Cal did not come home from town at night.

Sunday, July 27, 1941

All that were home went to church and to visit Grandpa and Grandma. They were not home so we went to Mary Tiahrt. Jake was there from Mt. Pleasant, Texas. He is married to a young woman named Sellers.

Henry Tiahrt is still mad at the AAA because he seeded too much wheat.

Monday, July 28, 1941

Edgar Hofer was here with a horse buyer to look at the horses I want to trade in on a tractor.

Wednesday, July 30, 1941

Made another stanchion in the barn. We are now milking 6 cows.

Went to town for the drawing. Had all kinds of tickets in but my name was not called once.

Thursday, July 31, 1941

Moved brooder house after 10 p.m. Cal phoned from Peter G.'s that we can get some oats there.

Pearl is at 4-H Roundup in Brookings. Edgar Hofer was here to talk tractor deal. I got him to help me milk cows.

Friday, August 1, 1941

Peddler Ernesti came. Girls did the buying.

Ruth, Marian and I went to the circus in Freeman. Not much to it. First they lure you in with a cheap entrance fee. Then they want more money when you get inside. We walked out when they asked for more money.

Tieszen Family Reunion
(L. to R.) Harry Tiahrt, Harvey Wiens, Marian Kleinsasser, Cal Kleinsasser, Sally Kleinsasser (friend), Esther Tiahrt, Ollie Mae Williams.

Saturday, August 2, 1941

The Watkins man, a Nelson from Menno, was here. They all think we have money after harvest.

Corn is still green. Grasshoppers are working.

Sunday, August 3, 1941

Tieszen family reunion at Marie Tiahrt's. All present but Dave and Susie. Jake brought watermelons up from Texas. The girls enjoyed playing with his step daughter, Ollie Mae Williams.

Monday, August 4, 1941

Girls had their teeth looked after. I had pulled a canine of Marian's that should not have come out before she was 12.

Tuesday, August 5, 1941

Shelter belt men are here to clean the trees. Ferd Thomas is here with his tractor to pull the cleaners.

Wednesday, August 6, 1941

Bought a fencer from Dave Tschetter and he helped me rig up the wire for an electric fence.

Cal came home. He claims he hurt his knee. He got sick while threshing.

Thursday, August 7, 1941

Cal is sick in bed with rheumatism. Dr. M. M. Hofer was here to see him.

Herbert Hofer sold us Fuller brushes.

Friday, August 8, 1941

Dr. M. M. Hofer was here and gave Cal an injection. He has been coughing for a few weeks. That may have been the beginning of his illness.

Tuesday, August 12, 1941

Pearl left by car with the College Choir for the General Conference in Pennsylvania. They will be gone 3 weeks. Arnold Tiahrt, one of the drivers, picked her up.

Cal is sick but some better, Dr. M. M. Hofer said.

The kerosene stove flared up.

With Pearl gone and Cal sick, the responsibility for cooking and choring fell to Morgan and his youngest daughters. "Who wants to get the cows?" he asked.

322

"I do," said Ruth and started for the pasture with Pepper, the large black dog, at her heels.

"Okay, Honey, you've got to come up with something for supper. How about *gedampfed Hahne?* Do you know how to make that?"

"Yeah, you put everything in a large pot and put it on the stove," she said glibly.

"Right! Chicken, carrots, onions, potatoes, and water. Add a little salt and pepper. And bay leaf. Know what that is?"

"Yeah. Do I have to cut up the chicken?"

"No, just put it in a big enough kettle. If you cook it slowly enough, the meat will fall off the bones.

Marian took the locker paper off the rooster and put it in the kettle. Then she added carrots from the garden. "Don't have to peel these. Just scrub 'em." Next came the potatoes, scrubbed, not peeled. Onions had to be peeled, though. As the tears ran down her cheeks she tried all the remedies she had heard of – sticking a farmer's match between her teeth, holding her breath, and finally, peeling the onions under water. Salt, pepper, bay leaf and water. If the chicken was young and skinny, Pearl sometimes added lard, but Marian decided she did not want to go down the basement for a messy cup of lard.

Everything was now in the pot, and the pot was covered. She lit the kerosene burner, turned down the wick and went outside to gather the eggs. Ruth and Pepper were coming down the lane with the six milk cows before them.

As Marian neared the house with the pail of eggs, she saw Dr. M. M. rushing from the house with his black bag. He waved and drove off in his new black car. He must have an emergency, she thought.

When Marian entered the house, she was almost overcome by a thick cloud of black smoke. "What in the world?" Then she remembered the kerosene burner.

"Never leave the kitchen once you've lit the kerosene stove. Those burners can flare up in no time," Pearl had warned. But Marian had forgotten the warning. She rushed into the kitchen, turned off the burner and ran outside.

"What's going on down there?" called Cal from his upstairs bedroom. "I smell smoke." He hobbled down the stairs and found the first floor heavy with black smoke. He rushed to the kitchen and found the burner off. Then he opened all the windows and doors and went outside where he found Marian, standing in the yard and watching the smoke come out of the windows. "What happened?"

"I forgot to watch the kerosene stove," she said.

When they returned to the house, heavy flakes of soot had fallen on all the tables and chairs. Sooty smoke blackened the kitchen and dining room walls. "Boy, will Pearl be furious when she gets home from choir tour!" said Cal, resting on a sooty chair.

"I wonder what Dr. M. M. thought," said Marian.

Saturday, August 16, 1941
Cal is up and around but still weak. He helped me with the milking.

Monday, August 18, 1941
Fensel took 10 pigs and I took 7 sheep to the Sioux Empire Fair. Cal stayed there with the livestock.

Wednesday, August 20, 1941
Cal got all the placings in the 4-H Duroc division.
Corn has some ears.

Thursday, August 21. 1941
Creamery picked up our sweet cream. They want to make sweet cream butter for the State Fair.

Sunday, August 24, 1941
All in church. I went to Joe J.'s to make out the program for the S. S. convention. Girls went to wedding of LeRoy Tieszen and a Zobel girl.

Monday, August 25, 1941
Sorted pigs and blocked sheep for the State Fair.

Tuesday, August 26, 1941
All went to the County Fair this morning. Cal got all blues and championship litter. He stayed there with the stock.
I had programs printed for the S. S. convention.

Friday, August 29, 1941
Cal is home washing sheep for the State Fair. I went to Tripp to bring our livestock back. Sheep took every placing possible. Got only $28 premium money for all.

Saturday, August 30, 1941
Got things ready for State Fair. Ruth and Marian got finger waves in town. Dave Tschetter will help here.

Sunday, August 31, 1941
Not in church. Took 13 hogs and 12 sheep to Huron.

Monday, September 1, 1941

Cal got champion Duroc gilt and boar. I got beat badly in blocking sheep. Too much competition.

Tuesday, September 2, 1941

Cal won second ($65) and I won third ($60) in Duroc futurities. I went home with Joe C. and Ed C. Graber.

Wednesday, September 3, 1941

Pearl started second year of College. Ruth and Marian go to Freeman School. Cal is still in Huron.

Thursday, September 4, 1941

One cow does not stay out of the cane field. The electric fence is not so good when ground is dry.

Friday, September 5, 1941

Park Lane's ad in the COURIER cited Cal's winnings due to 5% Ration Balancer he added to his grains.

Saturday, September 6, 1941

Cal did not sell any boars at the State Fair. He did not stick around the barns enough, I am afraid.

Sunday, September 7, 1941

John J. B.'s Katherine and Alfred W. Tschetter were married today. Had a very good supper.

Monday, September 8, 1941

Cal started College today. Ed Tschetter and Ben Schrag are cutting the corn for silage, charging $1 per acre. They started in evening and expect to cut all night.

Tuesday, September 9, 1941

Filled two corn crib silos (2 cribs high) using Frank Tieszen's cutter and P. P.'s tractor. Cut 4 1/4 hrs. Helpers were Johnny Kleinsasser, Abe Wiens, Jake Fast, Jake Waldner, Abe Becker, Walter and Edward Kleinsasser and Andy Wipf. Abe Wiens, Cal and I were in the silo.

Wednesday, September 10, 1941

Children all in school. Johnny Klein is working here. Repaired telephone line and dug out 4 bu. carrots.

Friday, September 12, 1941

Pete Ratzlaff and I went to the Spencer Co. Fair in Iowa. Large exhibits.

Saturday, September 13, 1941

Cal and Johnny hauled cornstalks and shocked some up north of the house.

Elmer Georgeson was buried today. He was on the Fraternal Burial Assoc. board. Raynie is still our undertaker.

Sunday, September 14, 1941

Listened to Dr. Gilbert afternoon and evening. He thinks Communists will win the war.

Tuesday, September 16, 1941

Johnny returned to Huron College. He feels much better than he did last winter.

Sunday, September 21, 1941

Marian had an appendicitis attack this morning.

Tuesday, September 23, 1941

Started to cut cane in southwest field. Tough job. Had to unhitch and come home at 3:30 when Chris Graber came to grind 2 loads of oats.

Cal went to Corn Palace with Andy Wipf.

Wednesday, September 24, 1941

Marian was very sick last night. Had stomach cramps. She just does not get the right kind of food. Everything is in too much of a rush. Took her to Dr. M. M. Hofer this morning. He said she had bowel trouble.

"Why don't you let me take her home and see if Mrs. Hofer can take care of her today, Morgan? I have some house calls to make. Then I'll check on her at noon when I go home for dinner," said the doctor.

"I'd be much obliged to you if you would, Doctor. I'm cutting cane and there's no one home to take care of her."

Marian knew where Dr. M. M. Hofer and his wife lived—in a big, two-story white frame house on the corner, a block west of her school. Dr. Hofer drove up to the back door and soon Marian was standing in the warmth of a large, immaculate, brightly-colored kitchen. "Mother," said the doctor, "this little girl is having stomach problems. Give her some Milk of Magnesia and make some milk toast for her. I'll be back at noon."

"Well, now, you just sit up at the kitchen table here while I get you some medicine and we'll have some milk heated in no time."

Mrs. Hofer's gleaming white stove looked like some Marian had seen in magazines. Around the stove were white built-in cupboards decorated with colorful reproductions of fruits and vegetables.

"Do you like milk toast?" asked the nice lady.

"I don't know. We don't have a toaster. We don't have electric lights."

"What does Pearl give you when you have an upset stomach?"

"Hot milk over soda crackers."

"Well, that's about the same thing. Watch how I make milk toast. Since you don't have electricity, Pearl or your Daddy could toast bread over the burner if you have a kerosene stove or in the oven of your kitchen range."

"Daddy says we're supposed to get the REA pretty soon."

"You mean the high line? I wouldn't bet on it. If we have a war, you won't get electricity."

"Do you think there will be a war?"

"I hope not. I'd hate to have Robert be drafted," said Mrs. Hofer.

While they waited for the mixture to cool a bit, Marian felt warmth – the kitchen, the lady, the breakfast. After she had finished eating, Marian was invited into the sunny parlor for a game. "Do you play cards?" asked Mrs. Hofer.

"No, we don't play cards at home. Daddy burned a deck of cards that Cal brought into the house."

"Oh, well . . ."

"I play Chinese checkers, though."

"Sorry, we don't have our Chinese checkers board anymore. Do you like to read magazines?"

"Yes, but I can't read all the words."

"Well, you take this pencil and draw a circle around all the words you don't know in this LIFE magazine while I finish my chores in the kitchen. Then we'll read the magazine together and practice the words you circled."

The forenoon passed quickly and after the noon meal Dr. Hofer pronounced Marian fit to return to school, where Morgan found her with Ruth at the close of the day, peering through the glass panes of the front entrance.

Cal went to Milltown with our car. Always something to chase around for. The College freshmen had a party.

327

Thursday, September 25, 1941

Marian feels much better. She went to school this morning.
I cut cane with the grain binder. It is too small in high places and too tall in the lakes.

Sunday, September 28, 1941

Went to grandparents after church. Saw wild ducks by the side of the road.

Tuesday, September 30, 1941

Went to sale west of Parkston. They had some 32-inch woven wire I wanted to buy. It sold for 34 1/2¢ per rod. New wire sells for 42¢.

Saturday, October 4, 1941

Took 2 lambs to Bones sales pavilion. I bought the top Shropshire ram for $50.

Sunday, October 5, 1941

Had S. S. convention in our church. John Toews and J. W. spoke in the morning and Classen in the afternoon. Had musical program in the evening. J. W. was here for dinner.
I turned the new ram in with the yearling ewes and ewe lambs.

Saturday, October 11, 1941

Pearl and Marian went to a shower at Adeline's for Gladys Hofer, who will marry Johnny Klein. John is working in Chicago. Ruth is at Jac Mendel's.

Sunday, October 12, 1941

No church today because Stahl church has mission fest and baptism. Cal, Marian and I went to Ben Spies in Valley Springs to look at boars.

Wednesday, October 15, 1941

Joe J. Walter finally bought a boar for $32.50. My horses broke the pole on the mower while I was home selling the boar.
The Fed. Land Bank board was here to see about my loan.

Thursday, October 16, 1941

Sooner milo is still not ripe. The gilts go up there every day and seem to do well on it. We have wonderful pasture on fields that hailed out since we got some rain. The hogs, cattle, sheep and horses are all on good feed.

Friday, October 17, 1941

28 sheep were gone. Found some at #98, one at Zach Wipf's and others on section line near Jake M. Hofer.

Saturday, October 18, 1941

Got a boar from Bert Broek near Hull, Iowa, for $40. He is just about what I want in a boar but too small. He is an April pig out of a good litter. Dark red, good feet, ears hang over his eyes too much. Very solid.

Sunday, October 19, 1941

Not in church. Sold a boar to Morrison Bros. of Mitchell for $40. Hunted pheasants at Henry Tiahrts.

Monday, October 20, 1941

Rev. Albert Schultz of Butterfield, Minn., started revival meetings at our church but we were not there.

Tuesday, October 22, 1941

Sold our John Deere grain elevator to Langrock of McCook Co. for $210. Plowed 6 3/4 hrs. with Ortman's tractor.

Thursday, October 23, 1941

A Graber was here for a ram but $30 was too much for him, I suppose. Sold one to Paul Z. Wipf for $20.

Found a neck yoke by the straw pile while plowing.

Friday, October 24, 1941

Cal started plowing this morning but bent the pan on the tractor so he went to school. Ortman came to fix it.

Sunday, November 2, 1941

All in church in morning. All in church in afternoon and evening but Cal. Rev. Albert Schultz preached all three times.

Monday, November 3, 1941

Started making a chute for loading hogs. Was at College for meetings. Dr. Suckaw and Rev. Toews speak.

Gave children $25 check for College Bookshop bill.

Wednesday, November 5, 1941

Set traps for skunks.

Marian accepted Jesus as her savior at the Schultz meeting at our church.

For two weeks the Rev. Albert Schultz of Butterfield, Minnesota, had been conducting revival meetings at the Hutterthal Church. And he was having a successful campaign, convicting young and old of their sin, and inviting them to make a new start by committing their lives to Jesus. Marian had watched her friends Angie, then Bertha, then Vivian, then Jeanette, and finally Sarah go forward to get "saved."

Marian had had stomach troubles that summer and fall. As she brought the cows home for milking she had watched the movement of the clouds and wondered if she were ready to die. Rev. Schultz had said one had to be ready to go in the twinkling of an eye. She had been in the hospital for appendicitis but Dr. Regan had not operated. Doc Ernest had said it might be kidney trouble. War clouds were gathering, Rev. Schultz said. The world was getting so wicked that Jesus could come at any time. Would she be ready? As she saw the clouds parting and the sun setting through them, Marian pictured Jesus coming through the clouds to establish his reign. How would Jesus find her? Had she confessed her sin? All her lies, laziness, quarreling? If she went forward, that meant she would have to give up a lot. Was she willing? Was she ready to be perfect? Maybe she could wait and make a confession just before Jesus came so she would not miss out on too much fun. If you were saved you shouldn't go to shows anymore or wear open-toed shoes or curl your hair, some said. Well, the shoes and hair part didn't affect her anyhow. Only older girls wore open-toed shoes and her hair was naturally curly.

When Daddy drove the car, he often complained of getting sleepy and asked the girls to talk to him to keep him awake. What if he fell asleep at the wheel and they all went down the ditch and were killed? There were signs with crosses at every major intersection where people had died. THINK and PREPARE TO MEET THY GOD they said. She had asked Daddy how to turn off the ignition if he had a heart attack, but she wasn't sure she could guide the car to a safe stop.

Some girls had gone forward night after night. When Marian asked her Daddy about this behavior, he said, "I guess it didn't take the first time."

Rev. Schultz had been visiting at the farm on Friday, Daddy said. He preached three times on Sunday. Monday and Tuesday the family hadn't gone to church. On Wednesday, when they returned to the church, Rev. Jacob B. was at the door, shaking her hand and saying, "I've been praying for you."

The meetings were coming to a close, Rev. Schultz announced. Soon he would be returning to Minnesota. There were just a few more nights in which to make a decision.

The singing began. "Throw Out the Life-Line," "Blessed Assurance," "Just a Closer Walk With Thee." It was request time. Other favorites were called for – "He Leadeth Me," "Oh, 'Tis Wonderful," "Jesus Alone Can Hear All Your Troubles."

Jacob B. read the scripture and prayed. The evening's sermon was based on the Prodigal Son, who had been wasting his life in riotous living and was reduced to eating the husks with the hogs until he came to his senses and came home to his father.

Marian looked at the wallpaper mural behind the pulpit. She could still see her mother in the picture, just as she had after her mother's funeral four years ago. Her mother was in heaven beckoning Marian to cross the bridge and make a decision to live for Jesus.

"Elsie, play the invitation hymn," said Rev. Schultz. Mrs. Decker began softly playing "Just As I Am" as the congregation bowed their heads. Then they sang:

"Just as I am without one plea,
But that thy blood was shed for me,
And that thou bid'st me come to thee,
O Lamb of God, I come, I come!"

"Won't you come now? As all heads are bowed, all eyes closed, won't you come to Jesus? Let's sing the second verse."

"Just as I am, and waiting not
To rid my soul of one dark blot,
To thee whose blood can cleanse each spot,
O Lamb of God, I come, I come!"

"Jesus is waiting. Yes, come forward, dear. Jesus will make it all right," said Rev. Schultz. Marian looked up. There was Elizabeth again, going forward for at least the third time that season. Rev. Schultz put his arm around Elizabeth. Marian looked at her friends in the second pew. They had all gone forward earlier in the campaign. "Let's sing the third verse."

"Just as I am, thou wilt receive,
Wilt welcome, pardon, cleanse, relieve,
Because thy promise I believe;
O Lamb of God, I come, I come."

"Now, before we sing the last verse, I know there is someone here tonight struggling," said Rev. Schultz. "Rev. Hofer, come and join me here in the front. I know there is someone weighed down by the burden of sin."

"Yes, Jesus," whispered Elsie, *sotto vocce*, at the piano.

"Someone we've been praying for. Someone who's tarrying. Tarry no longer. Come to Jesus. As we sing the last verse, come."

"Just as I am, thy love unknown,
Has broken every barrier down;
Now to be thine, yea, thine alone,
O Lamb of God, I come! I come!"

Marian felt an invisible hand pulling her up out of the pew. Another hand was pushing her from behind. Nervously she staggered to the front, burst into tears and knelt at the foot of the pulpit with Elizabeth.

"Praise the Lord!" said Rev. Schultz.

"It's an answer to prayer," said Jacob B.

"Yes, Jesus," said Elsie.

At the conclusion of the service, Mrs. Jacob B. came forward to dry Marian's tears and counsel her in the front pew while the two preachers worked with Elizabeth again. Marian's Aunt Katherine and Uncle Johnny J. B. came forward to welcome her into the fold by hugging her and saying some Bible verses with her.

Finally, as the faithful slowly withdrew from the little frame church to retire for the night, the hanging gas lamps were extinguished and removed from the sanctuary by the custodians, Mr. and Mrs. Joe K., who would ready them for service the next night.

Aunt Katherine and Uncle Johnny shepherded Marian outside into the cold night air. On the concrete porch slab out front of the church Morgan was talking to Joe P. about the price of skunk pelts. He thought he'd have some to sell shortly.

As Marian stepped into the back seat of the '37 Chevy, she found Ruth already sitting in the front seat. "I thought you'd never do it!" said Ruth.

Morgan pulled out of the church yard and looked steadily ahead and said, "I'm proud of you, Marian. I'm glad you made a decision tonight."

Saturday, November 8, 1941

Caught 2 skunks in 2 traps by the same hole, one medium size and one small. Sold 3 to Huber for $6.75 unskinned. Bought $9.65 worth of merchandise from K & K.

332

Sunday, November 9, 1941

Up too late for church. Got 90 sheephead from Math Kleinsasser. Cleaned fish half the forenoon and an hour after noon.

Went to Neu Hutterthal C. E. in the evening. Dave P. Gross spoke on C. O. camps.

Tuesday, November 11, 1941

Marian and I went to hear Prof. Toews and Dr. Suckaw of Ohio at the College.

Weather is warm — 36 to 40 degrees.

Saturday, November 15, 1941

Cal plowed and the girls helped me burn Russian thistles in the afternoon. Marie Walter is here helping Pearl.

As the evening shadows fell, Pearl said, "Honey, set up the separator while I do the milking. And take down the hits on the Hit Parade."

Marian turned on the radio and got a piece of paper and numbered on it from one to ten. As she stacked the separator discs and put all the clean parts together, Marian listened carefully to the popular songs as they were announced in inverse order of popularity that week.

"Number ten on the Hit Parade is 'Boo Hoo, You Got Me Cryin' for You'." Marian wrote "Boo Hoo" after the appropriate number. When she heard "I Got a Feelin' You're Foolin'," Marian consulted Pearl's HIT PARADE magazine for the correct spelling of *foolin'*. Other songs on the popularity charts this week were "Just Because" and "The Waltz You Saved for Me."

When Marie came in from the clothesline with a basket full of clean laundry to fold, Marian lost the announcement of one winner in all the confusion. "Be quiet! I can't hear the numbers," she shouted at Ruth, who complained that she should be helping to gather the eggs or fill the cob box. "Pearl told me to do this," Marian insisted.

Tuesday, November 18, 1941

Had a good turn-out at the 4-H banquet in Menno. Cal got the award for the Sow Litter division.

Saw Ray Hirsch at the Land Bank concerning my loan.

Monday, November 24, 1941

Packed straw around chicken barn. Robert Stern was here to check on trees for county bounty.

Thursday, November 27, 1941

Thanksgiving Day. Had turkey dinner at Jake L.'s Jake got the turkey from DeKalb Hybrid Seed Corn Co. as a premium.

Went to wedding at Henry Tiahrts. Arnold and Irene Hansen got married. Had supper and lunch after that.

Friday, November 28, 1941

Cal and I scraped dirt all day. Weather is warm, about 60 degrees. Barbara Hofer came to help Pearl butcher ducks.

Sunday, November 30, 1941

Took the Hiawatha from Canton to Chicago for the International Livestock Show. Joe R. Hofer is also here.

Monday, December 1, 1941

Had free lunch at Armour Packing Co. and saw horse show in the evening.

Tuesday, December 2, 1941

Visited Kraft Cheese Co., had free lunch at McCormick Club House, toured International Harvester plant and the Museum of Science and Industry. Fare and guide service was $1.65 plus 8c tax.

Went to Shropshire banquet and meeting in the evening.

Wednesday. December 3, 1941

Toured stock yards, NBC studios at Merchandise Mart and saw livestock exhibition in the afternoon. Went to Hampshire banquet with Frank Swope.

At the banquet that night in the ball room of the Sherman Hotel, Morgan said to Frank, "I can't believe I'm here. I used to dream about coming to a big Congress like this ever since I was a boy and Father told me about the one he attended in Columbus, Ohio."

Thursday, December 4, 1941

Visited Board of Trade at LaSalle and Jackson St., just 5 blocks from Sherman Hotel, where we are staying.

Left Chicago Union Station at 12:45. Phoned Rev. D. M. Hofer in the morning. He told me where John and Mary Stahl live, but it was too late to get there.

Got to Sioux Falls about 1 a.m.

Friday, December 5, 1941

Got home at 4 a.m. Have a cold. Drove home with a trucker from Stanley Corner after Pitts dropped me there.

Saturday, December 6, 1941

Signed a contract at Ortman's for a tractor. His deal now is: Pay $150 cash—$28.80 in advance for all unpaid balance. Tax 14.52 on $726. Freight $35. Balance of $576 in 2 payments, Nov. 1, 1941 and Nov. 1, 1943. I paid him $150 down.

Sunday, December 7, 1941

Did not go to church this morning. In the evening we went to Jake M. Walter's place to help them celebrate their 25th wedding anniversary.

Rev. Jacob B. Hofer stood before the family and friends assembled in the parlor for the Walters' anniversary. "This is a happy day and a sad day," he said. "We are happy that the Walters have been blessed with 25 years together. They've had a nice, large family and many friends, as this gathering attests. But these years haven't been all rosy. There's been Depression and drought, sickness and moving. But the Lord has been their constant companion and will be with them for many years to come, we are confident.

"Today we heard the news of the bombing of Pearl Harbor by the Japanese. It looks like we're in the war for sure now. But is it really any surprise? We've been expecting it all along. Many of our young men will be drafted. They will be faced with a major decision—either to serve their country in war or go into a Civilian Public Service camp. Some will give the ultimate sacrifice.

"We will face shortages at home, much worse than we've experienced up to now. There will be high prices for goods we need and temptations to our young people many of us cannot even imagine.

"As we give thanks for the anniversary the Walters are celebrating today, we pray for guidance in all of our lives in the days to come. Amen."

"Well, I guess the tin cans we collected will come back to us in the form of bullets," said Morgan as the family drove home.

"I wonder if we will get our tractor now," said Cal.

"That's the least of my worries," said Morgan.

"Will Cal have to go to war?" asked Ruth.

"I hope not," said Morgan.

"I'm glad I'm a girl," said Marian. "Girls don't go to war."

Tuesday, December 9, 1941

Ran over a gilt while Chris Graber was here grinding. We broke her leg, so we took her to Miller to butcher.

Thursday, December 11, 1941
Ruth got sick in school. Cal brought her home. Had a tube replaced in our radio.

Friday, December 12, 1941
I am not well. Doing chores is all I get done.

Saturday, December 13, 1941
Fall pigs are sick. I went to see Dr. M. M. Hofer. I caught a cold and it affected the glands in my throat.

Monday, December 15, 1941
Bought some Master Liquid Hog Tonic for the fall pigs and got some feed for them (50 lbs. oats, 25 lbs. barley, 15 lbs. corn and 10 lbs. wheat) to feed with the tonic.

Thursday, December 18, 1941
Made a straw loft in the granary chicken barn. Marian helped me put in straw after school.

"Get your overalls on," said Morgan, when he found her listening to the radio in the house.

"Aw, shucks, just when it was getting good and scarey!" she pouted but did as she was told. After changing, she found her father lifting huge forks full of clean straw from the hay rack and pitching them through what had formerly been a window but was now a door to the loft.

"I want you to climb into the loft and distribute the straw evenly over the floor boards. We want to pack it firmly so the chickens will be warm this winter and will lay more eggs."

Marian used the boards of the hay rack as a ladder, and Morgan gave her a final boost up and into the loft. She landed with a bounce on a pile of straw below. "Don't I get a fork?" she called.

"No, that's too dangerous. Just pick up the straw with your arms and move it to places that aren't covered."

Slowly and gingerly Marian began the task, first with small amounts but gradually with larger amounts of straw. Suddenly she screamed.

"What's the matter?" asked Morgan.

"Something just ran up my pant's leg! Help!" she screamed again.

"What the Sam Hill!" came the reply.

"I think a mouse ran up my leg!"

"Where is it now?"

"In my pants and going higher!"

"Try to shake it out."

"It won't come out. It's hanging in there."

"Well, of all the. . . .Why don't you put your fist around it and crush it?"

"In my pants?"

"Then take your pants off and shake it out."

"I need your help!" she cried.

"Well, I never. . . ." Morgan struggled up the hay rack and into the opening of the loft. "Now, take off your overalls. That mouse is more afraid than you are!"

At last the mouse was free. Comforting his daughter, Morgan said, "It was just a little mouse, Honey. It got scared when you upset its nest. It was just trying to find a warm place for the winter."

"Not in my pants!" Marian hollered and lit out for the safety of her scarey radio program.

Saturday, December 20, 1941

Cal and I hauled some spoiled silage out to the field. Went to town in evening to buy Christmas goods.

Monday, December 22, 1941

Took Marian and Ruth to town for piano lessons.

Helped clean stove pipes at church. We moved the heater over to the south side of the aisle, to the men's side.

Tuesday, December 23, 1941

John and Gladys Kleinsasser were here for dinner. I took them to P. P.'s.

Cal made a wooden stand for the kitchen sink.

Went to town for the drawing.

Wednesday, December 24, 1941

Cal hauled 2 loads of hay from Jake L.'s. Cattle are in poor shape. Sold our herd board to Gunderson of Parker for $40.

All at Christmas program in the evening.

After church the family unwrapped their Christmas presents. Ruth and Marian presented all homemade gifts – a comb holder made out of paper plates and yarn, a pin cushion, a picture painted with water colors. They received in turn a paper weight which, when turned upside down, showed Grandfather and Heidi in the snow, a kaleidoscope which made amazing pictures, a Bingo game and a jigsaw puzzle.

Cal got a pair of gloves and Pearl a nesting set of blue crockery bowls.

After a lunch of peanuts and oranges eaten around the dining room table, Pearl rose to take her gift to her bedroom. But when she placed the set of bowls on the cold floor below her window, there was a loud crash.

"What happened?" cried Ruth, as she ran to the bedroom.

"I think I broke my bowls," said Pearl. Slowly she gathered the fragments. Only one bowl was not broken.

"Pearl broke her present!" Marian reported to her dad as Pearl came to the dining room with broken crockery in both hands and tears in her eyes.

"I guess you were disappointed you didn't get any silk stockings," said Morgan. "That's why you broke your gift."

"I didn't do it on purpose," she cried.

Thursday, December 25, 1941

All in church this morning. Church was full.

Snowed most of day. Intended to visit grandparents but we turned around when we got to Abe Wiens' farm. Weather was too threatening.

Friday, December 26, 1941

Snowed last night. We are out of good silage.

Saturday, December 27, 1941

I went to see Dr. M. M. Hofer. Have rheumatism in my shoulder. Got an injection and pills. Mr. & Mrs. John J. Kleinsasser and Mr. & Mrs. John P. Stahl of Chicago were here for supper.

Sunday, December 28, 1941

John and Gladys left at 3:30 this morning. We were not in church.

Monday, December 29, 1941

Butchered 35 ducks. Paul E.'s, John J. B.'s, Mrs. Paul., Mrs. John L., Marjorie, Emma and Barbara Hofer helped.

Tuesday, December 30, 1941

Barbara is helping Pearl can ducks. Pearl is sick. I paid Fed. Land Bank $500 on delinquent interest.

1942
Youth in Rebellion

Thursday, January 1, 1942

Worst blizzard of the year so far. Moved sheep into back shed. They cannot see well on account of the snow.

Friday, January 2, 1942

Still drifting. Silage all gone. Very little feed.

Pearl went to College to work in the reception room. Solomon Wollman and Roland Hofer helped her.

Sold a 15 doz. case of eggs @ 28¢ per doz.

Fixed a rod on windmill that blew off last night.

Some roosters froze their combs.

Saturday, January 3, 1942

Drifting. Pearl is baking. Ruth is visiting at Jac. Mendel's.

Daisy died of old age and lack of feed. Cal and I skinned her, the last half after dark.

Nobody went to town tonight.

Sunday, January 4, 1942

Got up after 10 so did not go to church. Wind was blowing over the barn, so the windmill does not run steadily.

Monday, January 5, 1942

Windmill froze up. Weaned the calves since the cows are very poor. Cal sold horse hide for $5.

Tuesday, January 6, 1942

Children all in school. Am feeding sheep ground alfalfa and ground cornstalks with a little cane.

Wednesday, January 7, 1942

Had to pull car with team to start it this morning. Had telephone meeting at Carl Schmeichel's place. I was elected secretary. Had refreshments of apples, candy and nuts. Levy for this year, $6.

Thursday, January 8, 1942

Pipes froze under tank. No water for livestock.

Friday, January 9, 1942

Thawing today. Cal skinned a horse at Waldners and got $5.25 for it from Walter Kleinsasser. Livestock is eating straw from old pile.

Sunday, January 11, 1942

Had S. S. elections during S. S. hour. I was elected asst. teacher of Class 6. Mrs. Joe Math is the teacher.

Listening to Ford Hour on Pearl's radio. It is 10 to 9 and Marian just fell asleep.

Heard a good story: After a glowing introduction by a good speaker, the guest speaker said, "I did think, perhaps, they made a mistake when they picked me to speak to you, but that was before I heard this man's introduction."

Tuesday, January 13, 1942

Ruth is 12 years old. Donna Hofer came along from school. We got a quart of ice cream to celebrate. I bought some bowls that had MADE IN JAPAN painted out.

Wednesday, January 14, 1942

After taking children to school, I went to John J. B.'s to butcher. Got there quite late but at least I got there in time for dinner. Joe K., Joe A. and Joe J. Hofer families did the butchering.

One of Cal's sows threw her pigs. She was sick a while ago.

Friday, January 16, 1942

Fensel came to blood test the chickens. He found only 3 or 4 with problems (that he could not buy eggs from).

Pearl and Cal both went away. They do very little work when they come home from school.

Sunday, January 18, 1942

Pearl went away again in the evening. Cal did not go along to church in the evening. Marie Walter, Ruth, Marian and I went to the C. E. program. Many numbers on the program were not brought.

Wednesday, January 21, 1942

Paid Philip Mensch $7.42 for trees I got from him last spring. Paid $10 rent on locker. Took out health and accident insurance with Lincoln Mutual in Fargo, N. D.

Sunday, January 25, 1942

Jacob B. announced that we would go on Daylight Saving Time after February 9.

Tuesday, January 27, 1942

Jesse Hoover spoke at the Gym on conditions in France and of the relief work the Mennonites do there.

Thursday, January 29, 1942

Pearl and Cal went to play practice at the College. Hauled 2 loads of straw from P. P. Unloaded one load in back shed for sheep and the other one Cal threw up in the hay mow.

Saturday, January 31, 1942

Heard H. V. Kaltenborn, news analyst, on radio. He is on Tues., Thurs., Sat., and Sun. at 7:45 p.m.

Bought bushel basket of apples for $1.50 from Retzer.

Nobody went to town tonight. We have to save tires and gas.

Have a sick sheep. Lack of proper feed probable cause.

Sunday, February 1, 1942

All in church but Cal. Committee appointed to investigate church membership gave its report. Jacob P. Hofer objected to the report. Had a few arguments.

Monday, February 2, 1942

Another one of Cal's sows threw her pigs. We have 2 sick sheep. Got some mineral from Saner.

Wednesday, February 4, 1942

Peter Waldner M. S. ran across the field calling for help. He claims John M. S. hit him in the forehead. Jake Waldners and the girls came over here. Pete did not want to go home but we finally persuaded him to go.

Friday, February 6, 1942

Barbara washed clothes for us nearly all day. I went east looking for alfalfa hay to buy. Harold Ortman has an old stack. I paid him $30 for it.

Monday, February 9, 1942

Auction sale at Peter Waldner M. S. John M. S. was not at the sale. Best horse sold for $67.50, cows for $50. Cattle in poor shape. I bought a sickle for $1.25.

Tuesday, February 10, 1942

Gathered 105 eggs. We have nearly 50% production.

Went to basketball game between Scotland and Freeman H.S. Freeman won 32 to 27. Max Walter, Hank Kleinsasser and Calvin Warne are main players.

Thursday, February 12, 1942

Took case of eggs to Fensel's Hatchery. We get 30¢ per doz. or 8¢ above market.

Friday, February 13, 1942

College is on Daylight Saving Time, so children come home in time to do some chores.

Lowered trough and manger in northeast corner of barn so young cattle can eat there. We are using fewer and fewer stalls for horses.

Got 2 pedigrees returned because I did not have the breeding date recorded.

Saturday, February 14, 1942

Heard over radio that Singapore has fallen.

Got lime sulphur dip and worm capsules for sheep. Some of last year's lambs are not doing well.

Sunday, February 15, 1942

Pearl taught a S. S. class for first time. She was elected last Sunday morning.

Pearl and Cal went away with our car. Pearl is supposed to give a talk on Lincoln at the South Church.

Monday, February 16, 1942

All male persons between 20 and 45 are to register for war services. They expect 400 to register in Freeman.

Got new base for corn (42.1 acres). They made a 10% increase.

Am feeding sheep oil and soybean meal.

Wednesday, February 18, 1942

Marie Walter is to stay here the rest of the school year.

Andy Wipf will do some carpentry for me. He is to salvage the shed on west side of granary to make a hog brooder house.

Pearl and Cal went to play practice and came home at 12:30 a.m. Must be a long play.

Saturday, February 21, 1942

Pearl stayed up 'til 4 a.m. studying.

Sunday, February 22, 1942

This is my birthday. Girls were in church but Cal and I stayed home.

Pearl stayed up again quite late after coming in late. She will not last at that rate.

Monday, February 23, 1942

Snow storm. No school at College. They phoned the lines this morning.

I think we fed the sows too much alfalfa hay. Four of them slipped their pigs but when we quit feeding alfalfa and fed good grain, we had no more trouble.

Tuesday, February 24, 1942

Children all back in school. Had 4-H meeting at John L.'s. New county agent was there. His name is New.

Wednesday, February 25, 1942

Jacob L. Wollman bought 2 ewe lambs for $50. His wife was along to help him pick them out.

Sunday, March 1, 1942

All in church. Levy for C. O. camps is $1 for this period. Girls went to Bethany Church for College Choir program in morning.

Went to Silver Lake Church in evening. Rev. John Toews is leaving for Kansas. They had a farewell for him.

Monday, March 2, 1942

I let the small white calf out for exercise and one of the other cows killed it.

One sow had pigs. Most of her teats are inverted so pigs get no milk. Should have sold her on the market.

Tuesday, March 3, 1942

Joe L. and Joe P. were here to insure the old Isaac Tschetter place. Joe L. bought it.

Sprayed fall pigs with lime sulphur dip.

Friday, March 6, 1942

Sold 470 lb. sow with inverted teats at Menno Sales Pavilion. Menno buyers say they like small, light sows weighing around 200 lbs.

Saturday, March 7, 1942

Cal went to Brookings for the Little International Livestock Show. A bus from Parkston took about 40 club members.

Sunday, March 8, 1942

All in church. All but Cal went to Adeline's for supper. Pearl went away and got home late. Church must have lasted a long time.

Monday, March 9, 1942

Had 3 lambs this morning. One ewe wanted another ewe's lamb before she had lambed. It crawled away from its mother so she wanted to disown it. I locked them up together so I think they will get along.

Helmuth Schnaidt and I went to Huron for a sheep breeders' meeting with the State Fair Board. We suggested several changes.

Tuesday, March 10, 1942

Cal went to play practice and is not home at 12:30. Marian stayed at Jac Mendel's for the night.

Thursday, March 12, 1942

Went to Fed. Land Bank meeting. Bank furnished dinner for all its patrons and many others.

Friday, March 13, 1942

College gave Chekhov's THE FOOL. Cal and Pearl were in it. They had a big crowd.

Saturday, March 14, 1942

The 2-year-old ewe that had a pregnancy disease had triplets. One was dead, one weak but the other good.

We are delivering 2 cases of eggs per week to Hatchery. We gather 130-150 eggs from 210 hens.

Sunday, March 15, 1942

Joe K. and I traded children. Ruth went to Joe K.'s and Mary came here for dinner. After C. E. in the evening Ruth went to Joe K.'s again.

Monday, March 16, 1942

John J. Tschetter charged $2 for helping me fill out my federal and state income tax report.

Thursday, March 19, 1942

Had brakes checked by Richard Waltner. Ball bearings bad on one wheel, a part broken on hydraulic brake. Total cost, $2.77.

Saturday, March 21, 1942

Andy Wipf helped Cal haul home 3 loads of oat straw from Zach Wipf's. Horses played out. They did not get enough feed during the winter.

Sunday, March 22, 1942

All in church. Cal had left the car at Zach Wipf's, so he could get it out. Very muddy on our yard. Marian went to Joe K.'s after church.

When Marian stepped into the Joe K. Kleinsasser home, she was struck by a heavenly aroma emanating from the kitchen. Soon the large family was seated around the table. The family included Crippled Annie, Joe's sister, who had been carried from the church to the car and then from the car to the house. Annie was always friendly to Marian in church as the children filed out of their pews past Annie, who sat near the stove to keep warm. At the table now Marian sat between Bertha and Katheryn and across from Silas and Amos.

After prayer Marian discovered what had caused her mouth to water: a huge roaster of cut-up chicken with carrots and potatoes on the side. It had apparently been baking in the oven all the while they were in church.

"We have a hard time getting ourselves ready in time for church, let alone putting the dinner in the oven before we leave," thought Marian. "Mary and Sarah must do it."

Julia, Mrs. Kleinsasser, inquired whether Marian had had any more attacks of appendicitis. Then Marian remembered that it was Julia who had sent her the get-well card in the hospital. It was forwarded home because she had been released early. "I have side aches on my right side when I run too hard, but Daddy doesn't think it's my appendix."

After an afternoon of play in the girls' bedroom because of the muddy yard outside, Mary brought in a big box of peanut clusters. "Wow! Where'd you get all these?" asked Marian.

"Pa got 'em in town at Gelfand's at a bargain. The chocolate is a little pale and discolored from being in the show window too long, but they're still good."

Indeed they were. Marian bit into the chocolate-covered peanuts and then into the cream filling. "It's just like Christmas," she thought.

Monday, March 23, 1942

It dried so fast that some people were in the field in the afternoon. A wonderful change. Our rye is coming nicely.

Moved the little hog house on pasture north of the house and moved the sow with first pigs. They were in the barn 23 days.

Tuesday, March 24, 1942

Got a team from Paul L. and started sowing Pilot wheat in the afternoon on the east 80 south of the rye field. Sowed 6 acres.

Wednesday, March 25, 1942

Rained again. Cal left the car at Wipf's so he could get out.

Thursday, March 26, 1942

Blizzard. All livestock in barns except the colts. Cal stayed with Roland, Pearl stayed at P. P.'s and Ruth and Marian stayed at Aunt Emma's for the night.

"I can't see any lights at all," Ruth whined, as she peered out the tiny panes of the front door of Freeman Public School. "Maybe Daddy's stuck in a snow drift at home and can't come to pick us up." The panes were clouded with steam.

Ben Bessel, the janitor, had finished his sweeping and was locking the classroom doors with finality. "Pretty soon he's going to be locking the schoolhouse door and we'll have to wait outside," said Ruth, nervously.

"Remember, Daddy said that if some time he couldn't make it before school closed, we should go to Aunt Emma's and wait for him there," said Marian.

The janitor, Geneva's father, was standing tall behind them. "You got another place to wait? I gotta help Spomers with their chores tonight."

"We're going to Aunt Emma's," said Marian with importance. "Daddy said to wait there."

"You mean Mrs. Ike Kleinsasser?"

"Yeah. You know her?"

"Sure. That's not far from here. Tie your scarves up over your noses. All you need is room for your eyes to see out," he instructed them, helping to adjust their scarves. "Now, just walk one block west, toward Main Street, then turn left and walk one more block. Her house is at the end of the street on the right hand side."

"I know where it is. I been there hundreds of times!" Marian bragged.

Once outside, the girls could hardly keep their balance as the wind howled and buffeted them about. "Let's hold hands," offered Ruth.

"Okay, but it's easier to walk single file in the track. Funny there aren't any cars out. Can't even see the street lights very good."

As they trudged, they sank into snow up to their three-buckle overshoes. "We need five-buckle overshoes like Daddy has," said Ruth.

"It's not far. I'm still warm from waiting inside."

"Do you think Ben Bessel really knows where Aunt Emma lives? Geneva Bessel never came with us to Aunt Emma's."

"Everybody in town knows where everybody else lives."

"It doesn't sound right to me. Aunt Emma lives on the same street where Elaine Lipelt and Sally Kleinsasser live. And that's farther than he said."

"Well, all I know is we don't want to walk all the way to Main Street, because that would be too far."

"Let's turn here. I think this is the place to turn."

The two turned and walked, but nothing looked familiar. They walked some more.

"I think that's it up ahead," said Marian.

"Why don't we stop and ask somebody?"

"Okay, you ask. I'm gonna stand right here."

Ruth labored up the walk and steps to knock on the door. There was no answer.

"Maybe they can't hear with the wind howling like that," Marian suggested, the wind almost taking her breath away. Ruth returned to her sister, and together they resumed their walk. Suddenly Marian remembered: "The swan! Aunt Emma has a statue of a swan by her back door!" At each house they came to, they searched for the swan.

"Maybe we passed it already," said Ruth; "the swan could be covered with snow, and it's all white."

"But it has a bright orange beak. We should be able to see that sticking out."

By now it was almost dark. "I really think we should stop at the next house and ask," said Ruth.

At the door which opened to their frantic knocking stood a stout woman wrapped in a big blue apron. She was bathed in a rich smell of baking pork. Horrified to see the girls, she said, "What are you doing out in this weather? You're caked with snow! Icicles are hanging from your shawls!" She pulled them indoors.

"We're looking for our Aunt Emma's house."

"Who are you, Morgan's kids?"

"Yeah, and we can't find Aunt Emma's house!"

"Does she know you're coming?"

"No, but Daddy said we should go there if he couldn't pick us up at school some time."

"Well, I'll just give her a ring and tell her you're on the way. Jake will walk you over. It's just a block from here."

"I guess we turned a block too soon," said Ruth.

When the girls arrived with Jake's help, Aunt Emma and the swan were waiting for them. Waving good-bye to their guide, Aunt Emma said to the girls, "Come in out of that storm! I was looking for Virginia just before Tillie called. I hope Virginia makes it home okay. She's working down at the drug store."

Marian and Ruth hit the snow-clogged clasps of their overshoes to loosen the snow before they could remove them. "Here are some newspapers. Leave your boots in the entry for now. We'll shake the snow off later," Aunt Emma said, pulling the girls into the warm kitchen. "Does your Daddy know where you are?"

"No, but he probably has a good idea. He said for us to come here if sometime nobody picked us up before the school closed."

"Well, I'll give him a ring." Emma turned the crank on the wall phone several times. "Viola? Give me Morgan—6F310 . . .

"When you can get through, tell him that Marian and Ruth are at Mrs. Ike Kleinsasser's. Tell him I'll keep them overnight and send them to school tomorrow morning if the school opens."

"All right, Emma."

Placing the receiver back on its hook, Emma said, "Now get those wet clothes off and come over to the cook stove.

"Hang your mittens and scarves over the woodbox to dry," Emma instructed them. "Then stand in front of the oven door. But don't sit on it! It's not strong enough to hold both of you!" Then, tucking a stray wisp of her gray-white hair into her chignon, she said, "I wonder what we should have for supper? I've been so busy sewing all day that I haven't even thought about supper. But I do have some coffee on the stove. You may have some of that first."

"But we don't drink coffee!" Marian announced, horrified. "It stunts your growth!"

"This isn't real coffee!" Emma smiled. "It's made from roasted barley. And you may have yours with milk and sugar." Soon Emma was peeling potatoes. "Do you like your fried potatoes with onions or without?"

"With onions. That's my favorite, with pork 'n beans," said Ruth.

"I don't have pork 'n beans, but I do have eggs. My hens have started laying again."

"I like mine soft-boiled, so they run over the potatoes," said Marian.

"Well, that's good, because that's just how Virginia and I like our eggs. That's how Uncle Ike liked them too. I think we're going to be able to get along just fine tonight."

"Where's your radio?" asked Ruth, looking around the kitchen.

"It's in the parlor, but I'll turn it on loud enough so we can hear the news." Emma opened the door to a blast of cold air from the parlor and rushed back into the kitchen. "Brrr, it's cold in there," she said, closing the door behind her and rubbing her hands.

Through the closed door they could hear the farm market report from WNAX, "570 on your radio dial, Yankton, South Dakota." Then came the report of the blizzard with winds gusting to sixty miles an hour, drifts of snow blocking highways, and a preliminary list of school closings. "Tune in tomorrow for a complete list of school closings," the announcer said.

"I hope our school is called off for tomorrow," said Ruth.

When Virginia arrived, covered with snow, Aunt Emma shut off the radio. "Nobody's listening, anyway. We don't want to waste any juice." As Virginia changed clothes and Emma finished supper preparations, the little girls set the table. Soon they were all gathered around the kitchen table next to the range.

"You ask the blessing, Virginia," Emma instructed her.

"Lord, we thank thee this night for shelter and good food. Be with all those who are stranded. Lead them to safety. In Jesus' name we pray. Amen."

"I wonder if Daddy and Cal and Pearl are okay," said Ruth.

"Daddy's probably in the barn feeding the pigs and milking the cows," Marian said. "And Cal and Pearl probably stayed in too somewhere."

Just then the phone rang. "Hello? Yes, Morgan, they're here. They walked from school, like you told them. They're wondering where Cal and Pearl are. At P. P.'s and John L.'s. That's good. Yes, I'll send them to school tomorrow if there is school. . . .Well, yes, we would enjoy some pheasants from your locker. Number 26? Thank you, Morgan. . . .Whatever milk you can spare. I can always make cottage cheese out of the surplus. Thank you. Goodbye."

After supper dishes were washed, Aunt Emma polished the top of her Golden Oak wood-burning range. She shaved off particles of an old red brick with an old kitchen knife and began to apply the powder with elbow grease. To questioning glances she explained, "It makes a good scouring powder. I can't afford to buy all the fancy new products, so I make do with what I have. It's a trick my mother, Virginia's Grandmother Schmuck, taught me from the Old Country."

The four females spent the evening around the kitchen table near the range, for the kitchen was the only heated room. Virginia did her homework, Aunt Emma bound button holes on the suit jacket she was finishing, and Ruth and Marian drew circles around words in the FREEMAN COURIER that they could not pronounce. When they tired of that, Ruth asked, shyly, "Could we play with your dress-up clothes?"

"Well, they're upstairs in the trunk. And it's too cold to play up there. We'll bring the trunk down here. Give me a hand, Virginia."

Soon the little girls were digging into the trunk. First they brought out an ostrich plume, then a fur neck piece, a large "Merry Widow" hat, and lots of long, lacy dresses. They knew that Aunt Emma had been a "fancy dresser" when she was younger because they had seen pictures of her and Uncle Ike.

"When did you wear this feather, Aunt Emma?"

"I wore that the first year your Uncle Ike and I were married. It scandalized almost everyone in the Hutterthal Church."

"You weren't a member of our church, were you?"

"No, I had been a Lutheran, and Ike and I found the Mennonite church here in town more to our liking. But I might as well have been a heathen! My, how those ladies wearing their black shawls in the back row at Hutterthal carried on about my plume!"

After Ruth and Marian had played several different characters, Aunt Emma announced it was time to think about getting ready for bed. "Go upstairs and bring down some of your old pajamas and long underwear, Virginia. We'll see if we can outfit your cousins."

Emma moved several hot flat irons on the stove top to the front and stirred up a pot of Ovaltine. "This will warm your tummies before you get into bed. Put the pajamas on the oven door to warm before you get into them," she said as she wrapped the irons in layers of newspaper and then in an old pillow case. "I'll take these upstairs to warm your bed. You'll all three sleep together, so that'll keep you warm too."

When Emma returned from upstairs, the girls had changed and were sitting at the table sipping Ovaltine. "Now, I want you to fold your dresses neatly and put them on top of your shoes near the stove. Then they'll be nice and warm for you to wear tomorrow. I'll wash out your underwear and stockings so they'll be fresh."

"How's come Virginia has a scarf and we don't?" asked Ruth.

"Well, let's see if we can come up with a couple of flannel squares here in my box. You were right to ask, Ruth. One can lose a lot of heat through an uncovered head," Emma said, tying the folded triangles around the little heads.

"Now, upstairs, all of you! I'll be up a little later. I have a little finishing to do on Elsie's jacket." Then, calling upstairs after the three, she said, "You can say your prayers under the covers!"

They climbed into the double bed already warmed and covered with two feather comforters. There was a warm flat iron for each of them to find with her toes. At first Marian lay in the middle, but soon Virginia decided she would sleep better if she separated her two little cousins.

"How's come, if you're poor, you have all the nicest things?" asked Marian.

"Why, what do you mean?"

"Everything. Your room is all fixed up with ruffled curtains and a bed spread. Your feather ticks have pretty patchwork covers. And you have the nicest clothes of anyone at the high school."

"Well, I don't know about that. But Mother is a good seamstress. The patchwork cover is just made up of odds and ends she's accumulated over years of sewing."

"Do you miss your Daddy, Virginia?" asked Ruth.

"I miss him terribly. But we don't talk about him. He suffered for months before he died. It makes Mother so sad to talk about him."

"I miss my mother too. I wish she hadn't died. Then maybe I could have some pretty things like you do. . . . Say, maybe, if Aunt Emma and Daddy got married, ..."

Virginia laughed. "My mother is quite a bit older than your father."

"I thought you were gonna say that the Bible says they can't get married," said Ruth.

"No, actually, ... It's late now. Let's go to sleep."

"Okay. Good night, Virginia. . . . I hope there's no school tomorrow so we can stay here and play some more. . . .'I wish I may, I wish I might, have the wish I wish tonight.' I wish for no school tomorrow," said Marian.

Friday, March 27, 1942

Blizzarded all day. All livestock in barns. Paul L.'s horses are still here. I used them only a few hours for sowing on Tuesday. Back shed is very damp for sheep. Lambs should have sunshine. Brought kids home from town.

Saturday, March 28, 1942

Raging blizzard, sometimes blinding. Cal took Paul L.'s horses back with our wagon. I followed with the car to bring him home.

Sunday, March 29, 1942

Not in church. Still blowing in morning. Cal, Pearl and Marie all went away in the evening.

Monday, March 30, 1942

Docked 50 lambs' tails with our new docking tool. It does good work.

351

Tuesday, March 31, 1942

Brother J. W., his son John and their wives were here. Had 4-H meeting here tonight. Pete Ratzlaff and Melvin and John L.'s boys were here.

Thursday, April 2, 1942

Went along with Bernard T. Kaufman this morning. He took a load of Park Lane feeds to Kimball and Chamberlain. I got a load of alfalfa hay from Theo. Schumacher. Paid $13 for the truck load, not quite 2 tons. Good alfalfa but has thistles mixed in.

Friday, April 3, 1942

Good Friday. All in church in morning, home in afternoon. Pearl went to town to sing, she says, in the evening. Cal, the little girls and I went to Ortman to see about our tractor.

Saturday, April 4, 1942

Weather nice. Borrowed horse from Ben Ratzlaff. Sowed 9 acres Pilot wheat.

Sunday, April 5, 1942

Easter Sunday. Pearl, Ruth, Marian and I went to church. Cal and Marie stayed home.

Went to John J. B.'s for dinner and supper.

Ewe #227 had a very big lamb in the field while we were gone. It was dead when I found it. I gave the ewe two triplet lambs.

Cal and Pearl went away without doing one bit of chores.

Monday, April 6, 1942

Big Easter Monday musical program at the College but I was at home. Went to the concert in the evening. Had a good program and a good crowd.

Wednesday, April 8, 1942

Finished sowing wheat by time children came home from school. After school I disced a garden spot west of the house. Pearl sowed some of her garden.

Friday, April 10, 1942

Pearl, Cal and a load of kids from Freeman went to Sioux Falls to a rollerskating party. They got home at 2 a.m. Saturday.

Prof. Ben Waltner's Animal Husbandry class came to judge sheep. Cal, Harry Tiahrt, Paul Hofer, Jake Bolt, Willie Ortman and some Schweitzers were in the class.

Saturday, April 11, 1942

John M. Hofer is working here. We planted 3 bu. potatoes west of house.

Pearl was in Vermillion to attend a church college conference.

Sunday, April 12, 1942

Rev. D. S. Wipf preached this morning. The church was packed. Went to grandparents in the afternoon.

Pearl went with Peter Hofer to the Schultz church to sing.

Monday, April 13, 1942

Cal skinned a calf that had been sick and died.

John M. Hofer sowed 8 acres oats east of the machine shed and 13 acres of rye, oats & barley mixture in the southwest field.

I tried to get hay from several people but couldn't find any. Got some spelts, an old European variety of wheat, from Wm. Ortman.

Wednesday, April 15, 1942

Got a load of flax straw from Ike Tieszen.

As the children drove into the driveway after school they noticed a lot of commotion in the field south of the barn. "What in the WORLD?"

"It's a horse, lying down."

"That's Paul L. and Lizzie."

"That's Paul L.'s horse — the dappled gray one, and it looks like it's dead!"

Cal stopped the car on the driveway and they all ran into the field. "Oh, my God," said Pearl. "It's awful. That beautiful horse!"

Marian felt sick to her stomach. There was a huge mound of animal, foaming at its mouth.

"I feel just terrible, Paul. There didn't seem to be anything wrong with her when I hitched her up," said Morgan.

"She must've gotten overheated. It couldn't be helped," said his nephew.

"If Ortman had gotten our tractor in by now, this wouldn't have happened!" said Cal. "We ordered that tractor last year and still don't have it."

"You ordered a tractor?" asked Paul.

"Yeah, completed the deal with a down payment on December 6, the day before Pearl Harbor."

"Well, there's your reason for the delay. You may not get a tractor for the duration of the war now," said Lizzie.

"I'll be needing my other horse tomorrow," said Paul. "Could you lend me one of yours to make a team?"

"I'll let you have King. He's good and big—a heavy worker. I'll see if I can borrow Ben Ratzlaff's tractor. I believe he's done seeding," said Morgan.

"I'll skin the horse for you, Paul, and give you the hide," said Cal.

"Much obliged. I don't think I could do it."

Thursday, April 16, 1942

Paul L.'s LeRoy took home their surviving horse and King. We will get Pete Ratzlaff's tractor tomorrow.

Richard Kaufman brought my boar back. He paid me $5 for breeding 6 sows.

Saturday, April 18, 1942

Have the cattle and sheep on the rye field. There is not much to eat there but they have to live on something.

Docked 14 lambs for P. P. with our new tool. Johnny J. B.'s Johnny took it along home.

Sunday, April 19, 1942

Went to Tiahrts in the evening. Only Hy. and Buddy were home. Rev. Penner from Montana was showing slides of Indians at the Bethesda Church.

Pearl was singing in Monroe with the College Choir.

Tuesday, April 21, 1942

King, our horse, ran back home from Paul L.'s. He did not like it there, I suppose.

Pearl went to Sioux Falls with the College sophomores on a sneak day.

Friday, April 24, 1942

Fensel brought some chicks out but we were not ready for them. He took them back and said we could get some next week.

Paul L.'s Marvin came to get our horse, Nelly, to plant corn.

Saturday, April 25, 1942

Ruth was at a 4-H meeting at Holgates.

Went to Sam Preheim's sale. I bought a picture of Baby Stuart by Van Dyke for 35¢.

"What in the world did you buy that old thing for?" asked Cal as he saw his father remove the portrait from the car. "I thought you went to buy some tools."

"It's a famous painting and I got it cheap. The frame and glass alone are worth the 35 cents I paid for it. Tools went too high."

"It's not a painting. It's a copy of a painting."

"Maybe the girls will like it. I'll give it to them. Remember that picture of the baby waking from a nap in the crib? Marian and Ruth like that. Marian used to call it Baby Katherine."

"That's understandable. They could relate to that – a simple baby. But Baby Stuart isn't that kind of baby, with his fancy royal costume. What do they care about British monarchy?"

"Maybe they can learn some history that way – the difference between the Tudors and the Stuarts."

"Seems to me it belongs in a museum or a schoolhouse."

"That's a good idea! I'll give it to our school."

"Our school isn't even open. I'll bet Sam Schmidt will be thrilled with that idea!"

"Cal, didn't you study 'Baby Stuart' in grade school when you had Art Appreciation?"

"You mean every Friday when we pasted miniatures into workbooks and talked about color and composition?"

"Yeah! I used to teach 'Baby Stuart'. I'll bet the kids in Sunshine School would enjoy having a big picture to study next year."

"Is our school gonna be open again next year?"

"Patrons haven't decided yet. But I bet we do, with the threat of gas rationing and all."

Sunday, April 26, 1942

Had quite a discussion on non-resistance in Sunday School class. There is a real difference of opinion in our church. Ted and Walter Kleinsasser will be in the draft on May 7.

Monday, April 27, 1942

Made out my occupation questionnaire for Selective Service and the Telephone Company report for the tax commissioner.

Tuesday, April 28, 1942

I was fencing the alfalfa patch. The sweet clover we sowed last year in the alfalfa is growing nicely but the alfalfa is thin. Will have to sow brome grass in there next spring or this fall.

Wednesday, April 29, 1942

Got 400 started Leghorn chicks plus 28 Australorps from Fensel. We are crossing our chickens this year. They'll be Australwhites.

Thursday, April 30, 1942

The county is beginning the grading of our road. They are now at Philip Mensch's alfalfa.

The girls are making May baskets.

The dining room table was littered with supplies: ice cream boxes, butter boxes, crepe paper, construction paper, the stapler, paste, crayons, scissors.

"I wish we could put lilacs in the baskets, but it's so cold, they haven't even opened up yet!" protested Ruth.

"Even if they were open, it wouldn't be a good idea because they'd get limp and dried up by the time you got them to town and handed out," said Pearl. "It's best just to put candy and nuts in."

"How many you gonna make?" asked Marian.

"I'm gonna make enough for everybody in my room," said Ruth.

"Me too."

"Seems to me your anticipation is greater than your realization can be again," said Pearl.

"Waddaya mean by that?"

"It's like when you sit down at the table and put more food on your plate than you can possibly eat. Daddy says your eyes are bigger than your stomach. In this case, you hope to finish more baskets than you'll actually have time for. May baskets take more work to make than Valentines take to address. Maybe you ought to plan to make baskets only for your best friends."

"Let's make a list: Mary Lou Holgate."

"E. J. Holgate," said Marian.

"Bonnie Ellwein."

"Stewart Kaufman."

"Lorraine Mendel."

"Jean Kleinsasser."

"Bootsie Gross."

"Mahala Mutchelknaus."

"Donna Hofer."

"Sally Kleinsasser."

"Mary Kleinsasser."

"Clarice Schmidt."

"Rita Schmidt."

"Corrine Schmuck."

"Elaine Lipelt."

"Nita Huber."

"Sounds like you'd better get busy!" urged Pearl. "What kind of candy do you want to make?"

"What do we have the ingredients for?"

"Well, sugar is the main ingredient and, fortunately, we still have some of that left from canning season last summer."

"How about having a taffy pull like you did with the 4-H club?"

"No, that takes too long. Besides, you need more hands than we have to get it all pulled. We'd better stick to fudge and divinity. You get busy making the baskets and I'll start the candy," said Pearl.

Friday, May 1, 1942

Rained several times during the day. Weather is cold. Children got stuck coming home from school.

"How'd you get all your May baskets delivered in the rain?" Morgan asked his girls that evening when he and Cal came in for supper with their clothes soaked.

"We gave them out in school 'cause it was raining too hard to hang them on door knobs."

"Well, that way you escaped being kissed by the boys too!"

"Marian got kissed anyhow!" tattled Ruth.

"She did?"

"Yeah, look at her finger."

"Well, what is that, Marian, an engagement ring?" asked Cal.

"No, it's a Jack Armstrong ring that glows in the dark."

"How do you know it glows in the dark?"

"Cause E. J. pushed her in the dark broom closet and put it on her finger!" shouted Ruth and ran for her life.

Saturday, May 2, 1942

Picked up scrap iron and sold it. Got $7.05 for it ($10 a ton). Cal planted a few Russian olives in the shelter belt.

Had wheat election. I got there 5 minutes late so they did not let me vote. Ted Holzworth and Roth were on the election board. John L., Otto Stern and Dave S. Hofer were there too. I suppose all the boys will draw pay.

John P. Gross was here on account of sugar rationing sign-up.

Sunday, May 3, 1942

Got up too late for church. Weather so cold we started the base burner again. Cal took the car. Pearl sang at the South Church.

Monday, May 4, 1942

Had sugar rationing sign-up in our school. All came to school but Ferd Thomas and Art Becker, who came to our place in the evening. 58 signed up. Sam Schmidt was to do this as clerk but he said he had no time. All had some sugar but Albert Smith and Art Adrian. The most reported was Joe L. Thomas with 230 lbs.

Doris Kaufman came along with Pearl. They are busy studying chemistry. Dr. Congdon is putting on the pressure.

Wednesday, May 6, 1942

Rained yesterday and today. It is getting wet in the brooder house. The sheep and lambs are all wet. They do not get on the alfalfa field any more since we made new fence. The sick hog is not getting any better very fast.

Pearl took a big "bouquet" of red radishes to Dr. Congdon with her chemistry workbook.

Thursday, May 7, 1942

Got a load of feed from Joe Hofer in Shanard elevator. Bought 140 rods sheep woven wire @ 32¢. Had trough made at Thompson Yards for $5.

Visited Fred Dirks after dinner. He is quite sick. Does not get air sometimes.

Went to Alex Deckert & John M.S. Hofer to make a change on their sugar rationing.

Friday, May 8, 1942

Marian is at John A. Kleinsasser's place. She and her pal, Sally, have the mumps together.

"Hello, John?"

"Speaking."

"This is Wanda Kleinsasser, Sally's mother."

"Oh, yes. How are you this morning?"

"I heard that Marian came down with the mumps this morning."

"Yes, Superintendent Holgate just phoned for me to take her home. How'd you find out so fast?"

"Mr. Holgate just called to check on Sally and he mentioned Marian. Sally is home with the mumps and I thought it might be nice for the girls to be down together. If you like, bring Marian over here from school. She can stay here with us while she's sick."

"That's mighty generous of you, Wanda. I'll get her clothes together and bring her over from school."

"But dress her warmly, John. It's chilly out."

"Okay, Wanda."

When Marian learned of her destination, she cried, "Oh, goody! That'll be fun. Sally has some new Shirley Temple paper dolls we can play with."

Saturday, May 9, 1942

Our Allis Chalmers tractor finally came in at Harold Ortman's almost half a year after we ordered it. We got a steel wheeled model with lights and starter. We still owe $507 on it, but we won't have to pay rent to him anymore and we'll have a tractor when we need it.

Sunday, May 10, 1942

Pearl went with the College A Capella Choir to Fort Denison, Iowa, to sing for the boys in the C.O. camp. They went by car.

Monday, May 11, 1942

I was fencing all day. Very wet. Rye field has knee-deep water.

Cal slid off the grade this morning. We put lugs on the tractor and pulled the car out. That's easier than hitching up a team of horses.

Insured our crop, 165 acres, at a premium of $90.

Friday, May 15, 1942

I have been trying to drain water by ditching. There will be at least 29 acres drowned out, but that is much better than having 150 acres burn out.

Our eggs are hatching at 86%. Paid John M. Hofer with 12 doz. hatching eggs for his labor. He helped repair brooder house. Our first batch of chicks got coccidiosis because it rained in.

Julius Miller came out for a hog to butcher for the meat market. I had to pull him in and out of our place. Sold one sow, weighing 415 lbs., for $57.27. That's more than I used to get for a month of teaching.

Saturday, May 23, 1942

Ruth has the mumps. Fortunately, she waited until school was out.

Sunday, May 24, 1942

230 chicks were dead this morning when we got up and more are dying. The brooder stove overheated. Pearl had not set it right.

Monday, May 25, 1942

Ascension Day. Had Lord's Supper at church. Cal and Pearl did not go because the College had athletic contests. Road graders are working on the section line.

Tuesday, May 26, 1942

Cal plowed and dragged 'til midnight last night. He says dragging goes better at night than during the day.

Pearl graduated from the 2-year Normal Course at the College. Dr. Miller from Goshen College, Indiana, was the commencement speaker. He told a good story about a speaker's job: "Stand up to be seen, speak up to be heard and shut up to be appreciated."

Wednesday, May 27, 1942
Had a runaway with the horses and corn planter this morning. They bent one wheel badly.

"Girls, I need your help to pick up the hybrid seed corn that the horses spilled," directed Morgan.

"I can't. I still got the mumps," complained Ruth.

"It's nice and warm. The sun is beating down in the yard. It will do you good to get out in the fresh air," said Morgan.

Reluctantly the little girls took the gallon buckets that their father had thrust into their hands and eventually they arrived at the scene of devastation. Bright kernels of seed corn were sprinkled all over the ground. They started scraping the corn and dirt up by the hands full.

Pearl, having finished feeding her chicks, arrived to supervise the girls' chore. "I think Daddy wants to put that corn in the planter again. It's very expensive, treated seed corn. We can't feed it to the chickens or they'll die. You'll have to pick up each kernel separately because the dirt will foul up the corn planter plates."

"Oh, no!" moaned Marian and Ruth in unison.

"That'll take ages," protested Marian.

"We'll miss 'Helen Trent' on the radio."

"That's all right with me!" said Pearl. "Now get busy."

Thursday, May 28, 1942
Father-in-law and Dave J. R. were here. Susie, I believe, had Grandpa take back 60 acres that he had given her some 20 years ago and give her different land. They then made out deeds to give our children 30 acres of that land and Eva Wiens should get the rest. I did not sign it because I felt the arrangement was not fair.

Friday, May 29, 1942
Jamesville Colony boys came to shear the sheep for 20¢ each. They wanted 5¢ extra to tie the wool, so Pearl did the tying. One ewe had a lamb shortly after they were done shearing her. She seems okay, though.

The driveway was so muddy that Cal had to pull the boys in with the tractor.

"You boys register for the draft yet?" asked Morgan as he passed the mashed potatoes.

"Yo, all those over 20," said Eli. "How 'bout you, Cal?"

"Not old enough yet," said Cal, picking up a slice of bread. "Anybody been drafted yet?"

"Yo, but we go to the work camp. We don't go to war."

"I know," said Morgan.

"What would happen if any one of the colony boys went to war?" asked Pearl.

"They wouldn't belong to our Brotherhood no more. They would have to leave the fellowship. It is against our religion to put on the uniform and fight," said Amos. "We cannot go against our faith."

"But we pray that we get a farm deferment, like you people get. Our boys are needed on the farm, just like your boys are," said Eli.

Sunday, May 31, 1942

Could not get to church on time this morning because of the mud.

Jacob L. Wollman came in the evening to ask me to write a recommendation for him to get into the American Shropshire Assoc.

Pearl walked to Highway 81 to catch a ride to the North Church for Sally Tieszen and Bill Hieb's wedding.

Thursday, June 4, 1942

The sick cow died this morning. We have lost 2 cows and 3 calves this spring. Pigs are sick too and very thin. I think it is because of all the cold, wet weather.

Sunday, June 7, 1942

Northern District Conf. is being held at the North Church. J. John Frieszen and his children are here from Butterfield, Minn. I stayed at his place when the Conf. was there.

Monday, June 8, 1942

Took the Lord's Supper at the conference in the afternoon. The evening session was in charge of Jacob B. There were testimonies by missionaries now on the field and also by new workers being commissioned.

Pooled the wool. We got 719 lbs.

Wednesday, June 10, 1942

Cal and Pearl went to North Church for Young People's Day at the Conference. I planted corn. We all went in the evening. Rev. Walter Gering was main speaker.

Thursday, June 11, 1942

Finished planting last corn. First corn is ready to cultivate. Pheasants are doing damage to corn. Attended S. D. Dairy Cattle Congress in Marion for a while. They had good exhibits.

Saturday, June 13, 1942

Cal plowed the conservation acres 'til the plow broke. I cut alfalfa on section line. It is very good at places, drowned out in others and never got started in some. Cut some of the wheat where the graders want a borrow pit for the road. Graders are now working east of our mailbox.

Sunday, June 14, 1942

Miss Buller from Montana and Rev. Isaac from India, both missionaries, spoke in our church.

Ruth left for 4-H camp at Lake Lakodia, Madison.

Friday, June 19, 1942

Had heavy rain and wind last night which blew over some trees. Lakes are full of water again. Barbara Hofer was painting here. Pearl tried to take her home with the car but got stuck. So they both rode King home.

Sunday, June 21, 1942

Ruth, Marian and I went to the Gym to hear P. C. Hiebert of the Mennonite Central Committee concerning Civilian Public Service camps. He said they should be called Conscientious Builder Camps.

Tuesday, June 23, 1942

Cal finished the electric fence around the oat patch, so we turned in the cattle. The red cow jumped over and cut another one of her teats. One of the heifers got through right away too. After we put them back, they stayed.

Tuesday, June 30, 1942

Cal registered for the draft. Mr. Brown, Highway Superintendent, was here. He said we will get a ditch on our side of the road now to drain the lakes into the creek running to Silver Lake.

Friday, July 3, 1942

Graders are still working on the section line. They hauled quite a few loads of dirt on our driveway and yard, which I will have to pay for.

Pearl canned 2 boxes of cherries.

"You may each have three cherries," said Pearl to her little sisters as they were stemming the dark red Bing cherries.

"THREE CHERRIES!" shouted Ruth, astonished.

"Yes, that's all."

"You always let us have more than that before!" cried Marian.

"I know I did, but they're very expensive this year and we can only afford to buy two boxes. Besides, you get sick when you eat too much fruit."

"I'm gonna tell Daddy!" threatened Ruth.

"Go right ahead! You'll appreciate having the canned cherries next winter when it's cold and you don't have any fresh fruit."

"Waddaya mean by 'YOU'LL appreciate'? Aren't you gonna be here?" asked Marian.

"I don't know yet. I'm looking for a teaching job. I might be staying at home, but, then again, I might not. So you'll want to have all the sauce down the basement you can get."

"When can we eat our three cherries?" asked Ruth in a sullen mood.

"Any time. You may have one now, one when you've finished stemming the first box, and one when you've finished stemming the second box," answered Pearl. "Or, you may eat them all now!"

"I'm gonna eat all mine right now," said Ruth, hunting for the three largest cherries she could find in one box.

"Me too!" cried Marian and dug into the other box.

"Don't put them in your mouth without washing them!" Pearl cautioned the girls, who rushed to the pump in the kitchen and pumped a gush of water over the three cherries each held in her hand. "Come back to the table and eat them here so you don't get cherry juice all over your clothes! It's very hard to get cherry stains out," called Pearl.

Slowly the girls returned to the table and laid their cherries on the oilcloth cover. How pretty they looked and how soon they would be gone. "Maybe I will save mine," said Ruth.

"Me too," said Marian.

"But I'm gonna tell Daddy what you did!" said Ruth.

"That's all right. Tell him. And when you're done stemming the cherries, you can start shelling that bushel basket of peas," Pearl said, pointing to the corner.

"Ohhhhh," the girls groaned in unison.

"But you may eat all the green peas you want!" Pearl smiled.

Wednesday, July 8, 1942

The WPA put up a woven wire fence along the section line. Pearl and Cal were cultivating corn. Pearl was running the cultivator first, then later the tractor. It rained 3 1/2 in. at night.

Friday, July 10, 1942

The WPA is working their last day on our road. George Gross did a good job of blading.

Ruth and Pearl walked to town for a 4-H meeting.

Thursday, July 16, 1942

Started cutting succotash. Cut 'til 10:30 with lights before it started to rain again.

Tuesday, July 21, 1942

Benny Gross was here on furlough from the Army in California. He was one of Pearl's old flames.

Saturday, July 25, 1942

Pearl went to Dr. Payne's auction sale and brought back 5 oak chairs and some rugs for $19.80.

Monday, July 27, 1942

Cal and Pearl shocked wheat while I cut the prairie hay in the southwest corner.

Wednesday, July 29, 1942

Went to town in the evening. Some merchants want to close the stores on Wednesday nights because gas rationing keeps the crowd down. Got another permit for a retreaded tire. Finished shocking rye.

Sunday, August 2, 1942

Little girls and I went to Silver Lake Church to hear the CPS men's choir from Ft. Denison, Iowa.

Pearl and Cal were gone all afternoon and evening.

The Jamesville Colony people were here. They bought four ram lambs for $100. The little girls made supper for the colony people.

"Well, we got string beans, cucumbers and tomatoes in the garden," said Ruth when Marian asked what they would make.

"And potatoes, and we could open up a jar of duck meat from the basement," offered Marian.

364

When the food was ready and the table set, Morgan called the guests to the table and prayed, *Komm, Herr Jesus, sei unsere Gast und segnet wass du uns bescherret hast. Amen.*

"Please pass the cucumbers," said Ruth.

"Ah, you mean *Kratsivitz*," said Eli, passing the bowl in which the peeled and sliced cucumber rounds were swimming in fresh cream. "These look like Little Russian pickles like our folks brought over from the Old Country."

"That's what they are," said Morgan. "Best ones around. Better than any you can buy in the store."

"Our women folks save the seeds from year to year, just like the muskmelon and watermelon seeds. We brought them from Russia."

"And plum seeds?" asked Ruth.

"*Ja*, and apple seeds too," said Eli. "You girls did a real good job getting this supper for us. You're gonna make some lucky fellas some good cooks some day."

Tuesday, August 4, 1942

Pearl went to town to get Cousin Virginia to help her cook for threshers and Sally to play with Marian. We threshed about 20 acres of oats. Too much straw.

"Can Sally and I ride in the grain wagon?" Marian asked Cal as he drove the tractor up to the threshing machine to exchange an empty trailer for a full one.

"Sure, but you got to sit down. No standing on top of the grain. If I have to stop short, you could be thrown out."

The girls climbed into the wagon and sat atop the golden oats. "Let's take off our shoes," suggested Marian. The oats is going to get in our shoes anyway."

"It prickles," said Sally.

"Yeah, oats and barley prickle a little. Wheat and rye are smoother. Flax is even smoother."

Sitting on top of the grain they could better see the whole threshing operation and wave to the bundle pitchers. Ben Ratzlaff, the machine tender, came over to the wagon to tease and flirt. "This threshing crew gets better looking every day," he said.

"Okay, hang on," said Cal as he took off with the tractor trailing the grain wagon. He pulled out of the field where the wire fence had been removed and on to the ungraveled rural road and eventually on to the recently graveled section line which led to the driveway. The girls surveyed the deep green corn crop entwined with blooming white creeping jinnies. The sunflowers ripening, the wheat and barley and rye shocks dotting the stubble fields were beautiful to behold.

As they neared the farmstead they saw pigs cooling themselves in mud holes, sheep and cattle resting under shade trees or taking an occasional lick of the salt block.

Cal pulled up to the granary door. "You kids are gonna have to get out of the trailer now. You can go in the granary bin if you want to and help move the grain back from the door as I shovel it in."

"How's come we don't use an elevator anymore?" asked Marian.

"Dad sold the elevator the winter after we had no crop at all. Got $210 for it. He's usin' me as the elevator now," said Cal.

Inside the house Pearl, Virginia and Ruth were preparing dinner for the threshing crew. "You're just in time to help Ruth brush the potatoes," said Pearl, thrusting a pan of potatoes at them. "I'll get two more vegetable brushes and a pan and you can all sit under the elm tree and get these potatoes clean."

The three girls knelt under the tree and started brushing. Soon Pepper and several kittens came to investigate what was in the pan and Marian shooed them off with a spray of water droplets from her brush. "Don't. That's cruel," said Ruth. "C'mon, Pepper. Here, Boy, don't let her scare you off."

"When you're done with the potatoes, you can set up the wash bench," called Pearl through the screen door. "Use the enameled wash basins hanging in the back porch and hang clean roller towels on the nails."

When the potatoes were clean, Ruth rinsed them under the cistern pump and carried them to the kitchen. "You and Sally set up the wash bench. I'm suppose to slice cucumbers and tomatoes yet," she called through the door.

Soon it was time for Marian and Sally to ring the big iron school bell mounted on the garage. Slowly the threshing crew gathered at the house, threw their straw hats under the shade tree and washed the grime from their hands and faces, throwing the dirty water on the gladiolas Pearl had planted at the side of the house. "Smells awful good. Wonder what we're havin' for dinner," said Pete Ratzlaff.

"It's breaded pork chops," announced Marian, ruining the surprise.

The threshers filed into the house but the girls stayed outside to listen to the conversation through the screen door. After Morgan had prayed he said, "Okay, dig in. Help yourself to what's nearest you and pass it to the right. We can't have what one young man said at the table once: '*Soo viel pleasin' und gepassin', ich hob nit zeit zu essen.*'"

"That must be *Hutterische,* because I can't understand a lot of it," said Irvin Ratzlaff.

"Well, you Low Germans talk funny ALL the time," said Morgan, and they all laughed.

"I'm glad Pearl put the pork chops on the table right away. One place I was thrashin', the cook put the leftovers on first," said Irvin. "Then, when they were all gone, she brought out a platter of fresh meat. I should have had a clue to what was goin' on, because one guy in the crew was goin' with the cook and he kept passin' up the leftovers. We figgered out later that he knew her operation and waited 'til the good stuff came out."

"Mighty good eats, Pearl," said Pete. "Who's your helper?"

"Oh, I'm sorry, I thought you knew her. This is Virginia Kleinsasser, my cousin. Mrs. Ike Kleinsasser's daughter."

"And Jerome's sister! I knew your father. Mighty fine man. Good, honest implement dealer too! Shame he died so young."

Isaac Kleinsasser Family
Brother P. P. Kleinsasser on running board.

"Thank you," said Virginia, softly.

"I'm helping too," announced Ruth, standing beside Virginia.

"You I know. I just didn't know Virginia."

"Sally and I helped too," called Marian through the screen door.

"Another country heard from!" said Morgan, and all the men laughed.

Monday, August 17, 1942

I was supposed to go with Rev. M. A. Kroeker to inspect the CPS camp at Ft. Denison, Iowa, but we are still threshing at Pete Ratzlaff's. The creeping jinnies have grown up over many of the shocks. Rival wheat and rye are of good quality this year.

Wednesday, August 26, 1942

Pearl got a job teaching 7th and 8th grade in Irene at $100 a month. This is the highest pay I have heard of this year for a new graduate of the College. She ran the car down to Irene without putting in oil and ruined the engine.

Tuesday, September 1, 1942

Cal got Grand Champion litter over all breeds at the County Fair. Ruth also had a litter of pigs and some sheep in the 4-H club class. Cal stayed with the stock.

Monday, September 7, 1942

Cal got 2 red ribbons in ram lambs at the State Fair and 3 blues and champion gilt. I had some trouble getting my sheep judged in open class because pedigrees had not arrived in time.

Friday, September 11, 1942

I went to Irene to bring Pearl home for the weekend. It hailed.

Saturday, September 12, 1942

Went to Bob Haar's auction sale. Bought a study table for Cal, a set of books, MEMOIRS OF THE COURTS OF EUROPE, and an unabridged dictionary.

Friday, September 18, 1942

Cal walked to Highway 81 to catch a ride with the Tieszen boys, Melvin and Reuben. They all go to College. There are girls along too from Marion.

I butchered two Australorp roosters.

Marian and Ruth attend Sunshine #26 with Anna Becker as teacher.

Pearl did not come home this weekend.

Wednesday, September 23, 1942

Went to Kunkel auction sale. Car sold for $1070. I heard it was $150 more than he paid for it 2 years ago.

Thursday, September 24, 1942

Went to Menno Albrecht sale. A 1939 Allis Chalmers tractor sold for $940 on rubber. A John Deere elevator complete went for $430.

Killing frost last night. Cane is not cut.

Marie Walter came out after school. She attends Freeman H. S. She and the girls butchered two roosters for supper.

"Who's gonna catch the roosters?" asked Marian.

"Don't you have a chicken catcher?" asked Marie.

"Yeah, it's hanging in the chicken house," said Ruth.

"Well, we can put some corn in the chicken house, and when we got at least two roosters in there, we'll close the door. Then I'll go in and catch 'em by the leg."

"Okay, I'll get the corn," said Ruth, who ran off to the granary and soon returned with a small bucket half full.

"Put it in the feeders and watch 'em come," predicted Marie.

"Sure enough, here they come," said Marian.

When several had found the corn, Marie said, "Close the door behind me. When I catch one by the leg, I'll hand it to you. But hang on tight! They'll fight to get away and will try to peck you!"

"You get the first one, Ruth. I'm scared I might drop it," confided Marian.

Listening outside the chicken house the little girls heard a huge commotion, with roosters crowing, toppling feeders and waterers. Finally the noise subsided and Marie handed the first black rooster through the narrowly opened door by its legs. Ruth was there to receive it gingerly. "Hang on!" said Marie, and returned for the second rooster. Again they heard the commotion and again the subsidence. Luckily for Marian, Marie held on to the second rooster. "Marian, you bring the butcher knife from the kitchen."

The Australorp tried to escape Ruth's grip. "Stop it!" she hollered and threw her weight against the rooster now lying on the ground. Marie applied the knife and as the decapitated creatures flopped and flew around, sprinkling blood, Ruth went to the kitchen to see if the teakettle of water which Marie had lighted on the stove had reached the boiling point.

"Get the butchering pail from the garage, Marian," instructed Marie. When the water was hot, Ruth appeared from the house with the kettle. Marie emptied it into the pail and the first rooster was scalded, head first. "Take him into the shelter belt and start picking the feathers off," Marie told the girls. "I'll be along shortly with the second."

"You hold him by the legs while I pull feathers," said Marian. "You're taller." Soon black feathers lay mixed with yellow and orange leaves on the ground under the trees. "Who's gonna open up the roosters?" asked Marian.

"I guess I will," said Marie, as they walked back to the house. "You lay the newspapers out on the table." Deftly Marie cut off the feet and wings at the joints and disemboweled the roosters. When she had finished, she wrapped the entrails in the paper and said, "Take this out to Pepper while I cut the roosters into pieces

369

and get them on the stove. They're old and tough, so they're gonna have to steam after they're browned. You kids can peel potatoes."

Later, at supper, Morgan said, "You did a pretty good job cutting up this rooster, Marie. This breast piece isn't mangled too badly. You can always tell a beginner by how they cut up a chicken."

Saturday, September 26, 1942

Pearl was home this morning. She must have gotten a ride home from Irene with someone. She and Marie did the washing. Reuben Tieszen helped manure the barns.

Sunday, September 27, 1942

After church we went to Abe Wienses for dinner and then to Tiahrts for a while. Elmer was home from CPS camp at Ft. Collins, Colo. He does not like it there. He says he does not get enough to eat.

Pearl dug parsnips out of the garden and took a gunny sack full to Irene.

Monday, September 28, 1942

Helped Joe L. fill silo. He put up a cement stave silo. Bought it from Traub in Sioux Falls.

Tuesday, September 29, 1942

Signed up for a government wheat and barley loan in Parkston. I'll get the money through a local bank. Shot 3 pheasants coming home. After school Cal duckfooted the weed control patch.

Saturday, October 3, 1942

Pearl did not come home this weekend. Cal was sowing rye until it started to rain.

We butchered a yearling sheep. Had the liver and heart for supper and took the rest to the locker. Bought some chislic sticks to make chislic.

Sunday, October 4, 1942

Pearl came home from Sioux Falls where she was attending the SDEA convention. Adeline and John were here for dinner.

It rained off and on during the day. We carried chickens to the barns so they would not catch cold.

Tuesday, October 6, 1942

I butchered a rooster and the children got it ready for supper. Ruth also baked a cake. She found a fancy fluted pan in the attic which Katherine had used.

Rev. Willard Claassen of the South Church was here. Churches will make a drive to reduce the College debt.

Sunday, October 11, 1942

Had Sunday School convention in the College Gym. Pres. J. D. Unruh spoke on the difference between a regular soldier and a non-combatant. He says there is no essential difference. Both are part of the military. He made a great impression on the Hutters.

Wednesday, October 14, 1942

I helped Jake Fast make a fence between my land and Sam Schmidt's. Jake is living on Sam's farm while Schmidts are in Oregon doing church work. Our pigs got into Art Adrian's corn. Cal rented land from Mrs. Peter L. Thomas.

Sunday, October 18, 1942

Pearl did not come home this weekend. Cal and I went to Ben Spies looking for a good boar.

Wednesday, October 21, 1942

Sold a load of scrap iron to Wm. Gross.

Went to John J. B.'s for the evening. I gave a talk to the boys that will go to the C. O. camp at Hill City in the Black Hills. They had quite a crowd. P. P. made the opening, Jacob B. spoke and Peter J. S. made closing remarks.

The camp just opened with Paul Tschetter as director. It was a former CCC camp. The boys will be building Deerfield Dam, about 30 miles from Mt. Rushmore, under the supervision of the Bureau of Reclamation. There will be no support from the government. The financial burden will be borne by the historic peace churches.

Cal is picking corn.

Got formula for pig's necro from Kidman's Stock Powder Co.: 8 oz. blue vitrol, 4 oz. permanganate of potash, trace of potassium iodide, trace of iron oxide. Mix above with 1 gal. water. Use 1 pt. of this mixture with 40 gal. drinking water.

Saturday, October 31, 1942

I was elected secretary of our district Mennonite Aid Plan. Also elected to represent our district at Hillsboro, Kansas, for the triennial meeting on Nov. 5 & 6.

Tuesday, November 3, 1942

Election Day. Ed Weidenbach was the only Democrat running in the county. His opponent died, so he should get elected. We expect Bushfield to be elected Senator.

Wednesday, November 4, 1942

Left for Hillsboro, Kansas, at 6 a.m. Abe Wiens did the driving. Took Highway 81 to McPherson, Kansas. Got to Hillsboro at 8 p.m. Ate supper in a restaurant. Stayed overnight at J. P. Kasper.

Thursday, November 5, 1942

I was appointed to the credentials committee. Christian Thierstein of Kansas is the chairman.

Friday, November 6, 1942

Was elected to the finance committee of the Aid Plan. D. J. Mendel is general secretary.

Saturday, November 7, 1942

Visited Weeping Water, Nebraska, CPS camp on the way home from Hillsboro. It was a 441 mile trip to Hillsboro on Highway 81.

Sunday, November 8, 1942

Pearl is home. Had Mission Fest. Collection was over $600. John J. B.'s were here for dinner. Sister Katherine took some of our clothes home to patch. She said the boys at the CPS camp near Hill City are not getting enough to eat. They had to give up their ration books. It is very hard to get food, especially milk and meat. Katherine wants to organize a food drive.

Pearl caught a ride back to Irene from Freeman.

Lost 5 lambs from eating cane.

Monday, November 9, 1942

John J. B. and I bought a boar from Ben Spies for $80. It was sired by Masterful, Harold Timm's boar of Muscatine, Iowa.

Cut fence braces from ash trees.

Sunday, November 15, 1942

Gave a report on the Weeping Water CPS camp in church this morning.

Collected for the College.

Wednesday, November 18, 1942

Joel Deckert was here to see me about teaching their school. Their teacher is not an American citizen, so he will have to quit. I asked for $100, what Pearl is getting. If I get it, I will teach. The school is north of the Tieszen church.

Friday, November 20, 1942

Registered in our school for gas rationing. Got Pearl from Irene. Saw "The Hoosier Schoolmaster" at the Academy. It was fairly well presented.

Saturday, November 21, 1942

Had to bring some woven wire from the section line to complete the fence by the machine shed. It is hard to get wire.

Tuesday, November 24, 1942

Cal gave a duck to Melvin Tieszen and one to the grandparents for Thanksgiving.

Wednesday, November 25, 1942

Pearl came home from Irene with Miss Waltner.

Thursday, November 26, 1942

Had Thanksgiving dinner at Jake L.'s. Turkey and all the trimmings. We went home for supper because Cal wanted to study for his College quarter finals tomorrow.

Friday, November 27, 1942

Butchered 45 ducks. Had plenty of help from aunts and uncles. Some of the ducks will go to the CPS camp in the Black Hills.

Saturday, November 28, 1942

Barbara Hofer helped Pearl can 40 ducks.

"Wouldn't you girls like to give your goose to the boys in the CPS camp in the Black Hills?" asked Pearl as they were all filling half gallon jars with duck pieces.

"You mean ALEXANDER?" asked Ruth, horrified.

"Yes, he's the only goose we have."

"But he's a pet."

"I understand that. But he'll be all alone anyway now that the ducks have been butchered. And you could help feed the boys."

"Is that where Peter is?"

"Yes, and he said they're hungry, especially for some form of protein. They've been eating powdered milk mixed with peanut butter."

"Ugh!" said Marian.

"The dietitian calls it chalk but the boys call it choke. Here, your hands are small, Marian; I want you to get in this jar and scrub it out better. The jars won't seal if there's any foreign matter in them. They have to be absolutely sterile."

373

"Are you going to take the food out there?" asked Ruth.

"No, I wish I could go to the Hills. There will be two truck loads going. A. T. Kaufman will furnish one truck and John Gross the other."

"So Alexander would ride in a truck to the Hills?"

"Yes."

"I guess he'd enjoy that," said Ruth, resigned to giving up her pet for the cause.

Tuesday, December 1, 1942

Gas rationing starts officially today.

Fair weather turned to blizzard. Cal came home from College at noon but it was too cold to pick corn.

Wednesday, December 2, 1942

Hung a lantern in the cellar so food would not freeze. Car would not start. Tieszen boys pulled it to town.

Friday, December 11, 1942

Paid Fed. Land Bank $220 for hay and corn (proportional to yield).

Sunday, December 13, 1942

Girls had practice for Christmas program this afternoon.

Mrs. Paul J. Decker called her class up to the front where they stood on the platform, the pulpit having been removed. She directed from the piano where she sat, mouthing "Away in a Manger" and "Joy to the World" for the little ones to follow. "Some of you don't know your words yet. I want you to practice with your Mommies when you get home." They look so cute, Marian thought.

Sarah B., the maiden lady who had been a pious fixture in the church for years, called her class up next. She had passed out "pieces" for them to memorize by this first rehearsal. Unfortunately, nobody knew his piece yet, so it was a practice in pronunciation. Marian recognized some poems she had learned in the past and was glad to have graduated to the next level.

Marian and Angie's teacher was the preacher, Rev. Jacob B. Jacob B.'s son Jakie was also in the class and Marian had gotten a penny post card from him, signed "Love and Kises." Daddy had made fun of his spelling for weeks. "Love and Kises," Daddy said when it was time to go to bed. "Love and Kises." Daddy smiled at her from the back row where he was waiting for the rehearsal to end.

As Jacob B. had his class assemble on the platform, Marian remembered some of the good discussions they had had in his class: why saloons were always dark inside (sinners can't stand the light of day), where the saved departed, such as Marian's mother, had gone (to heaven), the price of honesty (absolute honesty to the rationing board would cause you to starve). This last statement created considerable discomfort in Marian.

"Does Jacob B. really mean that?" she had asked her father.

"No, he overstated the case a bit to make a point."

Jacob B.'s class practiced some choral speaking in addition to individual poems.

The oldest group practicing today, of which Ruth was a member, was taught by Jac. Mendel, also the church choir director, so he worked a little choral music into his class's portion of the program.

But there was more practice still needed, all agreed, as they piled into waiting cars to take them home.

Monday, December 14, 1942

Founders' Day at the College. Cal filled out his draft questionnaire with Atty. H. L. Gross. All went to hear Pres. E. G. Kaufman of Bethel College in the evening.

Tuesday, December 15, 1942

Went to Viborg for annual meeting of Fraternal Burial Assoc. Our undertaker, Raynie, was not present. He is taking flight training at the University in Vermillion. I was re-elected secretary.

Wednesday, December 16, 1942

Barbara Hofer took our dirty clothes to Adeline, who will wash them. Our Maytag won't work.

Bought some Christmas dresses for the girls. Cannot find a good coat for Ruth.

Saturday, December 19, 1942

Cal and I castrated some fall pigs and also a spring boar that had been returned by Wesley Kaufman as a non-breeder.

Pearl is not home this weekend. We got the clothes from Adeline that she had washed for us.

Paul Decker rented a boar from us and took it home in the trunk of his car.

Paid Fed. Land Bank $103, which was 1/3 of my Soil Conservation check.

Thursday, December 24, 1942
Had a good Christmas program in church.

"Look, Ruth still has the price tag on the sleeve of her dress," said Miriam, pointing and snickering at Ruth who stood in the middle of the platform, saying her Christmas poem.

Large hanging gas lamps hummed overhead. Little girls packed into long oak pews craned their necks to see for themselves if the price tag was still there. Marian was among them and overheard the remarks.

"Maybe she's proud it's a store-boughten dress instead of a homemade dress," surmised Angie.

"Who would make her a dress? She doesn't have a mother," said Pauline.

When her class's portion of the program was finished, Ruth took her seat, oblivious of the whispering. Marian turned around in the pew and whispered, "Take the price tag off your right sleeve." Embarrassed, Ruth blushed, clapped her hands over her mouth, and removed the tag.

"That's okay, Ruth. It's nothing to be embarrassed about," said Mrs. Paul E., patting her shoulder from the pew behind. While the Christmas packages were being distributed, the superintendent's wife scolded the girls for making fun of Ruth. "Shame on you! That kind of thing can happen to anyone. It was simply overlooked."

On the way home from church Cal asked, "What was all the commotion about on the girls' side of the church tonight?"

"The price tag was still on my dress," Ruth confessed.

"Well, at least they knew you had a new dress! Maybe they were jealous," said Morgan. "If Pearl had been here, she would have caught that before you went on stage."

Sunday, December 27, 1942
"You're not going to church?" asked Morgan of his son, who was sitting at the table, not dressed for church.

"No, I think I'll stay home today."

"How's come?"

"I've been in church for the last three days—Christmas Eve, Christmas Day, First Day After Christmas. That's enough church for one week. The preacher doesn't have much more to say than he's already said."

"That's not the point. It's Sunday, and there's Sunday School too."

"I don't care. I don't feel like going to church again."

"Well, you're 19 years old. I can't force you to go to church," said Morgan, resigning with a sigh.

"That's right, Pa!"

"Of course, you got an extra dose of church on Christmas Eve when you went to midnight mass at the Catholic church in Marion!'

"Well, at least that was something different."

"I'll bet it was! C'mon, girls, let's go or we'll be late again."

Monday, December 28, 1942

Pearl came home this morning.

John and Gladys Kleinsasser were here on furlough. He's stationed in New Mexico, training as a bombadier.

Gladys's brother, Samuel W. Hofer, had to have another blood transfusion. He lost his leg in a bad automobile accident.

Went to Harold Ortman to ask for an Allis Chalmers plow. He said he may not get any to sell.

Had a flat tire on the way home.

1943
Rediscovering Home Pleasures

Thursday, January 1, 1943

We did not go to church this morning. Ruth and Marian had school at Sunshine #26. Pearl is home from Irene.

Cal and I cleaned out the cistern in the morning and hauled manure out of the back shed of the horse barn in the afternoon.

The children went to see their grandparents after the girls got out of school.

I stayed home to get ready to leave for Pierre.

Saturday, January 3, 1943

Sen. Olson of Viborg came to my corner on Highway 81 at 12:30 p.m. to pick me up. We went to Sen. Buehler's and with him to Pierre. Arrived after dark.

Got a room at Earl Hammerquist's home. Sen. Buehler and I are staying together.

Learned that Mr. Piner, where I stayed last time, is sick.

Sunday, January 4, 1943

Republicans caucused in the afternoon and evening. Rep. Rev. Hove was elected Speaker of the House. I am pretty sure I'll get a job.

Monday, January 5, 1943

The House convened today. A. C. Miller read ex-Gov. Bushfield's speech. Gov. Sharpe gave a long speech. Went to the reception and stayed a while at the inaugural ball.

Earl Hammerquist, former Commissioner of School and Public Lands, is looking for a job in Minneapolis. His daughter Virginia is one of the pages. The desk force is the same as last session except Leone Schumacher is Bill Clerk. Doane Robinson, the historian, is Sergeant-at-Arms. My neighbor, Zach Wipf, was appointed doorkeeper.

Thursday, January 7, 1943

Had session at 2 and left for home at 3 with Buehler and Olson. Got home at 8. We stopped in Huron for lunch. I phoned Sister Susie (Mrs. John S. Waldner). It is nearly 1 a.m. and Cal is studying German.

Friday, January 8, 1943

Haar is supposed to bring some soft water for the cistern today and Fensel is to vaccinate the chickens so he can buy hatching eggs from us.

Sunday, January 10, 1943

Cal did not go to church with us this morning. Abe Buller and Tobias Kehn came to ask me to teach their school. Anna Waldner promised to come and do housework for us.

Monday, January 11, 1943

Took Cal to College this morning and got a load of cracked corn from Park Lane for $39 (78¢ per bu.)

Took Brother P. P. home with me. After dinner P. P. took me to Sen. Buehler's place in Emery. Picked up Sen. Oster at Ethan and Mrs. Schumacher at Mitchell. Got to Pierre at 7 p.m. for 8 p.m. session.

Friday, January 15, 1943

House passed the legislative expense bill this afternoon so we can get paid on the 18th. Left for home with Buehler.

When I got home, both Anna Waldner and Marie Walter were here to do housework tomorrow.

Saturday, January 16, 1943

Took Ruth and Marian to the dentist and brought Pearl home with us. She had gotten a ride to Freeman from Irene.

Anna and Marie did the washing although Maytag did not work well. They let a lot of cold air into the house because of the exhaust pipe sticking out the back door.

Sunday, January 17, 1943

We did not go to church this morning. C. E. was called off for the evening on account of the cold.

Cal took Pearl and Marie to Freeman in the afternoon and took the car in the evening. Pearl caught a ride back to Irene.

Monday, January 18, 1943

Too cold for the girls to walk to school, so they did not go. Cal rode to College with Dr. Tieszen's girls from Marion.

Tuesday, January 19, 1943

Had 25 min. afternoon session. Visited the federal government Indian school at 3 p.m. They have some 300 young people there beginning with junior high. Some of the high school boys are pages in the Senate.

Thursday, January 21, 1943

Had session at 2 p.m. There is not much activity yet. The horse trading will start after a while.

Marian sent my keys which I forgot at home. The letter was written Jan. 18.

Friday, January 22, 1943

Much warmer today. Got a letter from Pearl. Hammerquist's boy has the measles. Forty bills have been introduced so far.

Saturday, January 23, 1943

Got home from Pierre at 9 p.m. Cal was not home last night. I delivered 2 sows to Middleton Bros. at Canistota. Had flat tire on the trailer coming home.

Sunday, January 24, 1943

Nobody in church today. Did chores nearly all day. Water pipes froze up from the windmill to the horse barn.

Monday, January 25, 1943

I enrolled Ruth and Marian in Freeman Public School so they can drive with Cal and his crowd. It is too risky to let them walk across the field and fences to #26 when no one is home. We have to pay tuition, but that is all right.

Friday, January 29, 1943

This is the 25th day of the session. Nine representatives were absent. Our recess starts today. I am going home with Sen. Olson of Viborg.

Sunday, January 31, 1943

All in church but Pearl. She was grading papers. In the afternoon I took Pearl to Freeman so she could catch a ride with Regina Waltner.

Tuesday, February 2, 1943

Cal came home with Cpl. Herbert Hofer at 4:30 a.m. I sent two hogs to the Sioux Falls stock yards. Sold for $14.30 cwt.

Wednesday, February 3, 1943

Rode back to Pierre with Rep. Blake. Olson, Buehler and Oster were along. We took the Huron road. I had the shot gun along but did not shoot any pheasants. Had a flat tire near Highmore.

Had 9 p.m. session that lasted 35 min. Nine Reps. were absent.

Thursday, February 4, 1943

Convened at 2 p.m. and lasted 'til 4:35. Reciprocity bill on trucks passed, also the woman's jury bill.

Friday, February 5, 1943

Farmers Union had a meeting at the Locke Hotel. Had a good supper. Saw quite a number of fellows I knew.

Saturday, February 6, 1943

Had 10 a.m. session, recessed 'til 1 p.m., then had session 'til 2 p.m. Quite a few of the Reps. have left. It is 2:18 now and we are through with our desk work for the day. We have not been as rushed this year as in former years. The leadership is holding the line on how many bills can be introduced.

Sunday, February 7, 1943

Went to the Methodist church this morning. Harold W. Wagar is the minister. Went to church there again in the evening.

Monday, February 8, 1943

Passed a large number of Judiciary bills. Got my second pay check of $146.43. We are invited to the Hammerquists for dinner tonight.

I called the roll on one bill today.

We had our party last night. Olson, Sonnenfeld, Oster, Buehler, Solomonson, Bruett, Thoene and I were present.

Friday, February 12, 1943

Had a short program at 3 p.m. in the House. Harmon gave a good talk on Lincoln's political life. We adjourned at 4:48. Had a Lincoln Day dinner at the Catholic church. They charged a dollar a plate. Will ride home tomorrow with Olaf Blake.

Sunday, February 14, 1943

Ruth, Marian and I were in church this morning. Rev. Duerksen was the preacher. The church was quite cold. We do not have a janitor hired yet.

I learned that Cal got in trouble at the College for drinking wine. Somebody else bought it for him. When the children are small, the troubles are small. But when they get bigger, ...

The girls went to Paul E's for a Valentine party.

"May we take along the paper hearts and other stuff you brought us from Pierre?" asked Ruth.

"Certainly. There is more than enough to share with everyone. You can all design your own Valentines," said Morgan.

Before the party could begin, Angie had to check her muskrat traps, she said, and offered Marian and Ruth the chance to go along. She rode her Shetland pony from trap to trap along the creek while her guests followed along behind on foot.

"What would you do if you caught a skunk?" asked Marian.

"I'd skin it and sell the fur."

"Don't they stink?"

"Sometimes, but usually not. I got sprayed once. The smell was so bad we had to bury my clothes in a hole in the ground."

Angie's traps were empty that day. Ruth and Marian were glad, because they were eager to show what their dad had brought them from Pierre: red hearts on stiff paper, from jumbo to tiny sizes; white and gold paper lace; shiney Cupids and darts. There was more material to make Valentines than all the girls – including Geraldine and Pauline, Sarah and Miriam – could imagine. Finally, when forefingers flavored with white school paste were licked clean and the Valentines judged by Paul E. and Annie, the largest prize, a chocolate heart, went to Ruth for she had made the most beautiful one of all.

Wednesday, February 17, 1943

"Well, you're here bright and early!" exclaimed A. T. as he saw the girls sitting in the front booth of his brother's cafe on Freeman's Main Street. Their grips stood nearby.

"We came in with Cal this morning," said Ruth.

"Well, let's get your suitcases in the trunk. You can both sit up front with me."

They all climbed into Mr. Kaufman's gray Plymouth, Marian occupying her customary seat in the middle over the axle. "This looks like a new car yet. No wonder; he must be one of the richest men in town," thought Ruth.

"Are you Stewart's dad?" asked Marian.

"Sure am. You know Stewart?"

"He's in my room in school." Marian hoped that Stewart had not told his father about the accident she had had in the first grade when Miss Henley had not recognized her in time to go to the rest room.

382

"I know Denver too," said Ruth.

"Well, then, we're all acquainted. I've known your dad and Cal and Pearl for years. Knew your mother too before she died."

As he rounded the curve at Freedom corner and pulled onto Highway 81, A. T. pointed out landmarks along the way. When they passed the section line leading to the Kleinsasser farm, A. T. said, "I could have picked you up at home this morning. It's right on the way."

"There's nobody at home. Cal didn't want us waiting there alone," said Ruth.

"Oh. . . .Now tell me when you need to stop for anything, when you get hungry or. . . . Yes, your dad is one of the most progressive farmers we have around Freeman. And Cal too! He won Grand Champion litter, using Park Lane feeds, did you know that? We had his picture in the COURIER."

"I helped him paint the sign, RAISE A LITTER OF 14 PIGS," said Ruth.

"Did you, now? Well, that was fine."

Gray clouds hung overhead. Half melted dirty gray snowbanks littered the landscape. Gray, unpainted farm buildings were scattered on the almost deserted plain. Gray trees, now bare of snow, stood stark before the houses they were to protect.

Mr. Kaufman turned west at Stanley Corner and followed Highway 16 past Bridgewater, Emery, Alexandria, and Mitchell. "You hungry yet?" asked A. T. in front of a small cafe in Mitchell.

"Sure."

They all ordered hot beef sandwiches and orange pop at his suggestion. Dark brown gravy covered the white sandwich bread and mashed potatoes when their orders arrived. When Ruth had finished the last morsel of gooey mass on her thick oval plate, she reached for her money tied in a handkerchief. "The treat's on me. You can buy dessert somewhere else along the way," said Mr. Kaufman.

As they drove northwest to Huron and then west on Highway 14, the farmsteads grew even further apart. "There's a stretch of road where you can't see a farmstead for 35 miles. It's grazing land. Too poor for farming. Rolling too. If you plowed it up, the top soil would wash away."

At Highmore it was time for ice cream. "Your treat this time," A. T. said to Ruth.

"What flavors you got?" she asked the pimply-faced boy behind the counter of the small roadside cafe.

"Vanilla, strawberry, and chocolate."

They all decided on strawberry, much to the relief of the soda jerk, but when A. T. took his first bite, he said, under his breath, "Tastes like ground up corn cobs. That's war-time ice cream, if I ever tasted it."

"I don't think it tastes like corn cobs," said Marian, the perennial literalist.

"How do you know? Ever tasted corn cobs?" A. T. asked.

In Pierre A. T. took them directly to the Capitol, a hugely imposing, domed structure rising incongruously from the plain. They rode the precarious-looking cage of an elevator with an ominous view of cables and the dark underworld to the second floor where they followed signs to the House of Representatives. At the door they were met by their neighbor, Zach Wipf, who said, "I'll call Morgan out. He said you'd be comin'."

On the walls of the lobby were pictures of members of each legislative session. "I bet Daddy's picture is here some place and Uncle P. P.'s too. We have a picture like that at home," said Ruth.

"That's right! Your uncle was a politician too. That's unusual, to have two legislators from the same family," said Mr. Kaufman.

Soon Morgan came through the swinging House chamber doors and drew his daughters to his sides by large swooping motions of his arms. "Glad you got here safe and sound. No ice and snow, I trust?" he asked A. T.

"Nope, the roads were clear all the way. We had a good time. Your girls are good traveling companions. Even bought me some ice cream at Highmore!" he said and winked. "Well, I have a reservation at the St. Charles Hotel. I'll see you tomorrow."

Morgan took his daughters to the House gallery, introducing them to all they met. "I want you to show them the ropes," he said to Virginia Hammerquist, one of the pages. "I want them to come up here as pages some day. I have to go now. Mr. Matson went to his brother's funeral today and I'm Chief Clerk for the day."

In the gallery they found the front row of seats where they could look down on the strange proceedings. Pages, including Virginia, were running up and down the aisles, taking messages to members, delivering motions to the Speaker. When a Representative snapped his fingers, the page nearest him jumped up from her chair at the foot of the front desk and ran to do his bidding.

From the gallery Marian and Ruth waved at their dad, and he gave an inconspicuous salute. "That must be the Mrs. Schumacher he talks so much about," said Ruth of the lady to whom he was pointing out his children. "She's pretty. Look at all that dark hair!"

All at once they heard their father's familiar voice, but he was rattling off some unintelligible gibberish. "For a bill being enacted. . . ."

"How can anyone understand what he's saying?" Ruth wondered.

Then came a list of names: "Anderson, Blake, Bruett. . .," some names they had heard Daddy mention before, and an answer of either "Yea" or "Nay."

They ate at the Capitol coffee shop that night on Morgan's meal ticket. Everybody seemed pleased to meet them and, strangely, all these strangers seemed to know their dad. "Apple pie ala mode is what I want," said Marian to the waitress.

"You got it! That girl has a mind of her own, I can see that!"

There was an evening session to consider the ore tax bill. Before the session was to begin, Morgan took his daughters up and down the rows of desks to meet the Representatives. Many were friends of their dad and had served with him in 1937.

When the evening session was about to begin, Morgan sent his daughters to the gallery. Though the issue to be debated this evening was of great importance to the welfare of the state, there were fewer people in the gallery than there had been in the afternoon.

However, the lobby was crawling with lobbyists for the mining companies – Homestake, Baldmountain, Canyon, Gilt Edge. They would be prepared with amendments to slip to various friendly Representatives. They were not above writing speeches for sympathetic Representatives either.

The debate lasted for two hours with varying degrees of interest and participation. One Representative called "Congressman," Motley of Spink and Clark Counties, read his newspaper during most of the debate.

The proponents of the ore tax pointed to the need for diversified revenue. Property, sales and income taxes were not producing what was required to run the state. The ore was a natural resource belonging to all the people, not just those extracting it.

On the other hand, the opponents of the ore tax said it would eliminate the possibility of further development capital from outside sources. It would actually threaten the continuation of small operations. Furthermore, they said, only a growing industry produces increasing revenue and increased employment.

"Same old story," Morgan thought, as he called the roll. The ore tax lost, 41 to 32, with one member absent and one excused.

When the session ended, the girls were admitted to the floor. "I have some work to finish before we can leave," said Morgan.

"Can we ride the elevator 'til you're done?" asked Ruth.

"Okay, I'll look for you at the elevator."

The girls waited until most of the people were gone and then boarded the elevator for as many rides as they could get out of the operator. "Have you ever been up to the dome?" he asked.

"No."

"Well, tomorrow I'll get one of my pals to take you up there. It's a long hike up a circular staircase. Be sure to eat your oats for breakfast. The elevator doesn't go all the way up there."

Morgan found his daughters still riding the elevator. "Thank you, Mr. Brule. We'll see you tomorrow."

Outside, the night air was cold and damp. Stars shone overhead as they walked toward the Hammerquist home.

"Did you see Virginia tonight?"

"She went home early because she had homework to do," said Ruth. "She said we'd sleep with her in her room tonight."

"Well, be sure not to bother her. The pages have a tough time going to school and working at the same time."

"I smell popcorn," thought Marian when Mrs. Hammerquist greeted them at the door.

"And I smell cocoa," thought Ruth.

Mrs. Hammerquist invited them into the warm, brightly lighted and decorated kitchen. "Virginia has to finish her homework before she can join us for popcorn and cocoa."

"Here we are sitting around the kitchen table and talking, just like a regular family," thought Ruth.

"Have you heard from Earl recently?" asked Morgan.

"Yes, got a letter yesterday. He's working for the Minnesota Department of Education. They're a little more progressive in Minnesota. We're planning to move there in June after school is out."

"Well, it will be South Dakota's loss," said Morgan, sighing.

Virginia joined them and after a quick snack she took Marian and Ruth to her room. "You're used to sleeping together, aren't you?"

"Sure, we sleep together all the time," said Ruth.

As the girls changed into their pajamas and took turns using the bathroom, Ruth thought how lucky Virginia was to have her own room. And a warm bathroom! She didn't dare tell Virginia that they had to go outside at night or use a chamber pot.

In the morning Mrs. Hammerquist had large bowls of oatmeal and buttered toast for them. Virginia had already left for her geometry class. "How did you know we were going to climb to the Capitol dome today?" asked Marian.

"I didn't. Are you?"

"Yeah, the man who runs the elevator said we should eat our oats this morning so we could make it to the top."

At the Capitol elevator the girls ran into A. T. "I'm going to testify before the Poultry Sub-Committee. Wanna come along?"

"Sure."

"Let's tell your dad where you'll be," he said, and, taking each of them by the hand, he proceeded down the corridor to the House chamber. Marian felt very important. A. T. was considered to be a leader in Freeman. She wondered if maybe the people in Pierre didn't know that.

"Take care of my little girls," Morgan said to A. T., looking down at them from his raised desk at the front of the Chamber.

The girls did not understand what all the discussion was about in the committee — something about weights and measures, standards, licensing feed grain producers. They knew A. T. was well respected for developing formulas for making animals and poultry grow faster.

After lunch in the Capitol coffee shop, it was time for the climb to the dome. The elevator man had arranged for a guide.

"I can't go with you. I'm on duty at the desk," said Morgan. "Be careful on the steps. And if you get tired, stop and take a rest."

At first the going was easy. But gradually it got harder. Marian's legs started aching. "How about stopping for a while?" she asked Ruth.

"Let's keep on going," said Ruth, pausing. "I'd rather go up than look down."

As they proceeded, the dome before them grew lighter and brighter. Finally they reached their destination, a plywood-covered floor and a gray-windowed room, the walls of which were covered with graffiti. "Sue loves Bob, XXX," it said in bright red lipstick.

They stood on tiny stools to look out of the grimy windows. The view was impressive, all right. Their guide pointed out the Missouri River and Fort Pierre on the other side in a different time zone. There was the Indian School. There was the Locke Hotel and the Methodist Church.

"You ready to go back?" asked their guide. "It'll be easier going down."

"Yeah!" they eagerly replied in concert.

"I'll go first. You hang on real tight and watch your step. The steps are wider on the outside, away from the pole," he said.

The girls were relieved to get back on solid ground. The anticipation of reaching the top had exceeded the reality of seeing the dome.

Saturday, February 20, 1943

Had a 10 a.m. session. Many of the bills were referred this morning. The local option tax bill was indefinitely postponed. Eleven members were absent, so the opposition had a good chance to pull a fast one, and did. The girls and I went home with Buehler and Olson.

Ralph Hilgren wrote about the girls' visit to Pierre in his ARGUS column. He quoted them saying they wanted to return as pages.

Wednesday, February 24, 1943

Back in Pierre. Had a long session today. Saw the movie, "The Commandoes Strike at Dawn." It was a terrible murder picture. I fear for the results it will have on the boys growing up now and seeing those pictures. The little boys applauded each time someone got stabbed.

Thursday, February 26, 1943

Spent much of our time on preliminaries today. Kretschmar wanted to take the word "not" out of a committee report, but he did not succeed. We did not get to Senate bills at all. Just acted on House bills.

Sunday, February 28, 1943

Went to the Lutheran Church in the morning and afternoon and to the Methodist church in the evening. Mosby talked on his trip to Russia in 1936.

Monday, March 1, 1943

Had 1 p.m. session. Passed the tithing bill by a very close vote. Recessed at 5:30 and went to a feed and program at the Lutheran church. They had Swedish meatballs and Lutefisk. Glen Martens, I think, put on the feed. They discussed the farm program for 1944. Gov. Sharpe gave a good talk.

We reconvened around 7:30 p.m. Just now Jackson is running along in favor of SB18 on sabotage and Kretschmar is opposing it.

Tuesday, March 2, 1943

Plowed through a lot of bills last night. Session lasted 'til 11 p.m. Cal called from the St. Charles Hotel at 7 a.m. We acted on 20 bills today after 2 p.m.

Thursday, March 4, 1943

Cal has been here for several days. He looked for a chance to go home but there was none except by train. The ladies had tea at the Governor's mansion. Cal drove some there and also stayed for tea.

Friday, March 5, 1943

Cal went home with Olson, Buehler and Blake at 4 p.m. I could not go because we had to wait for the Senate desk force to catch up with the House desk force. We officially adjourned at 10:45 p.m.

Saturday, March 6, 1943

Left Pierre at 10 a.m. with Poelstra of Springfield. Got to Mitchell at 3 p.m. Caught a ride with Jim Wood, an ex-racer, who is trucking for the Buckingham Line. I called from Stanley Corner. Cal and the girls came to get me.

Sunday, March 7, 1943

Pearl did not come home this weekend. Marie Walter and Melvin Tieszen are boarding with us now. Lambs are coming in.

Monday, March 8, 1943

Melvin and Cal went to College with our car. John J. B. came over and asked me to go with him to see Judge Henry L. Gross about getting John M. out of the CPS camp. After dinner we went to Parker to see a Mr. Long at the Milwaukee R. R. depot. He is chairman of the Turner Co. draft board.

Tuesday, March 9, 1943

Had a meeting of the Fraternal Burial Assoc. in Viborg. Raynie is going into the Air Force. We hired a new undertaker, a Mr. Brakke.

Wednesday, March 10, 1943

Gave a talk at College Chapel on legislation as it affects education. Don't know how good it was but they were listening.

The county started graveling the road past our place.

Thursday, March 11, 1943

Lost a ewe this morning that Dr. Saner took a lamb from. Another ewe had twins, one of which got its leg broken by another ewe stepping on it. I am doing chores all day but still don't get done.

Melvin and Cal go to play practice every night.

Marian and I went along with them tonight. She took her piano lesson from Mrs. Oscar Gering and I had my income tax report made out by Hank Gross.

Saturday, March 13, 1943

Marie and the girls did the washing because Pearl did not come home. We took Melvin home to Marion in the evening and visited the grandparents. The girls played with Tina's girls, Arpah and Ruth. They live next door to the grandparents now.

Sunday, March 14, 1943

All in church. I taught Sunday School. Marie went home with Margie Pollman. Cal stayed home both Saturday and Sunday night.

Popped corn this evening. For topping we melted butter and duck fat in equal proportions.

Monday, March 15, 1943

Blizzarding this evening. All we need is more snow and all the roads will be blocked.

Tuesday, March 16, 1943

Ruth and Marian did not go to school because of the blizzard. Marie Walter stayed in town. Mel and Cal went to play practice.

Wednesday, March 17, 1943

Cal and Mel took the girls to country school because the wind is from the northwest. Insured Sam P. Hofer's farm in the Aid Plan for $6,000. He bought 160 acres for $9,200.

Sunday, March 21, 1943

A Miss Tieszen, missionary to the Belgian Congo, spoke at our C. E. tonight. Pearl was not home this weekend.

Tuesday, March 23, 1943

Went to Jack Lindeman's auction sale. His binder sold for $605 and the cattle between $125 and $140.

Cal spread the gravel that was dumped by our driveway so we could get in and out easier.

Wednesday, March 24, 1943

Went to AAA meeting in Parkston. There is talk in Congress about cutting out the appropriation for farm payments.

Cal came home from school and started dragging and sowing Pilot wheat.

We are feeding the sheep ground alfalfa, a little oats, some oil meal and soy bean meal. I turned out more ewes with lambs. We have only four left in the barn now.

Saturday, March 27, 1943

Pearl came home in the afternoon with P. P.'s. Marie Walter is here helping. Phoebe Walter came home with us from town in the evening.

Wednesday, April 1, 1943

Cal went back to College after being home Monday and Tuesday to sow. All I get done is chores.

Saturday, April 3, 1943
Broke our drill so we borrowed Jake Fast's. Cal disced and dragged the garden.

Sunday, April 4, 1943
Pearl came home so we were all in church. Had a memorial service for Pfc. Robert Hofer, Dr. M. M. Hofer's son, who was killed Feb. 17 in North Africa. He was a gunner. The College Gym was full. There was no room for many. Bishop W. Blair Roberts of the Episcopal Church in Sioux Falls was the minister.
Pearl got a ride back to Irene.

"I felt so sorry for Mrs. M. M. that her son got killed," said Ruth, as the family drove home from the service.

"Me too," said Marian. "She was so nice to me when my stomach hurt. She gave me milk toast and let me stay at her house. She told me about her boy and was worried he might have to go to war."

"The church service sure was different," said Ruth. "So formal."

"That's the Episcopalians for you. Just one step from the Catholics," said Morgan.

"Sorta like the Lutherans," added Cal.

"Well, I wonder how many more memorial services we're gonna have before it's all over," said Morgan.

"What would we do if Cal or you got drafted?" asked Ruth.

"It's not likely. The government needs farmers to feed the soldiers and keep the country going."

"Yeah, but what if?"

"I would just have to go, like everybody else," said Cal.

"What about you, Daddy?"

"They don't want old men like me. I can't even run anymore."

"They could put you in non-combat service," said Cal.

"What would you want to be in the Army, Cal?" asked Marian.

"I'd want to be a flier in the Air Force."

"I'd want to be a cook," said Morgan.

Monday, April 5, 1943
I was reclassified IV-A by the draft board. My draft number is Serial 7-656, Order No. 10486.

Tuesday, April 6, 1943
Cal disced and dragged 'til 3:30 a.m. and then went to College. I did chores all day. Got a card from Fred Ellwein that he got in a shipment of Case plows.

Wednesday, April 7, 1943

Dragged corn stalks 'til I wore out the bearings on the tractor. Went to Ortman for repair, which cost $10.10. Went to Bridgewater for a Case plow, but it was sold.

Cal was foreman at the College for a tree planting group. They had Clean-Up Day.

Friday, April 9, 1943

Menno and Freeman High Schools and Freeman Academy had a music festival. A professor from Madison Normal directed the choruses and a professor from Vermillion directed the bands.

Saturday, April 10, 1943

Cal finished sowing succotash. I still have the flax to sow. Flax does best on newly plowed land, but I still like to try some.

Monday, April 12, 1943

One of the new war tires cracked open about 1/3 around the wheel.

Tuesday, April 13, 1943

Cal and Marie are riding with the Tieszen girls from Marion. It is best this way. We have such poor tires and our gas does not reach out either.

Wednesday, April 14, 1943

Sowed flax, crested wheat and brome grass.

Thursday, April 16, 1943

Ruth and Marian had their picnic at country school. Just too bad that we have only eight months.

Friday, April 17, 1943

Got a 65 ft. rope for the horse barn in Marion. Cannot get any manila rope anywhere. The war rope will be jute at 40¢ per lb. Marie went home to Tyndall with her uncle, Josh Tschetter, and his wife.

Sunday, April 18, 1943

Not in church. Pearl did not come home. John J. B. was here to have me write a letter to get John M. out of CPS camp at Hill City.

Tuesday, April 20, 1943

Went to Marion to get a plow and woven wire but got neither. Goosen said he might get a Case plow designated for Hutchinson Co.

Katherine's brother John is home from Yankton Hospital, staying with his folks.

Friday, April 23, 1943

Good Friday. All in church today but Cal, who slept most of the day. Went to grandparents in the afternoon. The girls played with Arpah and Ruth next door. Tina gave our girls some hand-me-downs.

Saturday, April 24, 1943

Mel Tieszen is staying here. He built a fence around the garden. Went to Menno with George M. Hofer. Could not get a plow but got 20 rods of woven wire from the Menno Lumber Yard @ 30¢.

Sunday, April 25, 1943

Easter Sunday. Mrs. P. P. called that Edward is home on furlough from the Army.

Monday, April 26, 1943

All went to the Easter Monday Music Festival at the College in the morning. Cal and Mel planted trees in the afternoon.

Tuesday, April 27, 1943

Mel repaired fence on line between our land and Sam Schmidt's. It is impossible to get any posts or woven wire in Freeman. I will try to get our corn planter fixed. I had a runaway with it last year.

Wednesday, April 28, 1943

Cal and Mel borrowed Ortman's truck to get a load of alfalfa hay. Versteeg came in the afternoon. He charges $6 an hour to grind, so we ground only 1/3 of a truck load.

Thursday, April 29, 1943

Had Cal pay the real estate tax for the second half of 1942. Total $57.85.

Tried to haul prairie hay this afternoon, but it was too windy. Ruth and Marian were herding sheep on Ben Ratzlaff's rye field.

"It's your turn to chase the sheep. I did it last time," said Ruth as the two girls huddled together in the shelter of a boulder at the rock pile.

"I'm shivering. I can't," protested Marian.

"You'll warm up if you run."

"Why didn't we bring warmer clothes?"

"Because the sun was shining when we started out."

"Maybe we should hail Ben Ratzlaff on his next turn in the field. Maybe he would use his tractor to get our coats."

"Don't be silly. He's not going to unhitch his plow to get clothes for us!"

"The sheep are gonna be on the road in a few minutes. If one sheep goes, they'll all follow. You know how dumb they are! You get out there and do your job or I'll tell Daddy when he comes back!"

Marian ran from the shelter of the rock pile to chase the sheep away from the section line just before a car speeding on the graveled road came perilously close to hitting a straying ewe.

"Boy, you're lucky that sheep didn't get killed!" Ruth rubbed it in.

"Next time you can chase them back," said Marian as she pulled her dress over her knees and knelt in the lee of the rock.

Suddenly Ruth spied a familiar car turning toward them. "I think that's the Tieszen girls' car that just turned off 81. Let's tell Cal to bring us some clothes." Both girls ran to the road to stop the car by waving their arms.

"What's going on?" Cal demanded of the two as he stepped from the car.

"We're freezing. Daddy told us to herd the sheep. It was warm when we got out here but it got cold all of a sudden and we didn't bring our jackets."

"Oh, you must be frigid!" sympathized Delsie Tieszen. "And here we brought you some ice cream sandwiches. They'll only make you colder!"

"That's okay. We'll take the ice cream anyway!" Ruth assured Delsie.

"And I'll bring your jackets," said Cal. "Just hang on 'til I change clothes. I'll bring 'em out with the tractor."

When Cal finally arrived with their jackets he asked, "Why didn't one of you watch the sheep while the other one ran home for jackets?"

The girls looked at him and then at each other in amazement. "I never thought of that," said Ruth.

"Me either," said Marian.

"You were probably too worried about the division of labor, afraid that one was going to have to work harder than the other."

"Can we go home now and you watch the sheep?" asked Marian.

"NO! For pity sakes, I just brought you your jackets! You stay here and do your job. I've got plowing to do."

"What about Melvin? Couldn't he herd the sheep for a while?"

"No, he's going to help me."

"How about Marie?"

"Stop trying to get out of work."

"How long do we have to stay out here with the sheep?" asked Marian.

" 'Til the Old Man gets home or I come and help you get the sheep across the road. We don't have enough pasture at home and we're gonna make use of Ben Ratzlaff's offer to pasture the sheep on his rye today. Just make up your minds to that fact and stop trying to avoid your responsibility. You'd better watch those sheep now. They're getting close to the section line again!" insisted their brother as he sped off with the AC.

Saturday, May 1, 1943
Bought 100 rods woven wire from Parkston yesterday. Got an AC tractor plow from Ortman for $146.65. I used Abe Wiens' permit.

Friday, May 7, 1943
Plowing is the order of the day. Got 2 loads of hay from Emanuel Auch which I paid the Fed. Land Bank $4 a ton for. Cal went to Irene to get Pearl while I dragged corn ground.

Saturday, May 8, 1943
Pearl and Marie Walter are both here today. We planted potatoes and cleaned out the cellar.

Sunday, May 9, 1943
All in church but Cal, who was studying for finals.

I took Pearl to Irene in the evening. Cal went to Baccalaureate at the College. Rev. Walter Gering was the preacher.

Wednesday, May 12, 1943
Ground was covered with snow this morning.

Cal and I went to Parkston to get the rest of the 100 rods of woven wire I had bought and paid for, but they had sold 20 rods of it again to someone else.

Bought Cal a good suit and sport coat from Kayser.

Thursday, May 13, 1943
Cal had his College picnic. He left at 5 a.m. and came home after I had gone to bed. I planted corn all day.

Friday, May 14, 1943
Cal planted corn most of the day. In the evening all, except Pearl, went to Commencement exercises at the College. Cal and Melvin both finished the two-year college course.

Monday, May 17, 1943

Pearl's school is out but she is not home yet.

Marian and Ruth started vacation Bible school at the Silver Lake MB Church. They rode with Ben Ratzlaff and his children, Marjorie and Willis.

Tuesday, May 18, 1943

Finished planting corn. We planted all hybrid corn.

Got 400 Leghorn chicks from Fensel.

Pearl is not home yet.

Ruth and Marian drove to Bible school with Jake Fast and his children, Verlyn and Myron.

Saturday, May 22, 1943

Cold today. We are losing some chicks. Pearl is not home yet.

Jamesville Colony boys clipped the sheep. They charged 30¢ per head. Cal tied the wool. I took 600 lbs. of wool to town with the trailer.

Sunday, May 23, 1943

Ruth, Marian and I went to C. E. in our church. Marian gave a recitation, "Mother's Eyes." I gave an object lesson.

Tuesday, May 25, 1943

It was my turn to take the children to and from Bible school. Pearl is not home yet. I set two hens on duck eggs in the horse barn. We have sheep on rye, oats and barley pasture.

Thursday, May 27, 1943

Cal bought trees for planting.

John J. B.'s were here. Sister Katherine brought tomato plants. The boys planted. Pearl is not home yet.

Friday, May 28, 1943

I plowed up a little patch of oats because it had too many Russian thistles in it. We had Sooner milo in that field last year and it was not kept clean enough.

Saturday, May 29, 1943

Picked rocks in forenoon and dipped lambs in Cooper's dip in afternoon.

Sunday, May 30, 1943

We were not in church this morning or afternoon, but the little girls and I went to the College Gym in the evening. Rev. Homer

Leisy from Dallas, Oregon, is the preacher. He is an artist who paints his own pictures and then lectures.

Monday, May 31, 1943
Pearl was home this morning when I got up.

Tuesday, June 1, 1943
Plowed up the hog yard and seeded it with Sudan grass.

Thursday, June 3, 1943
So windy today that it cut the corn off. Many fields are black. We cannot see the rows on ours.
Little girls and I heard Rev. Leisy.

Friday, June 4, 1943
Went to Viborg for Burial Assoc. meeting. Our new undertaker is Linden Anderson of Elk Point. Raynie will have an auction sale on June 16. He has gone into the Air Force.

Saturday, June 5, 1943
Appraised hail damage on Mike S. Wollman's farm.
Arnold Dewald took a bull to Howard to a sale. He paid Harry Preheim $100 for it and sold it for $171 at Howard.
Corn is still in bad shape. Cannot see the rows yet.

Sunday, June 6, 1943
Left home at 4:30 a.m. and got to Mt. Lake, Minn., at 9 a.m. for the Northern District Conference. 1500 people present, meeting in the high school. Only about 200 were delegates.
Erland Waltner was re-elected president and I was elected secretary. Stayed with J. John Frieszen and Jake H. Tschetter. Rev. Leisy was conference speaker.

Thursday, June 10, 1943
Got home from Minnesota at 4:30 this morning. Paul E. was the driver. Paul L., Joe P., Alma Glanzer and Anna Gross were along.

Sunday, June 13, 1943
26 were baptized in our church this morning, including many of my former students: Samuel W. Hofer, Rosa Hofer, Melvin, Selma, Moses, Aaron and Miriam Glanzer; Marvin Hofer, and Ruth and Luella Schmeichel.

"My hair is straight! Jacob B. poured half the pitcher on my head, it feels like. I look like a drowned RAT," complained Marie to Margie as they sat in Morgan's car after the baptismal service, trying to style her hair in a more becoming fashion.

"I wish we didn't have to wear black dresses. When am I going to wear this black dress again? I'm not an old woman!"

"Some churches let their girls wear white for baptism, but we have to dress like the colonies! We're not colonies anymore!"

Marian sat mute in the back seat of the '37 Chevy, taking in the discussion. "Are you gonna come home with us today, Marie?" she asked.

"No, Honey, I wanted to tell you. I'm going over to Margie's to dry out. I'm gonna put up my hair, and then we've got dates to go to Menno tonight."

"Are you gonna come tomorrow to work for us, then?"

"Yes, I'll stay overnight at Margie's and get up to your place somehow, even if I have to walk."

"I think Ma and Pa and Edwin are ready to go," said Margie, and the newly baptized young women ran to the Pollman car, holding their purses over their heads to hide their appearance.

Marian turned on the car radio and waited for her family to finish their visiting and come to the car. Cal, the first, assumed his position at the steering wheel. "You're not supposed to turn on the radio if the car isn't running, Honey. It runs down the battery. I've told you that a hundred times."

"Marie got mad at Jacob B. for pouring too much water on her head," Marian told her brother, changing the subject.

"That's all right. It'll do her good!" he laughed.

Tuesday, June 15, 1943

More rain! Had school election. John P. Gross was elected chairman and Ferd Thomas clerk. I am to clean the school house before school starts for $20, haul coal at $2 a ton, and cut the weeds on the school yard for $2. We voted to buy a piano.

Wednesday, June 16, 1943

I plowed with the walking plow to drain some lakes. Water is standing in the corn and grain fields.

Thursday, June 17, 1943

Sold 5 hogs and 2 sheep at the Farmers Union in Sioux Falls. Got $13.35 cwt. for sows, $13.50 for butcher barrows, $7.50 cwt. for the ewe and $6.50 cwt. for the old ram.

Friday, June 18, 1943

Ruth and Marian caught a ride with Adeline and John to Spink Co. for Paul and Martha's wedding.

Saturday, June 19, 1943

I went to Spink with Jake L.'s. Went to Smokey Joe Mendel's for supper. I stayed at J. W.'s for the night.

Sunday, June 20, 1943

I helped J. W. get the meat and buns from Doland for the wedding. Nephew Paul and Martha Kleinsasser were married at the Ebenezer Church by J. W.

Monday, June 21, 1943

Sam Schmidt was here twice today. He wanted to rent the alfalfa from me that I had planted on the land I rented from Jake Fast when Sam left his farm to do church work in Oregon.

Tuesday, June 22, 1943

I started cutting alfalfa on Sam Schmidt's land which I rented at $3 per acre. The Co-op Oil tanks exploded. 22,000 gal. of gas and fuel oil burned up. Leslie Huber was burned.

I heard a good definition of a "schwindler": "Anyone what speaks on the back of your face and in front of your back."

Ruth and Marian came home from Spink with Adeline and John.

"What are these baby clothes doing here?" asked Marian of Adeline. "They're too small for Gwendy."

"What are you doing rummaging around in the packages I bought? Don't you know some things are private?" Adeline was furious.

"They were back here on the ledge and just slipped down. We couldn't help but see what was in them," explained Ruth from the back seat.

"Well, I never!"

Gwendolyn, age 2 1/2, was riding in front between her parents and began to cry over the commotion.

"What are you making such a fuss about?" John asked his wife.

"Well, I don't want them blabbing around that I'm in the family way," explained Adeline. "I don't know. I guess I'm just too hot. Why do people get married in June, anyway?"

"That's the best time. Then a man knows if his wife really loves him. If she cuddles up to him in January, it could be just to get warm. But if she cuddles up in June, he knows she really loves him!" said John as his car sped along Highway 16.

Marian and Ruth sat quietly in the back seat. They also cast occasional glances at each other as they were being initiated into the ways of family life.

Saturday, June 26, 1943

Hauled 2 loads of wheat to town for the Commodity Credit Corp. Delivered 233 bu. and bought 150 bu. @ 98¢ for feed.

Raked alfalfa in forenoon. Put up a fair sized stack at Sam Schmidt's. Cal and I changed off pitching. Pearl ran the bull rake.

A big post fell off the rafters in the summer kitchen and hit Marian on the head. She was dizzy and said she saw stars.

Sunday, June 27, 1943

All in church in morning and to Abe Wiens in afternoon. Cal went swimming in the Frank Tieszen lake.

Monday, June 28, 1943

Put up stack of alfalfa hay after 5 p.m. Cal is cultivating corn for the third time.

Thursday, July 1, 1943

Pearl canned Bing cherries. Marian is herding sheep and Ruth is herding cattle on the section line.

Cal and the girls had a 4-H club meeting in the evening at Thompson Yards.

"Well, I think we should write up our 4-H club news for the COURIER in a way to show we need a county agent," said Cal.

"How should we start?" asked Raymond, pencil in hand.

"Despite the fact that the county agent was fired, the Freeman Hustlers 4-H Club met on July 1 at the Thompson Yards. . . ." dictated Jake.

"Was he actually fired or was the money not appropriated by the county commissioners?" asked Raymond.

"Either way, it amounts to the same thing," said Melvin.

"Daddy said the Schambers are behind it," said Ruth.

"The club," continued Cal, "which had an outstanding record of achievement in recent years, is stymied. . . ."

"How do you spell that?"

"S-T-Y-M-I-E-D. The club is stymied by lack of professional leadership and requests that the county commissioners hire an extension agent," dictated Cal.

"Sounds more like an editorial than a report," said Bill Isaak, manager of the Yards, who was doing accounting in an adjoining room.

"Yeah, maybe you're right. Maybe we should send it in as a Letter to the Editor. All agreed? We'll do that. Now, the next order of business is to plan our picnic at the Gulches. What should we bring?"

"Wieners."

"Buns."

"Long forks."

"No, we can cut green willow sticks for roasting."

"Beans, beans, the musical fruit," piped up Marian at her first 4-H meeting since officially joining.

The boys burst out laughing. "I'm really surprised at you!" said Jake, in mock amazement.

Sunday, July 4, 1943

Gave a report on the Northern District Conf. in church this morning and herded sheep and cattle in the afternoon.

Tuesday, July 6, 1943

Cal finished cultivating corn for the 4th time. It should be taller for this date. John L. started cutting his Spartan barley, but ours is still green. Ruth is herding cattle every day.

Marian and I hauled alfalfa home from the section line field. She does a good job tramping it down and evening the load in the slings.

It was dusk as Morgan and his youngest daughter rode back to the barn atop the three slings of fragrant hay. The hay shifted gently in the hay rack as the horses moved slowly down the driveway. "C'mon, King, giddy-yap!" urged their owner.

Marian liked the view from on top of the hay rack. She could see Cal still out in the field cultivating. She could see the cows back in the pasture after milking.

"You're getting to be a good helper!" said her father.

"As good as Cal?"

"Well, not quite as good as Cal yet. But he's much bigger. You remind me of when he was your age, though, and helping me haul the hay."

"Did he even out the loads as good as I did?"

"WELL, say 'as WELL' as I did."

"As well as I did?"

"Oh, yes! But he was bothered by the mosquitos. Mosquitos were awful bad that year, just like this year. He said, 'These flies sure are bad, Pa.' I'll never forget that! He was sitting on top of the hay load, a little straw hat on his head, swatting mosquitos, getting welts on his face, and complaining about flies. Funny what a man remembers."

Sunday, July 11, 1943
Slept 'til 10 a.m. Visited P. P.'s in the afternoon. Nephew Paul is now a 2nd Lt. stationed in Florida.

Wednesday, July 14, 1943
Started cutting oats at 11 a.m. Creepers are very bad. Cal is shocking and Pearl is running the tractor. Marian is the lunch and water boy. Ruth shocked a little, then herded cattle.

Ruth drove the cattle home from the section line and into the pasture, locking the gate behind her. She clutched a huge bouquet of pink prairie roses which she had picked in the ditch along the fence row. "I didn't want the cows to eat the roses," she explained to Pearl.

"You don't have to worry about that! They're too prickly. I'm surprised you could pick them without gloves. The cows won't eat the thorns. That's what protects them."

Ruth took the pink beauties to the kitchen pump where Pearl handed her a blue Mason jar.

"I don't want to put them in a canning jar," she objected. "I want to put them in Mother's vase."

"All we have is Mother's antique marbelized brown and buff vase, and I don't want that broken. Besides, they'll look better in a blue jar – they'll match better."

"I don't care. I wanna put 'em in Mother's vase!" she cried.

"Okay, I'll get it for you. But you'll have to leave it in the middle of the dining room table and not carry it around."

Pearl went to the china cupboard and carefully lifted the precious vase from its position next to the antique mustard dish. "I'll fill it with water and then we'll arrange the roses together."

Slowly and lovingly the roses were placed in the tall, wide-mouthed vase which eventually dwarfed the roses. But Ruth was satisfied as she sat at the table admiring their beauty.

Sunday, July 18, 1943
Went to Paul E.'s to make out the program for the Sunday School convention to be held October 2 and 3 at the Emmanuel Church in Spink Co.

Tuesday, July 20, 1943

Mr. and Mrs. Satter were here to insure their farm in the Aid Plan. It is the Jacob M. Waldner place. She is Marie Waldner's sister.

Wednesday, July 21, 1943

Pearl, Cal and I shocked wheat. Started cutting flax. It is thin & weedy.

Friday, July 23, 1943

Cut alfalfa on the Sam Schmidt land. It is thin and short except in low places. Very hot. Horses puffing all day. Sam Schmidt's boys came over to go swimming.

"Your dad said we could go swimming in your lake," said Orville at the door, explaining their visit.

"You mean the duck pond south of the barn?" asked Pearl. "You'd have to share it with a lot of other critters. Come in for a snack. We just got in from the garden."

On the table lay a mound of large red-ripe, warm tomatoes. "You have ripe tomatoes yet?" asked Ruth.

"Naw, ours are still green. We got 'em in too late," answered Orville.

Soon the four children were seated at the table eating sliced tomatoes sprinkled with sugar.

"If you like, you may go down and watch the ducks," suggested Pearl, eager to get on with her housework.

Across the yard the children ran. Soon their shoes and socks were off. They walked around the pond whose borders were decorated with duck foot prints. Soon the children added their prints to those of the ducks. The warm mud oozed up between their toes. Ducks waddled up, quacking for corn.

Orville and Allen rolled up their overall pants' legs and started to wade into the water. "You're gonna get all wet and dirty," cautioned Ruth.

"C'mon, you come too," urged Orville.

Cautiously the girls approached the boys, now standing in water up to their ankles. Suddenly Allen slipped into a depression and muddied his pants' leg.

"Oh, boy, you're gonna get it when Ma sees that," Orville warned his little brother. "Let's take off our clothes so we don't get 'em muddy," suggested the acknowledged leader of the group.

"TAKE OUR CLOTHES OFF?" asked Marian in amazement.

"Sure! You turn your backs while we take ours off, we'll get in the water, and then we'll turn our backs while you take yours off."

The boys unhooked the suspenders of their bib overalls and threw them on the tall marsh grass. The girls did the same with their dresses and soon all were up to their waists in the muddy water.

Suddenly there came a shriek fron the front door. There stood Pearl waving a white dish towel and screaming, "Get out of that dirty water this instant and come up to the house! You boys are going to have to take a bath and go right home!" she said to the Schmidts.

Sheepishly standing in the grass, the boys attempted to slip their muddy bodies into their overalls. "STOP! Don't put your clothes on now. Get up here for your baths, boys. You girls wait there 'til the boys have gone."

After what seemed an eternity, Pearl called the girls to the house. Dumping the Schmidt boys' dirty bath water into the bushes, she scolded her sisters, "Shame on you! What came over you to get undressed and go into that filthy duck pond?" Not waiting for an answer, she continued, "Wash yourselves thoroughly. And be thinking about a suitable punishment for your actions."

"No candy for a month?" Ruth suggested to Marian in the oval tub.

"Something worse than that. Maybe sleeping in the corn field for a week with nothing to eat but field corn," offered Marian.

"The mosquitos would eat you up," Pearl said, upon hearing the latter suggestion. "We'll have to let Daddy decide."

As Marian walked to the pasture for the milk cows that evening, she saw the clouds parting over the setting sun. She wondered, "What if Jesus came now, between the clouds? I haven't paid for my sin yet. If he comes too soon, I won't be prepared. . . ."

Monday, July 26, 1943
Heavy wind about 7 p.m. broke the horse barn door and moved our machine shed.

Tuesday, July 27, 1943
Jake M. Hofer and A. R. M. Hofer appraised my loss at $80. I went adjusting for the Aid Plan with my car. Traveled 51 mi. Got $7 for appraising and $2.55 for mileage. Went to 7 places that had damage.
Cal and the girls pulled cockleburrs.

"Okay, everybody out of bed! The sun is high already and it's getting hotter. While I'm appraising, I want you kids out pulling cockleburrs in the corn field. The rain has soaked the ground so they'll be easy to pull, even the big ones," said Morgan, yanking the sheet off the bed that Ruth and Marian slept in.

"Oh, do we have to?" whined Ruth.

"I was going to wash today," complained Pearl from the kitchen.

"Washing can wait, but the cockleburrs are growing. You can hear 'em gettin' bigger! The sooner you get out there, the easier your job will be.

"I thought a new tractor and a new cultivator would eliminate all the manual labor," said Pearl. "That's why you always buy machinery before buying anything for the house," she said, putting the cereal bowls on the table in front of Cal.

"I cultivated four times, both ways. But the cultivator can't get those weeds close to the corn plant. I even stopped sometimes to pull out the big ones. The rains this spring were just too good for the cockleburrs. And if the neighbors don't pull theirs, the seeds get washed into our land," said Cal.

After breakfast Cal and the girls walked to the corn field. "Boy, if we don't get 'em now, we'll have to use machetes to kill 'em!" he said. "I'll take the first four rows. Marian, you take the next two and Ruth the two next to Marian. Pearl, take the four on the outside. Let's stick together. If you find any you can't pull out, Marian, just holler and I'll come over to do it for you. Ruth, you do the same for Pearl to help you."

The four left their shoes and socks piled at the corner fence post where they had hung a canvas water bag. Cal hung his shirt on the fence too. The ground was so saturated that their bare feet sank into the warm, black earth. Ruth and Marian giggled as they felt the mud ooze between their toes.

"This is a big sucker!" exclaimed Cal as he found his first. "Look, this is what you do. Pull it out, shake off all the dirt, then lean it by the roots up against the corn plant with the roots sticking up in the air. Don't let the roots touch the ground or the cockleburr will just start growing again in this wet soil. Got that?"

"Yeah," said Ruth and Marian in chorus, "we got it."

Through the corn field they trudged, looking left and right for the bright green bushes which the cultivator had missed. "If everybody pulled their cockleburrs, it wouldn't be so hard to get rid of these pests!" complained Pearl.

"Is this a cockleburr?" Ruth asked Pearl, holding aloft the tall green weed she had just pulled.

"No, that's a flannel weed. Feel how soft the leaves are? But go ahead and pull out anything that isn't corn. You know what corn looks like!" said Pearl.

405

"I don't think it's such a good idea to tell the kids to pull anything but corn. I think dad planted some squash and pumpkins with the corn at the end of the field," he said to Pearl. Then, to the kids he said, "Better to ask if in doubt."

"I think Daddy planted some sunflower seeds too, at the end of the field. Big ones, for eating," added Marian.

"Yeah, you're right. Better just pull the cockleburrs and flannel weed to be safe," said Cal.

Thursday, July 30, 1943

Threshing at Pete Ratzlaff's. We hauled a load of alfalfa after threshing. Got the hay unloaded at midnight.

Sunday, August 8, 1943

Rev. Ellis Graber was here for dinner. Then we went to see Ben V. Tieszen to arrange for a retreat in Freeman if we can get a good speaker. We traveled to different churches in the Conference to take pictures.

Tuesday, August 10, 1943

Finished threshing at Ray Senner's and moved to Art Adrian's. I went with Chas. Preheim to Olivet to see the county commissioners about hiring a county extension agent. We saw only Ernest Schamber, the county auditor. It seems they are trying to save money, but the 4-H program is suffering.

Sunday, August 15, 1943

All in church. I taught S. S. In the afternoon the little girls and I went to Ben C. Graber's. Mrs. Graber has a stove with an electric timer. She can put the meal in the oven, set the timer, and it will be ready and waiting for them after church.

Monday, August 16, 1943

Threshed at our place, oats in the morning and wheat in the afternoon. Also Cal's barley and my flax. Moved to Ben Ratzlaff's towards evening. We used Ray Senner's elevator. Tomorrow Cal will leave by train from Dolton for harvest in Montana. He wants to make some money.

Stopped in at John J. B.'s. Katherine said they waited for us to come for dinner yesterday. She said she invited Pearl after church, but I did not know anything about it. Pearl says she thought Katherine talked to me and I said we couldn't go.

Saturday, August 21, 1943

The girls cleaned the schoolhouse after I cut the weeds. Marie Walter helped.

"How's come we have to clean the schoolhouse? Why can't the teacher do that? Miss Becker did it all last year," said Marian.

"The patrons cleaned it up before Miss Becker started teaching last fall too. Remember when we discussed whether to bury or burn the old flag?"

"Oh, yeah, and you got mad when I mentioned it to Sally over our party line."

"This is the same special cleaning before school starts. We'll wash the curtains and oil the floor," said Pearl. "Daddy took on the job for $20. He thought we could do it. Besides, you'll have a new teacher this year – Miss Thomas – and we want it clean for her."

"Are we gonna get any of the money?" asked Ruth.

"Sure, we'll divide it up among the four of us!" said Pearl, generously.

They loaded the '37 Chevy with cream cans of water, rags, brooms, mops, furniture polish and all kinds of other cleaning supplies. "It sure would be simpler if there were hot and cold running water at school, like I have in Irene."

"We even have to carry water for drinking and washing our hands!" complained Marian, who had also had the "town" experience.

Soon everyone was hard at work. They washed the blackboards, windows and desks. "The curliques in these wrought iron desk frames sure are hard to get clean," complained Marie, trying to get in all the grooves with her rag.

"Who plays with all these old homemade games in these desks?" asked Pearl.

"We do, sometimes. But usually we play with games that the Fasts bring from home, like Monopoly or Chinese checkers."

"Well, I think we ought to pitch some of these games. I can remember playing with them before Warren Thomas died of diphtheria and the school was quarantined."

"I wouldn't throw anything away, if I were you," cautioned Marie.

"I won't. I was just thinking aloud about what ought to be done."

Before long Orville and Allen Schmidt dropped by. "Saw someone was here. Thought we'd come over and help," offered Orville.

"Well, you can air the flag," said Pearl. "Here, run it up the flag pole," she said, wanting to get the youngsters outside.

Soon the flag was flapping in the breeze, an invitation for Verlyn and Myron Fast to ride up in their bicycles. "Figured somebody must be here," explained Myron.

"May I ride your bike?" Marian asked Verlyn.

"No, I don't let anyone else ride my bike."

"Why don't you have a bike?" Myron asked Marian.

"I don't know. I just don't," answered Marian.

"You'd get to school faster if you did."

"We couldn't use bikes 'cause we cut across the fields and fences to get to school," explained Ruth. "It's too long to go around on the road."

"Oh, yeah, that's right."

"Do you know who our new teacher will be?" asked Orville of Myron.

"Yeah, Luella Thomas, Ferd's sister. Lives with Ferd and her mother," said Myron, proud to be able to impart the information.

"I heard we were gonna get a piano," said Orville.

"Yeah, she plays the piano. Maybe we can get her to spend a lot of time singing songs so we don't have to do so much schoolwork."

"That's a good idea. I hear she's real religious. Maybe if we ask her to play church songs, we can drag out the opening exercises."

Sunday, August 22, 1943

Ruth, Marian and I went to church this morning. Pearl was gone when we got home.

The girls and I went to the North Church where Rev. Ellis Graber showed slides illustrating the parables. He also showed Mennonite churches.

Monday, August 23, 1943

Had our threshing settling up party at Ben Ratzlaff's in the evening. They served ice cream and cake. I had to pay $97 for the machine and labor.

Slowly the families belonging to the Ratzlaff threshing ring began crowding into Ben's small house. Gradually they divided into three groups: the men around the dining table where there was plenty of light to "figure up," the women and babies in the parlor, and the older children on the porch outside.

"Let's play 'Hide and Seek'," suggested Melvin, the biggest of the group.

"In the dark?"

"Sure!"

"Okay, who's gonna be IT?" asked Willis.

"I will," said Melvin. "Everybody go hide. I'll count to a hundred. Then I'll call out 'Ready or not, here I come'."

Marian, Marjorie, Verlyn and Lois stayed close to the house, each finding a tree to hide behind in the shadows. Ruth and Lillian ventured further, hiding behind the toilet and the wash house. Myron and Willis ventured even further, stepping over a fence into the garden.

"Ready or not, here I come," called Melvin. All the hiders stayed as quiet as possible. Hiding in the shadows, they could barely see Melvin moving stealthily in the moon light. When they felt him getting too close, they tried to move without betraying their presence.

"I smell somebody's perfume," he said, swooping up Ruth and carrying her to the house, setting her down on the porch. "Who wants to be next?" asked the big boy.

"Me, me, me," called all the little girls.

Thursday, August 26, 1943

Pearl got a letter today offering her a teaching job at Kimball for $1,325.

Friday, August 27, 1943

Pearl went to Freeman to phone to Irene about her job. She did not want everyone on our line to know her business. She was supposed to be at the Conference Young People's Retreat.

In the evening we went to the College Gym to hear Dr. J. E. Hartzler.

Saturday, August 28, 1943

Pearl went to Irene about her job. She was not back with the car in time so we went to the College Gym with Dr. Saner, who had been here vaccinating the pigs. Jake L.'s took us home. Rev. S. F. Pannabecker spoke. The crowd was not very big.

Pearl came home at midnight. She decided to take the job at Irene for $1225.

Monday, August 30, 1943

Took the car to town to have it repaired. Pearl burned out a connecting rod when she went to Irene. Apparently it was out of oil.

Saturday, September 4, 1943

I drove to Irene to get Pearl and she went to town to get a finger wave.

Sunday, September 6, 1943

All in church but Cal, who is still in Mont. We have not heard from him for a week.

Monday, September 6, 1943

Marie is home from school today because of Labor Day. Ruth and Marian started school at Sunshine #26 with Luella Thomas as teacher. She gets $95 per mo. We also bought her a piano. She observed when I was teaching at Summit #51. She won't have any car expenses since she can walk to school from home.

Sunday, September 12, 1943

We were in Silver Lake Church this morning for a program by the CPS quartet from Denison, Iowa. Pearl did not come home this weekend.

The children practiced in our church in the afternoon for a Children's Day program to be given at the Mission Fest. Paul E. is in charge.

Tuesday, September 14, 1943

This is Cal's birthday, but he is still in Montana.

I got a letter from Wm. Stauffer of Sugar Creek, Ohio, that he can come to the Sunday School convention in Spink Co. on Oct. 16 & 17.

Saturday, September 18, 1943

Went to Irene this morning to get Pearl. She had an appointment to have her hair fixed at 11 a.m.

Sunday, September 19, 1943

Mission Fest in our church. Albert Schultz spoke in the forenoon. The children gave their program in the afternoon. The collection for missions was $1600+.

Monday, September 20, 1943

Went to see a bull near Hartford. Not very good.

Stopped at Sister Katherine's for dinner and again on my way home. She had her boys load up my car with watermelons and muskmelons.

Tuesday, September 21, 1943

Mr. & Mrs. Abe Wiens stopped in for a while. They brought a load of melons.

Wednesday, September 22, 1943

Rev. Solomon Walter of the Dolton Church stopped here. He is getting a revival speaker for his church and wants him in the College Gym if the crowds get too big. He claims Pres. Unruh won't let him have the Gym.

410

Tuesday, September 29, 1943

Paid Fed. Land Bank $937.65 for this year's share. Shot a pheasant on the way home. Went to Ben V. Tieszen in the evening. We decided to pay Hartzler and Pannabecker $62 each for their services at the retreat.

Saturday, October 2, 1943

Pearl is home but Marie went to the Corn Palace. We dug 25 bu. potatoes and I shot 3 pheasants. Art Adrian's bull was here again. I locked him up.

Tuesday, October 9, 1943

My sister Anna (Mrs. Joe M.) came up with P. P. She is visiting from Beadle and will stay with us a while.

Saturday, October 9, 1943

Sorted potatoes before storing them in the cellar. Mrs. Joe M. is busy patching and cooking. Pearl came home and went to town to have her hair fixed. I think there is some connection with the CPS quartet being here tomorrow.

Sunday, October 10, 1943

The CPS quartet from the Hill City camp sang at the Freeman church in the morning, at our church in the afternoon, and in the North Church in the evening. Paul Tschetter, camp director, gave a talk. Pearl went to all three services. Peter Hofer sings in the quartet.

Monday, October 11, 1943

Cal came back from Mont. He had been there since Aug. 18.

Saturday, October 16, 1943

Cal, Marie, Ruth and I were all picking corn.

Sunday, October 17, 1943

Went to S. S. convention at Emmanuel Church near Doland with Mr. & Mrs. Paul Decker. Bill Stauffer of Sugar Creek, Oh., was main speaker.

We took Mrs. Joe M. back to Beadle. Had noon lunch at Clarence Hofer, supper at Iky Tschetter and stayed overnight with J. W. Nephew John was home from Carleton College. Gladys and Mary Ruth both had baby girls named Beverly and Velma, respectively.

Monday, October 18, 1943

Left Huron at 7 a.m. and were home by 11. Cal and I got dead trees ready for sawing. Abe Kautz charged $1.75 for 45 min. of sawing.

Tuesday, October 19, 1943

This is Grandpa Tieszen's 80th birthday. I gave him a pheasant I had shot.

Friday, October 22, 1943

Shipped ram and wether to Sioux Falls with Art Hopf.
Went to Freeman H. S. to get Ration Book No. 4.
Cal picked corn all day.
Pearl came home from Irene with Andrew Gross. His daughter Lucille is teaching there too.

Saturday, October 23, 1943

Met with Finance Committee of the Aid Plan at D. J. Mendel's place to check his General Secretary's books.
Got some sheepheads from Math Kleinsasser. He has been fishing at the Jim since Oct. 15.

Sunday, October 24, 1943

All in church. I taught boys' class. The girls went to memorial service for Mr. Busch in the afternoon. He was killed in the war. He had been a teacher at the High School.
Cal went away with Mike and Paul Stahl in the evening.
I heard that cattle are dying from corn stalk disease, so I put the cows to the straw pile.

Tuesday, October 26, 1943

Pearl is home from teaching this week. Cal and I tried to get her to help pick corn, but that seems to be out of the question.
Cal got Ray Senner's elevator to unload the corn. We are using our tractor to power the elevator.

Friday, October 29, 1943

Pearl helped clean the church. Marie went home to Tyndall after school. The girls went to see "Little Women" at the High School.
Shot 3 pheasants with one shot.

Monday, November 1, 1943

Pearl is home. I think it has to do with Peter Hofer being on furlough from CPS camp. Cal and Peter picked corn 'til noon. Then Cal went to Kansas with Melvin Tieszen, and Peter picked in the afternoon.

Sunday, November 8, 1943

It is snowing and blowing. We were not in church.

*Phoebe Walter came along with Marie from town last night and
is here today.*

*The sheep are not under cover. We have a lot of corn that is
not picked.*

Monday, November 9, 1943

Marie and Phoebe walked to 81 to catch a ride to town.

*Found 7 lambs in the cornfield. I could not find them yesterday.
They seem to be all right.*

*Cal came home from Kansas in the evening, but Marie did not
come home.*

Saturday, November 13, 1943

*Marie and the girls cleaned the storm windows and Cal put them
in.*

"I never heard of such a thing – washing glass with kerosene!"
exclaimed Ruth.

"Sure, that's the best way. My folks always do it that way.
And we shine 'em with newspapers. You got lots of that around
here!" said Marie, crumpling a sheet of the FREEMAN COURIER
into a ball to show Ruth and Marian. "C'mon, let's go upstairs and
do it in the attic where there's enough room."

"We could carry the storm windows down here and clean 'em
here," offered Ruth.

"No, they're too heavy. Cal said he'd put 'em in, so he can carry
'em down," Marie said, leading the way to the attic with an arm
load of papers and a can of kerosene. "I'll wash with kerosene and
you kids can rub with newspapers."

They moved up the dark, curving stairway to the second floor,
only half of which had been finished into two large bedrooms. On
the unfinished side were playthings of former years: a wooden rocking horse, a doll bed with a hairless old doll asleep under the rag
rug Grandma had made for Marian, a tea table with chairs, and
china dishes. Marie and the girls made their way cautiously through
the accumulated clutter: boxes of empty Mason jars, old magazines
and books, piles of summer clothes and broken chairs.

In the back room were the storm windows leaning against an
antique cradle and washing machine. "I've never seen such a funny
contraption. Looks like someone would have to crank that wooden
drum handle to make the drum go 'round. Seems to me it would
be easier to rub your clothes on a scrub board," said Marie.

"Daddy calls it 'Mother's Folly' every time he sees it. He says
Mother insisted on having that machine, but once she got it, she
hardly used it," said Ruth.

"I can see why," observed Marie.

"How you comin' with the storm windows? Got any cleaned yet?" called Cal up the stair well.

"WILL have in two shakes of a lamb's tail!" replied Marie, and the three girls set to work cleaning.

"I can use some help with the ladder, Honey. Wanna help me?" asked Cal.

"Sure," said Marian and dropped the newspaper wad. "We're lucky it didn't stay windy. Otherwise it would be hard for you to hold a window up on the ladder."

"You better believe it! I feel like a steeple jack up here. What we need is some kind of a combination screen and storm window we can leave in and not have to fool with every year. Well, we're sure not gonna get it as long as the war is on."

"When is the war gonna end, anyway?"

"When one side kills off enough on the other side and they all get tired of fighting."

"How's come you didn't have to go to war like P. P.'s boys did?"

"I'm younger and I have a farm deferment. Dad persuaded the draft board that I was needed on the farm, since he had only one son. P. P. has a whole bunch of boys. The country needs agriculture for the war effort too."

"How's come some boys in our church go to the Army and some go to the C. O. camps?" asked Marian.

"It's a difference of belief. The Mennonite principles dictate non-resistance or non-combatant service, but some Mennonites don't go along with that anymore."

"The colonies—they all go to the C. O. camp, don't they?"

"Yeah, and most of the strict Mennonites. But we have the freedom to choose. We follow our own conscience. The colony boys would get booted out of the colony if they went to war."

"If you got drafted, where would you go, to the Army or to the C. O. camp?"

"I don't know yet. But I'm leaning," he said, balancing himself on the ladder.

Sunday, November 14, 1943

After church we went to John J. B.'s for dinner. John is home from CPS camp on a two-week furlough.

Thursday, November 18, 1943

Cal picked corn while I went to John M. S. Hofer's sale. Bought a roan heifer for $30 and an antique cradle for $1, which I donated

(L. to R.): Theodore Hofer, Cal Kleinsasser, John Hofer, Alfred Tschetter.

to the church for the baby room. We attended the Academy play, "New Fires," which was good.

Sunday, November 21, 1943
Cal led the opening for the C. E. tonight. It was his first attempt, and he did a good job.

Tuesday, November 23, 1943
Went to George Rollag's sale north east of Sioux Falls. Bought a John Deere cultivator. Mrs. P. P. phoned for us to come down to their place. Amos is home on furlough from the Army, stationed at Memphis, Tenn. Anne, Elizabeth and Alice were home too.

Sunday, November 28, 1943
All in church. I taught S. S. Cal took Pearl to the South Church where she got a ride back to Irene. The girls and I went to the College Gym for a program. Joe Glanzer from Beadle played the guitar and Paul Glanzer talked about conditions in a mental hospital in Pennsylvania, where he is doing his C. O. service.

Monday, November 29, 1943
Cal went to Chicago with trucker Herb Koster on a business trip for Wilmer Fensel.

Tuesday, November 30, 1943
Oiled the hogs. Pulled some Rockport Colony guys out of a mud hole at Philip Mensch's. They got some hay from Mensch but did not like it, so they got a little from us at $20 per ton.

I butchered two roosters.

Wednesday, December 1, 1943
Went to Burial Assoc. meeting in Viborg with Leon Weier. The Board decided to send Weier and me to Pierre to see Atty. Gen. George Mickelson about our charter. Got home after midnight because the Auditing Committee met after the Bd. meeting.

Thursday, December 2, 1943
It was 3:30 a.m. this morning when I got home. I cleaned up the driveway using kerosene to burn the weeds.

Saturday, December 4, 1943
Cal came home from Chicago with a '40 Mercury. He had a soldier along with him, AWOL from a camp in Oregon for three weeks. He was wearing civilian clothes. We gave him breakfast before he went on his way.

Cal started working for Ben Ratzlaff.

The Rockport Colony boys were here for more alfalfa hay. I sold them 2 tons @ $30 per ton. It was good second cutting hay.

Monday, December 6, 1943
Art Becker shelled corn for us. The corn ceiling was raised 9¢. It is now 99¢ per bu. here.

Ruth, Marian and I went to Joe K. Kleinsasser to make out 48 CPS certificates.

Tuesday, December 7, 1943
Ray Senner helped me put in cellar windows. Sold a boar to Adolph L. Waltner for $50.

Wednesday, December 8, 1943
Leon Weier and I went to see Atty. Gen. George Mickelson concerning the charter for the Burial Assoc. He was home in Sioux Falls so we did not need to drive to Pierre. He said he would make a decision and write me before Dec. 21.

Thursday, December 9, 1943
Cal and I put up a 26-in. woven wire (6-in. stay) between Schmidt's and our land, using a few iron posts.

Cal took the girls to the High School gym for a musical program. Marian got sick during the night.

Friday, December 10, 1943

We strung two barb wires on the fence between Schmidt's and our land. Did not have enough barb wire. We cannot buy galvanized wire. They are selling black wire made for the USSR.

Marian was home from school. She got very sick in the evening.

Sunday, December 12, 1943

In the evening Marian, Ruth and I went to our church to hear Rev. Weinbrenner, editor of THE MENNONITE. He did not have a big audience.

Our car froze up going to and from church. Cal's Mercury froze up too.

Monday, December 13, 1943

Very cold. The cistern pipe was frozen for the first time this season.

Tuesday, December 14, 1943

12 degrees below zero. Could not get either car started. Finally got the tractor started and pulled Cal's car to start it. It got too late to go to Founders' Day, but I did go to the Co-op Lumber Yard meeting.

Wednesday, December 15, 1943

Went to Co-op Creamery meeting. They paid out a 3 1/4¢ dividend and 5% on shares of stock.

Packed flax straw on north side of chicken barn.

Thursday, December 16, 1943

Christ Graber ground 800 lbs. alfalfa and a triple box of oats and corn. We filled the self feeder by the brood sows and stored the rest in the barn.

I sold 745 lbs. alfalfa to Fensel for 2¢ per lb.

Ed C. Graber came for his sow. In trade he will help fix our chicken barn. Bought 24 ft. sill and drop siding at Thompson Yards. The lumber yards do not have much of a supply. We will board up the entire east side.

Saturday, December 18, 1943

I chaired the annual church meeting again. Peter J. S. was secretary. The main new ruling is that all women will pay on the same basis as the men. The levy now is $10 per year per married member and $6 per unmarried member.

Sunday, December 19, 1943

Taught boys' class and had trouble with Elmer, preacher's son. He just cannot act like a human being. It would be best if he would stay home.

Tuesday, December 21, 1943

Went to my last Burial Assoc. Board meeting. George Erickson's and my terms expired. Chris Jensen and Fred Holm were elected in our places.

Thursday, December 23, 1943

Took a load of Wisconsin 38 barley to town. It sold for $1.23 per bu. Bought 35 steel posts and some presents for the children. The stores were crowded with people.

A. T. Kaufman said he would pay $35 per ton for ground alfalfa.

Children had their school program this afternoon. They raffled off a box of chocolates. Miss Thomas has added a lot of music to the school.

With Luella Thomas at the piano the eight children in six grades faced their parents seated somewhat uncomfortably in their children's desks for the Christmas program.

In Part I they sang the familiar carols which they had learned in church and practiced in school: "O Little Town of Bethlehem," "Away in a Manger," and "We Three Kings of Orient Are." Janice read Luke 2 while the others acted out the nativity of Jesus in bathrobes. The pastel chenille robes which Pearl had sent Ruth and Marian from Irene last Christmas came in handy.

Part II was the secular portion of the program. The songs were "Up on the House Top Reindeer Pause," "Jolly Old Saint Nicholas," and "Deck the Halls." Playlets such as "Virginia's Surprise" and "Grandma Loses Her Knitting" brought applause from the audience. The climax of the program was a recitation of Clement Moore's "The Night Before Christmas" by the oldest male student, Orville.

After the gift exchange and raffle, in which Orville's older brother Gordon, a Freeman Academy student, won the chocolate-covered cherries, cookies were served. Then the "real" Christmas tree was undecorated and given to the family which otherwise would not have a tree.

It was an ecumenical meeting of the parents who, though living within a few miles of one another and all being Mennonite, went to different Mennonite churches in different Mennonite denominations: Silver Lake Mennonite Brethren Church, Evangelical Mennonite Brethren Church, and the Hutterthal Mennonite Church (General Conference).

418

Friday, December 24, 1943

The children put on a fairly good program this evening in church. Ruth gave a dramatic piece and Marian recited "Silent Night" in German before it was sung by the choir.

Saturday, December 25, 1943

All in church but Pearl, who is not home.

In the afternoon we went to P. P.'s. Edward was home on furlough from the Army, stationed in Louisiana.

In the evening we went to grandparents. Dave J. R., Henry Tiahrt, Elmer Tiahrt, Arnold Tiahrt, Mrs. Marie Tiahrt, Mrs. Tina Tieszen and most of their families were there. Father-in-law gave each one a dollar bill. The children said their pieces.

Sunday, December 26, 1943

All in church again this morning. We had our Sunday School elections during the class period. I was elected to teach Class 3, a young boys' class.

Cal shot a pheasant and a jack rabbit.

"How's come they're called jack rabbits?" asked Marian as she watched Cal skin the rabbit in front of the kitchen stove.

"I don't know. Do you know, Pa?"

"I'm not sure, but Father said it was 'cause the ears looked like jackass ears. Used to call 'em jackass rabbits, and that got shortened to jack rabbits."

Tuesday, December 28, 1943

Went to Sioux Falls at noon to get the radiator cleaned out. Could not get it done. I am supposed to send it up next week.

While in Sioux Falls I went to see the play, "The Corn is Green." Ethel Barrymore was the chief actress. I paid $2.40 for a good seat but could not hear 'til the last act.

Sold the hide of the jack rabbit Cal shot to Stein for 50¢.

Thursday, December 30, 1943

Harry Tiahrt came over to help Cal tear off the shingles from the old machine shed.

Friday, December 31, 1943

Cal went away in the evening but the girls and I went to church. There was not a big crowd. Marian went home with Paul L.'s to visit with Vivian.

419

1944
And the Rains Came

Saturday, January 1, 1944

Not in church. Pearl did not come home for Christmas. She sent me this diary. She sent the girls Teddy Bear plush coats. Cal is working on his car.

Sunday, January 2, 1944

We got to church late, so I did not teach my class. Went to Elmer and Huldah Tiahrts for dinner. She is raising chinchillas for fur.

Monday, January 3, 1944

Cal started working with a hay baling outfit. They baled 601 bales today. He gets 1¢ per bale.

Marie came home today from school. She had been with her folks in Tyndall over Christmas.

Thursday, January 6, 1944

Went to Sioux Falls with trucker John A. Gross to take my car radiator to be cleaned out. He took three of my hogs to Morrell Meat Packing Co. They brought $13.20 cwt. I got 3 wooden barrels from Morrell for 77¢ each.

Paid Fed. Land Bank $350.

Friday, January 7, 1944

Went to Bill Tieszen's auction sale. Trailers sold for $119 and $145 each. All tractor machinery was very high.

I am reading GUADACANAL DIARY by Harry Tregaskis.

Saturday, January 8, 1944

Went to doctor about my stiff neck. He used ultra violet rays and gave me some salve.

I stopped at P. P.'s to see nephew Lt. Paul Kleinsasser, who is home from Indiana on furlough. He might get shipped overseas with his regiment. All the boys in his regiment got furloughs.

Sunday, January 9, 1944

Cal went to Irene with his Mercury to get Pearl and we all visited with Lt. Paul Kleinsasser at P. P.'s in the afternoon.

Monday, January 10, 1944

The water ran over in the chicken barn, wetting both barns. I cleaned them out and put in fresh straw.

Wilmer Fensel was here to look at our chickens. We will again sell eggs to his hatchery, beginning Feb. 1.

Tuesday, January 11, 1944

Cal went to make out the program for C. E. tonight. I am reading THE GOOD EARTH by Pearl Buck.

Thursday, January 13, 1944

I went to Rev. Abe Duerksen's sale. Bought a few small things. He is leaving for Canada to preach there.

Margie Pollman and Tabea Walter came along with Marie from school for the night. They had a little birthday party for Ruth, who is 14 today.

Friday, January 14, 1944

Beautiful day. I butchered a lamb while Cal was baling. It did not take long to do. We had the liver and heart for supper.

Cal and I saw a basketball game in the evening. Scotland beat Freeman High. Marie came home with us after the game.

Ruth says she heard the piano playing during the night last night when Margie and Tabea were here. She thinks it was her mother.

Sunday, January 16, 1944

John J. B. family stopped here after C. E. We popped corn and made coffee.

Monday, January 17, 1944

Sold a load of barley to Conrad Ellwein @ $1.23 bu.

Have the cattle in the corn stalks. We have no snow. Beautiful weather.

Tuesday, January 18, 1944

*Went to John J. B.'s for supper. They gave us quite a bit of sausage of different kinds from their butchering (*Fleisch Wurst, Leber Wurst, und Gritz Wurst.*)*

Thursday, January 20, 1944

Went to Geo. Janzen sale near Canistota. Weather was good and there was an immense crowd. The machinery went very high— Case planter, $135; binder, $500; gang plow (tractor) $217.

Saturday, January 22, 1944

Marie and the girls did the washing. They could hang it outside.

Sunday, January 23, 1944

Girls and I went to Abe Wiens in the afternoon and then to grandfolks in Marion. Mrs. Wiens is still in the hospital in Sioux Falls with rheumatic fever.

Thursday, January 27, 1944

Cal did not bale because of rain and snow. Marie did not come home from school. We had roast duck for supper. I butchered a sheep.

Saturday, January 29, 1944

Marie spent the day ironing.

Sunday, January 30, 1944

All in church. Cal and I wormed the sheep in the afternoon. He went away in the evening and I started reading SO BIG by Edna Ferber.

Monday, January 31, 1944

Cal came back from baling at 10 a.m. because it was too windy, so we hauled manure from the back shed all day. Went to town for manure spreader repair and bought two boxes of shotgun shells.

Tuesday, February 1, 1944

We are still hauling manure out of the back shed. There is plenty.

Wednesday, February 2, 1944

Went to Fed. Land Bank meeting. The bank paid for our dinners at the C & L Cafe.

Monday, February 7, 1944

Worked on the books of the Farmers Co-op with Ed C. Graber. Started saving eggs for Fensel. The girls pack the eggs.

Went to Freeman for Farmers Union meeting. Nephew John L. is chairman of our local, #888. Got into argument with Emil Nusz when I called the Mennonites a "faithful remnant."

Girls butchered 3 white drakes. They worked 'til midnight.

Thursday, February 10, 1944

Snowing and drifting. Many roads are blocked, according to the radio. We have most of the livestock in barns. Bucks and colts are out. Marie and girls are home from school. Marie's bus did not go.

Friday, February 11, 1944

Very cold all day. Went to town to make out a work sheet for the AAA program. Cal and I will farm some land in four sections this year.

Marie stayed home from school. Ruth and Marian walked to school in the afternoon.

"Sure, you can make it. The wind has died down," said Morgan, urging his daughters to go to school after dinner. "Miss Thomas is having school. You can see the smoke rising from the chimney."

"Lap your scarves over your foreheads and mouths. Just leave room to see out," added Marie.

By the time the girls had their woolen snow suits on, their rubber overshoes buckled up and their flannel scarves wrapped around their heads, they could hardly move. Nevertheless they set out for the three-quarters'-mile hike across the fields to school.

Drifts had hardened, making the crossing of fences much easier. In most cases they could simply walk over the fence on the drift. "Look," said Ruth, "the wind has hollowed out a boat for us. We can sit in it and pretend we're sailing to school."

"Daddy said he'd watch for us. We'd better keep walking or he'll wonder what happened to us," said Marian. Just in case their father was watching that moment, the girls turned back and waved broadly toward the farm house before trudging on.

"Good thing there are fence rows. Otherwise we might not know where to walk. We could be wandering all over the place," said Ruth, looking over the white expanse.

"Yeah," said Marian, breathless, as icicles formed on her scarf. "I'm getting cold. My fingers and toes especially."

"We're almost there," encouraged Ruth.

"I think I see the kids playing in the school yard," said Marian.

"Yeah, looks like they're playing Fox and Geese."

"Looks like Orville is IT!"

Soon the girls crossed the ice pond just south of the section line in front of the school. Snow covered most of the pond, but the wind had cleared some spots for them to slide on as they approached the section line.

"Come and get in the game!" hollered Orville. "It's almost time for the bell to ring."

423

"I'm freezing! I'm going to the school house," answered Marian. "Me too!" called Ruth.

"Okay, Sissies!" said Orville. But the girls were not deterred by the name-calling. They just hurried to stand in front of the large potbellied stove into which Miss Thomas with carefully gloved hands was throwing another piece of soft coal.

Sunday, February 13, 1944

Not in church though weather is warmer. Had our first lamb from Ewe #328.

Monday, February 14, 1944

Had my income tax made out by Mr. Smith of the State Revenue Dept. He did not charge for it. I did not have to pay any more tax because I had paid $16.50 victory tax at Pierre.

Tuesday, February 15, 1944

Marie went away on a date. Stahl boys were here in the evening. We had a chislic fry.

"You can help put the meat on the sticks, girls," said Morgan as he cut the loin of mutton into cubes on the wooden cutting board Cal had made in Shop class.

"How many pieces to a stick?" asked Marian.

"Depends upon the size of the pieces. Six or eight. There has to be room between the pieces so the hot fat can fry each piece quickly. But use the sharp end of the stick to pierce the meat, Marian."

Soon they had a huge pile of filled sticks on the oil cloth. "Now, get some lard from the large crock in the back room," Morgan said, handing Marian a large spoon. Morgan pulled the large black cast iron skillet to the front lids of the range and Marian dumped her spoon of lard into the pan. "Better get another spoon full," he instructed her as he shook the coals in the grate. "Ruth, throw some more cobs on the fire." When the cobs were burning well, he took the front lid off the stove and set the pan on the open fire. "Chislic needs a good, hot fire," he said. When the lard was spitting hot, he carefully laid six sticks of cubed mutton into the rolling pool and carefully turned them with tongs until they were cooked to a deep brown. Meanwhile the girls got more salt shakers out of the *Schrank* and put a two-pound box of soda crackers in the middle of the table.

"Get enough plates out for everyone, Ruth."

"That would be six—Cal, Mikey, Pauly, you and us kids," said Ruth, setting the table.

"I smell chislic!" said Cal as he and his friends descended from his upstairs bedroom.

"Where'd this come from? This is better than eating at Krueger's downtown," said Paul.

"Okay, eat 'em while they're hot," said Morgan, placing the fried chislic on a platter in the center of the table and turning to the range to cook some more. "Mutton is no good cold. The tallow gets hard."

Chewing on a salted piece of meat and holding a soda cracker in his hand, Cal mumbled to his friends, "Only thing missing is a cold bottle of beer."

"I heard that!" said Morgan. "There'll be no beer brought into this house while I'm alive!"

Cal winked at Mike and Paul behind Morgan's back.

Thursday, February 17, 1944

Went to Co-op Gas & Oil meeting at City Hall. They are supposed to pay out a dividend this year. Bill Senner has been doing a lot of business since so many people bought tractors.

Sunday, February 20, 1944

Went to Juke L.'s for dinner after church. Went hunting after dinner. Shot 3 pheasants. Jake stepped on a rooster that was hiding under a thistle.

Monday, February 21, 1944

Rev. Wm. Stauffer of Ohio was in our church this evening. He has been visiting CPS camps and churches for 11 months for the Mennonite Central Committee.

Thursday, February 24, 1944

Girls and I went to the South Church to hear Stauffer and see pictures of CPS camps. Cal refused to go along.

Friday, February 25, 1944

A. R. M. Hofer and I appraised Alfred Tschetter's farm and insured all his property in the Aid Plan.

Marian went along with Marie to Tyndall. Marian and Marie's sister Lily Rose are pals.

Saturday, February 26, 1944

Pearl did not come home again. Marie and Marian are in Tyndall, so Ruth is chief cook and bottle washer.

Wednesday, March 1, 1944

Went to Isaac Buller's sale. A drill brought $305, bought by I. I. Walter. A tractor brought the ceiling of $805.

Thursday, March 2, 1944

Took out partitions in horse barn and put different floor in one stall.

Took girls to Mrs. Oscar Gering for their piano lessons.

Sunday, March 5, 1944

Not in church because of lambing. Called vet. for sheep trouble.

Wednesday, March 8, 1944

Very windy. We have lost too many lambs in this miserable weather, so we are bringing them in the house to warm up.

"I'll warm up the milk; you pour it in the pop bottles with the funnel, Ruth. And Marian can put on the nipples."

"Aw, I got the hardest job!" whined Marian, playing with the lambs in a cardboard box on a chair in front of the open oven door.

"I'll help if you have trouble," said Morgan, stirring the milk in a saucepan on the stove.

"Poor little things," cooed Ruth, patting the two gray lambs on their nappy heads.

"Okay, the milk is lukewarm. Pour it in the bottles. But only about half full. They can't drink much yet."

"Is this all the lambs we got today?"

"No, there are other new lambs in the barn nursing at their mothers. These two lost their mother and there weren't any other ewes I could put them to."

"Poor little lambs," said Ruth, handing the half-filled bottle to Marian so she could attach the nipple.

"I need help!" Marian announced, looking at her father and holding up the large black rubber nipple.

Friday, March 10, 1944

Auction sale at Pumpkin Center. A 15-ft. disc sold for $180.

Cal got a haircut this afternoon. We all went to the College play, "Follow Thou Me." It was well rendered.

Sunday, March 12, 1944

Taught boys' class. Some of our people were in Huron for a service at Joe E. Wipf's Gospel Mission.

We had both dinner and supper at Paul E.'s. Annie cooked two big meals.

426

Monday, March 13, 1944

Went to Albert Mettler's sale. Livestock, except for horses, sold well. A young Hereford bull brought $185.

Wednesday, March 15, 1944

Abe Wiens came to try to hire Marie, but she is still in school. His son Harvey is still weak from rheumatic fever.

Thursday, March 16, 1944

Sold 2 white drakes to Mike P. Hofer for $4.50.
Cal went to Dolton to make out the C. E. program.

Friday, March 17, 1944

Organized a 4-H sow litter and sheep club here. Jake and Raymond Hofer, Willis Ratzlaff, and Ruth and Marian are members. Cal is the leader.

Had a meeting at City Hall concerning organizing a community hospital. Voted unanimously to go ahead. It will be open to any doctor wishing to use it.

Saturday, March 18, 1944

All went to Sioux Falls shopping. Marie's sister Bertha was along. I bought Easter dresses and coats for the girls. When we got home there was a letter from Pearl saying she wanted to come home, so Cal went to Irene with his car to get her.

Sunday, March 19, 1944

All in church morning and evening. Cal was chairman of C. E. in the evening. He took Pearl back to Irene after C. E.

Tuesday, March 21, 1944

John J. B. and Katherine were here to help butcher a yearling heifer. It was quite fat. We took 3 quarters to the Freeman locker and Katherine took one quarter home to can for us.

Thursday, March 23, 1944

Made out application for tires. Mine are bad.

Friday, March 24, 1944

Cal slept 'til 2:30 p.m. because he got up several times during the night to take care of the pigs that were farrowing.

We all went to the High School play, "Miss Tish." Marie was in the cast. Other actors were Marilyn Wollman, Arlyss Ratzlaff, Carlyle Groves, Bert Tiesen, Jack Isaac and Calvin Warne.

"Of course, you realize I gave you your start on the stage," Morgan said to Marie at the breakfast table the next morning.

"When?"

"When you gave a humorous reading, "Edith Helps Things Along," in 1936, when I was teaching your school."

"Boy, you sure have a good memory!"

"I don't see how you could forget such a major event in your life! Remember, I took you down to the College to have Miss Pankratz coach you before we went to the regional contest?"

"Yeah? What'd she do?"

"Oh, she helped you pronounce some of the words, helped you put stress on the right words."

"Well, I'll be! How'd you remember that, out of all your students?"

"I always remember the good looking girls the best."

Saturday, March 25, 1944

Not in church. Snowed quite a bit this morning. I found a crippled duck on our lake. I have never seen a duck of that specie before.

Went to our church in the evening. Mr. and Mrs. Brown, missionaries to China, spoke. They went to China in 1909 and are planning to go back.

Tuesday, March 28, 1944

Hauled our alfalfa hay from Sam Schmidt's land. It is good hay. Had to pull it home with the tractor because the ground was so muddy that the horses couldn't pull the load.

Saturday, April 1, 1944

Had a load of barley fanned at P. P.'s for seed. Have 150 bu. for seed.

Yesterday Cal went to Irene to get Pearl, and this afternoon she went to town and didn't come home at all. She was home only a few hours.

Tuesday, April 4, 1944

Took a load of oats to grind for feed and bought 27 bu. corn @ $1.03 from Park Lane to mix with oats. Corn is hard to get. Both Co-op and Shanard elevators were out.

Cal painted the drill, drag and wagon box.

Thursday, April 6, 1944

Straw pile fell over on one heifer but we got her out. The cattle eat into the pile and make it top heavy.

Friday, April 7, 1944

Went to Tieszen church in the morning and to Henry Tiahrts for dinner.

In the evening Rev. Dirks from Sioux Falls spoke in our church. He is a very forceful speaker.

Saturday, April 8, 1944

Cal cut a door into the cob house. We want to use it as a farrowing pen for sows out in the alfalfa field.

Marie went home to Tyndall for Easter.

Sunday, April 9, 1944 Easter Sunday

All in church. Pearl, the girls and I went to Abe Wienses. Dave J. R.'s and grandparents were there too. Eva is slowly getting better. From there we took Pearl back to Irene.

Monday, April 10, 1944

All went to College for Easter Monday program. Most of the churches in the community participated in the morning. Our church choir sang. There is a great variety in the quality of music among the churches.

We went home for dinner and then back to the College for the afternoon program, which was put on by the music department.

Red cow had a red bull calf.

Tuesday, April 11, 1944

Started sowing succotash this afternoon.

Saturday, April 15, 1944

Cal pulled his car to the section line with the tractor so he and Marie could go to town.

Sunday, April 16, 1944

Cal was sick this morning. We went to a mission program in our church in the evening. It was also Jacob B.'s birthday, so we had a shower for him.

Monday, April 17, 1944

Tried to move the coal shed into the alfalfa patch to use for farrowing sows, but it was too muddy.

Sunday, April 23, 1944

Did not go to church in morning. Went to A. R. M. Hofer's after dinner for short service and then to his funeral at our church.

429

Linden Anderson, our new undertaker from Elk Point, had the funeral for the Burial Association. It rained almost all day and then turned to snow towards evening.

A. R. M. had a steel casket and a cement vault that some boys brought out from Sioux Falls. The funeral cost about $600.

"You boys can come on in the house and get dried out by the stove," Morgan said to the young men from Sioux Falls as he opened the farm house door.

"Really appreciate that, Mr. Kleinsasser. We didn't want to track up the church with our muddy boots. Course, we don't want to track up your house, either, for that matter," said the lad with dripping parka, casting a cautious eye at the two young girls in the kitchen.

"Just pull off your boots by the door. Girls, spread some newspapers around for the boys to walk on. Mud, mud, mud. Have you ever seen so much mud?"

"Seems like it's either too dry or too wet in South Dakota. Can't seem to strike a happy medium," said the other, unbuckling his rubber boots.

"Girls, make some coffee for these fellas and get 'em warmed up before they go back to the city."

The girls obediently assumed their tasks, finding some store-bought cookies in a grocery box that was still unpacked from the weekly shopping trip the night before.

"Tell me, how often do you guys deliver a cement vault?" asked Morgan.

"Oh, about once a week. Not around here, though. First time we ever brought one down here. Mostly we sell 'em in the Sioux Falls area."

"Our people are not for encasing their remains in steel and concrete, I'll tell you. You know, 'dust to dust, ashes to ashes'. You can't very well return to the earth or rise from the dead if you're closed up in steel and concrete," said Morgan, smiling.

"Well, Mr. Kleinsasser, when the weather is this wet, people want to guard against subsidence of the earth and seepage into the remains. Also, they don't like the idea of little animals getting in and nibbling on the body or being dragged up to the surface of the cemetery by burrowing animals."

Ruth and Marian looked at each other in horror. "I never thought of that," Ruth said, as she became engrossed in the details.

Monday, April 24, 1944
Mud, mud, mud. No hay for cattle or sheep. Got a little old straw from Fred L. Thomas land.

430

Tried to get corn for grinding into feed, but government has frozen all corn to farmers within the four-state area.

Bought 39 lbs. lard @ 20¢ from John J. B.'s.

Tuesday, April 25, 1944

Went to Salem for hay but it was so poor I left it. He wanted $12.50 per ton for baled slough hay. Found another man with loose hay for $8 per ton.

Got a little corn at Marion elevator. Moved two sows to pasture north of house. We are using the chicken brooder house for them.

Friday, April 28, 1944

Went to Peter G.'s for supper and evening. Marian stayed there for the weekend. Lydia will bring her back to the College on Monday when she comes to the dormitory.

Saturday, April 29, 1944

Ruth went to Tyndall with the Walters. Cal and I are baching.

Monday, May 1, 1944

Jacob L. Hofer, Sr., gave us a bush cherry, plum trees, gooseberry bushes, rhubarb, horseradish and roses to plant from his garden.

Cal started sowing oats after 4 p.m. and ran out of gas at midnight. I told him to go to bed.

Picked up Marian at the College dormitory. She had spent the weekend at Peter G.'s.

"Well, what did you do at your Aunt Mary's?" asked Morgan.

"Not much. It rained most of the time. On Saturday we sold pickles to a restaurant in Mitchell."

"You did?"

"Yeah, Aunt Mary had a big crock of dill pickles left over, so we loaded it in the Model A and Menno, Dave, Lydia and I drove to Mitchell. Menno drove to the alley behind this restaurant."

"Which restaurant?"

"I can't remember the name. It was a big restaurant at a hotel. Dave went in to talk to the manager. The manager came out and Dave speared a large pickle for him to try. The manager said, 'Good and crunchy. I'll give you a dollar for the lot.' " Lydia said, " 'Okay, but we keep the crock.' Then Menno and Dave carried the crock full of pickles into the restaurant and came out with an empty crock."

Tuesday, May 2, 1944

Election Day. Rained all day, so there was a poor turnout. Dave Tiede beat Dannenbring for State Senate and Dave Wipf beat the other Tiede for the House.

Sunday, May 7, 1944

Went to College Baccalaureate in the afternoon. Rev. Willard Claassen of the South Church preached. Rev. J. J. Regier of the North Church preached for the High School Baccalaureate. Marie went home with her parents.

Friday, May 12, 1944

Our cattle were gone this morning. There is very little pasture yet. It has been too cold and rainy.

The girls and I went to College Commencement. Dr. J. Winfield Fretz of Bethel College spoke about "Mennonites, Past, Present, and Future."

Saturday, May 13, 1944

Cal dragged the field to rid it of Russian thistles. I went to town for feed but there was none to be had.

Went to brother-in-law Abe Tieszen for a load of oats and had it ground in Marion.

Sunday, May 14, 1944

Undertaker Mike Walter hit Cal's Mercury and bent his fender.

Went to Jake L.'s after church. Jake had speared quite a few carps in the lakes on his land. He gave us some to take home.

Monday, May 15, 1944

Went to Sioux Falls with trucker, Art Hopf. He got $13.20 cwt. for all the hogs that weighed between 180 and 270 lbs.

I saw Mr. Green at Morrell Packing Plant about the hogs which I took up last week. They had taken off 70¢ per cwt. because mine averaged 5/7 of a lb. too much. He said he would straighten it out.

John C. Mueller, township assessor, was here assessing our personal property.

Cal and Marie went to Dolton to make out the program for C. E., they said.

Thursday, May 18, 1944

Ascension Day. Got up too late to go to church. Dr. Saner vaccinated 49 pigs and 5 calves. Cal and Marie went away early.

Saturday, May 20, 1944

Cal rigged up the sheep clipper to run with the Maytag motor. The first sheep he sheared was a sight for a sheep man to see. Marian is tying the wool.

I planted 35 Diamond Willows and Cottonwoods in the lake in the northwest corner of our land.

Sunday, May 21, 1944

Cal and the girls went to Paul Decker's to make out the C. E. program in the afternoon. The girls played with VeAnna. We had C. E. at night. Cal was chairman.

Wednesday, May 24, 1944

Pearl called this morning that she wants to come home. I went down for her after dinner but had car trouble, so we got home at 6 o'clock. Pearl went back to town at 8 and left with John J. R.'s, taking Marian along. Cal went to town too.

I planted white corn 302 west of house.

Thursday, May 25, 1944

Finished planting west of trees with 458 corn. Cal is plowing and dragging.

The Low German relatives had a shower for Pearl at Arnold Tiahrts. They brought Marie, Ruth and Marian home.

Friday, May 26, 1944

Still plowing and planting. Cal can go through most of the low places now.

Melvin Tieszen was here for supper, left with Cal's car, and then came back to stay overnight.

Saturday, May 27, 1944

Cal plowed and I planted corn 404A in field west of big lake.

Cal, Marie and Marian went to church with Pearl and Peter Hofer to practice for their wedding. Ruth and I went to town after I got home from planting.

Pauline had a swollen udder, so I put on some Watkins udder balm.

Sunday, May 28, 1944

Marian, Ruth and I were in church this morning. I taught the boys' class. Marie and Cal stayed home.

Pearl and Peter A. Hofer got married at 6:30 in our church.

Wedding photo of A. Pearl Kleinsasser and Peter A. Hofer.

The men attendants were Cal and John Hofer. Ladies were Marie Walter and Esther Tiahrt. Junior bridesmaids were Marian Kleinsasser and Dorothy Hofer. Had supper at John J. R. Hofer. No wedding. Pearl did not ask for any.

"Anything you need from the store?" Morgan asked Ruth and Marian as they approached the convenience market at the filling station at Stanley Corner on their way home from Peter's folks.

"Yeah, we need some bluing to do the wash tomorrow," said Ruth.

"Bluing?" shouted Morgan. "Okay, we'll stop and get some bluing." He pulled up to the station and the girls got out of the car. Marian, still wearing her taffeta junior bridesmaid dress, held it high so as not to drag it in the mud that already covered her white patent leather pumps.

"The girls need some bluing," Morgan told the friendly, familiar-looking clerk behind the counter.

"Sure, we got bluing. You want the powder form or the liquid form?"

Ruth and Marian looked at each other and then at their father. "Better make it liquid. I had a bad experience with the dry form when I was a youngster," said Morgan.

"Oh, yeah?" the clerk urged him on.

"Yeah, I had ordered some bluing to sell and left it on the window sill. A big rainstorm came up and ruined the bluing and the window sill. After a while threatening letters started coming from the bluing company. The last one said that if I did not pay up, they would give the case over to our states attorney for collection."

"What did you do then?" asked Marian, alarmed.

"Well, I was scared. I didn't have any money to pay for the bluing, and I was sure I was going to jail. Brother Ike was home that summer and must have noticed that something was bothering me. He asked what the matter was and I told him. He said he'd take my case if I promised to work hard all summer. Well, you never saw such a helpful boy! I later found out that the states attorney mentioned in the letter had been dead for several years."

"So, here's your Mrs. Stewart's bluing," the clerk said, handing the bottle to Ruth. "How's come you're all dressed up?" she asked Marian.

"My sister got married today and I was in the wedding party," replied Marian.

"And you weren't?" she asked Ruth.

"No, it was a small wedding. Peter's youngest sister was the other junior bridesmaid. She and Marian are about the same height," explained Ruth.

"Did you give the bride away?" the clerk asked Morgan.

"No, I didn't. But I wasn't asked either. They didn't ask me about anything," he said, sullen, and walked dejectedly out of the store. The girls followed, Marian holding her fancy dress aloft.

Monday, May 29, 1944

Went to Sioux Falls to get my wheels aligned, but they could not align them because spindle bolts are worn. I had a "toe in" adjusted at Goodyear. They charged $2. I got two synthetic tires.

Hutters had a shower for Pearl and Peter at Joe J.'s.

Tuesday, May 30, 1944

Pearl and Peter were here. They loaded up all their worldly possessions on the trailer and took them up to his folks to store. Silly but true. They are leaving for Hill City where Pearl will get a job, I suppose. Peter is stationed at the Hill City CPS camp.

Friday, June 2, 1944
Cal plowed 'til 2 a.m.

Saturday, June 3, 1944
Planted 241 on Decker land. Cal plowed. Had heavy rain at 4 p.m. Went to town to apply for more sugar and gas. Got stuck in driveway.

Tuesday, June 6, 1944
Planted 241 and 302 white on Decker land. One strip has five lakes. Cal is plowing. Uses much gas and can't get much done.

Wednesday, June 7, 1944
Corn is coming up on Thomas land. We have some cut worm trouble.

Thursday, June 8, 1944
Drizzled all day. Packed 40 fleeces of wool and dipped smaller pigs. Girls did the washing.

Friday, June 9, 1944
Cloudy and cold. Cultivated in the afternoon with Ray Senner's tractor and cultivator 'til it started to rain.

Saturday, June 10, 1944
Cal cultivated 'til it rained. I went to town for gas for the Maytag. Cal sheared 9 sheep 'til the Maytag stopped. Marian tied the wool.

Sunday, June 11, 1944
Had terrific thunderstorm during the night. Must have rained 3 or 4 inches. Nice sunshine all day.

Girls and I went to Sioux Falls with Pete Ratzlaff. We visited his daughter Lillian, who was operated for appendix at McKennan Hospital.

Went to Dolton church in the evening. John S. Waldner family was there for a convention. Had midnight supper at John J. B.'s with Waldners. Sister Katherine served strawberries and cream from her strawberry patch.

Tuesday, June 13, 1944
It did not rain last night.

Friday, June 16, 1944

Rained and hailed this afternoon. Cal finished shearing at our place. We had 115 sheep. He is now shearing at Paul Decker, getting 40¢ per sheep.

Marian and I went to the Dr. Kaufman sale in the afternoon in Marion.

"You look around to see if there's anything we can use," Morgan instructed his youngest daughter.

"Okay," she said and began wandering around the household articles displayed on the lawn. There were dishes and glass ware, plain and fancy. Pots and pans, a hall tree, books, end tables.

Marian recognized some young people from East Freeman going in and out of the back door of the house and followed a group inside. Some girls were sitting on the davenport, talking. "I think it's just terrible how the public invades the privacy of people having a sale," said the blonde.

"So do I," said the brunette.

Marian sat down in soft chair. There was a low table in front of her with magazines and ash trays on it. One bowl had cigarettes in it.

"Hi!" said one of the East Freeman girls.

"Hi!" answered Marian.

"What's your name? You look familiar. I think I've seen you at the College Gym."

"I'm Marian Kleinsasser, Pearl and Cal's sister."

"Oh, yes, of course! You look just like your brother. Is he here?"

"No, he's shearing sheep."

"Shearing sheep? You mean he's a sheep shearer?"

"Sure. He shears sheep for lots of people, and I tie the wool," she said proudly.

"How interesting! Did you buy anything at the sale?"

"Daddy said to look around to see if there's anything we need."

"Well, you won't find it in here. Nothing in here is for sale. All the sale items are outside."

"Okay, I'll look outside then," she said. Marian heard the girls snickering as she left. Outside she met her dad. "I found a hall tree we could use. It's over there."

"Let's take a look at it," he said, taking her by the hand as they maneuvered among the sale items. "Looks like it's in good shape. Oak. Hand made. Looks like something Cal might have made in Shop class. How much do you think it's worth?"

"I dunno."

"Well, if you're gonna bid on it, you have to know in advance what your limit is, when to stop bidding."

"Five dollars?"

"Five dollars is pretty steep. I'd say two. Don't go beyond two. Anything else we should bid on?"

"They've got those deer in the front yard for sale."

"Well, I'm sorry, but we don't need fake deer in our front yard. We got enough real wild life to contend with. Looks like the auctioneer is movin' over to the hall tree now. If you want to bid on it, get over there."

Marian approached the auctioneer, who held up the hall tree for all to see. "How much am I bid?"

"Fifty cents," said a man in the crowd.

"Fifty cents? You must be kidding. This is a gen-yoo-wine oak hall tree, hand constructed. Minimum bid I'll take is one dollar."

"One dollar!" shouted Marian.

All heads turned to see the little girl whose emphatic voice they had heard.

" 'One dollar' I heard. Who'll make it two?"

"One fifty," said the original bidder.

"Young lady, do you want to make it two dollars?" asked the auctioneer.

"One seventy five," she said.

"Two dollars?" the auctioneer asked the man.

"Nope," he said. "Let the lady have it."

"It's yours, for one seventy five. Got your money?" asked the auctioneer.

"My Daddy here has the money," she said, pointing.

"Oh, Morgan! If I'd known you were behind this, I'd have taken the bidding higher."

"No, you wouldn't. You had only two bidders. She got it fair and square," Morgan laughed.

"You're right. Pay the cashier over there and take your hall tree with you."

Sunday, June 18, 1944

All in church. Visited Abe Tieszens for a few hours in the afternoon. Picked some June berries, mulberries and loganberries. Abe has kept Grandpa's orchard in good shape.

Had a Women's Missionary Society program in our church in the evening. The women did a good job.

Monday, June 19, 1944

Tried to get an application for a new tire, but the Kleinsasser boys at White Eagle are too particular.

Lily Rose Walter is here visiting from Tyndall.

Saturday, June 24, 1944

Crop insurance adjuster has not been here yet to estimate damage from hail on the 16th.

Sunday, June 25, 1944

Went to see Amos and Ted at P. P.'s this afternoon. Both were home on furlough from the Army.

Saw Joe A. Wollman. He has gotten very thin.

Monday, June 26, 1944

Hail insurance adjuster finally came — Ray Brown — for the Reegan Agency out of Sioux Falls. He did not give a fair appraisal. He said 38% loss on one field of oats, 19% on wheat, 14 on barley, 12 on succotash, and 10 on oats on Mensch's land. He gave me nothing on one field of oats and alfalfa. He should have seen it after the hail June 16!

Sunday, July 2, 1944

Girls and I went to visit Ray Senners in the afternoon. Went to John J. B.'s for supper.

"You're just in time for supper, Uncle Morgan," said Ted, laughing.

"Glad to hear it, glad to hear it! I'll see if it's all right with your mother."

Katherine heard her brother's remark through the screened window. "Sure, it's all right, *Hansele*. It's always all right for my baby brother to come for supper," she said, bussing him on the cheek. "Set three more places at the table, Sam," she said to another son who enjoyed helping her. "You're lucky I fried an extra spring chicken for supper. Sam, go outside and pick a few more peas. Girls, how about peeling a few more potatoes? Whoops!" she said, dropping a knife. "More company coming? Well, the more, the merrier."

"You could say, 'It never rains but it pours'," laughed Morgan. "Heard from Pete and Pearl yet?"

"Nope."

"Well, give 'em to time to get adjusted to married life. Johnny wrote that Pearl was trying to get a job somewhere close to the camp so Pete could visit her easier."

439

"If you ask me, she made a dumb move. Had a good teaching job in Irene. Gave that up. What's she gonna do in Hill City or Deadwood? Work in the Homestake Mine? Or give tours of Deadwood Dick's Saloon? Pete can't support her in CPS camp. She's gonna have to support him!"

"It'll work out, Morgan. Pete's a good boy. Of course, we're a little partial since he's John's nephew. I'm just glad Pearl didn't get Alfred, so my Katherine could get him."

Monday, July 3, 1944
Got 100 rods 26-inch woven wire @ 42¢ and 160 rods barb wire at $4.50 per spool. Sent the duckfooting weed control report to the AAA office.

Tuesday, July 4, 1944
Rained an inch last night. The girls wanted to go to Adeline's for ice cream, but I was afraid we'd get stuck on their road.

Saturday, July 8, 1944
Cal helped Senner lay a cement floor in his barn. I stretched another wire on the fence running north of the house. Found a dead ram. It may have bloated.

Monday, July 10, 1944
Special session starts in Pierre. I am home weeding cockleburrs with the girls. Children had 4-H club meeting at Ben Ratzlaff's in the evening.

Cal is cultivating for the third time and cut a field of oats on Mensch's land. It was poor oats.

I subscribed to the daily ARGUS LEADER. Ruth was sick today. Marian and Cal were sick earlier this week. I suppose I am next.

Sunday, July 16, 1944
Went to College Gym in afternoon to hear the Russing family sing and play. Peter G.'s were here for supper, after which we went to our church for C. E. Rev. Kinzie of Kentucky was the guest preacher.

Thursday, July 20, 1944
Cal shocked succotash and I cut oats that was sown in June.

Sunday, July 23, 1944

All in church. Went to Paul E.'s to make out program for the S. S. convention. Rev. Frank Harder of Broadland was supposed to come but never did. We waited 'til 9 p.m.

Wednesday, July 26, 1944

Melvin Tieszen and Cal are shocking. Ruth and Marian are on the binder tripping bundles. They cannot regulate the binder.

Friday, July 28, 1944

Started threshing. Melvin Tieszen pitched bundles.

Saturday, July 29, 1944

Cal went threshing and I cut alfalfa and bromus. Also some weeds in the grain field that we could not cut with the binder. Girls and I went to town in the evening. Bought a new tire for the trailer and a new wagon box from Haar.

"You can pick up the cream check after a while and buy the groceries," Morgan said to Ruth and Marian as he pulled into the only available parking space on Main Street in front of the saloon. "I have some business to do at Haar's. Then just wait for me in the car."

As on most Saturday and Wednesday nights, it was already late by the time Morgan and his daughters got to town for shopping. Cal had taken his shower earlier and had gone away with his '40 Mercury on a "heavy date," as Morgan put it. Some shoppers had already left town. Otherwise there would not have been a parking place on Main Street.

But Marilyn was still there, walking on Main Street, so Marian and Ruth joined her in the ritual "parade" up and down the block-long main business district of Freeman. The girls passed Gering's barber shop and Merchants State Bank, crossed Main and passed the Shack, Coast to Coast hardware store and Ellwein's and arrived at Corkill's Drug Store. There the familiar old cooking oil smell of the outdoor popcorn machine greeted them. But even though they had change gleaned from the piano top at home, the girls weren't hungry yet. They'd eaten supper just minutes before going to town. It was interesting, though, to see the congregants on the steps of Corkill's — mostly fellows of Cal's age and younger — surveying the scene of "parading" girls. The girls knew they were being observed and enjoyed the attention.

"Hey, Morgan," called Scratchy to Marian, "want a malted milk?"

"Later," she responded, enjoying being called by her dad's nickname.

"How did your dad get the name of Morgan, anyway?" Marilyn asked.

"From his initials, J. P. The kids in the Academy when he was going to school named him after John Pierpont Morgan, and it stuck."

Morgan and A. A. Hofer
"It's Only a Paper Moon."

By the time the trio passed the post office, Morfeld's Meat Market, Gering's shoe repair shop, the package liquor store (a tiny temporary-looking operation between two more substantial buildings), and First National Bank, the pedestrian traffic had thinned out so that the girls could link arms as they walked. They crossed Main Street again and turned north, pausing to look down the dimly-lit side street on which the Roxy movie theatre was located.

"What's the show tonight?" asked Ruth.

"I don't know. I'm not allowed to go down there to look," said Marilyn.

"The last movie we saw there was 'Gone with the Wind'," said Ruth.

"Really? You saw 'Gone with the Wind'?"

442

"Yeah, Daddy had read the book. It came in the mail through his book club and he thought we'd learn some history by seeing the movie," explained Marian. "But Bertha's dad saw us coming out of the movie and scolded Daddy for taking us to such a show. He said the movie was an evil influence. Daddy never took us again. But we had the book with colored pictures from the movie, so we just looked at the pictures and remembered the movie and talked about it."

"My favorite character was Bonnie Blue, the little girl who was killed falling off a horse," said Ruth.

"We read some of the book, but it was awful long and the print real tiny," added Marian.

"Pearl said she'd take us to see 'Bambi' last year when she was teaching in Irene, but she never did. Now she's gone," said Ruth.

As the girls approached K & K General Merchandise, Marilyn's parents were standing there, looking for her. "It's time to go home and get ready for church tomorrow," said her father.

Suddenly Ruth remembered. "We've gotta pick up the cream check before the Creamery closes so we can buy our groceries!" Down the street and past Schamber's the girls ran and found Mildred waiting for them in the Creamery office. "We almost forgot!" said Ruth.

"I knew you'd want this check," said Mildred, handing it to them as well as the pound of butter that was automatically deducted from their check. "Now I can close."

Back at K & K's, the girls noticed again the three older women with dark shawls covering their heads, speaking in *Hutterische* dialect. They interrupted their conversation long enough to smile greetings and nod to Morgan's *Diene*.

The store was nearly empty of customers, so it was not hard to find a clerk to wait on them. "Post Toasties, pickling salt, Kerr lids, jar rubbers, Butternut coffee, a pound of pressed ham and a pound of Longhorn cheese," Ruth read from their list to Spike.

"We got some real nice California Elberta peaches, 48 to the box, just ready for eating or canning. I'll give you a real good deal on 'em since it's late Saturday night," he said.

"Figure it all up and if the Creamery check is big enough to cover it all, we'll take 'em," said Ruth.

After Spike had helped the girls carry their groceries to the '37 Chevy parked in front of the saloon, the girls got in the car and began to wait. "Maybe he's still down at Haar's Implement. You stay here, in case he comes looking for us, and I'll go look for him," said Ruth.

"No," Fred Haar told Ruth. "He was here earlier and bought a wagon box but then left. Some time ago now."

443

"Maybe he was here looking for us," said Marian when Ruth returned to the car. "He'll prob'ly say we were galivantin' around when he was ready to go home."

"Yeah. 'Just as reg'lar as a clock', he'll say."

"Have you seen my Daddy?" Marian asked as she poked her head in the door of Leon Gering's barber shop.

"Saw him earlier passing by. But not lately," said her barber.

"Let's just sit here and wait. He can't go home without the car," said Ruth.

Slowly the lights of the stores were extinguished and managers began locking their front doors. "Wanna get some pop corn or an ice cream bar at Corky's before it closes?" asked Ruth. "Maybe we'll get lucky and get one with pink ice cream so we can get another one free."

"Okay, I'll stay here and wait for Daddy. Get me a pack of Fisher's sunflower seeds too, if there's enough money left."

When Ruth returned with pop corn, sunflower seeds and ice cream bars, she asked, "Remember when Mikey Stahl gave us each a fifty cent piece in front of Corky's?"

"Yeah."

"That's when he was still goin' with Pearl."

As the girls ate their ice cream bars, the clock on Merchants State Bank struck twelve and men started coming out of the saloon. Then came their father as well. It had never occurred to the girls that he could have been in that awful smelling place in front of which they had unconsciously held their breaths to avoid inhaling the stale smell of beer.

But when their father eased his tired frame below the steering wheel and backed the car out of its parking place, drove to the corner, made a U-turn on the now nearly deserted street and headed north out of Freeman, he smelled just like the saloon.

Slowly he drove east toward Highway 81 and then north toward home. The Northern Lights lit up the sky. The grasshoppers spattered on the windshield, and the cool summer breeze blew the smell of stale beer out of the wide open car windows.

"Did you get some pressed ham and cheese for breakfast tomorrow?" he asked, at last.

"Yes, and a box of Elberta peaches, just right for eating," said Ruth.

"That's good." He sighed and drove on.

Sunday, July 30, 1944

Not in church this morning. Went to Jake L.'s for cold crabs in the afternoon and to Adeline's for hot crabs at night.

John J. Kleinsasser and Gladys and little girl, Beverly, were there. He got a farm furlough.

Thursday, August 3, 1944

Rains almost every day. Cal threshes when weather permits. The girls and I weed cockleburrs.

Appraised damage on Jacob D. Wollman's hog barn struck by lightning.

Sunday, August 6, 1944

All in church. Went to Paul E.'s to make out program for S. S. convention. Rev. Harder of Broadland made it to the meeting this time.

Went to Young People's Retreat at the Gym. Dr. J. H. Langenwalter was the speaker.

Monday, August 7, 1944

Cal reinforced our oat bin with iron rods. We used channel wire on the outside.

Cal helped Ben Ratzlaff turn over shocks that got too wet to thresh. Started threshing at 3 p.m.

Wednesday, August 9, 1944

Started threshing Marion oats at our place. It is still making the best crop, even after the hail.

Thursday, August 10, 1944

Threshed wheat all day. We are getting very poor yields. I pitched while Cal took care of the grain, using Ray Senner's elevator. Marie Senner helped the girls cook.

"I make a vinegar and Wesson oil dressing for my cole slaw," said Mrs. Senner.

"That's okay by me," said Ruth.

"And I like to put a little celery seed in."

"I'm not sure we have celery seed. But we have poppy seed left over from making *Mag Kuchen*."

"That's fine. Poppy seed will be good. Heard from Pearl yet?"

"Yeah, she got a job in a mica plant in Lead."

"Mica? What's mica?"

"It's what you put in hard coal burner windows so you can see the hot coals."

"Oh! Isinglass! You mean isinglass. Well, that's good. I'm sure they mine a lot of mica in the Black Hills."

"She works in a factory stamping out rounds of mica," explained Ruth. "I think it's used for insulators. Part of the war effort, Daddy said."

"She's working for the war effort and her husband is a conscientious objector?"

"Well, Cal said our farming is for the war effort too, if we're successful. So far we haven't done too much for the war this year because it's been too wet," Ruth explained.

Mrs. Senner smiled. "Time to start frying the pork chops. You peel the potatoes, Marian."

Sunday, August 13, 1944
Cal left with the Stahl boys to work in the Montana harvest. The girls and I did not go to church. Went to see the grandparents in the afternoon and John J. B.'s in the evening.

Monday, August 14, 1944
I went with John J. B. to Sioux Falls to rent a tent for John M. and Gladys' wedding. The rent will be $25.

Heard we cannot get Erland Waltner to speak at our convention.

Tuesday, August 15, 1944
It did not rain last night. There has been no threshing this week. Ruth and I chopped cockleburrs with corn knives. We are going through one field for the second time.

Monday, August 21, 1944
Threshed off and on by Ben Ratzlaff's today. Adeline and John brought supper to us tonight, with pie and all.

Tuesday, August 22, 1944
Cut grass on the school ground. It is good prairie grass. Hope I can get it hauled out before it rains again.

Mrs. Jake Fast and Katie Ratzlaff will paint the schoolhouse inside. They needed the grass cut so they could drive onto the yard, they say.

Wednesday, August 23, 1944
Adeline and Barbara Hofer helped the girls can fruit. They canned 8 boxes of peaches, 2 of pears and 1 of apricots.

Thursday, August 24, 1944

The threshing crew came to help turn bundles. Had the oats turned once and now turned it over again. Finished threshing the barley on the Mensch land.

Have not heard from Cal in Montana.

Saturday, August 26, 1944

Rained again last night. Went to District #1 Farmers Union meeting in Yankton. Tiede was presiding officer. He got into a scrap with Skage. Those two do not get along. Got home about 11 p.m. Bought 2 school dresses for the girls.

Sunday, August 27, 1944

Wrote to my nephew Paul in France.

Monday, August 28, 1944

Shocked some oats in afternoon. It has nearly all sprouted. Turning shocks over does not work if it rains some more. There are hundreds of ducks on our lakes, most of them teals. There is plenty of grain for them unharvested.

Tuesday, August 29, 1944

Sorted 4 ewe lambs and 4 ram lambs for the kids to take to the county fair.

Wednesday, August 30, 1944

Rained again. Walked out to 81 and caught a ride to Mitchell with Davis and Nelson of Yankton. I took on the agency for Funk's G Hybrid corn.

Loaded the 4-H lambs on the trailer and hauled them to the gravel road for Dewald to take to Tripp.

Thursday, August 31, 1944

Mrs. Dewald phoned that Arnold brought the lambs back from Tripp. He claims there was no one on the fairgrounds to accept the lambs.

I took 8 pigs to the fair for Ruth and Marian. Marian got 4 blue ribbons. Together the girls got $45 in premium money. Paulson brought the lambs in the afternoon.

Friday, September 1, 1944

Drove to Tripp to get the lambs and pigs. I sold two boars.

Stopped at Jake P. Maendl. Mrs. Maendl wants to put up some pickles for us.

Saturday, September 2, 1944

Turned a few bundles. Most of the oats still out has turned to manure. Got nearly a load of prairie hay from the school yard. Cal is still in Scobey, Montana.

Sunday, September 3, 1944

Went to Gym in afternoon and evening. The Stahl church had Mission Fest there.

Monday, September 4, 1944

Ray, Ben and Jake came to help turn shocks over. School started for girls.

Tuesday, September 5, 1944

Finished threshing. Oats very bad, dark and wet. Quite a bit stayed in the field that we could not thresh.

Wednesday, September 6, 1944

Duckfooted weeds. Grandparents brought pears from their own tree and took the potato plow along.

Friday, September 8, 1944

Fenced all day. Cattle don't have enough pasture.

Adeline and John brought us some canned stuff—corn, apples and jam.

Saturday, September 9, 1944

Went to John J. B.'s to help get ready for John and Gladys' wedding. Before we left, a heifer bloated on alfalfa. We stabbed her and she got better.

"This is the kind of wedding I like," Morgan said, "the kind that lasts three days. Noodle soup the first day, stewed beef the second day and leftovers the third day. Actually, I'm partial to the noodle soup on the first day."

They drove on to the Hofer yard, which was already swarming with relatives helping. Even the bride and groom were helping. The tent had been erected in the middle of the yard, just east of the farm house.

After eating several bowls of homemade noodle soup, Marian and Ruth joined their cousins spreading fresh straw on the floor of the tent and setting up tables and chairs for the reception. "Let's pray it doesn't rain," said the bride, Gladys.

That evening Morgan and his daughters went to Freeman to get a wedding present for the bridal pair. "What are we going to get them?" asked Marian.

"I don't know. What do you think we should get them?"

"A blanket or towels or sheets and pillow cases," said Ruth.

"Just like a girl to think of something like that. I like to follow the tradition of giving a gift the groom can use if we are relatives of the groom, like a set of tools or something like that."

"But he's in CPS camp, not farming," said Marian.

"Eventually this war will end and he'll take up farming. Gladys is a city girl from Huron and they'll need all the help they can get to start up. Let's go to Wipf Brothers and look for some tools."

Sunday, September 10, 1944

John M. Hofer and Gladys Wipf were married by Jacob B. in our church this afternoon. There were a lot of people here from Beadle.

The wedding was at John J. B.'s. They had invited about 300 people. Looked like more than that under the tent.

Stewed beef, mashed potatoes, gravy, string beans, cabbage salad, cucumbers and a variety of homemade cakes were served by men and women with aprons tied around their waists. The tables virtually groaned under the weight of the abundance, as did the guests when they rose to make room for the next seating.

Aunt Katherine supervised the serving from the summer kitchen where coffee was cooked in a large copper boiler on a kerosene stove. The beef stewing in the large outdoor cast iron kettle provided a constant aroma as well as promised supply for the guests yet to be served.

Children darted in and out of the tent, crawled under tables and sat on the fresh, new straw that had been spread the day before.

After all had been served, a short program was presented. There were songs and readings, reminiscences about the bridal couple, and a sermonette by the pastor of the bride. It offered much good advice to the pair about "bearing one another's burdens" and leaving parents to become "one flesh."

Then it was time to open the gifts. One by one the presents were carefully opened. "We want to use this paper again on gifts some of you young people might get," Gladys joked. As each present was held high for the guests to see, the name of the giver was read aloud. There were the inevitable gag gifts to be taken on the honeymoon. Soon a box appeared whose wrappings were familiar to Morgan and his girls. Gladys held it up and tried to guess what it might be. "Sure is heavy," she said. When the box was opened, the contents were revealed: a hand saw and a claw hammer.

"Thank you, Uncle Morgan. I knew you'd get us something useful. We'll take these back to the Hills with us. I have some repairs to make in our apartment," said his nephew John.

Following the gift opening the guests were served peanuts in the shell, Tokay grapes, leftover cake and orange nectar. With wild abandon young and old discarded peanut shells and grape stems and seeds on the straw floor. The combination would be raked up the next morning and used for bedding in barns.

An accordion player who'd taken lessons from Myron Floren in Sioux Falls played for ring games in the yard close to the horse barn. Eventually couples wandered from the games to parked cars for more serious pursuits.

At last it was time to go home. Morgan rounded up his daughters, reminding them that "Tomorrow is another day, and a school day at that!" To his sister he said, "I'll be back tomorrow to help clean up – the food, I mean."

"Okay, Morgan. We'll be looking for you."

On the way home Ruth asked, "How's come Pearl didn't have a wedding like this?"

"She never asked for one. She was too proud, I guess, to ask. But, then again, our situation was different. With no mother at home, it would be hard to have a wedding at our place. She'd have to depend on everybody else. Maybe she was tired of doing that. And she couldn't wait 'til fall. She got married as soon as her school was out, when we were planting corn."

"When I get married, I want a wedding like John and Gladys had," said Ruth.

Tuesday, September 12, 1944

Mary Stahl is here from Chicago visiting and helping us. She shipped 95 lbs. of cucumbers to Chicago by train. She must have John pretty well trained if she expects him to put up those pickles.

Wednesday, September 20, 1944

Mary is still here painting and papering the inside of the house. She got a bunch of women from our church and Mrs. Ray Senner to help. We bought a linoleum rug for the parlor from Art Anderson's furniture store in Dolton.

Thursday, September 21, 1944

Ruth got another attack of appendicitis. Doc Ernest, Mary and I took her to Sioux Valley Hospital in Sioux Falls. She was operated on about 10:30. We went home after the operation.

Sunday, September 24, 1944

We had Mission Festival in the morning and Children's Day program in the afternoon. Marian gave a reading on "Great Men and the Bible."

I went to Sioux Falls to visit Ruth in the hospital. On the way home I shot 4 pheasants.

Had a good C. E. program in the evening. The collection for Missions was over $1500.

Monday, September 25, 1944

Alfred and Ferd Thomas got a boar. I traded them for 100 rods of 26-inch woven wire.

The school children collected milkweed pods in our ditches and on the stone pile for the war effort. I think they are used to make parachutes or as stuffing for bedding.

Tuesday, September 26, 1944

Adeline and I visited Ruth in the hospital. She is coming nicely but is very homesick and lonely.

Fuzzy Graber was here with his children hunting. They got only one duck.

Thursday, September 28, 1944

Got buttermilk from Co-op Creamery for the boars and signed up for the AAA program. I earned my allotment by duckfooting weeds.

Had our settling-up threshing party at Pete Ratzlaff's. I threshed only 909 bu. of grain and paid a $41 threshing bill.

Cal is still in Scobey, Montana.

Saturday, September 30, 1944

Ben Ratzlaff was here to help me pump the basement clean. We had several feet of water in it. Jars were floating around. Marie Walter was here helping to clean.

I went to Sioux Falls to get Ruth. She is staying at John J. B.'s to get built up. She is very thin.

Math Kleinsasser shot ten ducks on our lake and gave us three.

Monday, October 2, 1944

Went to A. R. M. Hofer's sale and sold 9 bu. Funk's corn. Went to a local Farmers Union meeting in School #54 and was elected a delegate to the State Convention in Mitchell on October 17-19.

Tuesday, October 3, 1944

Went fencing. Got stuck with the horses and hay rack on Mensch's land. Went home for the tractor and got stuck with that.

Visited Ruth at John J. B.'s. She feels pretty good.

Wednesday, October 4, 1944

Ben Ratzlaff came over this morning to pull me out of the mud hole but he could not. Ben fenced while I went to Ed Hofer for a cable. Then Paul Decker came with his old John Deere and pulled me out.

Rev. P. P. Tschetter preached in our church tonight. Brother P. P.'s got a purple heart in the mail. Paul must have been wounded.

Thursday, October 5, 1944

Marian and I went to a PTA meeting south of Marion in Miller's school. I gave a talk on "How a Bill Becomes a Law." I used some of the boys to demonstrate first, second and third readings of a bill.

Friday, October 6, 1944

Saw a Funk's G test plot west of town. Went to hear P. P. Tschetter preach in our church. Ruth was in church for the first time since her operation on Sept. 21. She came with John J. B.'s.

Saturday, October 7, 1944

Went to Herbert Hofer's sale. Bought a white kitchen cabinet, a bed spring, and a portable baking oven for the kerosene stove. Paid $13.50, $2.50, and .50, respectively.

Went to Bridgewater church for Sunday School convention.

Sunday, October 8, 1944

Went to Bridgewater church. They had Mission Festival in the morning and S. S. convention in the afternoon and evening. Rev. Frank Harder was elected chairman for next year. Jacob B., P. P. Tschetter and Jake Friesen preached.

Tuesday, October 10, 1944

Ruth went to school for the first day since her operation. She is staying at Paul Decker's.

Thursday, October 12, 1944

Had heavy frost last night. Shot 2 ducks. One pintail got away. They come for the weeds and land to hide.

Made out wheat sealing papers in town.

Monday, October 16, 1944

Cal came home from Montana late last night. He blocked 7 rams to take to the sale in Huron. We borrowed Grandpa's two-wheeled trailer to haul them.

Tuesday, October 17, 1944

Too many rams at Huron sale. Sold only one for $25. Went to J. W., Jr., and Paul in the evening. Left 3 rams with Junior to sell. Left 2 rams in Huron with J.W.

Wednesday, October 18, 1944

Went to Mitchell from Huron for the State Farmers Union convention. I got into an argument about the election of the president, so they put me on the tally committee.

Thursday, October 19, 1944

Stayed overnight at the Widman Hotel with a Mr. Herman from Phillip. Spoke several times during the meeting on the question of parity pricing.

Friday, October 20, 1944

Paid Finer $20 on the bill for wallpaper Mary Stahl ran up quite a bill.

Castrated 5 boars. Got a check from J.W. He sold 3 rams for me.

Monday, October 23, 1944

I am taking the children to and from school since Ruth's operation. We are picking corn. DeKalb 458 is very good, 404 not as good.

Wednesday, October 25, 1944

Bought an AC cultivator for $160 at a sale near Sioux Falls. Bought a single row picker from Ben Ratzlaff for $200. Ben is having his picked with a double row.

Sunday, October 29, 1944

Dr. J. D. Unruh was the speaker at our church this morning in interest of the College. Went to the Gym in the evening to hear Dr. Theodore H. Epp of the Back to the Bible Broadcast from Lincoln, Nebr.

Monday, October 30, 1944

I picked corn by hand while Cal got the picker from Ben's and picked two loads. It does a very dirty job.

Wednesday, November 1, 1944

Picking with the machine in west field, DeKalb 609. Corn is good. Paul Stahl is running the picker, Cal elevates the corn, and I am the cook.

Saturday, November 4, 1944

Cal broke the picker after picking only two loads. He and Paul Stahl went to Huron.

Sunday, November 5, 1944

Rev. Theo. H. Epp spoke in our church before 10 a.m. I took him to the Salem KMB Church, where he delivered another sermon. Otto Schrag had him over for dinner and then took him to Emery. I went to Sister Mary's for dinner and supper and then to hear Epp in Emery in the evening.

Tuesday, November 7, 1944

Election Day. Roosevelt and Truman won. Heard Epp at Gym. It was the last evening for his song director, Handel.

Wednesday, November 15, 1944

Snowed off and on all day. We picked two loads of corn by hand. Heard Dr. Kreider at Gym. Small crowd but good sermon. Afterwards I went to meeting about getting a hospital started in our community.

Sunday, November 19, 1944

Went to Harvey Wiens and Mildred Berg's wedding in the evening at Henry Berg's farm. It rained.

Tuesday, November 21, 1944

Jay Welch was here for the Funk's Seed Corn Co.

Wednesday, November 22, 1944

Cal picked with picker 'til it snowed, then picked by hand. Children had Thanksgiving program at school. I was there for a little while.

Thursday, November 23, 1944

Went to church for Thanksgiving service. Had pheasant for dinner and supper.

Sunday, November 26, 1944

Heard Orie Miller of Akron, Penn., at Gym in afternoon and evening. He spoke on our Mennonite principles in the afternoon and on the work of the MCC in the evening, especially pertaining to war relief.

Wednesday, November 29, 1944

Snowed. Gas line froze up on car. Went to REA meeting. As soon as our allotment goes through, we will start building if the material is available.

Friday, December 1, 1944

Melvin Hofer and Peter G., Jr., are here picking Cal's corn with their Case double-row snapper. There are many pheasants in Cal's field. Shot the limit today.

Sunday, December 3, 1944

Not in church. John J. B. family here for dinner. Girls and I heard THE MESSIAH in the Gym. Very well done. Mildred Waltner, sop.; Mrs. Ludeman, alto; Mr. Mills, bass; Mr. Gilbert, tenor. Warren Erickson, the High School music director, was in charge.

Tuesday, December 5, 1944

I was elected vice president of the Hutchinson Co. Fair Assoc. Cal and the girls made a lot of pumpkin pies from our field pumpkins. They are very good.

Thursday, December 14, 1944

Founders' Day at College. Donovan Smucker was the dynamic speaker. Heard him 3 times. Had a good pageant in the evening— "The Other Wise Man" by Van Dyke.

Friday, December 15, 1944

Mrs. John J. B., Mrs. Paul L., Mrs. Jake L., Mrs. Paul E., Mrs. Joe L., Mrs. Paul Decker, Mrs. Alfred Tschetter and Alfred were here to butcher ducks and do washing for us.

When the girls came home from school, they saw clothes hanging in the parlor. "You shrunk my sweater," Marian cried, pointing to a miniature pink garment more suited to a doll.

"I'm sorry," said Aunt Katherine. "It must have gotten in with the white shirts. The water was too hot for wool, I guess."

"Come on, girls, let's go outside and hang up the rest of these clothes," said Alfred. "The women folks have the butchering well under control."

"But the overhalls will freeze to the line. It's too cold to hang outside," protested Ruth.

"We've used all the lines available in the house. There is no more room."

"But they won't dry."

"They'll dry partially. Then, when you take them to the house, they'll dry in no time." Once outside at the clothesline, Alfred asked, "Pete and Pearl comin' home for Christmas?"

"I dunno. They didn't say," said Ruth.

"How's come your dad doesn't like Pete?"

"I dunno. Peter said Daddy told him once that he should work seven years for Pearl, like Jacob did for Rachel," said Ruth.

Saturday, December 16, 1944

Mrs. Jacob D. Wollman, Mrs. John L. and Mrs. Jac. Mendel canned ducks for us.

I was elected church secretary for a 3-year term.

Girls packed a box to send to Pearl and Peter in the Black Hills and addressed Christmas cards in the evening.

"What are you going to send Pearl and Peter?" asked Ruth.

"I'm going to send the picture I painted on glass at school during art class – the nice one with palm trees and camels – the Christmas scene. What are you going to send?"

"I'll send the one I painted of snow men."

"Good, then they'll have a pair. They'll really be surprised when the box comes!" said Marian, wrapping her glass pane in Christmas wrapping.

When the box was prepared for mailing, the girls tackled the Christmas greeting task. "Which relatives should we start with? The Hutters or the Low Germans?" asked Marian.

"Let's start with those who live farthest away so their cards get there by Christmas."

"Okay. Who lives farthest away?"

"Uncle Jake in Texas."

"Okay. Mr. & Mrs. Jake Tieszen, Mt. Pleasant, Texas. Is that enough of an address?"

"I don't know of any other. Ask Daddy."

"Will 'Mount Pleasant, Texas' be good enough to send a card to Uncle Jake?"

"Hope so. Better add 'Ollie Mae Williams' to their card," said Morgan from the next room.

"Who's next?"

"John S. Waldners in Huron."

"Mr. & Mrs. John S. Waldner, Lillian and Ramona."

"Where do John S. Waldners live, Daddy?"

"In Huron."

"Is that enough?"

"242 Nebraska, I think."

"Rev. & Mrs. J. W. Kleinsasser and Betty, Doland, South Dakota."

"No, they live in Huron now — 918 Kansas, N. E." called Morgan from behind his newspaper.

"Should Waldners' address have initials too?"

"Yes, S. W.," said Morgan.

"Who else lives far away?"

"Mrs. Joe M. She's in Huron with her daughter, Anna, Mrs. Paul I. Tschetter, but I don't know their address. Better hold that card and ask Aunt Katherine in church tomorrow what their address is."

"I'm getting tired," whined Marian.

"Me too. Let's finish tomorrow."

Monday, December 18, 1944

We thawed out and chopped out the hay rack loaded with cobs from corn shelling on the Decker land. We had gotten stuck. Then the wheels froze tight.

Went to Mitchell for Funk's meeting. Most S. D. dealers were there. Got a lot of good information.

Bought a used tire for Cal for $12.

Wednesday, December 20, 1944

Cal is packing straw around the supply tank.

A Delmont man saw our sign near the Highway and came to look at our brood sows.

Thursday, December 21, 1944

6 degrees below. Baled a little pile of straw on the Tieszen land and 100 bales from our big pile.

Friday, December 22, 1944

Cal and I went to get our used AC cultivator we had bought at an auction near Sioux Falls in October and bought Christmas presents for the girls.

"Aren't you going to wrap these for us?" asked Ruth of Cal and her father when she saw the packages in plain brown wrappings lying on the daybed after supper, exactly where they had been dropped upon the men's return from Sioux Falls.

"Why should we waste time wrapping them? You'll just tear up the paper in a few days anyhow," said Cal, munching on an apple.

"Yeah, but. . . ."

"We don't have a tree to put them under anyway," he continued.

"Yeah, but. . . ."

"You'll just be peaking into the packages anyway, even if we do wrap them up," said Morgan. "Why not peak now and find out if things fit. If they don't, we can take them back to Sioux Falls tomorrow."

"Oh, okay!"

Soon the girls had rummaged through all the packages and tried on underpants, vests, socks, dresses and sweaters. Only some dresses were too big.

"Those sweaters are wool. Remember, you can't wash them in hot water in the washing machine. But we bought dark ones so they won't get dirty as fast as that pink one did," said Morgan.

Saturday, December 23, 1944

Marian and I went to Sioux Falls to exchange some dresses. Stopped in at Henry Tiahrts in the morning and evening. Had supper there. Anna shortened a dress for Marian.

Sunday, December 24, 1944

All in church this morning. Pearl and Peter were there too.

"Did you get the box we sent you for Christmas?" Marian asked Pearl after church in the churchyard.

"Yes, we got it. But the pictures were broken. You have to pack glass better than that," said Peter.

"But it was a nice idea. And I could tell from the pieces that they were pretty once," said Pearl.

"Where are you staying?"

"At Peter's folks."

"Did you get the box I sent you?" asked Pearl.

"Yeah! I like the friendship bracelet," said Marian.

"And the milk glass relish dish," said Ruth.

"Those dishes are precious things you'll want to be careful with and save for later—when you get married and establish your own homes. Would you like to visit us in the Black Hills? I could send you train tickets."

"Oh, yes!" they shouted in unison.

"Are you going to be at Grandpa and Grandma Tieszen's house tomorrow night?" asked Pearl.

"I think so."

"Well, we'll see you all there then. Good-bye! See you tomorrow!" said Peter, whisking Pearl off with his arm around her.

Monday, December 25, 1944

All in church. Went to John J. B.'s in the afternoon and to the grandparents in the evening. Cold but no snow.

Tuesday, December 26, 1944

All in church. Got coal from Freeman Lumber Co. Was elected secretary of our co-op telephone co. at a meeting at Nachtigals. Girls went along to play with Mary.

Wednesday, December 27, 1944

Baled our own straw. Got 268 bales from one stack and 81 from another. Ray Senner, Ben Ratzlaff, Melvin Tieszen, Alfred Hofer, Cal and I baled.

Dr. Saner was here to treat a calf with scours. Got a recipe for a calf diarrhea cure: 2 T. honey or syrup, 1 t. soda, 1/2 t. salt, 1 pt. warm water. Mix into calf's milk. One quart is enough milk for a small calf.

Sunday, December 31, 1944

All in church in morning. Had Watch Night service in evening. Girls sang in an ensemble. They sang 'Give Me My Roses While I Live.' Sounded like a Del Rio, Texas, cowboy song.

In the churchyard after the service, Morgan's nephews, Jake L. and Paul L., huddled with him in the cold.

"Well, Morgan, *Wie geht's?*" asked Paul.

"*Es geht, aber es geht sehr schlecht,*" answered Morgan.

"Remember, 'the first hundred years are always the hardest'!" said Jake, quoting one of his uncle's favorite expressions.

"Yeah!" said Morgan, looking up at the stars, "it can only get better."